PRIDE AND PARANORMAL

ADRIENNE BLAKE

To

Noelle,

Enjoy reading and
thank you,

Adrienne Blake.

CITY OWL
PRESS

PRIDE AND PARANORMAL
Souls and Shadows, Book 1

CITY OWL PRESS
www.cityowlpress.com

Cover Design by Mibl Art. All stock photos licensed appropriately.

Edited by Tee Tate.

For information on subsidiary rights, please contact the publisher at info@cityowlpress.com.

Print Edition ISBN: 978-1-64898-068-8

Digital Edition ISBN: 978-1-64898-067-1

Printed in the United States of America

I'd love to dedicate this book to Mom and her love for trashy books. I still remember clutching her copy of Pride and Prejudice and asking me what I loved about it. Everything Mom. All of it. Thank you for making me read it.

Chapter One

THE FLAMING CAULDRON

THE PARKING SPACE WAS TOO TINY. THERE WAS NO WAY MY POOR LITTLE Beetle was going to squeeze into the one solitary spot in front of the pub, but this was an emergency and there was no other spot in sight. My best friend, Charlotte Lucas, never went out drinking in the middle of the week. She was far too busy with her work. So I was more than surprised when I got the call asking me to meet her at The Cauldron.

My family lived in a quiet little valley in Misty Cedars, Pennsylvania, surrounded by mountains. It was the kind of out of the way place easily missed in a blink. I glanced furtively up and down the street. No one was watching, so I pulled out my wand.

"*Minorem ad quietiora*," I said, pointing at the two cars flanking either side of the parking space.

A shot of green light pulsed from the tip of it, circling both. They wobbled, just a little, like they'd been hit by a strong gust of wind, but in less than five seconds, they were suddenly each about a half foot shorter, opening up the space. I backed into the now wider spot, and after turning off the engine, I wound down the window and sat perfectly still. A parking violation was hardly a major offense, but if a Hag appeared out of the shadows, they could still cart me off to Bitterhold for the night.

Unnecessary magic in a public area was an arrestable offense. How would I ever explain that one to Mom and Dad?

Climbing out of the car, I glanced around me. Sensing all was clear, I hurried inside.

Charlotte was sitting at a high table, checking her phone when I saw her. The Flaming Cauldron was a dark basement drinking hole, with slate flooring and a magically illuminated bar that always reminded me of the aurora borealis. The magic was mostly cosmetic—there wasn't any obvious source of electricity, but there was just enough light to see and be seen.

A young warlock worked the bar—there were usually two on duty. The other was a vamp. I had no clue where she was tonight.

"Hey, Benny. No Sue tonight?"

Benny was a good-looking warlock who had his life history tattooed all over his body. More than once he'd asked me to check out some of the more personal tats, and with a show of feigned reluctance, I'd always managed to turn him down.

"Hey, Iz. Nah, she's not here. Anemia. Again." He worked while he talked and was busy stashing dirty glasses into a dishwasher under the bar. "Luckily, we're not too busy. What can I get you, babes?"

We'd known each other long enough I wasn't offended by the *babes*. "I'll take an Angry Orchard," I said. "And whatever Charlotte ordered."

"I'll bring it over," he said.

I turned and strolled past the handful of tables currently occupied by a group of young werewolves to join Charlotte. A small light illuminated the center of our table, resembling a white orchid. The small flower was suspended in the air, emitting a warm, incandescent light that became dimmer and brighter as was needed.

"You found a spot then?" Charlotte took a sip of her drink and looked over my shoulder toward the entrance. "I had to park halfway up the street."

"I, um, improvised."

Charlotte's eyes opened wide in disbelief. "You didn't. You know you're lucky you didn't get caught. This place has been crawling with Hags lately. If they catch you using ley line magic in broad daylight where anyone can see it..."

I slid into the seat beside her. "Don't worry, I was careful. I checked everywhere at least a dozen times before I used my wand. I promise, no one saw me."

"For someone who works in the legal profession, you sure like to live dangerously."

The bar went silent, and Charlotte, who had a better view of the place from her seat, shot me a pointed look. Curious, I turned to see two Hags making their way over to the bar. Years of unfiltered ley line magic had taken its toll on their skin, which was leathery and covered in warts. Wisps of hair protruded from the top of their heads and out of their ears. Their features drooped so pitifully it was hard to tell their sex. They were bereft of any kind of shape, and only their height hinted at what they once might have been. My heart stopped. Had they been watching after all? Had they come for me?

In a shadowy corner of the bar, a hooded figure sat perfectly still, hunched over a half-full beer glass. Whoever it was, they were the only person not following the Hags as they made their way toward Benny. When the Hags were just a few feet away, the individual jumped from its barstool and sprang up on the counter, running along the length of it. Glasses smashed, and plates of food went flying as they made for the emergency exit on the other side of the bar. A bolt of white light flashed overhead; its tip wrapped around the neck of the escapee, who went down with a violent crash. Their hood down, Charlotte and I stared aghast as a female goblin writhed against her restraints but to no use. The more she fought, the tighter the restraints held her.

When the Hags reached her, with a click of their gnarled fingers, the goblin rose from the ground, hovering in midair, her hands still grappling with the rope. The first Hag turned to leave, and as she left, the goblin floated through the air behind her. The second surveyed the bar area, and with a similar click of their hand, chairs were uprighted and broken glasses mended, until everything was put back to how it had been before. The Hag bowed to Benny and then followed her companion and captive to the exit. The door closed behind them, and only then did anyone dare breathe. Everyone began chattering at once, and order was restored.

"You know, that could have been you." Charlotte picked up her glass and stared at it thoughtfully.

I buried my private fears and laughed. "Oh, come on, they'd hardly do that for a parking violation."

Charlotte shook her head. "You never know. And in any case, have you looked closely at those Hags? They weren't born like that—unfiltered magic did that to them. It'll happen to you, too, if you're not careful."

I laughed out loud. "Oh, Charlotte, really. You know I do mostly earth magic. The plants pay the price, not me. In any case, I hardly ever use the ley lines. They're strictly for emergency use only."

"Like getting a parking place? Look, just be careful. You don't want to get old before your time."

"What did she do, the goblin?" I asked, wanting to deflect the subject from me.

"No clue. Probably dealing in illegal love potions. There's been a lot of it about, I heard, and the Hags are clamping down."

I nodded. "That would do it."

Charlotte shook her head indulgently, reminding me of Mom. "Did you eat already?"

I was glad of the change of subject. I'd had enough talk of Hags for one night. "Yes, you?"

"I had a little something before I left." She looked me up and down appraisingly. "You know, I love what you did to your hair. Did you braid it yourself?"

I automatically reached for the intricate braids I'd conjured the night before, and I ran my fingers over them, checking to make sure everything was just as it should be and that the magic still held. Four longer braids fell forward over my shoulders down to my boobs and I checked the ends. I considered it was probably not a good idea to mention I'd used ley line magic rather than fussing with them myself. My sensible friend would have had a fit. "Um, yes, yes, I did. You like it?"

"I do," Charlotte said. "You're so lucky. You have perfect bone structure. You look good no matter how you wear your hair. And I wish I could wear mascara too."

"I don't see why you can't," I said.

"My mom says it makes me look like a fierce raccoon."

We both laughed at the familiar joke. It was true, though. Charlotte and I couldn't look more different. I had an athletic build, with dark-auburn hair and clear skin my sisters would die for. Not that I was the best at taking care of it, because I liked to goth it up—with purple lipstick and heavy on the kohl around the eyes. My magically-knitted leotard-style dress had a V-neck, exposing just enough boobage to tease, with long leaves of black forming the skirt, which stopped just above my knees. I hated shoes, preferring to run wild without them at home, but here I wore a pair of open-toed sandals, showing off my black nail polish and ankle tattoo of a hummingbird. Half the time, people took me for a vamp. Easy mistake.

In contrast, Charlotte was slim, but her figure was otherwise unremarkable. Today she wore a simple, off-the-shelf dress adorned with an equally neutral scarf, high heels, and a matching purse. Her blond hair was cut into a short bob, and her pale face was devoid of any makeup. It bugged her to no end, but the fact was she had sensitive skin and could only get away with a few products. We'd tried a few spells to ease her condition, but so far, no luck.

Benny arrived at our table with our drinks in hand. "Do you want to run a tab?"

"Sure."

Benny grinned at the wink I gave him and shot me one of his own before returning to the bar.

"So what's the big to-do?" I asked Charlotte once the cute warlock left.

"You'll never guess who I had dinner with last night."

"Who?"

"Charlie Van Buren!" Charlotte seemed so excited I thought she might launch from her seat.

"The matchmaking guy?"

"Yes, him. It looks like Dark Coven is let at last. My dad arranged the lease, and we had him over for dinner last night. Hell, Iz, he's so gorgeous —much better than in the magazines, and he has such nice eyes. Not to mention, he's single. He was telling us all about it, all about Wendy and the big breakup." Charlotte shuddered and covered her eyes for a moment, embarrassed. "God, you know I think I drooled all the way from Mom's appetizer right through to dessert. He probably thinks I'm a total idiot."

I laughed. "I somehow doubt that."

Charlotte grinned. "But it's true. Anyway, I managed to sneak a picture of him on my phone while he was talking to Dad in the kitchen. Wanna see him?" She picked up her cell and began swiping.

"Not especially."

Truth was, I was dying to see him, but I wasn't going to tell her that. Charlie Van Buren was all anyone talked about these days: the self-made warlock who'd made a fortune with his supernatural dating app, Magical Moments. I hadn't tried it myself, though if my mother was to be believed, it would solve all my man troubles. Apparently, it never failed—users got a love match every time.

"Yeah, I believe you." Charlotte smiled at me sideways, knowing me better. Of course I was as curious as everyone else about the new tenant of Dark Coven. "Ah, here he is." She turned her phone to me. "What do you think?"

Hmm. Charlie Van Buren was certainly hot. I could see why everyone was swooning. He had sandy-brown hair with just enough natural wave to be appealing but not overly fussy. And he was tall. Charlotte's kitchen had a high ceiling, and he was way up there in mortal danger from the pendant lighting.

"Nice," I said. "So he's only leasing Dark Coven—he didn't want to buy it?"

"It's up in the air, I think," Charlotte explained. "I think he just wanted something easy while he sorted things out with his ex."

"Lucky for the neighborhood."

Charlotte's eyes glazed over as she stared off into space. Who could blame her? The population of warlocks in Misty Cedars had thinned out over time. The east side was too suburban for most young warlocks, and since most of us were third-generation or less, we had little money. And the Hags prohibited conjuring any—unless you fancied a solitary cell in Bitterhold. It was the price we paid for sharing an economy with nonmagical beings, who my generation affectionately referred to as numpies.

"You're lucky. At least your dad is in a position to meet new people as they come and go. Once in a blue moon, Dad invites someone over from his university, but they're mostly old farts he knew when he worked there. All book nerds and bibliophiles. He definitely doesn't know anyone as hot as this Charlie guy."

I amused myself by running my hand around the orchid light, checking the redness of my fingers as the light illuminated my skin.

"Oh my God!" Charlotte's sudden outburst almost made me spit out my cider.

"Christ, what is it?" I followed her horrified gaze over to the door, thinking maybe the Hags had come back for me after all.

A group of young people had just entered the bar and were looking around, checking the place out. I recognized Charlie Van Buren at once but had no clue about the other four people with him. One thing I knew for certain: they were all magical. Their pulsating auras said witches and warlocks as clearly as if it were stamped on their foreheads.

Charlie's ready smile and eager expression made it clear he was out to have a good time, although I couldn't say as much for his four companions. Charlie traveled with two men and two women, all looked around his general age, and all were dressed impeccably well. They looked a little ostentatious in this spit-and-sawdust basement bar, and from the sneers on their faces, they knew it.

One in particular caught my eye. Charlie was tall, but his companion was even taller, and I would have been totally into him if it weren't for the permanent scowl glued to his face. Still, that wouldn't matter one bit if he were nice, because the wizard was hot—like smoldering hot. My keen gaze feasted on his broad shoulders, tanned complexion, and strong but manicured hands. I hoped to Gaia that scowl was only temporary.

Charlie headed straight for the bar as his friends surveyed the place.

"I heard this place was supposed to be happening," said the more sophisticated of the two women.

"Clearly we were misinformed," the tallest man said. He had a deep, commanding voice that made my skin tingle in the best possible way. I could hear him from our table in the corner and watched as he surveyed the place, like a lord overseeing his minions.

One of the werewolves walked by. The taller woman pulled the shorter one close and stuck her nose in the air, as if some nasty smell had irritated her. I always liked the musky werewolf aroma myself, but this lady had issues, and from the stiff gait of the others, I figured none of them liked the place. Not my type of crowd at all.

"We could go back to Charlie's place," the shortest man suggested. "At least there's free liquor there."

At that moment, the taller woman managed to catch my eye. I smiled, seeing no reason not to, but my smile was not returned.

"Too late now," said the taller man with the scowl. "Charlie already ordered the drinks. We're going to have to stay for one at least." It was his turn to stare directly at me. "You're going to have to put up with the local riffraff for one round."

I could feel the color rise within me. Riffraff indeed. "Anyone would think their poop didn't stink."

Charlotte laughed. "Or if it does, it smells of roses."

I snorted into my drink.

"This place does somewhat remind me of one of my late father's stables," the shorter woman said.

"Yes, or the pigsty. I'm definitely getting eau de swine." The other girl giggled.

"You're not wrong. The resemblance is remarkable." As he said this, the tall man glanced directly at me. I would have said something smart to Charlotte; however, I was so taken aback that for the moment I was struck dumb.

"Did he just say that? Did he just call us *pigs*?" Charlotte leaned into me, and her acknowledgement brought me to my senses.

"Just me, I think. Or maybe not. They're probably think they're being amusing. Stupid asses. Thank Gaia we don't have to talk to *them*."

Resigned to their fate, the group at the door moved over to the bar as Charlie handed back their drinks. They talked among themselves for a while but were now too far away for me to catch what they were saying.

Charlie glanced over at our table. Seeing Charlotte, he grinned warmly.

"Shit," I said in horror. "They're heading this way."

Charlotte kicked me under the table as, indeed, the group of five moved in our direction. Charlie was the first to arrive on the scene.

"Well, hello!" he said, his tone friendly as he leaned in to hug my friend. "I didn't realize you would be here tonight, or I'd have invited you along. This is a great place. I'm so glad you recommended it last night."

Charlotte's grin betrayed her delight. "I'm glad you found it. I honestly didn't think you'd be coming so soon."

"Ah, well," Charlie continued, "I have the urban family with me, checking out my new digs. I had to take them out somewhere, or they'd be driving me up the wall. They'd all just hang around and do nothing, given the chance."

Charlie and Charlotte chuckled, but I could clearly see his friends weren't impressed. Judging by their faces, one would think they'd all just trod in pig shit. I thought that kind of fitting under the circumstances. I fixed my gaze on Charlotte and tried to pretend the others weren't there.

"Everyone," Charlie said, "this is my new friend, Charlotte. Her dad is Bill Lucas, the man who runs the local real estate office and who fixed me up with Dark Coven."

His companions all nodded at once.

"Nice to meet you all," Charlotte said. "This is my friend, Izzy. Izzy Bennet."

I managed a polite enough smile, although I didn't feel it. I was surprised Charlotte could be so nonchalant under the circumstances, but then I supposed they hadn't just called *her* a pig. Satisfied, Charlie continued, "These are my sisters, Caroline and Louisa, Louisa's husband, old Hursty, and my best friend in the world, Fitz Darcy."

"Fitz? Is that German?" I asked with more politeness than I felt.

"I was born in Maine, but my mother was Pennsylvania Dutch," he replied in a clipped tone.

I spotted an intricately carved silver skull ring on his finger, which looked expensive, curious about its meaning. I also had a funny feeling I'd seen one like it before, but right now I just couldn't remember where.

"Have you lived here long?" Fitz asked.

"My whole life."

"I see," he said. "And it's the best place to be, you think?"

"Yeah, why not?" I said. "In fact, we love it down here. The Cauldron's the best paranormal hangout in the county. They have the best bands, the best people, in fact, the best of everything in my opinion."

"I suppose it rather depends on what you're used to," Caroline said. "I guess it's, um, what would you call it, Louisa?"

Louisa was the shorter of the two women. She glanced around the bar, taking it all in. "It's very, err, rustic, maybe?"

"And happening," I continued. "It might not be the most sophisticated place in the world, but it has a great atmosphere when there's a bigger crowd, and the people you meet here are great."

"I'm sure they are," Caroline said. She'd finished her drink quickly and looked anxious for the others to do the same. Her friends were at least taking their time, and I smiled on the inside.

"Did Charlotte say your last name was Bennet?" Charlie asked. He rubbed his chin thoughtfully.

"Yes. Yes, it is. Why?"

"I believe I may have bumped into your dad earlier this evening."

"You did?" I stared at Charlie with more than my usual curiosity. "Are you sure it was my dad?"

"Yes, I think so. He's a retired professor, no?"

"Why, yes, he is. How did you meet him?"

"I saw him at the bank, just as it was closing. We have the same financial advisor, and he introduced us. Nice man, your father. He seems to know a lot."

I laughed despite myself. "I suppose he does, but then he was a literary professor at Yule."

"That's so cool," Charlie said. "I sort of ran into him at the bank. He mentioned he had five daughters—are they all as pretty as you?"

I couldn't help but laugh out loud at that, and when I was done, I noticed Fitz staring at me intently. I had no idea what the man was thinking and, quite frankly, cared even less. "Shit no, my sisters are much prettier. I'm the ugly one." I half expected some kind of reaction from Fitz, but he didn't respond at all.

"You're a witch, right?" Fitz asked. "Only..."

He was looking at my clothes. "Yeah, totally a witch. Not a vamp. I'm just into goth. I get that a lot."

"I see."

"We're all witches and warlocks, and proud of it," Caroline said, her tone sharp. "I never see the need to display anything other than what I am."

"So am I," I said. "It's just a fashion thing."

"And it suits you," Fitz said. "I meant no offense."

"None taken."

Under the table, Caroline pulled on Charlie's shirt.

"Um, well, I guess we'd better be off then," Charlie said. "Lots of places to go and visit before the night is done. I'm running down the list you gave me, Charlotte. Can I buy you both a drink before we head off?"

"Err, no, it's okay," I said, not wanting the others to think we were sponges.

"Thanks for the offer, though," Charlotte added. "Maybe some other time?"

I glanced at Charlotte, realizing she had the hots for him. She probably wanted to get him all on his own, so he'd have the chance to molest her with his magical dating app. Fair enough.

"Right then, well, I suppose I'll be seeing you all soon."

"Good-bye."

They deposited their half-full glasses on the table in front of them, and I sighed with relief as, at last, they made to leave.

Charlotte still looked starry-eyed, as if they'd done us a great favor by noticing us at all. But I couldn't share her good feelings, I was still too upset by that great brute of a man and the pig comment he'd made the second he'd walked in the door. I smiled to myself. Like he was anything to talk about. Twit.

I was quiet as they left the bar, organizing my thoughts and thinking about everything they'd just said to us, especially that Fitz. The second they were gone, I turned in my seat, and for the rest of the night, we did nothing but talk about the town's newest arrivals.

Charlotte, who was a darling, couldn't stop singing their praises, whereas I, part witch, and clearly part demon, couldn't stop laughing at their nonsense. On the upside, the two of us had nothing but praise for Charlie. He wasn't just smart, he was nice. But Charlotte and I had mixed views on his friends, and though she tried to persuade me to see the good in each of them, all I could think about was the snarky comments they'd made and was well on the road to disliking them.

Chapter Two

DARK COVEN

WHEN I WAS SEVEN YEARS OLD, MY MOTHER GAVE ME MY FIRST WAND. And a cleaning kit. From that day on, I spent every Saturday morning opening up my box and giving the wand a good spit and polish before we all went to the weekly coven meet.

As I rubbed mine slowly with wax-free polish and a lint-free cloth, my mind wandered back to the night before.

The truth was, Fitz Darcy was the best looking warlock I had seen in yonks, and if he'd been the least bit amenable, I'd have been all over him like a warming charm. But no—not only had he been standoffish, but he'd also been downright insulting to me, which had hurt. As far as I could make out, I'd done nothing to deserve his spite, which pissed me off. My only consolation was he might not be around for long, and since Charlotte wanted us to befriend them, I could keep civil for a few more days.

"Are you going to be much longer?" My sister Jane popped her head around the door, and I could see she was anxious to get going.

"What? Oh, yeah, sure. Just finishing up."

Carefully, I put my wand away. Saturday mornings were always coven time, and I wouldn't be up for much without a functioning wand.

For as long as I could remember, the coven had gathered in Charlotte

Lucas's barn. Prior to that, so I was told, everyone had gathered over at the Dark Coven estate. When I was young, the old witch who owned it died, so the property had been put up for lease, and our coven had been forced to find a new meeting place. Not that I cared. When we were younger, the barn was a perfect place to play and practice magic, and that was good enough for me.

"Is everyone else ready?" I asked, not wanting to be the last.

"Everyone except Mom, I think. She's on the phone with someone. She shouldn't be long; she was ready to go a minute ago. They just called."

Typical Mom. She couldn't just let the phone ring and leave; she had to go back and pick up. "All right, I'm coming now. Hold up."

I grabbed my things and bustled out of the room after her. As always, Jane looked fantastic in a pair of torn jeans and a billowy, off-white linen top. She was the only person I knew who could wear something so casual and look like a million bucks with her long, flaxen hair tied in a simple knotted updo.

"Yes, yes, of course," Mom said. "It won't be any trouble at all. Yes, I know the way. No, no, that's okay. I'm glad you caught us. We were just going out the door. You're too kind. Yes, yes, thank you for letting me know. Yes. See you soon. Good-bye."

Mom was funny about so many things, including the old-fashioned rotary phone she kept in the hall by the door. She swore cell phones messed with a witch's delicate aura. She was standing by the phone now, one hand on her hip, the other cradling her forehead like a woman in a conundrum.

I gathered with my sisters now; indeed, everyone was in the hall except Dad, who generally begged off attending every other meet to enjoy a few solitary hours alone in the house with his books. We all stared at Mom. Her mouth was wide open, yet she seemed uncharacteristically lost for words.

"Well, would you believe it?" Mom flattened her palm to her chest as she struggled to gather her thoughts. "I just heard they're having the meeting over at Dark Coven, like the good old days."

"What?" I said, filled with a sudden sense of foreboding. "What's wrong with the Lucases' barn?"

Mom adopted the air of someone more in the know than we were. "Oh, stop your whining, Izzy. The new tenant obviously wants to start off on the right foot, that's all. I suppose he wants to get to know everybody. What a nice man! I have to say, I'm hoping he takes a shine to one of you. It's about time I got a daughter off my hands."

Lydia snorted. "I'll have him. I hear he's totally loaded."

"Then I want him," Kitty cried. "Since I'm older than you, I should get hitched first."

"Not with that face." Lydia pointed at her and laughed.

Mary, our middle sister, stood with her back to the wall, her nose in her Kindle, oblivious to us all.

"Anyway, I'm quite excited to sneak a peek at the old house," Mom continued. "The place has been locked up for years. I think this is a brilliant idea. And I hear he's not bad looking, either." Mom winked at Jane, nudging her, and I fought a cringe. Still, I didn't argue. I knew if Mom had heard Fitz last night, she'd have been singing a different tune now, but I'd chosen not to tell her and that was on me. I didn't want her to know. If she found out he'd called one of her daughters a pig, she'd have put some serious hurt on him, and that would have brought on the Hags. It was better she knew nothing at all.

"Lydia, are you sure you should go out in that skirt? I can see your backside when you bend over!"

"Oh, Mom, this is what everyone's wearing now."

I raised my eyebrows, but Mom only smiled and waved her thoughts aside like they didn't matter. "Well, if you say so. Come on, girls. We're going to be the last people there if we're not careful."

Jane and I shared a knowing glance. I knew my big sister well enough to know she disapproved of Lydia's provocative dress sense just as much as I did, but we both knew it was futile to make a stand now.

As always, Mom's oversized bag was hanging on the hook by the door. Why she carried so much with her all the time, I'd never know. She couldn't conjure a spell worth a damn, and her potions were little more than tonics. Still, she loved having tea with the elder coven witches, and mingling made her happy.

Resigned to the inevitable, I let all my sisters trundle out ahead of me, and I followed the party from the rear. Maybe Fitz wouldn't be there, and even if he was, there was no reason for me to forewarn them about him. They'd soon find out what an asshole he was for themselves. All he had to do was open his big fat mouth.

Mom climbed into her battered old Chrysler minivan and opened the side doors. Kit and Lydia scrambled into the back, where they immediately started giggling at something on their phones. Mary, armed with her trusty Kindle, got into the front passenger seat next to Mom, and Jane and I settled for the middle-row seats, surrounded by all the coven bags, and a mess of candy wrappers on the floor.

As soon as we were underway, I turned to Jane. "It's a bit much, don't you think, him taking over like this? He's been in town, what, all of five minutes, and now he's running the place?"

Jane shrugged. "Oh, I don't mind at all. To be honest, I'm rather curious to see the old place, aren't you?"

I nodded. "I suppose so." Perhaps I was being unreasonable; after all, I hadn't whispered a word about what Fitz had said last night, so Jane didn't know any better. Maybe it was pride, but I just couldn't bring myself to share the insult Fitz had given me. Not yet anyway. "It does feel a little odd, I mean. I know the elders encourage sharing coven meets, but we really don't know these people. What if they practice some strange kind of magic that we're not familiar with or take umbrage at something we do? I really think these people should have waited a bit before diving in feetfirst and hosting."

"I hadn't thought of that," Jane replied. "Hopefully the elders have. Look, I'm sure everything has been thought of. If not, we can always take it up with the Hag Council later. You worry too much."

Jane was probably right.

Turning aside, I stared out of the window as we passed a row of small cottages. Misty Cedars was an odd little place, an hour or so west of New York, where paranormals clustered in the older parts of town and nonmagical folk lived in the newer developments. Lately, things were changing. Urban sprawl was making our once remote village very desirable, and with a heavy heart, I watched as the removal men hoisted old Mrs. Robinson's cast-iron cauldron into the back of a Harpy-Haul truck.

I waved to Mrs. Robinson as we passed, and though the dear lady waved back, I saw the tears in the old witch's eyes.

"Another good one down," I remarked.

Jane looked over me to see what I was staring at. "Oh yes, and I heard the developers got her house for a song. She only missed a few payments, poor dear. They're planning on building some swanky townhouses or something."

I shook my head. "It's such a travesty. These older witches just don't understand the ways of the numpy economy. How many more are going to lose their home?"

Jane rested her hand over mine and squeezed it. "We all agreed we would live by the same laws. What can anyone do?"

"Nothing. They won't be happy until they've pushed the whole magical community out. It's just so sad."

"Yes, it is," Jane agreed. "But her family are taking her in up in Salem, so maybe it won't be so terrible for her after all."

"Sucks, all the same."

We passed the last row of new townhomes on the estate and were soon driving along the side of a cornfield. The stalks were still green—it would be a few more months before they were harvested.

Dark Coven was an old estate house, with a long, winding private drive, cushioned in the middle of acres of farmland just outside Misty Cedars. It hadn't entered much into my consciousness until about a year ago, when we heard the owners had been granted planning permission to make renovations. I supposed the carpenters, plumbers, and masons had come and gone, and today, at last, we would all see the fruits of their labor. And yes, I was itching to see what they had done to the place, in spite of my complaining.

"She unfriended you because you're an idiot, that's why!" Lydia's bombastic tone snapped me out of my thoughts.

"How would you know?" Kit countered.

"Because she told me in a private message."

"Show me!"

"I will not."

My mother turned in her seat to reprimand them both, and the car veered to the wrong side of the road.

"For the love of weres, Mom, watch the road, will you?" I said, holding onto the door for fear she might roll the car. The road might have been empty, but the tall corn made it impossible to see what was coming around the corner.

With a sigh, Mom steered straight, like it was a pain in the butt to do so. Jane and I exchanged more anxious glances but said nothing. All we wanted to do was get there in one piece.

Jane stared thoughtfully out of the window. "So you've met him, this Charlie person? What's he like?"

"He's nice," I said. "And not bad looking at all, though not my type. And he seems very sociable. I think you'll like him."

"I guess I'll be lucky if I get a look in," she continued. "I hear he has a ton of friends staying with him. And all the girls in town are interested. I'd be surprised if he even learned my name."

"I don't know about a ton. He was in a group of five when I met him, and two of those were his sisters."

"Were they all nice? You know, our sort of people?"

I bent down to pick up my purse, pretending to need something while I thought about how to answer. "They're nothing like their brother. They seemed quite trendy. I suspect they get most of their clothes from Warlocks on Fifth Avenue. Don't get me wrong, he was dressed nice, but was more, I don't know...down-to-earth, maybe?"

Jane nodded, satisfied for the moment. She turned to look back out of the window, and I did the same. Hmm. It would be interesting to see how those two got along. They were both so nice. Jane had always been a little introverted, and though a few guys had asked her out, she'd never really shown a lot of interest. Even if she liked them. She wasn't shy, really. She just wasn't particularly expressive. For a while, I'd wondered if she might be gay, but I doubted it. Mary maybe, but not Jane. Ah, well, que sera. What would be, would be.

Mom turned the last corner, and the great house loomed in front of us. The building was centuries old. Dad had told me once that it predated the Salem witch trials, which was as old as it got around here. Whoever built it had built it to last. The original building had a gray facade, with diamond-paned casement windows, a deep overhang on the upper floor, and a very prominent chimney stack running right up the middle.

Over time, it had been added to, with great stone annexes flanking on either side and a modern, though tastefully matched three-car garage off to the left. It looked like there might be an apartment above that too. How the other half lived, I thought.

These days, there was a long, circular drive in the front, currently crowded by row upon row of cars. Without slowing her pace, Mom shot up the drive, heavy on the gas, and I braced myself for impact as she almost collided with a parked Mercedes toward the back of the second row. Just in time, she missed it—thank the Hereafter—and I pressed the button, anxious to escape from the car.

"Watch out. That's my car!" came a voice from the window. "And we're not going to be running out of sandwiches any time soon. There's no need to be in such a hurry!"

Mortified, I recognized the disdainful voice of Caroline Van Buren, who was staring at me from an open ground-floor window. I turned, horrified to see Fitz Darcy standing right there with her, snarfing on a chicken drumstick in one hand and holding an elegant wineglass in the other.

Oh, for the love of weres. Just my luck. I blushed for shame as everyone bundled out of our car: Mom fussing over the bags in the middle, Kit close to tears, and Lydia climbing out ass-first, treating everyone to a frilly set of purple panties. Only Mary and Jane spared my blushes, and I braced myself for more *fun* to come as we walked along the gravel drive to the entrance.

"What's wrong?" Jane asked.

"Bit of a headache," I lied.

Jane caressed my upper arm. "You poor thing. I quite understand."

Jovial host that he was, Charlie Van Buren was waiting for us just inside the door, a huge grin on his face as we approached. I liked the cut of the shirt he wore—not too formal, although some of the senior warlocks preferred traditional dress at these gatherings. A numpy would probably consider the cut a little gothic, maybe. I thought it romantic, but not overbearing.

As soon as he saw Jane, he appeared to catch his breath but then recovered. Cupid's arrow maybe? I would live in hope. I glanced at Jane, but although her expression was less readable, the subtle gleam in her eyes suggested she approved of what she saw.

"Hello, hello!" he exclaimed, as he stepped out to greet us. He looked at me and did a double take, and then his grin broadened.

"Oh, Izzy, it's you! I didn't recognize you without your goth clothes on. Ha-ha. You look lovely. Is that dress your own work? Amazing. Is your father not with you today?"

"No," I said. It was easy to return a smile so freely given. "I think he enjoys having the house to himself for a bit. He rarely comes to the coven meets these days. It has to be something special to draw him out of his den."

"Ah, well," he laughed. "I can understand that."

"Let me introduce you to my sister Jane."

Jane stretched out an elegant hand, and Charlie held it a moment longer than was necessary. I glanced sideways at my sister, but she remained composed, and if she noticed his particular attention, she didn't show it.

"And this is my—"

Mom barged in between us, shooting out her hand before I had a chance to finish. "Nice to meet you. I've heard so many lovely things. So many. How do you like the place? Are you settling in okay? Do you plan on changing anything outside at all? I loved your roses as we came up the drive. If you wouldn't mind, I would love a cutting," she gushed and prattled on. "And the hemlock. My, my, this is a wonderful place. It's so kind of you to offer your house for the coven meeting, so thoughtful."

"Um, sure. Take whatever you want."

Charlie seemed so natural and sincere, and I liked him more already.

"And these are my younger sisters, Mary, Kit, and Lydia," I said, resuming the introductions.

I didn't catch what any of them said as my three younger sisters talked over each other, but I felt the push from behind as they were all eager to get inside.

Charlie merely grinned, and since he wasn't looking to find fault, I relaxed a little. "Are we the last to arrive?" I asked.

"Mmm, I'm not sure," he confessed. "I haven't met everyone yet. Come on inside, there's plenty of food and drink, and we can start all the coven business in a bit. Um, Jane, I'd like you to come and meet my sisters. Izzy met them last night. I'm sure we'll soon be the best of friends."

Wow. After carefully looking Jane up and down, it was like the rest of us had disappeared. Though we were still talking away, after that, he had eyes only for her, and his attention remained transfixed on her lips. I had hope.

"Well, this place is incredible," Mom exclaimed. "Gosh, look at all your furnishings. You really pushed the boat out, I must say!" She picked up a small black china ballerina, sitting on a side table just in front of the door. "This doesn't look cheap. I bet you wouldn't find too many of those down at Target."

I tried not to cringe.

"Actually, it wasn't horribly expensive," Charlie said. "It's a weakness of mine, but I rather like antiquing. I don't think I paid all that much for it, and I've even less an idea of its worth. I should research it a little more, I guess. If only I could find the right book."

"I quite like antiquing myself," Jane said. "Dad has a ton of books on the subject at home. You should come and check them out one day if you have time. You might be able to find out something of its history."

"Oh, it doesn't matter. I never have much time to read." Charlie reddened. "But of course, I would love to come and look—if you don't mind."

"Not at all," Jane said. "I'm sure Dad would be thankful for some male company. A houseful of women can be a bit much for him at times."

Charlie's cheeky grin was enchanting. "Oh, I don't know, it doesn't sound too bad to me."

The place was spartan but showcased in a way that exhibited great taste in design. Inside, the hall wall was exposed brick, and the ceiling was lined with timber beams. A few occasional tables were strategically placed with lamps, pottery, and flower arrangements, and a great iron pentagram took center stage on the wall. The renovators had done a marvelous job updating it, without losing any of the original character or class.

Charlie took us through to the left, although we could have found the kitchen ourselves—all we had to do was follow the noise. The kitchen was modern, although I couldn't see much of the décor because almost the entire coven currently filled it. Really, I thought, we could probably fit our whole house inside this one room. Like those in many magic practitioner's homes, Charlie's kitchen was divided into two sections: one for cooking and one for mixing spells and potions. Right now, everyone lingered on the food side; the center island was strewn with all sorts of goodies, and our friends were busy diving into the best food catering could provide.

My three younger sisters were already in the middle of it all, laughing loudly with their friends, and shoving copious amounts of food into their ever-gaping mouths.

"Ah! There's the Lucases. Back in a tick!" My mother dashed to the far corner of the room, ready to digest as much gossip as was to be had.

True to his word, Charlie steered us through the kitchen and over to a small room next door. A handful of senior coven members had gathered there. I smiled cordially as we passed them, but we didn't stop—we were headed straight for his two sisters, who were still standing over by the window, a little apart from the rest of the gathering. Fitz wasn't with them anymore. Good. I would have found his presence distracting and unwelcome.

"Caro and Lou, this is Jane Bennet, Izzy's sister. You met Izzy last night at the Flaming Cauldron, remember?"

Caroline and Louisa looked me up and down, momentarily surprised, I guessed, at seeing me out of my goth gear. They nodded. I assumed I'd passed the fashion-police test this time.

The two sisters also scrutinized Jane and, seeming to find no fault, managed to smile in return. I couldn't have been prouder of her; not even a couple of stuck-up squirrels like these two could fail to be impressed by such beauty or by Jane's natural charm, which made them look like a pair of out-of-date pretzels.

"Nice to meet you," Caroline said genuinely enough.

"Caro and Lou are staying with me while I sort the place out." Charlie grinned, not taking his gaze off Jane.

Caroline laughed and placed her hand on Charlie's arm. "Of course, we had to. Poor Charlie here has no sense of fashion at all, and if we left him to it, you'd find nothing here but a couple of worn-down old sofas, a laptop, and a giant television."

"Nothing wrong with that." Charlie shrugged with a smile. "Sounds rather homey if you ask me."

Caroline rolled her eyes and shook her head. "Well, really, what *am* I to do with you?"

She glanced from Jane to Charlie, and back again. A lightbulb clearly went off in her head because she parted her lips into a knowing smile. "So, um, Jane, how long have you lived in Misty Cedars?"

"Oh, pretty much my whole life," Jane said.

"What about college? Didn't you go away then?"

"I went to Yule. It's a good school. Our father was a professor there."

"Oh, yes, Yule. That is a wonderful place. Did your father meet your mother there, too?" That question came from Louisa, and I sensed she already knew the answer as she didn't even bother to mask her knowing sneer.

"No, in fact, Dad met Mom at a coven harvest hop, back in the mid-eighties."

Charlie grinned. "I heard those days were a bit crazy-wild."

I nodded and had to smile along with him. "My dad would certainly agree with you."

Caroline's gaze took me in from head to toe. Like Jane, I was dressed informally in Jeans, but I was aware my homemade black top was covered in lint from where I'd been handling the wool.

"Are coven meetings always so informal in this town?" Caroline asked. "We generally get all dressed up in New York. I believe it gives the meetings an air of stylish sophistication. I don't suppose you're into that around here. More barn dance and May poles?"

"Really, Caroline? This is a casual gathering. Let's not put on unnecessary airs and graces, hmm?" Charlie said.

Caroline smiled and shrugged, but I could see she didn't like being chided by her brother. I swallowed the words I'd been about to spew at her. Poor Jane looked relieved. I gave her a little smile to let her know it was okay—I wasn't going to erupt. Not this time.

My mom chose that moment to find us. She came armed with a plate full of sandwiches and hummus and offered some to Jane and me.

"No thanks, Mom, I'm not hungry." I said.

"But it's really good," she protested. "I don't know where this lot came from, but it sure beats the crap we buy at Libras. Oh, Mr. Van Buren, I really hope you host the meeting here again! Everything is so wonderful."

Caroline smiled politely through this, and I realized she was waiting for an introduction. "Um. Mom. This is Caroline and Louisa Van Buren. Charlie's sisters."

Mom had stuffed a small prawn sandwich wedge in her mouth but managed to beam a welcome. She swallowed hard and uttered a breathy, "Howdy. My other daughters are running about someplace in the kitchen. Oh, I remember being so young myself, surrounded by young warlocks, having the time of my life. It's getting harder and harder to find nice warlocks nowadays, don't you think?"

Neither sister answered, but pursed their lips and exchanged a knowing look.

"Ah, Fitz," Caroline said, looking over my shoulder. "I thought you'd abandoned us already. Have you met Izzy's mom? And this is her sister, Jane."

The man in question had appeared suddenly at my side, and though I didn't immediately turn to greet him, I felt very conscious of his arrival. I could hardly forget the pig comment, and I stiffened, praying to Gaia he wouldn't talk to me. Still, I suspected he'd overheard everything we'd said. Well, everything Mom had said, anyway. No one else was saying anything about eligible single young warlocks, thank goodness.

"Nice to meet you both," he said.

I wouldn't say he was sarcastic, like Charlie's sisters, but there was a cold formality in his voice that suggested to me he couldn't care less whether he was introduced or not. I noticed my mom was looking him up and down, still uncertain of what to make of him. I suspected it wouldn't be long before she figured him out. She was a crazy old witch, but she had her moments.

"Charlie," Fitz continued, "I believe everyone who's coming is here. I think it's time we started."

"Sure, if you think that's everybody."

I noticed how Charlie deferred to his friend. Not that there was anything wrong with that, but it seemed unnecessary. After all, Charlie was a self-made warlock, and it was pretty obvious he could take care of himself. Weird character flaw, maybe? Who knew?

More importantly, I was dying to see a coven meeting taking place in an authentic seventeenth-century setting. How cool was this going to be?

Sure, I'd attended plenty of groups in my time, but we'd never worshipped in any place quite so old as this. My curiosity was piqued, so I put all other thoughts out of my mind and, along with the others, followed our host down to the basement.

Chapter Three

THE SPIRIT

I LOVED OUR COVEN. THEY WERE ALL FRIENDS AND NEIGHBORS, MOST OF whom I had grown up with or known for a long time. Some lived close by in Misty Cedars, and a few traveled regularly across the valley to worship with us. We were a mixed bunch of lawyers, doctors, gas station attendants, and Walbrook shelf fillers. Worldly status had no place here. We were one as a family, united by a common belief.

When the order to move came, there was a general shuffle as many donned their ceremonial robes, and in under a minute or two, we transformed from a motley crew to a serious band of coven practitioners.

I pulled my lilac robe over my head, the color indicative of my unmarried status. All right, I suppose it was a bit un-PC, but it was our tradition, and we liked to honor the old ways as much as we could.

Mom checked out all the robes too, but her attention was on the unmarried warlocks. They wore pale-gray robes with crescent moons emblazoned on the front. I knew her only too well and braced myself for the tirade I knew was coming.

"I really wish one of you would hurry up and get married," Mom said. She handed the last two robes in her bag over to Kitty and Lydia. Her focus languished on the newly married Tilly Moffet, née Smallbottom, standing just a few feet from us. She was just now pulling her new red robe over her hair. "I would love to see at least one of you in red before I die."

"There's no rush, Mom," I said.

"I think red would suit me better than this awful lilac thing," Lydia observed, raising her hands to look with disgust down her robe. "And why does it have to be so long? It covers everything up."

"Thank God for that." Jane laughed. "Especially since you left your skirt back at home."

"Oh, ha-ha! Very funny. But you'll see! You're all just too damned picky, and I swear, I'll get hitched before the whole lot of you, just wait and see."

In ye olden days, this would have been impossible, since the eldest must be married off first, then the second eldest, then the third, and so forth. The youngest just had to wait their turn and suck it up. But thankfully the rules were more relaxed nowadays, and no one had to wait. They could run off and get hitched any time they liked. I'd have no problem if Lydia found herself a husband before I did. As long as he was kind to her, wealthy enough to give her everything she wanted, and loved her more than life itself, I'd be happy for her. Come to think of it, that was what I wanted too. But what were the chances? What man could possibly put up with my temper? I was going to end up unmarried, unwanted, and living with lots of cats.

I rolled my eyes, and Jane ushered my younger sisters to follow the crowd. I guessed Charlie was leading them from the front, although I couldn't see him at the moment. We slowed as we all bottlenecked at the basement door. I looked for Fitz, expecting the big jerk to tower head and shoulders over everyone else, but he was nowhere in sight. Neither was Caroline, for that matter.

The cellar at Dark Coven was deep underground, and it seemed an age as we slowly descended the narrow staircase. I held my breath—there was no railing, and I hated heights. As much as I could, I clung to the cold stone wall with one hand, noting the stale air, though not detecting any unpleasant mold or rising damp. When I got to the last step, I breathed a sigh of relief—although I was surprised, since I could see nowhere to worship as we'd arrived in some sort of dimly lit cellar.

I exchanged glances with Jane, who looked as perplexed as I did.

Charlie was clearly visible up front now, as he led everyone past the barrels of wine and around a corner. Instead of congregating there, as I thought they would, everyone just disappeared. My curiosity was piqued until I realized—*shit!* There was another set of stairs just around that corner. There was a subbasement!

"Don't worry, we're not holding the meeting here," Charlie said. "There's another room farther on. This way, folks!"

I held my breath as my family disappeared into the darkness. *Crap. Why did they have to put these things so deep underground?* I knew the answer of course; we were witches, whoooo-oo—covens had to be careful, especially back in the day. I didn't have to like it though.

"Just a moment," Charlie said. He pulled out his wand from under his robe. "*Revelar!*"

There was a brief flash of light and a great creak as a heavy door opened to reveal a secret passage.

"Is that cool or what?" Charlie grinned. "A secret coven door! William Lucas showed me when we first inspected the property. When I saw that, I knew I had to have the place."

There were grunts of approval among the coven, and the group began to move forward again.

I inhaled, ready to brave it when I heard lowered voices behind me on the other side of the barrels. I was still hidden by the shadows, out of sight, and was just about to reveal myself when I realized who it was, and instead, I froze.

"Well, someone's totally smitten, I think. Did you see him checking out her butt in the kitchen? His eyes were glued to it the whole time. When they weren't glued to her face, that is." Caroline. Her voice dripped with disdain.

"Yeah, I noticed," Fitz said.

"She's certainly very pretty, don't you think? His type for sure. When in Rome, I suppose. I'm glad someone's found something to do in this shit hole of a valley. When do you think he'll get bored with this and head back to New York?"

"Not for a while, I should think. We've only just arrived." Fitz again.

"Sheesh." I could almost hear her eyes roll in the darkness. "Well, she's a nice enough girl," Caroline continued. "But that family. Uh! Her sister Izzy is all right, I believe. What do you think?"

"She looks tolerable enough now, I suppose, but did you see what she wore when we met her? Pathetic woman, I'd never dip my wand in anything so crass. So no, I don't think I'm in any danger of meeting the love of my life here."

I held my breath. *Like he was something special!* At least I'd been upgraded from a pig. I smothered my chuckle.

I was on the point of stepping out of the shadows to maybe punch him in the nose when I heard a familiar voice coming up the stairs.

"My goodness, here you are. I wondered where you'd gotten to. What are you doing up here still? I thought you were over all this stuff by now."

"Mom," I cried.

"Come on, take my arm, and I'll help you down the steps. Don't worry, we'll take it slow."

Probably prompted by the sound of my Mom's voice, Caroline and Fitz had come around the corner, and I could tell from their looks they were wondering how much I'd heard.

To hell with them. I had more important things to worry about. Like those stairs. I took a deep breath and did as my mom suggested, holding onto her arm and taking it one step at a time.

Still, without knowing it, they'd done me a small favor. Still reeling from the insult, the stairs became less of a challenge.

The subbasement was made entirely of stone and lit by colored ceremonial candles, strategically placed at all four points of the compass. A five-pointed pentagram had been cut into the stone floor, and a simple rose had been etched into the center of it. That touch was unusual, but pretty, even if there was a whopping great crack in it now. The coven members all hovered loosely around the outside, waiting for worship to begin.

Mom led me over to where the family stood in one corner. Jane was talking to Charlie, and I half smiled at his undeniable attention. Well, Caroline had been right about one thing, I supposed. It was like my sister was the only person in the room—Charlie had eyes for no one else. I only hoped she would make something of it this time and not let this one get away like the others had done. At least this one was worth keeping. Well, I thought so anyway.

"You okay?" she asked as I approached.

"You know what I'm like with heights," I said, since Charlie was listening. I'd tell her later. "So are we gonna get this party started?"

"What, oh? Yes, I guess I should." Charlie moved to the edge of the circle and turned around to face everybody. He cleared his throat, and his natural charm resonated through his voice.

"If I could have everyone's attention. Welcome to my home. I know many of you have wanted to see inside this building for years, and the Lucases here graciously accepted my offer to host today's meet at Dark Coven."

He smiled and motioned toward them, and there were a few hoots and *yays* among the crowd.

"I am told the oldest part of the house was built in 1653, predating the Salem witch trials, by a German settler escaping religious persecution. I believe the pentagram etched into the floor appeared on the original blueprints, but those were lost many years ago. His daughter, Goody Becker, who was burned at the stake for her beliefs, is said to haunt the place on the anniversary of her death, which I believe is today, as it happens, so I'll let you know if she makes an appearance while I settle in."

His chuckles dissipated when there were no snickers in the crowd. I wondered at the flippancy of his statement and shrugged it off as newcomer nerves. There were plenty of ghosts in the older part of town, some fair, some foul, but we all knew they walked among us. I tried to imagine what this Goody Becker would be like and what it had been like living back in the day. Pretty shitty, I guessed. Those were bad times. No Internet.

A cold shiver ran through me, and I instinctively looked around. I had never met a ghost myself, but people told me the first sign was a drop in temperature. But I saw nothing.

William Lucas stepped up to Charlie, and after conferring with him for a moment, the younger warlock nodded.

Charlie cleared his voice. He raised his wand over his head and said, "Xerarquía de cobertura."

In that moment, a golden light spilled from the tip of his wand and swirled about the members. As it touched each witch or warlock, their aura became deeper or more transparent. Nobody minded. The spell was customary when different covens mingled to worship. The spell determined everyone's place in the hierarchy, the stronger the aura, the more senior the witch or warlock.

"If the senior members of the coven would take their places on the inner circle, and if everyone else would line up directly behind them, we can begin."

Seniority in the circle had nothing to do with affluence, and everything to do with standing and magical ability. So I was surprised when Fitz passed through the crowd and took one of the primary spots in the main circle.

Even our host didn't assume that right; Charlie had deferred to the elders by standing in the second ring beside my sister, Jane. I shot a glance at her, but she didn't seem bothered by this show of arrogance, and looking about, neither did anyone else. Not even Finn Lucas, the elder cousin, who would normally take the spot Fitz had taken. I suppose I shouldn't have been concerned, since no one else was, and his aura was stronger than anyone's, yet I couldn't help feeling Fitz was taking liberties.

As High Priest of the host coven, Bill Lucas raised his wand and said the incantation to raise our protective circle.

"I humbly ask that the Goddess bless our circle so we may be protected here, in this space. So mote it be."

A quiet fell over our group as, wands in hands, we closed our eyes to focus on the energy around us all. Today was a balance day, our sole objective to bring peace to those that needed it ahead of the lunar cycle that typically brought chaos and disruption.

It was hard for me to clear my mind of all thoughts; there was too much crap going on up in my head, but until we thought as one, the magic wouldn't happen, so I bit my lip and tried my best to focus.

Our goal was to achieve total quiet. We didn't want to disturb anything, or disrupt the world, or do anything evil as numpies often supposed we did when we gathered in our circles. It wasn't about that at all. When we were one collective mind, we could reach deeper into the universe and provide a safe place for any soul seeking comfort, either from within our circle or outside it.

As each witch and warlock reached this state of harmony, they opened their eyes and raised their wand hand; all wands pointing to the center of the circle, channeling all energy to a focus point. My thoughts were calmed by the collective power of the coven, and at last I raised my own wand, completing the arc above us.

As my energy connected, purple streams of light emitted from the tip of each wand, and the whole coven was illuminated by a faint and pleasant glow. My soul felt peaceful, and I absorbed the chi of my friends and family who in turn shared mine.

Never in all the years we'd worshipped together over at the Lucas Barn had our magic drawn anything to us beyond a sense of communal peace. Perhaps not too many souls lingered in that pleasant place, but Dark Coven had a history, and an entirely different story to tell.

The temperature dropped even more, and I shivered. Then, to the coven's astonishment, a faint figure appeared under the apex of the wand lights, shrouded in a kind of gray vapor. The person was tiny, and at first, I thought it was a child, but then the mists cleared, and I saw it was a young woman. She was possibly in her twenties, but it was hard to say because her face...

I wanted to cry, not just because the skin on her cheeks bore the marks of fire, but also because I could feel her pain; we all could—we were one in the circle, joined in spirit by a common chi.

Timidly she turned, almost as surprised to find herself where she was as we were to see her among us. I wondered, was she a ghost or a demon? I had little experience with either, so it was hard to say, but I could sense no malevolence in her, only a deep yearning. I wished I could read her mind as clearly as her emotions.

She mouthed something, but had no voice, and I found myself aching to hear what she had to say to us. She reached out her hands, beseeching, but we dared not break the circle and reach back—there was no way to know who or what she was, and like it or not, some spirits were evil. And even if someone did happen to extend a hand, the ethereal-looking spirit might disappear at the slightest touch.

Frustrated, the small woman turned in the circle, her black-eyed, lifeless gaze falling on each and every one of us—until at last, she faced me. I felt a sudden sense of joy as she smiled, and her hands rose again, imploring, asking for Gaia knew what. The collective curiosity of the coven overwhelmed me, and I gasped, taking a step back to the wall and inadvertently breaking the circle.

The woman disappeared, and the candles flickered out, leaving us all in utter darkness.

Chapter Four

GOODY BECKER

"ILLUMINOUS."

Before anyone had time to panic, the candles flickered back on. Fitz lowered his wand, and we all stood aghast for a second or two. Then everyone in the coven began talking at once.

"Oh hell, did you see that?" someone cried.

"It must have been Goody Becker. I can't believe she appeared after all this time. So the stories must be true," Mr. Lucas said.

"I wonder if she'll be coming back?" Lydia asked.

"Maybe we could try summoning her again?" That was Charlie.

"Did you see her face? Poor little Goody. How she must have suffered." Mr. Lucas again.

"And what was that thing with Izzy? I thought she was going to pass out," Mom said.

Slowly, all eyes turned to me, but I had no answers, only the same questions everyone else had.

"What?" I said. Like I knew anything.

"That was cool." Lydia stood clutching her hands to her chest in glee. For once, I couldn't have agreed with her more. "You frightened her off though."

"I did no such thing!" I protested.

"Maybe she didn't like your face." Lydia poked her tongue out at me.

"I doubt that!" Mom said. "My Izzy is not bad looking at all."

"Oh, Mom," I said, fearful of where she was going. "Were you even in the same room? Did you see what just happened?"

Mom opened her mouth to answer, but thank fae, Jane stepped in and shut her up. "So does anyone know much about this Goody Becker?"

I could have kissed my sister.

"Only what I learned when I signed the lease," Charlie said. "Which wasn't much."

"Imagine being burned for your beliefs," Kitty said. She shuddered.

Fitz had been reading something on his cell phone, looking totally bored. Maybe mysterious specter appearances weren't a big thing where he came from, but my heart was still racing. He must be a cold bastard, I thought. Or maybe it was some kind of act, to make him look superior to the rest of us.

He slid his cell phone in his pocket and sighed.

"Actually, a lot of those burnings had nothing to do with religious fervor. They were more to do with rites of property. The women targeted were often old, or widowed, with no one to speak out for them. If they had a desirable piece of property, all someone had to do to get their hands on it was accuse them of witchcraft, and everything they owned would be forfeited. They were sitting ducks for any gold digger looking for an easy conquest. Your Goody Becker may not have been a witch at all. She might have been a victim of someone else's greed."

"I bet she was a real witch," Lydia said, her eyes wide with over imagination. "And has some crazy romantic story to tell, that's why she appeared today. She's probably looking for her long-lost love."

"Maybe," Kitty agreed. "That's why she kept staring at Izzy. Maybe her love was a woman, and Izzy is the spitting image of the woman she's been pining for all this time!"

I snorted at their nonsense and rolled my eyes. "As always, your imaginations are running away with you." I caught Caroline and Fitz exchanging knowing glances and cringed. "Can we just focus, people? This is important."

What I didn't add was I *had* felt a connection with the spirit, but what it meant, I hadn't the faintest idea. It wasn't any kind of romantic vibe, I felt sure of that, but what? How does anyone understand the motives of a nonspeaking ghost?

"Have you ever used a Ouija board?"

Wait, what? Was Fitz a mind reader? I took a step back from the group, feeling suddenly vulnerable. "Excuse me?"

"A Ouija board," he continued. "The woman was trying to say something. We could all feel that. Maybe if she could communicate with us, she could tell us what was troubling her. It seems perfectly obvious to me. But maybe, out here in the sticks, you've devised some other method to commune with the dead."

As soon as he said the word *sticks*, Mom puffed up her chest. "As a matter of fact, we don't generally commune with the dead at all. Out here in the sticks! Or anywhere, for that matter. We prefer our dead to rest in peace."

"Unless they're hot, and then they can haunt me any time."

Lydia and Kitty fell into a fit of giggling.

I scowled at Lydia. Was my entire family hell-bent on making us look ridiculous?

Still, I smiled and lowered my gaze to the floor. Mom and I rarely agreed on much at all, but I could see we were in complete accord in regard to Fitz-up-his-own-ass Darcy. Say what you like about my mom, but put down her friends and family and she would turn from bumbling brain to ferocious Mormo in a spell-casting second. We had that in common, I supposed.

"I think Fitz just means we might have devised some other method to communicate with her," Jane said. "He didn't mean to be rude, Mom."

"Oh, I know what he meant," Mom said, but her lips were tight, and I knew she didn't want to hear about it anymore.

Who knew what Fitz was thinking behind that furrowed brow of his? And what did I care? Caroline was smirking by his side, I suspected she was enjoying the hostility clearly brewing between him and our mom. Well, good luck to her. If her heart was on Fitz, she could keep him. It wouldn't be any skin off my nose, that was for sure. Hot bod or not, I wouldn't want to suck face with that twiddle-twat if he was the last warlock on earth.

Throughout the entire discourse, my sister Mary had listened intently, as if every word said was a matter of great import. "Ouija boards have long been recognized as an effective method of conversing with the dead. The Catholic Church thought it was evil of course, but there are plenty who have used one effectively."

"Thank you for that wonderful Wikipedia insight," Lydia sneered. She took Mom's hand. "Anyway, can we go upstairs? It doesn't look like this spirit thing is coming back, and I'm really hungry."

Fitz cringed, and I cringed too, because he did.

"What about Goody? Maybe we should all come together again and try to get her back? Does anyone have a Ouija board?" I looked hopefully at Charlie, but he shook his head.

"Sorry, not here anyway." Like him, everyone else was shaking their heads.

"I have one," Fitz said. For a second, I was hopeful. "Just not here." My hopes were dashed. "In my experience, they're not all that anyway. A bit of hocus pocus for the numpies. What a ghost really needs is a focusing soul to latch onto, the more the merrier, in fact…"

"So shall we just reform and try to summon her back?" I suggested. "Maybe if we don't break the circle, we can find out a little more."

"I'm not sure I'd want to bring her back," Mom interrupted. "You young'uns might find this all diverting, but it's very tiresome on my poor nerves. We met here today to bring peace to the coven, not for all pandemonium to break loose. I've had enough for one morning, if you don't mind."

I looked around for support. Charlie, to his credit, looked prepared to do whatever anyone wanted, but most of the coven members were shaking their heads. I guessed one visitation was enough for most of them.

"I'd try again, of course," William Lucas said, "but I fear we are all out of harmony now. I vote we call it a day, with our gracious host's permission?"

"Yes, yes," Charlie agreed. "Well, there's plenty to eat upstairs. I guess we should wrap this up. Um, William, would you do the honors?"

"Yes, of course. Everyone, please take your places."

I confess I was a little disappointed. Nothing so exciting had ever happened to me at one of these gatherings, and I was eager to learn more. But except for maybe Lydia and Fitz, no one else seemed interested in trying again. I was surprised by everyone else's lack of curiosity, but perhaps the elders were wiser than I was, and I decided it was probably best not to argue. For now, anyway.

The circle formed for a final time, and we all chanted the closing ritual.

> Powers of the West, the North, East, and South,
> Thank you for joining our circle today,
> Blessed be, Gaia, Mother of Earth,
> Hail and farewell as you go on your way.

"Well then, that's it," Mom said. "Now you can eat all you want to, Lydia. But we quick about it. I want to get back to your father and tell him everything that's happened. He'll be so sorry he missed all the fun."

I wasn't so sure about that. "You go ahead. I'll catch up with you later, Mom. I want to have a word with Charlotte's mom about this knitting thing. I can walk home after I'm done."

"Walk home?" Mom said. "But it's almost five miles."

"I don't mind," I replied. "I like the fresh air."

"Knitting thing?" Caroline asked, raising her eyebrows.

"Yes. I knit. I like reading too. In fact, I have a lot of interests. We don't live in a bubble here in Misty Cedars, you know. We have hobbies too."

"No one suggested otherwise," Fitz said.

Why was I so annoyed? I had already decided not to like the man, so what did it matter what he said or thought about our dining habits or general pastimes?

"Well," Charlie said, looking a little alarmed by the growing hostility. "This was certainly an eventful meet. I'm sure we'll all be chatting about it for days."

"I know I shall," Jane answered.

Charlie beamed, clearly pleased she was smiling at him.

"I think it safe to say this was one of the most eventful coven gatherings we've had in a while," Jane said. "I hope you plan to host a lot more of them in the future. It was so entertaining."

"Indeed I will," Charlie said, encouraged by her kindness. "As long as the Lucases don't mind. I would hate to step on their toes."

"I'm sure they'll be delighted," Lydia said. "Nothing ever happens over at theirs. The meets at the barn are rather boring, and this was a lot funner."

I shot her a look.

Lydia ignored me. "Now can we go upstairs? If I don't eat soon, I will pass out from hunger, and you might have another ghost on your hands."

"Yes," Mom said. "Come on, girls. We'd better get back up those stairs. Izzy, do you want me to help you?"

Ugh. My heart sank at the very thought of climbing them again.

"I will escort you if you'd like," Fitz offered. "You'll be quite safe with me."

His kind gesture surprised me a little. "Thanks, but I think I can manage. Going up is never so bad as coming down."

Since Mom was likely to leave before I got up those stairs, I pulled off my robe, ready to hand it to her. As I yanked it over my head, I noticed Fitz staring at me, curiously. For a moment I wondered if my top had ridden up, but checking it, everything was in place. Whatever.

In ones and twos, the coven began to ascend, returning to the upper levels. I purposely held back. I knew I could do this, but I didn't want anyone behind me or watching me when I tried. I felt self-conscious enough about this whole meeting as it was, without adding my sense of stupid to the mix.

Fitz, on the other hand, refused to go up with the others. Even though I'd told him I'd be fine, he still stayed with me, out of some pumped-up sense of gallantry, I imagined.

"You go on up," I insisted. "I'll follow in a moment."

"Actually, if you don't mind, I'd like to go last. I'm enjoying the, um, ambience of the place. You don't see many places this old, and the vibe really is quite something."

"Suit yourself. I'll see you later."

What else could I say? I couldn't force him to go up ahead of me. He was a grown warlock after all.

I turned and began to climb. I couldn't look back, only forward. To look down would make me dizzy, and I didn't dare risk falling, as there was no railing to save me if my legs gave way. I wondered how people coped with vertigo all those years ago.

As for Fitz, whatever *vibe* he'd been enjoying was already over. I was conscious he remained around four steps behind me all the way as I climbed. The man clearly was as stubborn as I was, so pretending he wasn't there, I made my way carefully, holding onto the cold stone wall for support, taking it one step at a time until I reached the top. It occurred to me that the smug, insolent twerp had wanted to follow me all the way upstairs so he could look at my ass. *Son of a bitch*.

Chapter Five
MAGICAL MOMENTS

WHEN I GOT HOME, LYDIA WAS SLOUCHED IN THE CORNER EATING something else, Mary had her nose in a book, and Kitty and Mom were folding the ceremonial robes on the kitchen table. Jane and Dad were nowhere to be seen. Situation normal. Yet I was wound up tighter than a two-dollar watch.

"Could you guys have been any more embarrassing, do you think?"

"What?" Mom asked, barely looking up. "Oh dear, have we unsettled your delicate sensibilities again, Izzy? Wonders will never cease."

"Can you stop trying to fob us all off on any man who would have us? You make us sound so damned desperate."

"Watch your mouth, Izzy," Mom said. "There's no need for that kind of talk. Anyway, I didn't do or say anything wrong. You're just highly strung. And despite all your big words, I bet you'd be just as delighted at finding a nice man as the next girl. So instead of picking on me, why don't you do something about it? Like try that thing, what's it called?"

"Magical Moments, the dating app," Mary said without even looking up from her book, as if they'd rehearsed this.

"Yes, Magical Moments. You never know, you might get lucky and find someone who'll take you and your bossy ways."

"I doubt it," Lydia sneered.

The others all grinned, and exasperated, I shook my head and bounded upstairs to my room, flopping on the bed as soon as I got there.

I kicked off my sandals and closed my eyes. What the hell had just happened? Perhaps no one cared because she hadn't addressed them, but Goody had focused on me. ME!

What did it mean? There had to be a reason, right? I wish I knew more about ghosts, but we'd never really talked about them before, and I had no clue what to do next. Maybe Charlotte would know? I leaned down to the floor, grabbed my bag, and rummaged for my cell phone. As soon as I had it, I sent a message:

Me: Hey Charlotte, how are you? You weren't at the meet?

Charlotte: No, sorry. Headache. Would have messed up the balance. Heard there was a ghost???

Me: Oh Gaia, yes! Incredible!

Charlotte: What happened?

Me: She just appeared—a birthday thing apparently. OMG, her poor face!!

Charlotte: Mom said.

Me: Do you have any idea how to summon them back? Ghosts?

Charlotte: No. Why would you want to?

Me: Because I felt she had something she wanted to tell me.

Charlotte: What would she want with you?

Me: Dunno, just had a feeling.

Charlotte: Wish I could help.

Me: No worries. I keep wondering what would have happened if I hadn't broken the circle.

Charlotte: Well, next time there's a meet, maybe she'll appear again.

Me: I guess.

Charlotte: Find out what you can about her. Not all the dead are friendly.

Me: Good point.

The wait-and-see approach wasn't exactly my style, but I didn't know what else to do. I resolved to look up Goody online once we were done, and if there was nothing there, I could always walk down to the local library after work tomorrow. After all, Charlotte was right. Who knew what she wanted? I'd never heard anything bad spoken *of* her, but she had been burned at the stake. That would piss anyone off.

Charlotte: Was Charlie there, and Fitz?

Me: Oh, not you as well.

Charlotte: What do you mean?

Me: Oh, you know Mom.

Charlotte: So? Move out?

Me: Yeah, right.

Charlotte: We could room. 50/50?

I stared up at the ceiling, focusing on the light over my bed and wondering if I stared too much, if I'd really go blind like Mom always said I would.

Me: Tempting, but no.

Charlotte: Why not?

Me: You know.

We'd discussed this before. Dad had been retired almost a year now. He'd been a professor at Yule University for years but had been forced to leave before he was ready due to ill-health. Not only that, but he'd had to take a numpy's mortgage to support us all, and since Jane and I were the only ones with any money coming in, he needed us at home. I couldn't support Dad *and* a second place.

Me: No can do. Unless I win the lottery...

Charlotte: Go back to school? Earn a bit more?

Me: Maybe.

If only school wasn't so damned expensive.

Charlotte: I hear ya. Time to go. Thumping head. Talk later?

Me: Sure.

As soon as she was gone, I opened Google. I got that no one else was that interested, maybe it wasn't a big deal to them, but it was to me. I typed Goody's name—there weren't too many hits, and I opened each and every one. My phone arm flopped on the bed. My search had revealed little more than I already knew about her, which was kinda disappointing.

And then I thought about something else Mom had said. I navigated to the app store and pulled up Magical Moments. It only took a second to download and set up an account. When I was done, an image of Charlie came out of the phone and started talking to me. I squeaked in surprise and almost dropped the phone.

"Merry meet, *Izzy*. Thank you for downloading Magical Moments. Looking for Mr. or Mrs. Right? Well, I have just the witch or wizard for you. Magical Moments has hooked up thousands of couples in the last few years, and we guarantee a true love match, every time! Just put your finger in the box, and we'll analyze your data to find the perfect mate for you. Just one click of a button, and it'll be sparkles and unicorns—that's our promise to our customers. Whether you're looking for Mr. Right, or Mr. Right now, we've got you covered. All forms of payment accepted. So what are you waiting for? Come meet your perfect love match and begin your magical moments!"

Charlie's image faded and was replaced by some very attractive prospects, including some pretty Elf boys and even Goblins, some of whom I had to admit were not bad looking at all. They smiled or wiggled their eyebrows or licked their fangs suggestively. One closed his eyes and puckered his lips, inviting me to kiss him, ewww!

I laughed out loud and closed the app. Really? Mom might think I needed a man, but I didn't. And if it was meant to be, I wanted to meet one organically. Not via some program that knew nothing at all about me. Binary love. Um, no, I wasn't buying into that at all. I wasn't that desperate, not yet anyway. I was an intelligent, vaguely attractive young woman with an amazing sense of humor and epic knitting skills. It was only a matter of time before the right young man came knocking on my door looking for socks. Or knowing my luck, climbing in my window to stare at me moodily as I slept.

After securing my phone on the bedside table, I turned over, closed my eyes, and took a nap. I dreamed of goblins.

Chapter Six
ROSINGS PARK

GEORGE WICKHAM WAS THE HOT NEW PARTNER AT LOWE, WYATT, AND Wickham, and he perched his beautiful six-foot-two frame on the end of my desk.

"How was your weekend?" His tone was low, with just enough of a rasp that I forgot myself, forgot everything but how he grinned down at me, waiting for an answer.

I doubted the senior partners at our paranormal law firm would approve of my ogling the warlock. Wickham stretched his neck, dropping his arms into his lap, pulling my attention to his shoulders, wide as an ox, and I was transfixed. Those dancing green eyes staring down at me didn't help, were equally drugging, and that smile alone, fixed right at me, stirred up the baser parts of me I didn't like to bring to work.

His perfectly tanned body was a whole shade deeper than it had been last time I'd seen him. Another weekend out on his girlfriend Fae's Skater, I guessed. Well, Daddy's yacht, anyway. Some girls had all the luck.

"Mine? Oh, it was good, really good. In fact, I saw my first ghost at our coven meeting. It really was something to see."

"Really?" George's eyes widened, and he parked his perfectly fine ass on the edge of my desk. "That sounds exciting. Tell me all about it."

I was surprised that the new junior partner would get all fluffed up over a simple haunting. I hadn't seen one before, but they were supposed to be commonplace enough, even if it had been a surprise to me. And if nothing else, George Wickham was clearly a man of the world.

"What do you want to know exactly?" I asked.

"All of it, really. I, um, well, hauntings are sort of a pastime of mine." He picked up my stapler and opened it to look inside. "A bit of a hobby, if you like. I find it all really fascinating. So tell me everything. From start to finish. Don't miss a single thing."

Who knew? "Oh, I see. Okay," I said, thinking. "Let me try to remember. Well, we'd just formed a circle, and were all meditating, opening up to the Goddess and focusing our chis."

George nodded but didn't interrupt me.

"That's when she appeared, right under our collective streams. The ghost, or demon, or whatever she was."

"Could you see through her, or did she look solid?" George asked.

"She was a bit transparent, yes."

"She was definitely a ghost, then. That's how you tell."

"Oh, right. Anyhow, the air became really cold. I almost died when she stared into my soul. Then she vanished. The candles blew out, and the cellar was plunged into darkness."

"Could she speak?" George asked.

I shook my head. "No. I think she was trying to, but we couldn't hear the words."

"Pity."

"Why? What are you thinking?" I asked.

"When the dead walk among us, they typically have something to say. Otherwise, why bother?" George wrinkled his brow. "Did anyone have any idea who it might be?"

"They're pretty certain her name was Goody Becker, a witch who used to live at Dark Coven back in the day. She's rumored to have haunted the place for ages before she was burned at the stake."

"Umm, interesting. Can you pull her up on the Internet?"

"I looked already, but there's not much." I pulled up Google on my computer and typed in her name.

"Pennsylvania witch burning—haunts on her birthday—yada—same old, same old—mystery—speculation about hidden treasure—predates Salem witch trials—not a lot to go on."

George grinned and stared at his beautifully manicured hands. "Yeah, well, that's not much, is it?"

"Do you want me to send you the link anyway?" Any coinvestigator was better than none, I thought.

"Sure. I might have a read of it later when I have some free time. It might be fun to get to know the natives better."

He moved like he meant to tussle my hair, which I'd worn loose around my shoulders today, so I quickly dodged out of his reach. "Hey, no touching the hair!" I laughed.

"Just playing." He smiled back. "I know better than to mess with a witch's locks. It's a hanging offense."

"You're not wrong."

I had to admit I liked flirting with the new boss. He was charming and playful, and saw the funny side of most things, which I liked. This new woman of his, Fae, was a lucky girl to have him. If they ever thought to split up, I could do worse than have a stab at him myself, although I fully knew the danger of workplace romances, having been burned in the past.

He glanced over at the senior partner's door, which right now was closed. "If you like, you can come with me later to interview a new client. It shouldn't be too difficult a job, just a wills and testament thing for an old vampire."

I shuddered. Vamps gave me the creeps, especially the older ones. They smelled funny, like bad wine, but a wine you couldn't help but drink. "Ugh, not unless I have to."

"Don't worry, you'll be quite safe with this one. I know he isn't practicing any more. That's why he wants a lawyer. He's over at Rosings Park."

"Oh, I see." Rosings Park was a well-known assisted vampire suicide house for vamps all over the world. I looked out of the window. The sun wasn't at its fullest, but it was shaping up to be a beautiful day. "Isn't it a bit early for vampires?"

"Yes. Let's have an early lunch to talk about the paperwork, and if it's okay, we can go in the early evening. You don't mind a little overtime, do you?"

"If you think it's okay?" I said, grabbing my bag.

"Sure, why not? Some field experience is just what the doctor ordered. Unless you want to read Pixie citations for the rest of your life?"

"Umm, no," I laughed.

I hadn't heard a sound from the cubicle next to me, but I knew my colleague, Mary King, had been hanging on our every word. She had a thing for George herself and would be jealous as sin right now, and the naughtiest part of me felt a little triumphant. George was hot. Who wouldn't want to spend the day with him, girlfriend or no?

Rosings Park was established some years back, offering the tired undead a respectable way out once their prolonged existence became intolerable to them.

When I'd first heard of it, I'd thought it was unethical, but over time, my opinion had changed. Rosings Park was the only place of its kind, and although I approved of it in principle, it still gave me the willies.

George and I walked along the hall leading to Matthew's room. It was lavishly decorated, resonate of a long-dead age. There were paintings on the wall of someone's stuffy ancestors, and marble busts and suits of armors clung to the widely spaced walls.

"This place must have been something else in its heyday." I marveled at the imagery around me, trying hard to take it all in.

"Different times," said George. "But the super-rich have always liked to show off their wealth, whatever the age. Nothing has changed about that."

I nodded.

We passed several nuns in the corridors. They smiled sweetly at us, though none stopped to inquire who we were.

"One thing I don't get though," I said.

"What's that?"

"Nuns?" I whispered. "Why nuns? Don't they bat for the other side?"

"They're medical nuns. Sponsored by the Vatican."

"I see. They're wearing their crucifixes. Is that wise? Won't it torture the vampires?"

George grinned. "They're necessary to protect the nuns. All it takes is one out-of-control vampire losing their shit and going for blood. There are lines they just cannot cross."

I nodded. There was a long sideboard against the wall, decorated with five vases full of lavender. The aroma was intense here, and I gagged and pointed to the vases. "That's a bit much, don't you think?"

"We're near the bedroom wards. You have to remember that vampire pheromones, even very old ones, are incredibly alluring. The nuns here are handpicked for their temperance, but even they have their limits. Apparently, the lavender helps mask the scent."

I grinned, trying not to imagine the nuns losing their self-control.

One of the nuns who ran the place joined us in the waiting room. "Mr. Devereux is ready for you now. Please take the stairs up to the next floor."

"Thank you," George said.

Matthew Devereux was sitting up in his bed, his laptop perched on his knee, a plastic cup of pills left untouched at his side. Like all vampires, I'd supposed he'd been beautiful once, though now he was anything but. His lank, silvery hair had lost its luster, his sea-gray eyes were sunken and watery, and his mouth, which once might have smiled in delight, was down turned and deeply wrinkled.

I knew vampires could live for hundreds of years, but I had never seen one so ravaged by time as this vampire was. As he closed the lid on his laptop, my gaze fell on his yellowing nails and gnarly knuckles. He wasn't pretty, but more importantly, when he looked up at me, I could see his eyes were cold and unkind. I shivered. Perhaps coming here hadn't been such a good idea after all.

Slowly, Matthew's attention turned from me to George.

"You have papers for me to sign?" Matthew asked.

"I do," George said. "Everything has been done as you requested." He held out the manila envelope he'd been carrying, but Matthew turned his head and gestured toward the table by the bed.

"Good. Leave them there, and I'll look them over when I'm alone this evening. It will keep my mind off...other things."

Matthew's attention turned back to me, and I could feel my blood begin to quicken. Heck, I hated vampires.

"You're afraid of me," Matthew said. "I can smell it."

"A little," I confessed. "I haven't met many vampires quite so..."

"Old?" Matthew finished for me. "Well, I don't suppose you have."

He peered at me more intently, and I sensed a mental tendril reaching into my head—or trying to. But it was too weak, and my natural defenses rebuffed his probe. I stared back at him, and he looked away.

"I'm not the power I once was, obviously."

It had been rude of him to try communicating that way without asking me first. But all at once, I felt a terrible sympathy for this old vampire at the end of his days. "I bet you can do better than that if you try really hard," I said,

"I doubt it. You're young, and you're strong."

I shrugged. "You're probably right."

"What are you both talking about?" George asked.

"I was just lamenting that your friend here finds me repulsive." I opened my mouth to protest, but Matthew raised his hand. He then turned it over to examine it. "Yes, I am so very old now. I wasn't always this way, but all vampires become ugly in the end. We're not truly immortal, you know. We just take a very, very long time to die. And I've been waiting for death for so long now. All I want is for this to be over, for this...life...to be done."

"Why?" I managed. "Can't you bite someone and be young again?"

A twisted, bitter smile tweaked the corner of his mouth, and he turned his head to stare at the small window that looked over the grounds and out to the lake. I noted the glass was dark, to prevent ultraviolet light from entering the room.

"I think you've read too many novels," Matthew said. "But then you are very young. I am not Countess Elizabeth Báthory de Ecsed, I don't bathe in the blood of virgins, and I don't become my perfect self every time I take the blood of a human—no, all this is pure romantic nonsense. I suppose we are beautiful for a while, but like all things in this world, we age, wither, and die. I have lived too long, and I have seen too much. The playmates of my childhood have long been in the ground, and I yearn to be with them once more. Life has no flavor for me now. I simply want to die."

I didn't know what to say, so I nodded. I couldn't imagine living in a world without those I loved—without Mom, Dad, and Jane, even Mary, Kitty, and Lydia.

"I think I understand," I said. My words felt feeble in my mouth, but Matthew smiled.

"Hmm. Perhaps you do understand some things. If I had been younger...well...perhaps that's best left unsaid."

Matthew sighed and reached over for the envelope George had left for him. "These things are so very dull," he said, weighing the unopened package in his hand. "Perhaps you can humor me with the short version." He patted the side of his bed, like he wanted me to sit down on it.

"I, um, I don't..."

"Miss Bennet is not privy to the contents of the letter. But let me assure you, everything is exactly as you requested. I have included an inventory of all your possessions and made exact calculations regarding the disposal of your worldwide assets. You have nothing to worry about, I promise you. It's all in there. Take your time, but sign it tonight."

"Huh." Matthew's nostrils flared in distaste. "The promise of a lawyer. Hmm. Time. I rather seem to be running out of that."

He put the unopened package down on the table and sank back into his pillow.

"Sit with me a while, Miss Bennet. I will miss very little in this life except perhaps the company of a beautiful woman. There is nothing quite like it in the whole wide world. Would you do that kindness for me? I know you're afraid of me, but could you offer me that?"

I turned to George, not sure what I should do. He shrugged and busied himself by pulling an armless chair over to the end of the bed.

"You'll understand that I can't just leave Izzy alone with you," George said.

The vampire rolled his eyes but didn't object. He closed them for a while, and I began to wonder if he'd fallen asleep. That said, wild horses wouldn't have dragged my ear to those lips to check.

"Tell me something of your life," Matthew said. "I see from your aura you are a witch, are you not?"

"Yes, yes, I am."

"I doubt you have seen much of interest, but tell me, what excitements have you faced in this little town of Misty Cedars? Let me see the world through those young eyes of yours."

"Umm, okay, err...where to begin?" I felt stupid, put on the spot like this.

George was behind me, and I looked back to him for help. His mind was already elsewhere, as he flicked through his iPhone, reading messages. "Tell him about the ghost," he said. "That was kind of interesting."

Thanks for the vote of confidence, I thought. "Um, okay."

I tucked a stray lock of hair behind my ear and turned so I could see out to Rosings Park's grounds through the colored window. Matthew felt a little too close and a little too clever for comfort. It was okay to sit here, this close, but I didn't want to look him in the eye.

"I imagine you're probably more familiar with local legends than I am," I said. "Have you heard of the ghost of Goody Becker?"

Matthew's reaction surprised me. The corners of his mouth curled, like someone recalling an especially pleasant memory.

"Heard of her? More than that. I courted her. Dated, as you might say now."

For the first time, I sensed no irony in his smile. The flash of remembrance brought warmth to his features, and a gentleness I never would have thought possible softened his eyes. Perhaps I imagined it, but for a brief second, I saw a reflection of the young vampire in him.

He closed his eyes, and his head fell back on his pillow. But then he recollected himself, opened his eyes, and sat up straight again. "Nothing came of it, of course. She had a fear of the undead and ended things before they got, um, interesting. So yes, you could say I knew her. Better than many."

There was a slight shuffle behind me, and I sensed George's ears had pricked up. As for me, I was conscious that my mouth had fallen open. Ignoring my earlier reservations, I stared at him in amazement.

"You and she were in love?"

"She was a beautiful woman, rather like yourself. And intelligent. Perhaps too clever for her time, and in the end, that might have been her undoing." His attention went to the window, though I wondered what he was seeing in those ancient eyes of his. He fell silent, and I began to think he'd forgotten we were even there.

"You mean about the burning?"

"What? Oh, of course, what else? That was a vicious business.

Regrettably, she had long since severed her ties with me, and I believe I was in Paris at the time. If I had known of her troubles, I would have come to her at once. I still loved her, you see."

My heart softened to hear him talk so. It had all been hundreds of years ago, but the unusual gentleness in his speech betrayed his feelings.

"So if I understand you correctly, you think you saw her ghost?" Matthew asked.

"We definitely saw a ghost," I said. "Whether it was Goody Becker or someone else, I really couldn't say."

Matthew leaned forward. "What did she look like? Where did this take place? Did she try to communicate with you? What did she say?"

"It happened at Dark Coven. We were having our meeting there. She was tiny, that's for sure, but she didn't speak to anyone, not exactly. I almost died when she looked at me..." I blurted without thinking.

Matthew raised a hand and stared at it. I wondered if he was imaging another hand against his own, another hand from another time.

"She was, indeed, a small woman. I could wrap her little fingers in my hand, thus." Before I could object, he took my hand in his and closed his cold fingers around mine. I shuddered, and he let me go. "Yours is considerably bigger. Hers were the hands of a child. What else? How did she look?"

"Her hair was loose about her shoulders, and it was dark—I can say no more than that because the image was faint. And her skin was horribly scarred..."

Matthew closed his eyes in disgust. "You know, in Salem, the witches were hanged, not burned. Their death was a kindness in comparison. The person who condemned my Goody—he was vicious. I tried forever to hunt him down, but he was cunning, and always one step ahead of me. If I take one regret to the grave, it's not finding the man who tormented her."

"Who was it?" I asked.

"His name was Thackeray Collins. He would be long dead now, I suppose, but still, I would have liked his death to have been at my hands. He deserved no better."

"There were a lot of religious zealots in those days," I said. "No witches were safe."

"Ha! Witchcraft had nothing to do with it. Anyway, not in the sense you mean. No, this was a matter of good old-fashioned greed. Collins was a Puritan clergyman, to be sure, but in this case, God didn't come into it. His motivation was pure self-interest."

"I don't understand," I confessed. Then I recalled what Fitz had said at the meeting about unscrupulous men accusing helpless woman of witchcraft so they could possess their property. I imagined Thackeray bloody Collins was such a man.

"Why would you? But perhaps it's best to leave the dead buried."

Matthew sank a little deeper into his pillow, and I heard the air slip slowly through his lungs.

"I am tired now," he said. "Come back tomorrow and we can continue our discussion. Right now, I need to sleep. George, make sure to bring her with you when you come back for these papers. I like her company. It's more companionable than yours."

"As you wish," said my boss. He rose and returned his chair to the wall, and I slid off the end of the bed.

The old vampire's eyes were closed now; perhaps he had no time for good-byes, or perhaps that wasn't the vampire way.

Odd. After all my reservations before, now I found I didn't want to leave. He had asked me for my story and then entertained me with one of his own. A better one. And though the sand was running out on his life, the vampire was determined to enjoy the time he had left with us. I wished he could have told me more, but this was his story, and he clearly wanted to tell it in his own way.

"Come on, let's let him rest," George said. "I'll buy you a late supper, if you like?"

I followed him over to door and glanced back. Matthew's eyes were still closed, but though he looked as ancient as before, there was something different about him now. A spark of life still lingered in those old bones, perhaps? I wasn't sure.

Like it or lump it, I would have to wait until tomorrow to find out what else he had to tell. And truth be told, I could hardly wait to hear it.

Chapter Seven

A LATE SUPPER

"I DIDN'T THINK VAMPIRES LIKED THE LIGHT?" I SAID. IT WAS SET NOW, but a little sun had still been in the sky when we first talked to Matthew. "I know the glass was tinted, but would that be enough to protect them?"

George was treating me to a fish taco salad and cold Chianti. As I finished my glass, he poured me another.

"Are you trying to get me drunk?" I asked. "What if my boss finds out?"

"Umm, no. Shut up and just enjoy yourself. As for vamps, well, I don't think any of them like the sun shining directly on them. But there's plenty at Rosings I've seen brave a little. At least, from a distance. Some of them have found a way to tolerate it. Don't ask me how."

"Hmm." I chewed my taco thoughtfully, trying to recall everything I knew about vampires. And George. He hadn't been with the firm more than a few weeks, yet he appeared to know so much about Rosings Park. "Did you do a lot of work over at Rosings? In your old job?"

"Some." He picked up a taco and bit the end. I grinned as a dollop of tartar sauce smudged the corner of his mouth. Apparently aware of it, he smiled back at me and licked it off with the tip of his tongue.

"It's a funny business, don't you think?" George said.

"What is?"

"This assisted suicide stuff," he said. "What do you make of it?"

"I don't know," I admitted. "I'm not the one dying. I try not to judge."

George nodded and swigged down half his Chianti in a single gulp. "Dying is a lucrative business. There's a lot of it happening."

"Is that what you did before in your old place?"

George wrinkled his brow.

"Settle things for the dying?"

"Something like it," he said.

"So what made you leave and join our little firm?"

"It was a good opportunity. Although I have to confess, I didn't always want to be a lawyer."

"Oh?" I pushed away my nearly empty plate and wondered if there was time for dessert. "What did you want to be?"

"Um, I can't tell you that. You'll laugh at me."

I crossed my heart. "Witch's honor, I won't do any such thing."

George looked at me thoughtfully. "How are you liking the new tenant of Dark Coven?"

"Charlie Van Buren? Quite a lot as it goes, he seems very nice. Why do you ask?"

George puckered his lips and nodded. "Yes. I've met him once, I think. By all accounts, he's a good man. His friends..." He scrunched up his nose and shook his head.

"Oh? I didn't know you knew them." Surprised, I pulled the dessert menu out from behind the condiment aisle. My attention was drawn to the triple chocolate fudge cake. I wondered if George would think me greedy if I ordered it à la mode.

"I do, as it goes. In fact, I knew Fitz's sister quite well. We were great friends, all of us, once upon a time. What do you make of him?"

"Fitz? I think he's a bit of a snob, actually. So to answer your question, not very much at all. All he ever does is look down his nose at everyone. Charlie's really nice, but his friend—I could take him or leave him. And from what I gather, I'm not alone. My mom can't stand the sight of him. I've never met his sister."

An amused smile crept onto George's face, and he grabbed a dessert menu of his own.

"Anything good?" he asked, nodding toward my menu.

"I'm a chocolate girl."

"I'll have the same then." George returned his menu to the stand and beckoned the waitress over. "Two of those, please." He smiled, pointing at the image on the menu.

The girl blushed. "Yes, sir."

"Can you make mine à la mode?" I asked.

She nodded. As soon as she left, I leaned across the table and spoke in a near whisper.

"Well, tell me the scoop then. Do you know anything wicked about him? Fitz, that is."

"I know he doesn't think very highly of us peons, but then I think you've worked that out for yourself."

I nodded. "You're hardly a peon."

He smiled. "Maybe not. Not now anyway. But there was a time..."

George hesitated, and I wondered what it was he was trying *not* to say. "Well, if you must know, he denied me my rights under a trust."

"What do you mean, denied you your rights?"

"Fitz comes from old money, like, practically dating back to Camelot type wealth—you know, incalculable? My family had been tied to his for years, attending the same coven, sharing in their fortune, and so on. You wouldn't know it, but my dad and his were lifelong pals—not in the same league, mind you. We never had two cents to rub together, but we did okay, and his dad and mine were tight."

"Okay," I said.

"My dad served his for years, and Fitz's father, well, he was a regular Joe and put some money aside for me in a trust. He knew my dad was always broke. Don't get me wrong—my dad was great, just bad with magic and money, and he left me with nothing more than a shoddy wand and a decent work ethic."

I nodded. "You must miss him very much."

"Every day. Anyway, when I came of age, I was supposed to get a stipend. I'm not entirely sure what I would have done with it—maybe open a care home for elderly witches or warlocks, I dunno—but when it came to it, Fitz put a block on it, and I didn't receive a dime. And I guess he didn't like where things were heading with his sister."

"Wait—what? He can't do that. That's illegal."

George shrugged and sat back as the waitress placed two dessert plates in front of us.

"There was just enough ambiguity in the trust to make its terms uncertain. A decent man would have honored it anyway, but we're talking about Fitz, so..." He picked up a fork and snipped at the wedged end of the cake. "But you know, there's always a silver lining. I wasn't that skilled at magic, so I went into the law to make sure no one could hoodwink me like that again. Now I make a comfortable living on my own, no handout needed. Life could be worse."

"That's awful," I said. "Why would he do that?"

"I'm a lot prettier." George laughed and shoved a large chunk of chocolate cake into his mouth. "Jealous, I suppose. Oh, don't worry. What goes around comes around. Karma can be a bitch, and one day he'll get his comeuppance, you'll see."

"You couldn't contest it?"

"Maybe if I cared enough, but as you see, I'm doing all right. And I get to work with the sick and dying anyway, so in the end, I got what I wanted in a roundabout way."

"I guess so." I still thought Fitz had to be a total shit though. "I'm surprised he gets on so well with Charlie," I said. "I mean, the two of them couldn't be more opposite."

"True, but Fitz isn't a total ass. He has his moments. And I don't think Charlie knows anything about the bad shit—why would he? He's got plenty of money of his own. That dating agency of his is doing phenomenally well."

"I suppose."

If I'd thought Fitz was a dick before, now I thought him possibly evil. An image of him looking so pious and at peace in the coven circle came to mind, and I wanted to scream and punch him in the throat! Sometimes life just wasn't fair. Poor George! More power to him for having gotten over it all, though. If it had been me, I knew I never would.

George began to pour a little more wine for me and gave me a look I knew only too well. Tempting, but no. I put my palm over the rim of the glass. "I'm good, thanks. Does Fae drink?" I asked.

George sat back in his seat and sighed, though he didn't look defeated yet.

"No more than most," he said. "But since she's not here, what does it matter?"

"Oh, I dunno, but I know I've had enough." *Change the subject.* "So Matthew Devereux, do you think he'll go ahead with this suicide thing? Or chicken out?"

"I couldn't say," George replied. "Some do, some don't. I would say he knows his own mind, though, wouldn't you?"

"That's for sure. I don't think I've ever met anyone quite so in control of himself. Is that a vampire thing?"

"Possibly. You have to be careful around them. They're very good at mind manipulation."

I nodded. I had experienced that tonight firsthand. Matthew would have invaded my mind if I'd let him. "I have to say, I'm a little nervous about seeing him again. I mean, I'd like to know more about Goody and all that, but now I'm away from him, I'm not sure how I feel about going back."

"You have to go," George said sharply. "You made a promise."

"I guess. But it wasn't your head he tried to creep around in."

"All the same."

I sighed. He was right, I supposed. And I did want to learn all I could from him.

I sipped the last of my wine, and when I looked up, George was smiling at me again with an unmistakable twinkle in his eye and purse to his lips that meant trouble. I didn't need any vampire superpowers to guess what he was thinking. Was that all men ever thought about? Ever? *Oh, well, not this witch, baby. Your luck has run out.*

"I guess I'm just tired. Do you mind if we go? That chocolate cake about did me in."

George's shoulders drooped, and defeated, he tossed his napkin on the table and raised his hand to signal for the check.

"Sure," he said. "If that's what you want?"

"Absolutely. Do you want me to pay half?" I volunteered.

"Not necessary. I'm expensing this."

I nodded, hoping the waitress would be quick about it. I was feeling awkward, and the sooner we were out of this place, the better. It had really been quite a day.

Chapter Eight

A GIRL'S NIGHT OUT

"OH, COME ON, IZZY, PLEASE. I REALLY, REALLY, *REALLY* WANT TO GO."

It was the most impassioned thing I'd ever heard Jane say.

"Well, go then," I said, hanging my purse over the knob of my bedroom door. "You really don't need me to be there. You can go by yourself."

Jane sat on the end of my bed and gazed distracted to the floor. She said nothing and stared into an empty space. Give me screams, give me hisses, give me spit—anything but this. Her silence was torturing me.

"Oh, all right then, I suppose," I said at last. "Just because it's you."

With a sigh, I kicked off my work shoes and changed into my comfier sandals. Apparently sometime this afternoon, Jane had gotten a text from Caroline asking her to join her and Louisa down at the Flaming Cauldron for a drink or two. She'd shown me the text.

Bring Izzy too, if you like :)

I was flattered by the afterthought. "I thought they hated the place. Where's Charlie tonight, anyway?"

Jane snapped out of her reverie. "Oh, the guys went up to the mountains to do some zip-lining, apparently."

"Ugh. Rather them than me. Any chance they might come back while we're there?"

Jane shook her head. "None, according to Caroline."

"Well, at least that's something. That Fitz dude gives me the creeps. What time do we have to be there?"

Jane frowned, probably remembering what I'd told her Fitz had said about me. "They said to get there by five for happy hour."

I glanced at my watch. Great. That was like twenty minutes away. I looked at Jane, who had clearly cleaned up after work and smelled all fresh and lovely.

"Well, they'll have to take me as they find me," I said, staring down at my clothes. "There's no time for me to change."

Jane was too pleased to argue and ran off to her own bedroom, leaving me free to do whatever I needed to do to get ready.

As soon as she was gone, I collapsed on my bed and stared up at the ceiling. *Who did I piss off up there to deserve this?* I thought.

Still, it was nice to take five minutes for myself. I could hear Lydia and Kitty fighting somewhere in the distance, but I closed my eyes and shut everything out of my thoughts. I needed to chill the hell out before I took on the poisoned sisters.

Ever since I was ten, I'd been able to project out of myself. It was my favorite kind of magic, the kind to promote calm and peacefulness. As I lay there, my temporal self sank deep into the mattress while my spiritual self left my body and floated a foot or so above the bed. I was relaxing and floating at the same time, and it was the quickest way for me to unwind whenever I felt stressed. It was a bit like what the numpies called yoga, only much more fulfilling, and I got to see myself fly. And with all the madness in our house, I did this quite a lot.

Soon enough, there was a knock at my door, so I opened my eyes and allowed my spirit back into my body.

Jane stuck her head around the door. "Oh gosh, were you discorporating? Sorry!"

I exhaled and slid my legs over the end of the bed, relaxed and ready for anything. "Yes, I was for a bit. But I'm good to go."

And I was. My hair didn't need any special attention, and my makeup might be a little smudgy after closing my eyes, but it wasn't that bad.

I could have zapped myself into shape with a dash of ley line magic, but the truth was I couldn't give two hoots what the ugly sisters thought. They would have to take me as they found me.

With less grace than my sister deserved, I forced myself up and grabbed my purse from the back of the door. I followed her downstairs and snatched my car keys off the windowsill next to the front door.

"You wanna drive?" Jane asked.

"Sure, why not? They're your friends, so you can drink. I'll be your designated driver."

"Thank you," Jane said. "That's very thoughtful."

It was a nice night, almost nice enough to walk to the Flaming Cauldron, but I figured the sooner we got there, the sooner we could get back again. Jane never really drank much as it was, and since I was off the sauce tonight, we could be in and out in a flash. Win-win. We could be home before the owls were out. We climbed in my Beetle and zoomed into the evening.

Caroline and Louisa were sitting at a high table in the middle of the bar, sipping Flaming Cauldron cocktails, the specialty of the house. They were odd little red cocktails, served in a martini glass, with fires that never burned lips and never seemed to go out.

Caroline clicked her fingers, and although the bar was busy, Benny the red-blooded bartender was over in a thrice, ready to do her bidding. His colleague, Sue, was back behind the bar, serving a short werewolf and looking as anemic as ever. It crossed my mind she might be in thrall to a greater vampire, since she looked like someone was feeding on her, but I was too polite to ask if this were true.

"I'm glad you could both make it," Caroline said. As always, she was impeccably dressed, her makeup looked professional, and she clearly enjoyed the attentions from the randy barman, even though I knew she would put him down in a heartbeat if he had the nerve to ask her out.

"What will you have?" Caroline asked. "This one's on me."

"I'll have whatever you're having," Jane replied.

I eyed my sister cautiously. I knew she wanted to make friends, but I also knew from experience that the shit she was drinking was strong. If she was trying to keep up with these two sophisticates, she might be in for it. Oh well, I was there to keep an eye on her, just in case.

"Just a water for me, Benny," I said.

"Whatever you like, sweetness." He winked at me and I smiled.

"I thought you didn't like this place," I said as I sat down and shimmied until I was comfortable.

"Well, it's not Fifth Avenue," Caroline said. "But we tried the other bar in town for lunch, and this is the nicer of the two."

She meant Emma's. I wasn't about to contradict her since Caroline was right. It was a bit of a dive bar. Still, I didn't like her saying it.

"We'll get used to this place in time, I'm sure," said Louisa. "We're so used to being spoilt for choice, back in the Big Apple. Still, it won't be for long. We'll be going back to New York soon enough."

"Have you fixed a date?" I asked, more cheerfully than perhaps I should have.

"Not yet, but soon," Louisa replied, smiling.

Caroline shot me a death stare, which I pretended not to notice.

"Ah, our drinks." I grinned at Benny as he put the glasses down in front of Jane and me, and he returned my smile with gusto. Pleased to see he was still my lapdog at heart, I took a sip of my water.

"So," Caroline said after taking her first sip. "I understand your dad was a professor? I'm sure he's living the life now, enjoying his retirement and all that."

The attack had launched early.

"Well, I know he would have liked to have kept working for a while longer," Jane said. "I think he misses academia, and I think we all drive him up the wall half the time. He's adjusting to it though. He'll be fine."

"Did your mother ever work?" Louisa asked.

"No. She had her hands full raising us." My sister winced as she took a sip of the flaming cocktail.

"Did you eat anything?" I asked.

"No. I'll take it easy." Jane put her drink down in front of her.

"You'd better."

"Of course, my dad's also retired," said Caroline. "He signed off in his forties. Couldn't wait to get out of the rat race, that's what he said. He's living the life now, though, out there on the golf course with his old corporate chums. But then he'd always been quite particular about putting money aside, and he has a wonderful investment man—the numpies are so good at that sort of thing. Your dad and he should have words sometime. I'm sure he'd be able to help him."

"Thank you," said Jane. "That's very nice of you."

The cold ice sent my teeth on edge as I crunched down on it. Was my sister really that innocent or just a good masker?

"It was so nice to hear from you both," Jane continued. "A pity we didn't get to see your brother and the others again, but another time perhaps?"

"I'm sure." Caroline's smile was twisted. "I did mention I was thinking of hooking up with you both, but he was desperate to do the zip-line thing. He's really quite the adrenaline junkie; my brother hardly comes up for breath, I swear. He won't be happy until he's broken his neck doing something stupid. Do you do any sports? Louisa and I love our Pilates."

"I'm not very sporty, no," Jane replied. She took a larger gulp of her drink, which was still flaming, and it seemed to tickle her nose as she twitched it.

"What about you?" Louisa asked, turning to me.

"I like to jog sometimes. Mostly I power walk."

"Ah, jogging. Not really my thing," Caroline said. "It's supposed to be really bad for the knees. But power walking, that's an excellent exercise for people on a budget. I fully approve!"

I couldn't care less whether I had her benediction or not. *Snooty cow*, I thought. But then I remembered I was there for Jane, so I kept schtum a little longer. *You just keep on pushing me, Miss Van Buren*, I thought. *Just keep on pushing.*

"These flaming cocktails are amazing," Louisa said. "Shall I order another round? Since the boys aren't here, we might as well get shit-faced."

"I dunno..." Jane said.

"Oh, go on, let's have some fun!" Caroline raised her glass in the air, and a moment later, Benny was back at our table, ready to serve. "Another round of the same?"

"Not for me, thanks," I said, tapping my glass. "Designated driver."

"Make them all doubles," Caroline continued. "Izzy can have a double water. Ha-ha!"

Oh, so funny!

Benny was quick to return, laden with drinks. Caroline and Louisa finished their first glasses quickly and deposited them on Benny's tray. Jane took a few sips, and I could see she was trying to keep up, but I knew she was wasting her time. These two were obviously seasoned partyers.

"So we were discussing the local talent," Louisa said. "Of course, I'm off the market, but there's no harm window shopping, is there? Who's at the top of your list then?"

Funny, the first thing to pop into my head was George, although he was already taken, and I knew I had no chance there. Unless it was just for the other, which I was definitely *not* up for.

"Well, there's Benny at the bar," I replied.

Caroline half turned and smirked.

"Easy on the eyes, I suppose. Is this a full-time gig for him, or does he have his sights on something bigger?"

"I don't know." I sipped my water and looked in Benny's general direction. "You'd have to ask him. I've never heard anyone complain about him, though. In fact, he comes highly recommended."

"Well, I'm sure we could all do better than the local bar staff." Caroline ran her index finger around the rim of her glass. "Come on, Jane, you're falling behind. Hurry up and we'll order another."

I was about to suggest Jane do no such thing, but she glanced at me and shook her head. *Oh well*, I thought. *Your funeral.*

"You work for a law firm, I believe," continued Caroline. "There has to be some decent action in there. And your clients, well, a paranormal legal must have contact with all sorts of naughty people. I do love a bad boy myself. Take Fitz, for example. He's totally badass."

"Fitz Darcy?" I said. "That's not how I'd describe him."

"No?" Caroline chugged back the last of her flaming cauldron and smacked her lips. "Those are damn good drinks. Anyway, where was I? Oh yes, Fitz. The man is absolutely loaded. Knows everyone. Been everywhere. Massive house up in Maine in the exclusive dragon district. It will be a lucky girl who gets him."

"So why don't you whip him up?" I asked. "I mean, if he's such a catch?"

"Given the chance." She grinned. "I imagine it's just a matter of time."

To be honest, I hadn't noticed Fitz show any particular interest in Caroline, but then again, I barely knew them. And what did I care?

"There's no one else quite like him, you know. And he has such a fabulous ass." The drink had definitely loosened Caroline's tongue, and I wondered how many she'd had before we'd got to the bar. "Come on, come on, drink up."

"Don't if you're not ready," I said to Jane.

"I'm good," my sister said. She smiled into her glass. "And these are rather moreish." She took a deeper draught of the cocktail, and I noticed Caroline's eyes light up defiantly.

If it weren't for Charlie...

"I heard you went to visit an old vamp at Rosings Park," Louisa said. "I have to say, that place gives me the creeps. But young vamps, wow, some of them are so hot, don't you think?"

"Where did you hear that?" I asked.

"Oh, I think Charlie mentioned it. Maybe. I dunno."

I shot Jane a look, and she gazed sheepishly down into her glass.

"The trouble is, they don't age very well," Caroline chimed in. "A lot of them are loaded, though. I'll give them that."

"Would you go with an old one just for his money?" I asked.

"If he wouldn't bite me and it was absolutely guaranteed that he would die before I did, sure, why not? It's not like they can take it with them. Don't look so shocked, Louisa. I wouldn't be the first babe to bed down with an older guy, and I sure as hell wouldn't be the last. Anyway, Louisa has a thing for werewolves."

Louisa flushed pink and hid behind her glass. She took a long sip before responding. "Oh shush, Caroline. You'll never let me forget that, will you?"

I smiled in spite of myself. "Oh, do tell. We love a little juicy gossip."

"There's nothing much to tell," said Louisa. "I had a tiny crush once, but it was nothing. Caroline is being silly."

Pity. It might have been fun to hear more. There were a few weres in Misty Cedars, but they mostly kept to themselves. Shifters were just as bad, although they tended to mix more than the weres.

"Silly my foot, you had your tongue down his throat at your bachelorette party."

This time Louisa went positively beetroot. If Caroline was like this with her friends, I wondered how shitty she would be to an enemy.

"You're an asshole, Caroline," Louisa said.

"But you love me," Caroline teased.

I wasn't so sure about that.

Jane was looking a little flushed herself but continued to sip her cocktail at a steady pace.

"Don't you think we should order something to eat?" I suggested.

She shrugged. "I'm okay for now. Maybe in a bit."

Caroline smiled. "She's a big girl. I'm sure she can handle herself. Anyway, we're all here to protect her, and I have my superpowers after all."

With a flourish of her hand, her own glass slipped right through the wooden table, and I instinctively looked under it to see where it had got to. There it was, hovering inches from the surface. I righted myself up, and as I did so, Caroline waved her hand again, and the glass came back through the table without spilling a drop of the red liquid.

"Cool party trick," I said.

"Works better with my wand."

"You'll always have a job as a magician if your marriage plans don't work out."

Caroline treated me to another death stare. Before she had a chance to retaliate, I slid off my stool. I needed to pee pretty bad.

"Back in a minute," I said, "bladder alert."

The bathrooms at the Flaming Cauldron were pretty well maintained, with hand lotion and hair spray laid out for the guest's convenience. As a special consideration for their particular clientele, they also offered an assortment of dried herbs and powdered roots, arranged in tiny wooden boxes. I reached for the lavender and mixed it with some of the oil in the medicine dropper, rubbing it into my temples and onto the back of my hands. I would have liked some eyebright, just to keep my wits about me, but the bathroom store was limited, and I had to go with a soothing potion.

It was taking all my willpower not to lash out at Caroline, and I thought the only thing really stopping me was I sensed she wanted me to lose it. She would like that, I was sure, to prove to her friends what rednecks we really were.

If only Jane had the sense to see through her snarky comments, but Jane was desperate for Caroline and Louisa to like her, so for now, I just had to put up and shut up.

Resigned to the inevitable, I straightened my shoulders, took a deep breath, and went back out to face my new demons, hoping the night wasn't going to turn to shit.

The volume was increasing by the second, and it had nothing to do with the tunes coming over the jukebox.

With every drink they chugged, their voices grew louder, and we were drawing the wrong kind of interest from all around the bar.

"I think it's time we went home," I said to Jane. I wasn't kidding. This was her fourth cocktail, and she was taking it down on an empty stomach. She was white as a ghost and was beginning to sway in her seat.

"I don't want to go home." Jane giggled, but her eyelids were starting to droop, and she slurred her words. "I'm having way too much fun."

"Don't worry, we'll look after her," Louisa said. "We can call her an Uber if she needs one."

"Thanks, but I'd rather not." I stood up and wrapped the strap of my purse over my shoulder. "Ready?"

Whether Jane was ready or not was immaterial. She had turned a nasty shade of green. "Come on, pretty troll, let's get you home."

"I just...need...some fresh air," Jane gasped. She almost kicked the high table over as she slid off the end. "Can we go outside?"

"She didn't have that much," Louisa observed. "We've had twice as much, I'm sure."

"Well, Jane's just not used to it," I explained. My sister didn't look too steady on her feet, so I thought it best to get her outside fast.

The bar was packed, and we had to dodge a rowdy group of half-troll lacrosse players. They watched us with amusement, though an intoxicated witch wasn't exactly big news in this place.

"Yeah, yeah, nothing to see," I said as I waved them off.

Out under the streetlights, Jane looked positively goblin green.

"I think I'm gonna be sick," she said. Sure enough, a moment later she was bent double, and a ghastly spew of red stuff shot from her mouth.

"Having a bad time of it?"

I turned to see Charlie and Fitz stepping out of Fitz's car. Going by the alloys, he was driving something posh, and I didn't recognize the emblem. It was Fitz who spoke, and his expression was as inscrutable as ever.

Great. Caroline would probably jump with delight if she knew what the men had just witnessed.

"She can't hold her liquor. She'll be fine."

"How much did she have?" Charlie asked. His brow furrowed with concern.

"Not that much. Four glasses I think, but she doesn't usually drink, and she has no tolerance for it. She'll be fine in a bit."

Jane stood up, and there was a nasty-looking dark stain down her top.

"I'd better drive her home."

"Where's your car?" Fitz asked.

I stared up the steep street and knew my Beetle was somewhere up there in the dark. Parking had been tight when we'd got here, and there had been no room to even hex into a spot.

"It's a fair walk, but I think she can make it," I said.

Jane responded by upchucking again.

"Put her in my car," Fitz said. "I'll take her back to Charlie's, and you can both follow behind us."

"It's okay, I can get her home," I argued.

"And have her mom see her like that? No. Let's get to Charlie's, where we can clean her up a bit first. You don't mind, do you, Charlie?"

"Not at all."

"That's settled then. Come on."

Before I could object, Fitz supported her arm and walked her carefully over to his sporty something. When he opened the door, I peeped inside. It sure looked expensive.

"She might puke again," I said. "Do you really want that all over your dash?"

"I'll chance it," he said.

Gently, he coaxed Jane down into the bucket seat, and she groaned. To my relief, she turned her head to the side and only dry heaved.

"It looks like the worst is over," Fitz said. "I'll see you both back at the house."

Carefully he closed the passenger door and sped round to the driver's side. A moment later, he pulled slowly away from the curb, and the two of them were gone.

"Well, really," I grumbled, turning to Charlie. "He didn't waste any time."

"Don't worry, she's in safe hands. You can absolutely trust Fitz. Does she often get that way?" he asked.

"Absolutely not!" I protested. "She's not that fond of booze. She really wants them to like her, so she drank more than was good for her."

"Ah," Charlie said. "I can relate. And those two can certainly put it away. So, um, where's your car?"

I pointed up the road, and we both turned together.

"You don't want to say hello to Caroline and Louisa?"

"I'll talk to them later. Let's see how Jane's doing first."

"I thought you two were zipping?" I said. "We weren't expecting to see you tonight."

"We were, and then we were supposed to go out for a few drinks on our own, but Caroline texted us to say you were all in the bar, and Fitz and I thought, why not?"

"Where's Old Hursty?" I asked, remembering his other friend we'd met that first time at the Cauldron.

"At my place. He's not one for sports. I wouldn't be surprised if he was in bed already."

"I see."

He fell silent, and I wished I had the gift for mind reading. Then he said, "Has your sister said anything about me at all?"

I smiled a little on the inside. "Like what?"

"Oh, I dunno. Anything really." He clammed up again.

"My sister is a tad shy when it comes to guys, but I think she likes you. I guess you'll have to ask her. Ah, here's my car."

I was grateful for the interruption, and for the next minute or so we were busy, buckling up and such. Knowing he'd arrived in such an amazing car, I wondered what he'd make of my old jalopy. To his credit, if Charlie had any reservations about her roadworthiness, he kept them to himself.

"So how long have you known Fitz?" I asked.

"Oh well, just about my whole life. We even roomed together at college. Those were fun times."

"I bet." The word Fitz and fun didn't compute in my brain. "Has he always been so stuffy?"

Charlie grinned and turned to look out of the window at the passing lights. "I know what you mean, but he's not bad, not once you get to know him. He's just a bit awkward around new people."

"You mean, poor people."

"No, I didn't say that." Charlie faced forward and grabbed his knees. I wondered if my speed was a little scary for him. "Give him a chance. He'll grow on you in time. And trust me, he's a good man to have around in a crisis. There's no one better."

I grunted and focused on the road. He had certainly taken command of the situation back there at the Flaming Cauldron.

"Is he always so high-handed?" I asked.

"He does what he needs to do to get the job done."

"I see."

Dark Coven was a short distance up the road, and I slowed down and turned on my high beams. It was really dark out here, and the probability of hitting a deer or raccoon was high.

Fitz's car was parked in front of the house, and I pulled up behind it. Charlie slipped out of the Beetle and dashed inside. I dashed after him as quickly as I could, not wanting to be left behind.

"Fitz!" Charlie cried. He ran up a set of broad stairs, and I followed him.

It wasn't hard to find the other two. Halfway along the landing, I saw my sister on her knees, her head down the toilet. Fitz sat on the edge of the bath, holding her hair out of her face with one hand, a hot flannel ready for her to use in the other. Nice.

"How is she?" Charlie asked as we approached.

"She's fine."

"Did she puke in your car?" I asked.

Fitz shook his head. "Thank Gaia, no. There was some dry heaving, but apart from that, I think she's getting better. Does she have to work tomorrow?"

"Yes. She works in a daycare."

"Then we'd better sober her up and clean her up tonight. Charlie, does your sister have a robe she can wear while we wash her clothes?"

"There really isn't any need," I said. Jane turned to me, and in the stark light of the bathroom, I noticed just how bad the stain down her front was. "Um, maybe you're right."

"I'll go look," said Charlie.

"We'll fill her full of water to flush her system," Fitz said. "Water really is the best magic for this kind of thing."

"I know a good incantation for it, too," I said.

> "Spirits who are near us be,
> Save sweet Jane from misery,
> Take her headache and dehydration
> And teach this poor soul moderation!"

As I spoke the words, a small cloud formed over Jane's head, and with a pop like an exploded balloon, it began to rain, sobering her up.

"That's a good one," said Fitz. "I haven't heard it before."

"My dad taught it to me."

Jane groaned and put her arm on the toilet as she tried to stand. In a trice I was there with her, helping her to her feet. I noticed Fitz hovering nearby, ready to help if he was needed. Charlie appeared in the door with a gown, which I took from him.

"Thanks!"

Both men cleared out of the bathroom, and I locked the door.

"How did you get into this state?" I remonstrated.

"I dunno, I guess I knocked it back a little too quickly."

"I'd say."

Jane looked at the door, and for a second, I thought she might be sick again. "Oh God, why did *he* have to see me like this?"

I knew she meant Charlie, and frankly, I couldn't have agreed more. What the hell would either of them be thinking of us now? Still, no point crying over their good opinion. Or vomit.

"Get out of your things and take a shower. Let's get you cleaned up so we can both get home."

"I'm sorry." Still, Jane did as she asked, though she kept apologizing profusely. As soon as she was safely under the jets, I scooped up her things, closed the bathroom door behind me, and went off in search of the others.

I found them both in the kitchen, and they looked up when I approached. They both looked down at Jane's bundle of clothes.

"I'll show you the laundry room," Charlie said.

"Thank you."

Charlie's laundry room was about the size of my bedroom. It was just off the kitchen; he pointed to a cupboard.

"You'll find whatever you need in there, I think." I heard a beep, and Charlie reached for his phone. "Excuse me, it's Caroline."

While Charlie went off to talk to his sister, I focused on navigating the cockpit-like control panel that confronted me. There were more buttons on this thing than a 747. Thankfully, it was a lot easier than it looked, thanks to some diagrams, and I soon heard the reassuring gush of water and the hum of the drum turning.

I wandered back into the kitchen where Fitz was making something hot to drink.

"I'm making tea. Do you want some?"

"No thanks, I'm good," I said.

There was a large table to the right of the kitchen area, and I sat down at it and watched while he maneuvered around Charlie's kitchen. Fitz certainly seemed at home, and though Charlie hadn't been here long, somehow Fitz knew where everything was.

As he bustled about the cutlery drawer, I heard a raised male voice and realized it was Charlie, shouting. Fitz must have heard it too, but he continued pouring water into his mug, ignoring it.

"Caroline can be a handful when she's had a few," he said simply.

"Can't we all."

He glanced my way. "You seem perfectly in control."

"Designated driver," I said, miming my hands on a steering wheel.

Fitz shrugged and grabbed some milk from the fridge. He was dressed for zipping, his athletic top showing off his defined muscles and rather pert backside.

Fitz looked up, and I averted my gaze just in time. Anyway, what was the use in a fine butt if the rest of the package was damaged?

With nothing to say, I stared at the grain of the table, calculating how long the wash and dry cycle would take—the sooner I was out of here, the better.

Fitz sat down at the chair by my side, his hot drink in hand. I had nothing to say to him, so we sat in an awkward silence. We stayed like that until Jane came down, wrapped snug in Caroline's bathrobe, her hair turban-tied in a towel. She looked a lot better.

At that moment Charlie returned to the kitchen, and seeing her on her feet, he made a beeline for her. "Can I get you something?" Charlie said. "A cup of coffee? Some water? I could make you a sandwich if you like."

She shook her head, turning slightly green. "Nothing to eat, thanks. Some water would be nice."

Once he had her sitting safely at our table, her wish was his command, and he made straight for the refrigerator and pulled out a jug of filtered water.

"Feeling better?" I asked.

"Much. A drink of something and I'll be fine."

"That'll teach you," I said. "As soon as your clothes are dry, we'll get going."

"There really isn't a need," said Charlie. He handed Jane a glass of cold water, and she sipped it carefully. "She can stay here for the night—you both can. I have plenty of guest rooms. I'll just have to make a bed up for you both. It wouldn't be any trouble."

I could see how eager he was to have us both stay over. Well, at least Jane for sure. But we were both working girls.

"I think we need to go," Jane said. "It's very kind of you, but I'm a big girl. I'll sleep better in my own bed. I have to be up early in the morning for work."

Charlie's shoulders slumped, but Fitz looked as inscrutable as ever. "Whatever you think is best," he said.

I turned to Charlie. "What did Caroline say? Did she mind us just shooting off like that?"

Charlie grinned. "Never mind her. She enjoys a good reason to moan. I told her about your Jane, and she calmed down a bit." He faced Jane. "She sends her love and hopes you're okay."

"I'm fine," Jane said. "Well, I will be in a bit."

"Well, since we're not going out, if it's all the same with you, Charlie, I'm going up." Fitz pushed back his seat and returned his empty cup to the sink. "It's been an eventful evening."

Charlie's grin remained plastered to his face, but I couldn't tell if Fitz was being pleasant or sarcastic. He really was an odd sort of dude.

"Night then," I said, perhaps more curtly than was called for.

"Good night," Jane said. "And thank you."

Fitz nodded to her and, without another word, headed off to the stairs. He was a weird one for sure, but strangely, as soon as he was gone, I felt a little uncomfortable. Perhaps it was my inner gooseberry; three was an awkward number after all, but all the while the washing machine tumbled, I found myself staring at the stairs. I secretly hoped Fitz would come back down again, if only to make up our numbers.

Regardless of what I wanted, he did not return. All I could do was pray the 747-styled tumble dryer would do the job quickly, so we could get the hell home before Caroline and Louisa got back from the Flaming Cauldron.

Charlie and Jane talked for a while, but I didn't listen to what they were saying. I wandered around the kitchen and out into the hall while waiting for the washing and drying cycle to finish. I examined the various statuettes and paintings, and I thought about the cellar downstairs, with its ancient pentagram, and I recalled the ghost of Goody Becker. I extended my senses but couldn't find any trace of spirits lurking in the vicinity. Maybe that was just as well.

I was relieved to hear the beeps from the laundry room. Reaching inside, I found Jane's clothes were toasty warm. I fished them all out and returned to the kitchen.

"Come on," I said, "time to change."

Jane stood up slowly, massaging her head. She wobbled a bit on her feet but managed to follow me back into the laundry room where I helped her change. Once she was all dressed, we went back to the kitchen.

"Thank you, again," Jane said to Charlie.

He scratched his chin. "Not at all. Anytime you feel like upchucking again, my laundry is at your service."

Jane managed a weak smile at his humor.

"Come on, let's get you home." I nudged her to the door, anxious to be off home.

Outside, we climbed into my car, and Jane gave Charlie a wave; he waved back. *Sweet.* As we headed down the long drive, I glanced in my rearview mirror. Charlie was still standing on the steps, watching as we drove away. I couldn't help but think that despite everything, the night had been a success.

Chapter Nine

THE BREW

IT WAS ANOTHER EXCITING MORNING AT CASA BENNET. THE BREAKFAST ritual was in progress. I watched with amusement as my sister Lydia danced around the kitchen in next to nothing while she waited for her Pop-Tart to jump out of the toaster. Dad looked her up and down over his newspaper; he shook his head sadly and, sighing, disappeared behind his copy of the *Misty Cedars Times*.

"O EM GEE, I can't believe they're actually coming to Misty Cedars!" She grabbed the hot tart out of the toaster and dropped it on her plate.

"Who are, dear?" Mom was sitting in the next room, her feet up on the ottoman resting the swelling ankles she didn't have.

"Why, The Brew, of course!" Lydia said, blowing on her fingers.

"All this fuss and nonsense over a cup of tea?" Dad said, as he nibbled on a piece of buttered toast.

"Don't be crazy. Come on, The Brew! You must have heard of them. They're only the coolest band in the entire universe, and they're coming here soon. This can't be happening!" Lydia was almost singing.

"The answer is no."

Lydia glared at the back of Dad's newspaper like he was the dumbest creature on two legs. "I haven't even asked for anything yet."

"But you will. And the answer is still no."

Lydia snorted and chewed thoughtfully on her Pop-Tart. I knew when my sister was scheming and sensed trouble ahead.

"How long will they be in town for?" I asked.

"A couple of weeks at least, I think. They're getting ready to tour their new hit single, 'Toil and Trouble,' and I think the lead singer's family lives here so they're taking a break before things get wild. Hell's bells, it's so exciting, isn't it?"

It made sense. Why else would such a huge band want to hang out in a little town like ours?

"Charlotte told me they'll be performing live at the Flaming Cauldron for one night only. Apparently, they're doing it as a favor to the owner. How cool is that? Her dad can get a special deal on the tickets if we ask her."

This was awesome news. I wouldn't mind seeing them myself and made a mental note to talk to Jane about it later when she came home from her daycare job. I hadn't seen her this morning and hoped she was fully recovered from last night's shenanigans. I'd sent her a *u ok?* text, but she'd only replied, *yep*, which told me nothing.

"Mom, can you lend me some money so I can buy the tickets? I won't be starting at Walbrook's for a few more weeks, but I can pay you back when I do. Please?"

"I'm sure something can be worked out, sweetie," Mom called from the other room. "Leave it with me and I'll see what I can do."

Dad folded his paper and returned his breakfast cup and plate to the sink. Without saying a word, he looked sadly at me, and then with his head bowed, he disappeared into his annex. Something was wrong, and I knew it.

While Lydia rummaged about in the fridge looking for something else to eat, I rinsed my empty coffee mug out and put it on the rack to dry, and quietly went after Dad.

He wasn't sitting or reading, as he typically did, but was standing by the window, staring thoughtfully out into the garden. He turned and gave me a weak smile as I closed the door behind me.

"Everything okay, Dad?" I asked.

He didn't answer at first but resumed staring out of the window. After a minute, he sat down at his usual desk.

"Your mom and me, we were pretty wild when we first met." He smiled fondly, with that look he always got when he remembered moments from his early days.

"I know, Dad," I said. "You told me."

"Then Jane came along, then you, then the others. Boom, boom, boom, one baby after the other. They were great times, and we had a lot of fun." He chuckled and shook his head. "That fertility spell, oh boy, did it work, heh. When the other professors jumped on the numpy's pension plan, I should have joined, but I didn't. There was so much time ahead if us, and I told myself I would do it later. Tomorrow, always tomorrow." He sighed. "And now my daughter wants to do the most natural thing in the world, to go out and party with people her own age, and I have to say no to her. If only we could conjure a pot of gold—I know I'd do it."

"Are things really that bad?" I asked. "I know things are tight, but we're doing okay, aren't we? It's not as if the house isn't paid for. We've got that covered at least."

Dad's frown deepened, and he sat back hard in his chair.

"I'm very proud of my daughters, and when you went to college, I didn't want you all saddled with student loans."

"I know," I said, sitting on a stool opposite him. "You were very generous." I felt tense, and not for the first time I wondered where the money had come from.

"I took out a small mortgage on the house. It wasn't a lot, just enough to get you through your studies. I thought I had years of work ahead of me, but then, my heart."

Dad put his hand to his chest, reminding me of the bypass surgery he'd been forced to undergo a few years back.

"How bad is it?" I asked. "I can contribute a bit more each month if you need it."

"Don't worry. We'll be fine, I think," he said. "As long as I keep a tight rein on expenses. In fact, I met with my financial advisor to talk about it and invited Billy Collins over for dinner soon to see if he has any ideas."

"Ugh."

Billy Collins was a distant cousin. He had been born with a smidgeon of magic, so he was forced to make his way among the numpies. Still, he was doing well and had scratched his way up to the general manager position at the Misty Cedars Banking and Loan.

He gave me the creeps. Worse than that, we suspected he was a bit of a stalker. Jane often reported him bumping into her at awkward hours here, there, and everywhere. Just thinking his name made me shiver. And he was coming over to our house for dinner. *Fantastic!*

"That's wonderful," I said flatly. "Last time I caught him checking the china. Anticipating an estate deal, no doubt."

"Now, now, Izzy, don't be naughty. Blood is thicker than water. He says he has an idea about how to help us pay back the loan sooner."

"By spiking up the interest rate, I suspect." I said. "You know he's always had his eye on this property. All he sees is the dollars and cents in it. He knows any developer could make a killing with this land. I don't trust him one bit, not at all."

Dad sighed and rubbed the bridge of his nose under his glasses. "I'm sure you're wrong. He only wants to help."

"Himself," I finished for him. I was being mean, and I knew it. "Sorry, Dad. Look, I know what Lydia's like. She'll keep on at Mom until she gets her way, so I tell you what. I'll buy her a ticket when I get paid. Hell, I'll buy us all tickets. I mean, how often does a cool band like The Brew come into town? It'd be a shame if we all didn't go. So don't worry—I'll take care of it."

Dad smiled at me; not his best smile, I knew, but it was an improvement on the first. "You're a good girl, Izzy. I don't know what I'd do without you."

"Neither do I." I laughed, making a joke of it all. "God, look at the time, I'm gonna be so late. My boss will kill me."

I rose and, after kissing him on the top of his head, left him alone and headed off to change. Maybe I could get a 401(k) loan from work and help him with the payments. After all, he'd helped me and Jane through college. It was the least I could do in return.

If only we had a philosopher's stone, like those spoken of in the old legends. Maybe I could use it to turn my Beetle into gold! Or on second thought, perhaps something smaller that could more easily be made into gold bars or coin. Bloody Hag Laws. What was the point of being magic if you couldn't make a killing with it? But I knew the Hags would be on me in a heartbeat if I tried to spell up some currency. Inflation was inflation, and counterfeiting was a hanging offense! I'd be carted off to Bitterhold before I could say *Abracadabra!*

No. Whatever our problems were, they couldn't be cured with a swish of my wand. I had to be smarter than that. Only how?

Chapter Ten

PIXIES BY THE LAKE

GEORGE KNOCKED ON MATTHEW'S DOOR, BUT THERE WAS NO ANSWER. He grabbed the knob, and the door opened. Matthew wasn't in bed.

"Should we wait inside?" I asked.

"Yes, I don't suppose he'll be long. He knows we're coming."

The bed was made, and there was his open manila envelope on top of it. George made a beeline for it and picked it up, immediately pulling out the contents.

"Damn, he didn't sign it," George said.

"Maybe he has a question?" I moved over to the darkened window and looked outside. The sun was low in the sky and would be setting in an hour or so. There was a long, oblong, man-made pond, directly in front of Matthew's room window, covered in lilies, which was stocked with an assortment of very large koi. Beyond that was the Rosings Park lake. It was certainly beautiful, if austere, and not a bad place for anyone to hang out during their final days.

A lone figure was walking toward the house from the lake. He was a tall man, dressed in a flowing robe that trailed all the way to the ground. His face was mostly concealed by his hooded cloak, but I recognized Matthew at once. I wondered if the cloak helped him walk in the sun. There had to be something protecting him from its rays.

His pace was slow, and though he was surrounded by beauty, he appeared lost in his own thoughts. Well, he had a lot to think about, after all.

"He's down there," I said and turned to tell George when my heart almost jumped out of my chest. Matthew Devereux was standing right behind him, waiting in the door. I hated it when vampires did that. I spun round to look back out of the window. The lone figure was gone. It was him all right.

"The polite thing to do was to have waited," he said to George.

George blushed a little red and put the envelope back down on the bed. "Err, yes. You're right. I wasn't thinking."

Matthew stared at him in silence, and I wondered if he liked George or not. The vampire was near impossible to read.

"Do you like pixies?" Matthew said, turning to me. "There's an abundance of them down by the lake. Perhaps you would honor me with a walk that way. It's a fine evening, definitely not one to be cooped up inside."

I'd glimpsed sparks flitting about down there and thought they might be fireflies. Learning they were pixies filled me with pleasure. "You don't mind the remaining sunlight?" I asked.

"This robe protects me when I walk in the day. Well, toward the end of the day. Nothing will protect a vampire from the sun at dawn, not even demon magic. But it works well enough in the early evening."

"Where did you find it?" I asked.

"A young witch, rather like yourself, fashioned it for me, many, many years ago. So I could share days like this, walking beside her."

"Goody?" I prompted.

Matthew nodded. "Love will always find a way." He stepped aside, leaving room for me to pass by him into the corridor. He began to walk beside me, leaving George to follow in our rear. I suspected Matthew didn't care whether George joined us or not. And for some reason, neither did I.

We walked back along the long corridor, past the old portraits on his floor, and then down the wide, spiral staircase to the main lobby. George remained a fair distance back, maybe close enough to hear. I couldn't say. He didn't seem to mind leaving us to it; every time I looked over my shoulder, he was examining some portrait or work of art. The door was just ahead of us, but he paused at a small display case under an old Seth Thomas clock. It chimed the hour of ten as we approached.

"Look here," said the old vamp, pointing a gnarly finger at a leather-bound book on display under the glass.

I leaned forward to examine it. The leather was shop-worn, and there was a small pentagram the size of a quarter embossed on the front cover. I suspected what it was even before Matthew told me.

"That's Goody's Book of Shadows," he said.

"Oh, I see. What is it doing in there? I didn't know Goody had any connection with Rosings Park?"

"She didn't." Matthew straightened and walked to the door, and I followed him. "She was never here in her life. Couldn't have been. Rosings Park was erected at least a century after her death—she would not have been aware of its existence."

"I don't understand," I said.

"There's no mystery," he explained. "It is customary for the dying at Rosings Park to leave a little something of their life behind. Goody was the only woman I ever loved, and that tome was one of two of her possessions I kept."

"Two."

"Yes. The other I could never part with. Not even in death."

Matthew reached into his cloak and removed something small from inside. It was a locket, and the gold chain dangled loosely between his fingers as he unconsciously stroked the front cover. He handed the locket to me.

"There. That is Goody," Matthew said.

"Really?" Surprised, I pinched the clasp and stared at the face inside. Most miniature portraits I'd seen were little better than blobs, a rough likeness of the subject. This one had been painted by a master—the details were amazing, and it was like looking at a high-resolution photograph. I felt as if Goody was actually staring out at me, assessing me with her keen gaze. Goody looked no older than I was now, with dark hair and laughing eyes.

I thought about the tortured ghost who had come to our coven meeting, remembering her ravaged features, and I was filled with a sudden desire to cry.

Matthew put his hand on my shoulder, and I wondered if he sensed this.

"No one should have gone through what she did," I said.

"No, they should not."

I handed back the locket and glanced over at George. He was standing by the case, no doubt curious about the tome.

"Come. Let us step into the garden."

The moment we were outside, the evening sun hit my face, and I closed my eyes and bathed in its unusual warmth. Even with my eyes closed, I felt Matthew's gaze upon me.

"Forgive me," he said, as I opened my eyes. He was pulling the hood a little protectively around his face. "I have often marveled at the effect of the sun on the living. It is a sensation I have never felt myself. It is why I like walking in the daylight. I like to...imagine."

"You were born vampire?" I asked.

"I was."

We turned left around the pond, and I watched the koi as they followed us, hoping for food. Every now and then, I would hear the gentle *plink* as the braver ones broke the surface of the water and then dived down again.

"You are a patient woman," Matthew said. "I know you want to know more about me, but you aren't pushy at all. I like that about you."

I chuckled. "Oh, believe me, I can be. I can be a ball of fire when I want to be."

"I don't doubt it." He returned my smile. "But you have been very kind to me. Dare I say...gentle. Compassion is a rare quality in a human, and even rarer in a witch. You are a special woman."

"Thank you."

"Goody was like that. Kind. I think she loved me. Oh hell, I know she did. She just couldn't deal with what I was. She wanted a full life, with a family. Children were something I could never give her."

I nodded. Certain paranormals could crossbreed, like witches and humans, but the undead, never. Life could never be gotten from an un-life, though a vampire could breed with another. It defied the laws of nature.

"And you never found anyone else to love? A human, perhaps?"

"No, mostly we attach to our own kind," Matthew continued. "But for every rule there's an exception, no?"

I nodded.

"Goody was a witch. A lovely one at that, but for the longest time, I paid no heed to her. Well, tried not to. Why would I? We don't often bite witches, and if we do, it's to kill them, not to drink from them or bring them under our thrall. You have certain enzymes that disagree with our rather delicate digestive systems. It's your natural defense against us. But we will bite, when provoked. Goody never provoked me."

"So how did you two get together?"

We had reached the end of the pond, and the lake was a short distance away. It was partly surrounded by naturally occurring shrubbery, and I liked it all the better for not feeling so man-made.

"You're probably too young to have given much thought to destiny," Matthew said. "I'm sure you know what it means, I don't mean that of course, but the passing of time gives one a particular perspective. I believe Goody and I were meant to meet. Like Anthony and his Cleopatra, or like Napoleon and his Josephine. Look, over there at that cluster of rhododendrons by the rock. There's a nest of pixies just inside. They're most active at twilight. Let's go take a look at them."

Odd. In an instant, he had changed from the old, tired vampire, longing for death, to an excited little boy on a treasure hunt of his own. I could almost feel his heart beating faster from the joy of it. He had given me a glimpse into a side of him I would never have guessed at, and it made me smile.

There were several large rhododendrons along the lake edge, and these were perhaps the prettiest shade of pink I had ever seen. There was an unnatural hush in the air. The pixies were hiding, and I knew it. The old vampire knelt down, and with a gentleness and strength I would never have expected, he lifted the rock just in front of them.

"There, do you see them?" Matthew asked.

I bent over, and sure enough, there was a whole family of pixies staring up at me from behind a pile of smaller stones. They looked pissed at being disturbed in such an intrusive way. Their tiny voices were too quiet to hear, but judging by their angry expressions and tiny fist shaking, I could guess at the expletives now being uttered.

"Sorry," Matthew said, smiling. He carefully lowered the rock just as it had been before. "That never gets old. I love to watch the little people. Always have done. Do you know, some say the Moonstone came from the pixies?"

I shook my head. I had never heard of any special moonstone, so I took his word for it.

We continued to circle the lake, and I looked back to where George was following us a little way behind, though still within earshot. As ever, he had his nose in his iPhone and appeared to be paying no attention to us at all. I knew better. He barely glanced at the pixie rock as he passed it. No treasure inside to interest him, I supposed.

Satisfied at least that he didn't mind the walk, I returned my attention to Matthew. Every time I looked at him, he felt younger. Not looked. He was still as old as ever, and it was hard to imagine what he looked like as a young man. But it was as if his energy was increasing; like the evening itself was reviving him, giving him a fresh lease on life. It was a weird thing to see.

"Goody Becker came to me on Midsummer's Eve, 1652, just as the light had faded and the night had begun for me. I had just risen and was drawn to the window by the sound of girlish laughter coming from somewhere on my property.

"Her coven was playing some silly game, and she had sneaked into my garden without permission and was rambling through my roses, looking for something.

"I had no time for trespassers and marched onto the porch to scare her off. She had no business being there, and I planned to ensure she never came near my property again."

Matthew closed his eyes to absorb a memory and looked as I must have when I was soaking up the sun earlier.

"I can see her before me, even now. She wore a pretty pink frock, and her dark hair fell loose about her face. Running around barefoot on the hunt had brought a flush of color to her young cheeks. She was eighteen years old and bursting with life. I remember her merry jet-black eyes, displaying no fear at all when she saw me, even though she was in the presence of a young vampire she must have known was in his prime. She won me over right there, in my gardens, all those years ago, in 1652."

He opened his eyes. They were no longer cold and unfeeling, as they had been when I'd first met him, but were alive with desire and yearning.

I smiled, imagining myself in that scenario. "What did she say when you confronted her?"

"I didn't confront her, that's the thing. I found myself totally lost for words; a young vampire entirely captivated by this young girl's beauty. I felt clumsy and stupid, and just stood there, staring at her like a total fool."

For some reason, the idea of this old vampire lost for words in the presence of a beautiful witch touched me deeply. Suddenly I wanted to hug him, and perhaps would have if it weren't for those fangs.

"I often wonder," Matthew continued, "how things would have turned out if we'd never met. If she hadn't ventured into my garden that evening. Perhaps, if she hadn't, she might not have died as she did."

I stopped in my tracks. "How so?"

Matthew continued to walk on, and I followed him. Behind us, George had caught up a little. "As I said before, they were playing a foolish game. It turned out Goody was looking for a small piglet her high priest had released. It had some bauble about its neck, I can't remember what, it was such a long time ago."

"Sounds fun," I said.

"It was a popular sport back in the day. She was certainly enjoying herself. We both heard a scuffle behind her, and ignoring me completely, she ran off in search of her prize.

"The stupid pig was running amok in my rose bushes. I remember it squealing as it tore itself on the thorns. Goody was trying her best to catch it, but it was hard in the dim twilight, and then she cried out. But it wasn't the thorns. She had found something else, and it wasn't the pig—I had freed that little terror, and it had already scurried off over my lawn. I tried to kick it for good measure, stupid animal."

"What did she find?" I asked.

"Her fate. When she came back out of the bushes, she carried a rather unusual stone. It fascinated her, and she asked if she could have it. I could deny her nothing, not even then, so I told her she could keep it."

We had reached a small bench, big enough for two people to sit on at the end of the lake. Matthew took a seat, and I sat down next to him. For a while, he just stared into the water. Then he sighed.

"So many hours I have thought about that moment and what would have happened if I hadn't fallen under her thrall."

"What was unusual about the stone?" I asked.

There was no more room on our bench, and George leaned against a large rock a few feet away from us. I stole a glance in his direction, wondering if he was annoyed this was taking so long, but he didn't seem bothered at all. He had put his iPhone away and was staring at the surface of the water. I knew he was hanging on Matthew's every word.

"My house back then was on the edge of Misty Cedars. Some say it was erected when the first settlers disembarked from the *Mayflower*, but I know it was even older than that. Jamestown vampires, I think. Anyway, I was born in it and knew it to have many secrets. I had heard legends of a lost stone, thinking it little less than a magical myth. It was said to bring its keeper uncommon luck. Not success, mind you, not every endeavor was sure to succeed, but more than your typical luck. That's what Goody found that day. The lost Ashcan stone. The locals know it as the Moonstone."

I didn't think being burned alive was especially lucky but thought it best to keep my mouth shut.

"How do you know it was that stone?" I asked. "I mean, it might have been just a pebble after all?"

"Shortly after finding it, her life changed for the better. The harvests were bad that year—hers flourished. Her youngest sister had contracted smallpox and miraculously survived. It was 1652, and people noticed these things back then.

"Somehow word of the stone began to spread, and fearful it would be taken from her, Goody removed it from around her neck and entrusted it to her sister for safekeeping. Perhaps if she'd left it on her person, it would have kept her safe, but by passing it to another, she'd effectively lost its protection, and they took her. The rest, as you know, is history."

"What happened to the stone?" I asked.

"No one knows. They searched her house, but it was never found."

"And the sister?"

"Miraculously escaped their persecution."

"What happened to your house?" I asked.

"When I heard of her trials, I returned from Paris at once. Too late, of course—I can travel at great speed by land, but my powers fail me on the ocean. It was weeks before I got back to the New World. As soon as I learned what they'd done to my poor Goody, I went into a rage and burned down several of the houses in town, including my own. They'd dumped her body in an unmarked grave, and I tore it from the ground and returned her home."

"Where is she?"

"We had a secret place we liked to meet, and I put her to rest there. One day I hope to join her. I've never spoken of it, but it's all there, in those documents George is waiting for me to sign. If you know what you're looking for, that is."

My boss coughed, and we both turned. He had been quiet all this time, but now he was looking at his watch.

"I'm sorry, but we will have to get going soon," George said. "I have an early start in the morning. We'll need to take those papers and go."

"I could come back in my own time if you'd like?" I suggested, no longer afraid to be with him.

Matthew rose and checked his hood once more, wrapping it round his face like a sort of security blanket.

"I would consider it a great honor if you did," he said. "I've enjoyed your company, but George is right. I have taken up much of your time this evening already. We should be heading back."

With the greatest reluctance, I stood up. He said nothing at all as we returned to Rosings Park, though I was desperate to hear more of the love story between him and Goody. Ultimately, I knew she had spurned him, he had told me that much himself, but there had to be more to their tale. The secret meetings, the cloak, his passion, all of it. I was hungry for romance and would risk much to hear more.

But it was not to be today. I'd have to wait for an opportunity, and as the huge doors of Rosings Park loomed ahead of us, I knew I'd have to make the time pretty soon, before the secrets of his love died with him, and their story was lost forever.

Chapter Eleven
BILLY COLLINS

THE NEXT DAY, I ARRIVED HOME AFTER WORK TO THE ROAR OF laughter. Kitty and Lydia were fussing around the outside of the house with a string of fairy lights, and Mary sat on the garden wall, and for once, her Kindle was nowhere in sight. She smiled at me as I approached.

"What's the occasion?" I asked. Then my notice fell on a cream-colored Ford Taurus on the drive, which could mean only one thing; our cousin Billy was here.

I groaned. "When did he arrive?"

"About half an hour ago," Mary said. "Jane managed to escape to her room before he spotted her, but we weren't so lucky. We had to be nice to him for a whole ten minutes before we could get out of the house."

I nodded. "Where is he now?"

"In with Dad," Mary replied. "They're in the back and are not to be disturbed. Money talk. Suits me fine. If you hear them come out, let me know, and I'll go hide someplace else."

"Sure."

Lydia planted a ladder squarely in front of the door and climbed the first two rungs.

"What's all this about?" I asked Mary.

"Lydia thought the front of the house needed sprucing up. But I think she's just going to make the place look tacky."

Lydia, who was halfway up a short ladder, scoffed. "What do you know, bookworm? Just because it wasn't your idea."

Unperturbed, Lydia pulled out her wand and aimed it at the string of lights. The glowing string hovered over a hook she'd just hammered in, and then it wrapped itself around the hook.

I left the girls to their activity and wandered inside. Mom was on the phone to her sister-in-law; it was a weekly ritual, never to be missed whatever the circumstances. Mom loved to complain, and Auntie Bri liked to listen, so it was a match made in heaven.

An unusual fragrance caught my attention as I put down my things; the air was alive with one of Jane's infusions. I recognized the scent of blackberry and bromeliad, which invited protection and money. Smart girl. At least someone around here was thinking with her head.

I could hear muffled voices and hoped everything was going okay. Unlike Dad, Billy knew all about money, but whether he'd apply his knowledge in our favor was another thing entirely.

Since Mom was preoccupied, I walked quietly up the stairs in search of Jane. I found her sitting in her room, typing an email on her laptop.

"You look a lot better," I said.

"Thanks," Jane replied. She didn't look up.

"Anything interesting?" I asked.

Jane blushed. "I'm just replying to an email I got from Charlie. He's invited me to go with him and his friends to see the band play at the Cauldron."

"That's great!" I exclaimed, bouncing down on the end of her bed. "Look, I don't want to rain on your parade, but you know Lydia wanted to go, and I said I'd get tickets, so we'll all be there in the crowd."

Jane shrugged. "The more the merrier."

"Make sure he knows you're after his body. Plenty of girls would step into your shoes if they could."

Jane smiled. She continued to type and then paused. "He must be online—he just replied."

I smiled. "Or he's glued to his phone hanging onto your every word."

"Don't be silly," Jane said, but she was smiling.

"What did he say?"

"He's letting me know Fitz is going, and definitely Caroline. He's not sure about the others."

"Whoever is there, I'm sure it'll be fun!" My mind returned to the business downstairs, and I wondered how Dad and Billy were getting on. "By Gaia, I hope Billy isn't going to be here for much longer."

"I wouldn't get your hopes up," Jane replied. "Rumor has it he's here for supper."

I fell back on Jane's bed, exasperated. "Ugh. Shit."

"Look, he's not *all* bad. He's here to help us after all. Remember that. He's a good egg, really."

"If you say so. I still say he's part goblin."

Jane laughed. "That's probably why he's so good with money. Talking of supper, I guess I'd better get downstairs and start on dinner. I suspect Mom hasn't."

"When does she ever? When I came in, she was stuck on the phone with Auntie Bri."

Jane clicked on her mouse and rose from her seat, stretching. "You coming?"

I rolled my eyes but laughed anyway. "I suppose, if I have to." I forced myself up off Jane's comfy mattress and got to my feet to follow her downstairs. Within seconds, Jane's nose was in the fridge. She was pulling out a few bowls full of veggies she'd already prepped and started laying them out on the counter.

"Need me to do anything?" I asked. I knew she'd refuse my offer, and I was okay with that.

"Nope, I got it. Just keep me company."

My knitting kit was in a bag on the table, and I grabbed it. Since there was nothing for me to do, I thought I'd work on my casting-on spell. While Jane filled a pot with water, I sat back and focused on the needles.

"*Lanzando nerebus fastando,*" I said, carefully pronouncing the phrase. My needles went up perfectly poised, and the wool wrapped around the needles, just as they were supposed to, but the knot was too loose, and the whole thing fell apart. Frustrated, I grabbed at it and untied the knot. "This is hopeless," I moaned. "I might as well have cast it on myself."

"And then you've learned, what exactly?" Jane asked. "Be patient. You're almost there. A few days ago, you couldn't even tie a knot in the wool."

"I suppose so, oh wise one."

"Oh, and it's *nereboos,* not *nerebus,*" she added casually, cutting up some carrots.

"Thank you, Hermione." I laughed.

I fell back into my seat and continued to practice while Jane pottered about. We could hear faint voices coming from the other side of the wall, but I couldn't make out much of what was being said. Billy was talking too quickly, as he typically did, and Dad really wasn't saying much of anything at all. It sounded to me as if he was making a sales pitch, not offering financial advice, but it was hard to tell for sure.

After a few minutes, Mom came into the kitchen and sat down at the table beside me. She motioned over toward the annex.

"Are they still in there?" she whispered.

I nodded. "Yup. What did Auntie Bri have to say? Anything fun?"

Mom pulled a banana out of the fruit bowl and began to peel it. "You know Bri, living the life as always. She's still up in Maine, partying with her sisters in the coven. They have the best life up there. I can't remember the last time your father and I went on vacation together."

Mom sighed and took a bite of the banana. Auntie Bri had no kids, so she was considerably better off. She and Mom's brother, Uncle Ed, lived the life of snowbirds, with summers spent in Maine and winters in Florida. Good luck to her, I always thought. I would love to be a snowbird, if I had the chance.

The voices behind the wall grew a little louder. I let my needles drop to the table as the door to the annex opened.

Billy Collins was an oddity. His features were regular enough, and he had dark hair and a muscular build, but something about him was put together wrong. I don't know, maybe it was his eyebrows, which grew a bit too close together, giving him a werewolf look. Or maybe it was his eyes, which were sharp and calculating, a tad too goblin. Whatever it was, he was an odd sort of dude.

As the door opened, he beamed, his nose stuck in the air, sniffing.

"Ah, what delights are you making for us tonight, sweet Jane?" Without invitation, Billy pottered over to the stove and started lifting one pot lid after the other. When he wasn't looking, Jane shot me a weary glance, and I smiled; we both knew what he was like.

Dad remained standing quietly in the doorway. I guessed their meeting had gone well, since he looked rather pleased with himself. Maybe Billy had come up with a solution for Dad's money worries after all. If he had, I would gladly cook him supper too.

When Billy opened the oven door and peered inside, I thought Jane was going to clunk him with a wooden spoon. "Oh Jane, that smells divine, how can you make simple pork roast smell so good? What's your secret ingredient?"

Jane slammed the oven door shut. "Ground werewolf. Now sit down and let me cook."

I noticed he was making love-sick puppy eyes at Jane. I wondered if there was a way to let him down gently, but then again, did he deserve to be let down gently? "Did you know Charlie Van Buren's back in town?"

Billy raised an eyebrow. "I had no idea you knew him. He usually moves in quite snooty circles. That is to say, I mean, not that you don't—"

"We know what you mean," I said, rescuing him from his own stupidity. "He's taken quite a fancy to Jane. He's taking her to see The Brew when they play at the Cauldron."

Billy stopped dead in his tracks. He put down the potato pot lid and slid down onto a chair at the end of the table. "Like, on a date?"

"Yes, of course, like on a date." *What else could I have meant?*

I could see the heartache working behind his eyes, and I had to admit, I felt a little sorry for him.

"I see." And then he seemed to recall that Jane was in the room with us, and he recovered his poise. "Well, that's just marvelous. He's a great man and does a good deal of business with our firm. Of course he would have noticed Jane as soon as he came into Misty Cedars. What red-blooded male wouldn't?"

I admired his gracious recovery and slipped my knitting into the bag, as it was time to clear the table.

"How long before we eat?" Dad asked. "I'm famished." I could tell he was amused at the turn of the conversation. He had that particular twinkle in his eye he always had when Billy was in the house.

"Twenty minutes," Jane replied.

"I'm pretty hungry myself," Billy said, looking at the fruit bowl thoughtfully. "I was telling your father how well I'm doing at the bank. The Board of Trustees has shown uncommon confidence in my ability. Perhaps you don't know the chairman, Kate De Bourgh, but I was appointed at her particular recommendation."

"Yes, I understand you're the manager now," I said, not really interested in hearing any more about it than I already had.

"Uh-huh. Yes. Youngest manager in the state, to be sure, thanks to Kate. You know what she said to me the other day?"

I shook my head.

"'Billy,' she said, 'there's no man I can count on more than you to cast your vote sensibly at our quarterly meetings.' Of course, I assured her that whenever she needed my support, she could count on it, totally. After all, our visions for progress are so generally the same, we always seem to be voting the same way anyway." He sighed, happily. "But enough about that. Oh, you know what else she said? She said, 'Billy, if you really want to rise in the sphere of the paranormal banking world, you should find yourself a wife. Make sure she's a pretty one who can hold her own at big corporate events.'"

"Really," I said, pulling a bunch of plates out of a cupboard and trying not to drop them. He was sending me to sleep! Would he ever stop talking about himself? "I didn't think that sort of thing mattered in this day and age. Being married, that is."

Billy snorted, like he knew better. "Yes, well, you would think so, wouldn't you? Maybe there's nothing down on paper as such, but you only have to look to see all the senior execs, men and women, all have partners. I suppose it promotes a sense of the bank's stability."

"So what? You'll get married just to guarantee a leg up at the bank?" I asked.

"Well, yes, but you know, we're none of us getting any younger. I wouldn't mind coming home to a cooked dinner and a pair of warmed slippers. It might be the very thing."

Over by the door, Dad disguised his laugh as a sneeze.

"Bless you," Mom said.

"You really live in the dark ages, don't you?" I said as I reached for the salt and pepper pot. "No self-respecting witch ever warmed her husband's slippers, unless it was to set his feet on fire."

Maybe I was being unkind. After all, there was nothing wrong with old-fashioned values. Just as long as they weren't being forced on me. "I'm sure you'll find a lucky lady soon enough," I said.

"I sure hope so," Billy said. "Especially if I want to keep Kate's good opinion, which I do." He was looking at me sideways, and unused to his particular interest, I wondered what exactly was going through that odd little brain of his.

"Ten minutes," said Jane. Something had clearly tickled her as she had a huge grin on her face.

"I'll tell the others to get washed up," I said. I didn't really need to; Kitty and Lydia had a knack for showing up when all the work was done. Still, as they were all acting so strangely, I was glad of any excuse to get out of the kitchen.

"Oh, are you going out?" Billy asked.

"I'll be back in a sec. Lydia needs to come down off that ladder before she breaks her neck."

I turned my back on him to tear off some paper towels we used as napkins. I folded the sheets diagonally, so they looked the part.

"Only, I was thinking," Billy continued. "It's a nice night. Perhaps I can persuade you to join me for a walk after dinner?"

At first, I was pretty sure Billy was addressing himself to Jane, but when she didn't reply I turned around, only to find him staring directly at me.

Mom and Dad glanced at each other with raised eyebrows.

Wait a gosh darn minute! Was Billy actually setting his sights on me? Because I'd told him Jane wasn't available? Was I his second choice because I happened to be in the vicinity? That seemed likely. Did he really think he had a chance with *moi*? Or that I might somehow be interested in him? Gaia, I should have kept my big mouth shut.

My first thought was to laugh, but the poor guy had probably just rescued us from disaster. Laughing wouldn't have been a nice thing to do, if that were true.

"What, oh, um?" So for the first time in my life, I was completely at a loss for what to say. "Ugh, well, sure. Okay." *Shit*.

Jane grinned as she stirred the gravy, and I felt her attention on me as I left the room. There had been a subtle shift in the workings of the universe, and I'd been the last to catch on. Great. Just what I needed. I'd now inherited a bumbling bore for a stalker. How cool was that?

Billy beamed as Jane planted a steaming plate of pork roast and potatoes in front of him. Without waiting for anyone else to be served, he dived into his plate and began chomping noisily, no doubt wanting to share his appreciation of my sister's cooking with the rest of the family.

"Would you like something other than water, Billy? A beer maybe?" Dad asked. The perpetual smile on his face convinced me that their meeting had gone well. In fact, the whole atmosphere at our table was upbeat. I supposed everyone was making the same assumption I did.

"No, no. Water is fine, thank you. "

Mom smiled, contented. I knew she wasn't a big fan of drinking, and his reply pleased her.

"Jane, I must say, you're a wonderful cook," Billy said between mouthfuls. "Are all your sisters as amazing as you are in the kitchen?" He stared directly my way.

I snorted. "Not me. I can barely boil an egg." As it happened, I was a pretty fair cook—not as good as Jane—but I wasn't going to admit it. I had higher aspirations than being stuck in a kitchen all day, thank you. Or warming slippers, for that matter.

Billy's smile faltered for a second, but he quickly recovered.

"Ah well, I'm sure you have many other talents." He smiled, clearly pleased with himself, and began mashing down his potatoes with the back of his fork. "I try my best to compliment where I can. You won't find me finding fault in other people. Not if I can help it."

"Even when they're being a little bit ridiculous?" I asked.

"Um, I forgot to ask," interrupted Dad, "how soon will you hear about that item of business we were discussing?"

"Oh, by tomorrow I'd expect," Billy replied. "These things never take too long. It's the one thing about being the manager of the bank—I can cut a few corners here and there."

Lydia was staring at me slyly, and from the way her attention kept bouncing from me to Billy, I could easily guess the mischief in her head. I knew trouble was afoot, and I gave her a warning glare, but it didn't do any good.

"Oh Billy, you must come with us to see The Brew!" she blurted.

"Yes, well, thank you, but I'm not entirely sure that's my thing, you know?"

Relieved, I took a bite of my own supper, but Lydia wasn't done yet.

"We're all going, you know, including Izzy. It's going to be amazing. It's a special performance. In fact, they probably won't ever play here in Misty Cedars again. You'd be mad to miss it."

If I could have reached my sister under the table, I'd have kicked her.

"Oh, well, in that case," Billy said. "I'm sure I could find the time. Are there any tickets still available?"

"Actually, I think they're all sold out," I said with secret satisfaction.

"Aww, what a shame." Billy sighed.

"No, they're not," Lydia pressed. "You can still get a ticket from Charlotte's dad. You should have a word with him. I'm pretty sure he's got some left."

Great. Thanks, Lydia. She was right. Charlotte had told me as much herself only a few hours ago.

"Then I will indeed. I'm sure it'll be a lot of fun; it's been a while since I danced to a bit of music. I'll call him later and see if he can help me."

Lydia looked very happy with herself, and I felt like poking my tongue at her, but I managed to hold back.

Billy was the first to finish his plate. He looked around the table expectantly.

"Would you like some more?" Mom asked.

"I wouldn't say no."

Mom beamed, happy to please him, and gave him the rare honor of serving him herself.

"Oh my," he said, gazing at his rather full plate with delight. "I shall be fit to burst if I get through all this."

We all knew he would. Billy's appetite was legendary.

"Ah well, you and Izzy will be walking it off after dinner, I'm sure."

Thanks, Mom. Was my entire family conspiring against me? Even Dad looked a little amused and did nothing to come to my rescue. I looked down at my own plate and pushed it away.

"Not hungry, Izzy?" Lydia laughed.

"No, not much."

"Never mind, maybe you will be after your walk," Mom said. "I'll put your plate in the fridge for you."

"Thanks." The fates were conspiring. Lucky me.

When dinner was over, Billy and I stepped outside, just as the sun was dipping behind the mountains in front of us. The sky was a wash of oranges and purples, very pretty as sunsets go, but this was one I would rather not have enjoyed.

I looked up at the lights Lydia had just arranged. She hadn't done a bad job at all, and they looked super cool.

"Which way shall we go?" Billy asked. As he spoke, he pulled out his wand. "*Illuminous.*" A beam of light lit the end. I did the same.

The path to the left led to a pretty little stream and was my preferred way to walk when I ventured out on my own or with Jane. By turning to the right, we would take a street past the cookie cutters and could loop back home quite quickly. It was the shorter route, and that's the way I headed tonight.

Billy was right beside me, and for a little while all was well, and we exchanged nothing but a few polite pleasantries. It was a pity that things had to change.

"I must say, I am delighted that you asked me out to see The Brew. I'm not very, um, good at that sort of thing, and I was delighted you made things quite easy for me."

"Err, Billy, I didn't exactly ask you out."

"Well, no, maybe not directly, but the result is the same. I have heard of this band, and although music like that really isn't my thing, I think I may grow to like these guys."

"What exactly *is* your thing?" I asked.

"A little jazz, perhaps. Some light classical, you know."

"Sounds good."

"Of course, Kate De Bourgh has excellent taste in everything. I've been to her house, you know. Oh, you should see it. It's not far from mine, but boy, it's a big one."

"Is she married?" I asked. "Have you ever thought about asking her out?" *If only.*

"Ha, no. Like she would even condescend to look at me twice. She's way out of my league. I'm surprised you even mention it. The woman has more wealth than anyone I know."

"That doesn't mean she can't be loved."

"Ah, love. Amour, amour." He waved his wand in the shape of a heart, and then he tapped his chest. "It beats a little faster when you're in love, don't you think?"

"Err, I wouldn't know," I confessed.

"Really? A gorgeous girl like you? You surprise me."

"I mean, I've dated and all that, and met some really nice guys, but I don't think I've met *the one* just yet. Not even close."

"Maybe you have and just haven't realized it?"

"Uh, no. I haven't."

Undeterred, Billy's grin remained resolutely plastered to his face.

"Your father and I had a very good chat earlier on."

"I know. I was there."

"I'm sure you gathered I was able to come to…an arrangement. I'm sure he'll tell you all soon enough, but needless to say, he's a lot happier this evening having spoken with me."

"I'm glad to hear it."

We passed the window of an old lady I sometimes talked to when I walked this way. I'd found her unusually open minded for a numpy, and she was fascinated by my magical talk.

I could see her looking out of her bedroom window, and she waved at me. I cringed, knowing the inevitable conclusion she would come to, seeing me with Billy. I returned her wave but walked a little faster.

"You seem in a hurry," Billy said.

"It's getting cold, don't you think?"

Billy looked upward. The sun was set now, and the stars were clearly visible in the sky. "Not really. I was enjoying your company too much to notice."

This was getting intolerable and getting way out of hand. I might find him a bore, but he was a decent enough man, and he was doing his best for our family. The kindest thing to do would be to let him down gently.

"Look, Billy, I..."

"Say nothing, sweet Izzy. I'm not a fool. Let's just enjoy the evening, shall we?"

"Okay," I said.

With another flourish of his wand, Billy conjured a single silver rose. He took it and handed it to me. "For friendship," he said.

"Um, thank you," I replied. That was clever. I wondered if he'd prepared the spell earlier—for Jane.

"And to hope."

I had no answer for that.

On the upside, it was the last he spoke of *Amour, amour.* For the rest of our walk, we returned to pleasantries, but I still felt a tremendous relief when I saw Lydia's new lights ahead of us.

"Well, good night," I said, as we approached the drive. I was turning on my heels to make a sprint for our front door, but Billy was too fast. He grabbed my hand and bent over as if to kiss it.

Dang. I managed to escape by pretending to sneeze, inadvertently blowing all the petals off his rose. It fizzled and disappeared.

"Oops," I said. "Ah well. Thank you for the thought. See you later." And before he could make another gesture, I turned and went inside.

Chapter Twelve

TROLLS AND HARRIDANS

"'OH BILLY, YOU MUST COME WITH US TO SEE THE BREW!'" I ROLLED MY eyes as I mimicked my kid sister's comment to Billy.

Mary King had listened to my ramblings, but now she shrugged and perched her backside on the end of my desk. She stared at my near-empty in-box. Pushing her index finger under the thin pile, she raised it and then let it drop. "The senior partners are piling stuff on *me* all the time. How come you're so damned lucky?"

Personally, I didn't think having nothing to do was lucky at all. It was rather boring, to tell the truth. I was reputedly the best paranormal legal in the firm, and George was the hotshot go-getter. That was why they'd paired us up, for pixie's sake! He was supposed to help me up to the next level. Yet here I was, with nothing to do, bored out of my wits, while Mary King's in-box looked fit to burst. It wasn't fair!

"You think it's because he's new?" I said in a hushed voice. "Are they breaking him in slowly or something?"

"Maybe," Mary said. She narrowed her eyes, and I couldn't help feeling she knew something I didn't.

I picked up the solitary file on my desk and opened it. It was nothing interesting—again. Just another property right-of-way dispute between a bridge troll and a harridan witch with a mouth like a cesspit. She was certainly giving the troll a hard time!

I watched again as the familiar hologram of the exchange spiraled from the file and appeared in front of me. Too bad for them both, an eyewitness had recorded the entire exchange. Same old, same old.

I'd typed up their individual depositions and had given the file to George for review over a week ago. It shouldn't have taken him this long to return it to me.

"Talking of." Mary motioned over to the partners' offices and slid off my desk, tout suite.

As she returned to her cubicle, I leaned back in my chair and saw George heading in our general direction, a promisingly thick file in his hand. Something had wiped the usual smile from his face though, and judging by the heavy five-o'clock shadow, that something had kept him up all night. He certainly wasn't looking his best.

"Hey, boss" I said, flipping the troll-versus-harridan file casually back in my in-tray. "What's up?"

"I was reading through Matthew Devereux's estate documents last night," he replied. "Are you sure everything's in there?"

I glared at the file he brandished inches from my face. "Course, why? I checked it all myself before I gave it to you." I took the file from him and flicked through the contents. "What do you think is missing?" I had a pretty good idea he was looking for Goody's resting place, hoping that would lead him to the moonstone. Why didn't he just come out and say so, though? Did he think I was an idiot?

George scratched his stubble thoughtfully as he stared at the front of the file. "I need to take the documents back to Matthew, Monday evening. Would you like to come with me again?"

"Yes, I'd love to," I said. It wasn't a lie. I really hoped Matthew had more to tell me. I found his story intriguing. "Monday though? Isn't that cutting things a little fine? Doesn't he..."

"Yes, but he won't see me before then. Apparently, he's entered a period of grace."

"Oh." That took me by surprise. A period of grace was like a stay of execution. Some used it to make peace with the hereafter, or whatever it was the undead believed came next. Dad called it the eternal nothing.

I experienced a sudden surge of hope. "Don't some vamps talk themselves out of the suicide after grace?"

George shrugged. "It's been known."

Maybe it was none of my business, but I really wanted Matthew to change his mind. And perhaps it was selfish too. After all, if there was nothing left for him to live for, why should he stick around?

"I can do next Monday, sure." And then a new thought occurred to me. "Hey, what are you doing Friday night? Is Fae coming into town?"

"Um, no, not this weekend. She's...err...busy." His face lit up mischievously. *If I didn't know any better...* "Why? Did you have something fun in mind?"

"We're all going to the Flaming Cauldron on Friday night. A big crowd of us. I bought tickets for me and my sisters to see The Brew while they're in town. You wanna come?"

"Sure, I love them! I buy all their stuff. Are there still tickets?"

"Let's see," I said. I made a circling motion with my finger over my phone. The call went through, and Benny answered.

"Flaming Cauldron. Izzy, is that you?"

"Hey, Benny, sorry to bother, are there any tickets left for The Brew?"

"No, but I kept you one, knew you'd be calling."

I laughed, tickled with pleasure. "Thanks, Benny, you're the best!"

"You know it, girl."

I made a downward cutting motion with my finger, ending the call, and smiled up at George. "Sorted."

He grinned hugely. "You know people!"

"Benny's a warlock. He's a useful friend to have. So we're on?"

"Indeed we are."

There was a devilish twinkle in George's eye, and his gaze wandered down to my legs. *Has he broken up with Fae*, I wondered? And even if he had? I suddenly doubted if asking him had been a good idea after all.

I handed him back his file. "Even your friend Fitz is making an appearance, from what Jane tells me. You should come, if only to tease him. I'd love to see his face when he sees *you* turn up."

George's smile faltered, and he knitted his brow. "You're right, I really should." He didn't sound so sure now though.

"Great, 'cos you'll be doing me a big favor." I laughed. "Seeing you might keep my annoying cousin off my back. He's been sticking to me like glue of late, but another man around might scare him off."

"Oh, right." George half laughed. "Well, I'll have to check with Fae, of course, but I'm sure it'll be fine. Umm, how much was that ticket? Let me pay you for it now."

"Um, thirty-five bucks."

George reached into his pocket and pulled out his wallet. He counted out the bills and handed them over.

"I think the family is eating first, so as soon as I have it, I'll drop your ticket off in your office and you can meet us there, if that's okay?"

"That's fine." Without another word, George sauntered off, leaving me to my very pleasant thoughts.

Chapter Thirteen

BROOMSTICK

Since the Flaming Cauldron was going to be packed solid, Charlie had invited Jane to a dinner at his house before the big event. We agreed to meet them just before the gig.

Lydia, Kitty, Mary, and Billy had met me at the office for a quick bite at the local diner. From there we could walk to the Flaming Cauldron, since parking downtown for the event was going to be near-impossible. George had promised to meet us there around six thirty. The early evening was a little chilly, so I slipped one of my home-knitted sweaters on to keep warm. I thought it looked pretty cool. Goth, of course, but then all my clothes were that style.

Kitty and Mary were wearing jeans and a sweater, but Lydia was wearing a tee that was little more than a sports bra, and a skirt that was way too short. We walked at quite a brisk pace, and I supposed that kept them all warm.

Only Billy seemed unhappy with the walk. He did his best to keep up with our pace, but from the huffing and panting, I could tell daily exercise wasn't his thing. I guessed that was the downside to a sedentary banking job.

"Jesus, you can hear the noise from here," Mary complained.

"You didn't have to come, you know," Lydia quipped. "It's not like anyone would miss you if you stayed at home."

"Lydia, that's unkind." I wouldn't care a jot that my sisters were at it already, but I hated that Billy could hear them banter. What must he think of us? Fighting like alley cats in the middle of the street.

When we reached the Flaming Cauldron, there was already a line of people all waiting to get inside. The bass seemed to be bouncing off the brick wall, and the level of general excitement was high.

Mary stood behind them all, but Billy, trying desperately hard to hide he was out of breath, marched over to the steps leading down to the bar.

"We have tickets," he said to the door man. The name tag on his bulging pecs said Bob.

"So do all these people," Bob replied, uninterested. "You'll have to wait in line like everyone else. You have to be stamped in."

"It's okay, Bob. They're with me. I'm Fitz Darcy, and we're friends of Jed, and he's expecting us."

I turned to see Fitz Darcy standing right behind me. He looked unusually casual, in expensive black jeans and a black goth shirt. Handsome too. Once again, I found myself thinking it was a pity that he was so spoiled, aloof, and self-centered.

Bob looked up, and his expression turned respectful at once.

"Yes, sir, certainly Mr. Darcy. Come right in."

He unhooked the rope barrier to allow us all through.

"Thanks, Bob."

With a natural authority, Fitz walked past Bob and offered his upturned wrist to Bob's companion, a very pretty half-elf goth girl with silver ringlets in her hair, who was busy hexing ultraviolet bracelets around everyone's wrist. I'd worn them before. They were typically good for four hours, after which they would fade and disappear. Caroline swept after him, closely followed by Charlie and Jane. They all held out their wrists for the bracelets.

"You better hurry up before Bob here changes his mind," Jane whispered to me as she passed us.

Billy didn't have to be told twice and almost tripped over his own feet in his haste to catch up with Fitz.

"Oh my, well, what an unexpected surprise! Fitz Darcy himself." Then to me in particular, "Did you know that he's the nephew of our chairman, Kate De Bourgh? I must go and introduce myself!"

"Wait," I cried. The last thing I wanted was for Billy to ingratiate himself with Fitz. As it was, having Billy along at all was annoying as hell, but I cringed at the thought of Fitz meeting him. I'd been dreading this moment, ever since Lydia invited him along. "Hold up! I don't think that's a good idea."

Billy ignored me entirely and planted himself directly in front of Fitz so he couldn't be ignored. "Well, what a wonderful night this is going to be, after all. I thought myself the luckiest man to be here with Izzy, but meeting you is just the icing on the cake."

Oh Gaia, he'd said it.

Fitz looked puzzled at the odd man, and then his gaze rested on me. I couldn't quite read his expression, but what did it matter? The only thing I wanted in the world was for a chasm to open in the ground and for brimstone to suck me down into the depths of Hades. Or some such.

Instead, I was nudged forward by my three little sisters, all anxious to get inside to secure a good spot.

"I don't believe we've met," said Fitz. His words were civil but without warmth.

"Ah, but we have now. I'm William Collins. I run the bank here in town —I work for your aunt Kate. But my friends call me Billy, and so must you. Nice to meet you."

Fitz nodded politely.

"Oh, and I'm a distant relative to the Bennets. It's so wonderful to bump into you like this. I've heard so many fantastic things."

Billy was holding everything up. Bob looked like he wanted everyone to keep moving, but seemed reluctant to say anything, perhaps out of respect for Fitz. The result was an angry crowd mumbling behind us. But Billy just stood there, oblivious to it all. Fitz, on the other hand, looked over Billy to the crowd beyond and, seeing the problem, pulled Billy graciously to one side.

"It's nice to meet you, err, William?"

"Call me Billy."

"Err, sure. Billy. Let's continue this discussion inside, shall we? We're holding up the line."

"Oh yes, yes, of course, of course."

Without another word, Fitz led the way into the Flaming Cauldron, and Billy hurried along behind him. It seemed I was all but forgotten in Billy's haste to ingratiate himself. What was it with everyone? Fitz wasn't *that* special.

Lydia, Kitty, and Mary now had their bracelets, and as soon as mine was on, we were successfully swept behind the others and pushed inside the Flaming Cauldron. I gritted my teeth and groaned inwardly. It was shaping up to be one hell of a night.

The Flaming Cauldron was barely recognizable. Tonight, it was like an entirely different bar. All the tables and stools had been put away, leaving standing room only, and though it was still early, the bar was almost filled to capacity.

Silver and white neon specters and ghouls danced around the ceiling, providing the only source of light, and a graveyard mist swirled around the temporary stage.

I was looking around the bar, wondering where the best place to stand would be, when a warlock wearing a cream suit with big lapels and loads of bling carved his way through the crowd and appeared right in front of us.

It was Jed Colonel, owner of the Flaming Cauldron. He was a remarkably handsome warlock, with drop-dead gorgeous sea-green eyes and pure white bangs that drooped forward, almost hiding their beauty. He owned the club with his husband, Joe Forster. Typically, neither of them made an appearance in the club, but I supposed this was a special occasion.

As soon as Jed reached us, he lunged at Charlie and squeezed him so hard I was surprised his eyes didn't pop out.

"Yes, you made it! I was so excited when I heard you and Fitzy might be coming. Hey, Fitzy, my love. How are you doing? It's been almost forever!" He turned and squeezed Fitz with the same enthusiasm, and to my surprise, Fitz didn't just bear the hug with good grace—rather, he gave as good as he got.

"Where's Joe tonight?" Fitz asked, looking around as if expecting Joe at any moment.

"Poor dear has a terrible cold," Jed said. "It's such a shame because he would love to see you again, but the noise and the crowd would probably kill him, so he decided to stay home and try to hex it out. He sends his best love to you both!"

Billy had been standing by, his mouth slightly ajar at this outward show of bonhomie. He thrust himself in between the men, shook Jed's hand vivaciously, and then pulled him into an awkward hug.

"So great to meet you," Billy said.

Jed's jaw dropped, but his smile never faltered. "Same to you," he said. He glanced over Billy's shoulder, first at Fitz, then at Charlie, looking totally perplexed. "And you are?"

"Billy Collins at your service."

"He works for my aunt," Fitz said, as if that explained everything. I didn't know if he was being funny or not.

"Um, let me introduce you to everyone," Fitz said. "You know Caroline, of course. These are the Bennet sisters. We have Jane, Izzy, Mary, Kitty, and Lydia. Have I got that right?" Fitz asked, looking directly at me.

"Yes, perfect," I said, wondering at the odd tingle that ran down my spine when he said my name.

Jed shook each of our hands warmly in turn. "So nice to meet you all. Look, I'd love to hang, but there's a rowdy group of musicians in the back demanding my attention." Then he said to Fitz and Charlie, "I saw you arrive from my office, so I just popped out to say hi. Don't forget, we're having a few cocktails after the show. You promised you'd come. Don't let me down."

"You're with the band in the back?" Lydia gasped. Her eyes were starry, and her gaze kept fleeting behind the stage.

"Absolutely. You can meet them after the show, too, if you like? It's just a private party, a few friends and a few drinks. You're welcome to join us if you desire?"

My sister began bouncing up and down on the spot, clapping her hands. Oh hell, wasn't she wearing a bra? All the men were mesmerized by the boobage action, even Jed.

"That's very kind of you," I said, wanting to draw their attention away from my sister's chest. "We'd all love that."

"Great." Jed grinned. "Now I must go. The support band is getting ready to start again. By the way, you should head over there to the notice board. It has the best view of the stage. Toodle-oo!"

"Holy crap, we're gonna meet the band!" Lydia squeed.

"And you'd better be on your best behavior when we do," I cautioned. "Or I promise you, I will tell Mom everything, you hear me?"

We all fought against the solid mass of bodies to reach the spot Jed had suggested. There was a small ledge along the wall, and by standing on it, we were able to see clearly over the heads of the mob.

Mary, who up until now had been silent, pointed to a flyer on the wall. "Hey, there's supposed to be a karaoke after the show tonight. While you all party with the band, would you mind if I did that instead? You know how I love karaoke."

I cringed. Although my sister tried her hardest, we all thought she had a little banshee blood in her because her voice could remove limescale from a toilet—without magic.

"I dunno," I said. "I mean, maybe they won't tonight because of the band?" I hoped more than believed this to be true.

"Well, if they do," Mary said, "I'm doing it!"

Jane was staring at her feet, but I could see she was grinning.

The support band, Broomstick, according to the logo on the drums, were done with their break and were busy tuning their instruments for their next session. But my thoughts were entirely elsewhere. George had said he would show up around six thirty, and though I looked over to the entrance, there was still no sign of him anywhere.

I checked my watch to see if I had the time right. When I looked up, I noticed Fitz, who right now was standing beside me, was looking at me. He wasn't scowling, but he wasn't frowning either.

"Are you expecting someone?" Fitz asked.

"Um, yes, actually. My boss was supposed to be here. Well, he said he would come. I was just wondering where he was, that's all."

"Your boss, as in George Wickham?"

Like you don't know already, 'Mister knows everyone in town,' already.

"Yes, that's him. Do you know him?"

"As a matter of fact, I do."

I was bursting to tell him what I knew, and that although everyone in town was sucking up to him, I knew what Fitz Darcy was really like, behind the smiles and sexiness.

But in my job, I knew better than anyone that it was unwise to go mouthing off in public. Didn't mean I didn't want to. "Oh, that's nice for you."

Fitz looked at me funny, and I imagined all sorts of thoughts were going through his head. He'd probably guessed George had confided in me. Too bad. For him.

The lead singer of Broomstick stepped up to the front of the stage.

"Hello, Misty Cedars. Are you ready for some more musical sorcery?"

The crowd all cried *Yes!* at once.

"All right! Here we go!"

And then all possibility of conversation was over. The heavy bass vibrated through the entire building, and at the first strum of the electric guitar, we all began to dance. Everyone, that was, except Fitz. He just stood there like a stiff banana, looking acutely out of place.

To Hades with it. Maybe Fae had put her foot down and told George he couldn't come? Not that it should matter—she was his girlfriend after all, and I had no right to expect anything of him. I was going to enjoy myself, no matter what. And as for Fitz, who gave a hoot? It wasn't like I cared about him. I threw my arms up wildly in the air, and as soon as the rhythm entered my soul, I forgot everything else and danced.

Chapter Fourteen

BANSHEE KARAOKE

THE LAST BEAUTIFUL GUITAR RIFF FROM "I'LL LOVE YOU AGAIN WHEN The Moon Rises" faded out, and the spellbound crowd erupted into mad cheering. It had been a fantastic performance. The Flaming Cauldron might only be a little venue for them, but they might as well have played to a big stadium, they were that good.

The singer strode to the front of the stage and grinned.

"Thank you, everybody, for coming to our show! It's so great to be home, to see family and friends, and heed my advice, folks—never let them get too far away from you, hold them close, and treasure them forever, because without family, without friends, nothing has meaning. Thank you, Misty Cedars! We love you!"

The crowd roared again, delighted to be recognized. At last, a few people began to leave, and Benny appeared behind the bar, signaling business as usual.

We stood around expectantly, not sure what was going to happen next. Normally we'd have left with the others, but we'd been invited "backstage," and since the invitation had really been for Charlie, Caroline, and Fitz, my sisters and I were unsure what to do next.

We didn't have to wonder for too long. Once again, Jed was fighting his way through the crowd, motioning to us all to join him.

Lydia didn't hesitate. She bounced off the ledge and was soon at his side, jumping on the spot like an excited rabbit. I guess she wanted to make sure she wasn't left behind. Fat chance of that.

Mary, too, was quick to join him, displaying a rare moment of passion for our quietest sister. "Now everyone's leaving, will you be doing the Friday night karaoke?" Mary cried over the bustle.

"Yes, as soon as the tables are back in place. You a singer then?" Jed asked.

"I like to think so," Mary replied.

"No one else does," Lydia teased.

"Lydia!" Jane shot our youngest a reproachful look.

"Come on back," Jed said. "The band will be with us in a bit—they're stashing their gear in the van."

We shuffled through the sea of departing fans, and Jed opened a black door between the bar and the stage. I held onto Billy, not because I wanted to, but strictly for damage control.

"Can I stay down here?" Mary asked.

"Sure." *She won't come to any harm doing karaoke.*

In all my years in Misty Cedars, I'd never been invited into the private rooms of anything before. The first thing I noticed was Benny, his muscular frame shown to full advantage as he hoisted up a crate of clinking bottles. He looked our way for a second, but once he saw we were with Jed, he turned around and continued replenishing the bar.

The back of the bar was the opposite of the front. It was totally unglamorous, all dark, with rough stone floors and stack upon stack of crated bottles. The place reeked of spilled beer and booze.

Jed led us straight through and up a flight of spiraling iron steps to another door, which opened to a large, well-lit roof office. At the rear of the room were two very neatly kept matching desks, but the thing that caught my attention at first was a pewter genie lamp, with a swirl of rainbow-colored mist oozing out of the spout. It was sitting in a large window seat, surrounded by exotic-looking flowers. I wondered if it was there for show or a real one. Probably the latter.

It seems I wasn't the only one to wonder. Lydia made a beeline for it and, snatching the lamp up, began rubbing it ferociously with her palm. A very sexy, totally naked genie popped out. Unabashed by his nudity, the genie yawned and rubbed his eyes. He looked none too happy at being disturbed.

"Um, would you mind putting that down?" Jed said. "Max doesn't like being woken up before midnight. He says it's quite rude."

Caroline shot Fitz a look that could only be interpreted as, *How crass was that?* I blushed for my sister's sake and was annoyed she had exposed herself yet again.

Kitty, who was now right at her sister's side and gawping at the tiny nude, took the lamp from her sister and set it back in place among the flowers. "Sorry, pardon my sister, she can be a dick sometimes," she said.

Max snorted, and then, like he was about to dive off a board at a swimming pool, he plunged arms-first, back into the spout and disappeared.

"That was cool!" Lydia said. "Sorry, I've never seen a real genie before."

The lamp wasn't the only priceless thing on display. There was also some incredibly fine art and kissing cupids—two beautiful, opaque cherubs that kept hugging and touching each other on the tops of cupboards. They would vanish with a puff the second their lips connected in a kiss, and then the petting and touching would start all over again. I found them mesmerizing. Jed smiled at me and nodded, as if he understood what I was thinking. He really had an eye for art.

Lydia wandered over to a regular window and leaned into it as far as she could, hoping to get a look at the band as they packed up in the alley behind the Cauldron.

Jed strolled over to a cabinet along the wall just before the desks. He waved his palm over something that looked like an Apple mouse. The lights in the room dimmed at once, and the back wall seemed to melt away. An elaborate entertainment center opened, complete with music system, an enormous television, and lots and lots of alcohol, all lit in a beautiful shade of mystic green. A pretty little pixie in a bottle-green frock was perched on the end of the bar, ready to attend to us.

"Whatever you want, just ask the pixie," Jed said. "She will get it for you. Food, beverages, anything."

"Hey, can I have a glass of wine?" I asked and watched with wonder as the tiny pixie popped out to siphon some wine from a bottle using a long tube that looked like a chicken baster. She poured the alcohol into a glass, and I took it from her.

"Thanks!" I said.

The pixie winked at me and started on the next request.

"We'll be launching a new side operation in the Spring," Jed said. "FCC, Inc. We need to hire and train some more pixies first, and then we'll be venturing into big weddings, Magimitzvahs, that sort of thing."

"FCC, Inc?" Charlie asked.

"Flaming Cauldron Catering, Incorporated."

"Ah."

"I didn't think many people were so into the big weddings these days," I said.

"You don't?" Fitz said. He'd been standing beside Jane and Charlie all this time, totally silent, but watching everything that went on.

"Most of us can't afford it," I said. "If I had to choose between a big wedding and a down payment on a house, I know which one I'd pick."

"Economizing is a good thing, I suppose," Caroline said. "I do so hate it when people live beyond their means. I think it's wonderful *you're* so practical, making your own clothes, finding ways to save money." She took in my self-knitted sweater with a single sweep of her heavily mascaraed lashes. "When I get married, I want the whole enchilada, the big church, flowers, the dress, everything. I'm really quite lucky in that I won't have to make any particular sacrifices to get what I want when my big day comes."

"I see," Fitz continued. It was as if he hadn't heard a single word Caroline had said. He stared at me, intently. "But practical considerations aside, are you against marriage, then?"

"No. Why should I be?" Maybe I was wrong, but I got the distinct impression Fitz was spoiling for a fight. I thought maybe the others did, too, because the atmosphere suddenly became quite tense. I wished to Gaia someone would say something to break the tension. Surely, we weren't the only two people in this room?

"They're coming up!" Lydia shouted, and boob-bounced over from the window to rejoin us.

A few minutes later, sure enough, the four musicians from The Brew burst through the office door and came over to where we were standing near the bar. The lead singer, Denny Finn, we knew by report was a were, and ruggedly handsome. His aura was pure brown, and his hair and eyebrows were the classic thick chestnut color of a thoroughbred.

He was dressed in tight black jeans and a black tee with a blue witch on a blue broomstick emblazoned on the front. I'd seen their emblem on the drums as well.

In one hand, he carried a bottle, and he wrapped his other arm around Fitz and squeezed him in a great were hug.

"Fitz, man," he said, then pulled back to chug from his bottle. "How's it hanging?"

"To the left," Fitz replied.

I only just avoided spraying wine everywhere. It was the first time I'd seen Fitz crack a real smile. It changed him completely. For a moment, he wasn't a long streak of misery.

Denny turned to Charlie. "And Charlie!" The two men did some crazy high-five thing. Billy stood by, almost on tiptoe as he waited to be included in the greeting, but I held him back.

"Don't you dare!" I whispered between gritted teeth.

Denny leaned in and kissed Caroline politely on the cheek.

"Can I get you all another drink?" Jed asked.

"Nah, not for me," Denny replied. "I'm good with the old H$_2$O. I never touch the hard stuff. I leave it for you street guys."

The other band members were at the bar, being served beer by the cute little pixie. Their roving gazes touched on Lydia, Kitty, and Jane, but they didn't seem to notice me, the least-endowed Bennet sister. Maybe if I bounced up and down, I might attract some attention. The bass player was pretty decent-looking, pale and edgy, like a recently resurrected corpse, and his black leather pants looked as if they were sprayed on.

"That's just water?" Lydia gasped.

"Yup. I never drink anything else." Denny's eyes narrowed with interest as he checked out my little sister. "And you are?"

"Lydia, Lydia Bennet." She almost danced on the spot at his notice of her, and I made a mental note to keep a close watch on my little sister tonight.

All at once I could hear this awful screeching coming from the bar below. Denny winced, and he turned to stare at Jed. "What the heck was that?"

Jed shrugged. "Karaoke," he explained.

"Oh, that's Mary," Kitty laughed.

Kill me now, I thought, as Mary's dreadful screech rose up from the floor below. Denny winced but said nothing.

"What a delightful signing voice your sister has," Caroline said. She sniffed her pinot grigio and chugged it in a single gulp. Her gaze fell straight back to me.

"What can we say, she loves to sing," Jane said. "It makes her happy anyway, and that's a good thing, right?"

Caroline raised her eyebrows but didn't offer another response.

"So, Fitz, how did you like the show?" Denny asked. "I saw you swaying over by the wall." He grinned at everyone. "You know, he never could lighten up and dance, even when we shared a room at Yule."

"Oh, you were at university together?" I said.

"Sure were. We all were. Me, Charlie and Fitz, the three Musketeers. We were the terrors of Yule. You know I missed you guys," Denny said jovially. "How long has it been?"

"Two years, I think," Charlie replied.

"Coming up to three, actually," Fitz said.

"As long as that," Denny said. "Wow. Mind you, me and the band, we live on tour. Nonstop shows, one after the other, bam bam bam."

"Must be the life," Billy said, finding his way into the conversation at last. "All those women throwing themselves at you." He stared directly at Lydia, and I cringed. "You guys must have a whale of a time."

By Gaia, I hated him for doing that to her, and my dislike for my cousin tripled on the spot.

"Well, I can't deny we get a lot of attention from the opposite sex, but I'm a one woman sort, I am. I'm waiting for that special someone..."

Mary's shrill voice cut through the conversation like a meat cleaver, and we all covered our ears.

Jed put his glass down and raised his hands, palms out. "Sorry, guys. I better go and see how they're doing downstairs. Back in a bit."

"So how long are you in Misty Cedars?" I asked Denny.

"Just a week. I promised my Gran I'd pop in and see her. We're off to Japan for a tour and will be in Australia after that. She made me promise I'd see her before we left. So here we are."

"I really loved 'Toil and Trouble,'" Lydia said. "Are you working on anything new?"

Denny grinned. "As a matter of fact, I am. A love song, but I can't quite seem to get it right."

I smiled. The Brew were known for their dance energy. I couldn't imagine for a second what kind of love song they'd produce.

"I'd love to hear that sometime," I said. Lydia gave me a sharp look. Oops.

"You would?"

"Sure," I said. "Is it nearly finished?"

"Almost," Denny said. "I tell you what, though, the crooning wizard you should talking to is Fitz, here. Man, he sings like a choir of horny angels."

We all turned to Fitz in surprise. Even Lydia was momentarily lost for words.

"You can sing, Fitz?" Jane asked.

"A long, long time ago." Fitz had turned a little pink around the gills. "I can't believe you brought that up, Denny."

Denny grinned. "He could have played with us if he'd wanted to, but no. Fitzy, here, never liked playing to an audience." His expression became serious. "But you know, you'd really be doing me a favor if you played it for me now. I can't quite get the cadence, and I remember you had it down beautifully."

"Then it's a good thing you put your instruments away." Fitz smiled. "Oh well, maybe next time."

"I can get you a guitar out of the van if you like," said a voice over his ear. It was Colin Carter, the band's drummer.

Fitz glared at him. "Look, I don't wa—"

"Sure, if you don't mind," Denny said. "Ignore Fitz." He nudged him jovially on the arm. "He'll be fine once he gets started. He always had a little stage fright."

"No problem," said Colin. "I'll be back in a minute."

Fitz looked rather sick. "You know, I haven't had an instrument in my hand since, pfft." He couldn't finish the thought and merely rounded it off with a dismissive gesture.

"You didn't fancy being in the band then?" Lydia asked him. "Wow, just think what you could have been. The Brew are like the most exciting thing since broomsticks went solar powered."

Everybody laughed; everybody, that was, except for Fitz.

"My bad luck then, I guess," Fitz said politely. He certainly didn't sound like a man with dashed hopes.

To all our relief, my sister had stopped singing at last. I hoped she hadn't been dragged off the stage. Mary was pretty thick-skinned, but there were a lot of people down there, and I would hate for her to be laughed at. But really, she'd brought it upon herself. How often had we tried to tell her?

Apparently, Jed had been tactful because he and Mary came back together, and she was smiling happily, just as Colin returned with a guitar case. He handed it to Fitz, who looked mortified.

"I really don't..."

"Oh, just man up." Denny laughed. "You know you can do it."

Fitz didn't look so sure.

"Did you have fun?" I asked Mary.

She beamed at me. "There were banshees in the audience," she declared. "And they loved me!"

"I'm sure they did!" I grinned.

Denny settled himself in the window seat, and Fitz stood with his bum slightly hitched on one of the desks. He fiddled about tuning the strings, mumbling incoherently under his breath and shaking his head. I caught, "I can't believe I'm doing this," and then he mumbled some more.

Fitz took a deep breath, straightened up, and hit his first chord. Then he began to sing.

> Palm to palm you circle me,
> The fire's bright, you're all I see,
> I follow the path where you have danced,
> And marvel at this crazy chance,
> That your soul unbound, did call to me,
> The world has gone, you're all I see,
> I surrender to you, eternally.

Flickering flame burning bright and strong,
Reveal your magic in your song,
By candlelight, we two embrace,
Enchanted in this hallowed place.

We all listened, spellbound by Fitz's music, unable to speak. He had a beautiful, deep baritone voice, and I was mesmerized by his singing. It touched me deeply, and for a moment, I forgot how much I hated him and wondered what it would be like to have someone write such lyrics for me. Indeed, I was so entranced that it didn't dawn on me he was staring at me the whole time, as if I were the only person in the room. When he finished, the spell was broken, and I looked away. I heard a faint sigh, and then he laid the guitar down gently on the desk behind him.

"You wrote that?" I asked.

"Not exactly. I wrote the music. My grandfather wrote the words for my gran when he was courting her. Back in the day. I think it was for candle magic, but I adapted the lyrics a bit." He hesitated before asking. "Did you like it?"

"Very much so," I said. "It's beautiful."

Fitz's cheeks reddened, and a shy smile lit up his face, making him more handsome than ever.

"Did it scare her off?" Lydia laughed. "Your granny?"

"Oh, hush now, you Philistine!" I said.

Fitz ignored her and stared thoughtfully at the instrument.

"Wow," Denny said. "Of course, I remember the chorus now. That's what I was struggling with."

"You could have called and spared me this embarrassment," Fitz said. "I'd have been happy to tell you over the phone,"

"I thought it was wonderful," Jane said.

I noticed she was sitting on a sofa along the wall, and Charlie was next to her. They were sitting thigh to thigh, and if other people hadn't been present, I think they would have been holding hands. I was kind of annoyed that they thought they couldn't.

Caroline grinned. "Well, Fitz, you've been keeping that a close secret.

But it's out now. I hope to hear a lot more of your singing in the future. You have an exquisite voice."

Fitz nodded politely, but I wondered if he was really listening to her. Instead, he was looking directly at me. I gazed down at my knitted sweater and wondered if he really hated it that much. It wasn't supposed to look poor—it was meant to look trendy, damn it! Or maybe he was just staring my way, oblivious to what was right in front of him, still absorbed by his own performance. That was more likely.

"Yeah, come on, people," Jed said. "Let's put on some music and have some fun."

With a snap of his fingers, some lights clicked on over in his entertainment center, and a song began to boom through the speakers. Everyone got up and started mingling, Lydia and Kitty with the band members, Jed hooking up with Jane and Charlie. Fitz and Caroline remained glued to the desks, and I was left to the attentions of Billy and Mary.

"He was really good," Billy said. He kept looking over his shoulder as if expecting Fitz to tap on it or something. "Say, how about you and me pop downstairs and have a go at that karaoke? What do you say? Shall we show everyone how it's done?"

"Um, I'm good, thanks. I have a bit of a frog in my throat right now. Ask Mary. I'm sure she'd love to."

Mary's eyes lit up, and Billy looked a tad disappointed but then immediately brightened up again. "No, no. I'm here with you. It wouldn't be right for me to run off with another woman now, would it?"

Oh Gaia, how I wished he would. Really.

Chapter Fifteen

BESOTTED

"I'm in the mood to dance. Would you like to dance with me, Izzy? I'm no Denny Finn, but I'm a bit of a dynamo on the dance floor, if I do say so myself."

To make his point, Billy raised his hands and gyrated his hips like a '70s porn star. *Just ugh*. I'd been dreading this moment all night.

"It's really nice of you to ask," I said, "but actually I was wondering if we should be heading home soon. We have to walk back to get the cars, and I like to get to bed early when I can."

"I'm sorry to hear that," a voice right behind me said. It was Fitz. "Since I was going to ask you the same thing."

I froze. This was unexpected. Billy, I saw coming a mile off, had planned for it, and knew what to say, but Fitz took me totally off guard.

"I, erm, well..."

"It's okay," Fitz said. "I guess my timing is off. I heard what you just told, um..."

"Billy," Billy said.

"Thank you. Yes, Billy."

"I wouldn't mind going down with you," Mary said to Billy. "To sing, 'cos Gaia knows I can't dance."

"I, um, yes, well, I suppose we could do that, sure," Billy said. "If my date will allow it?"

"This isn't a date." I frowned and slapped my palm to my forehead. "You're free to do whatever you wish."

Billy's jaw dropped, like this was news to him.

"Why don't we all go down?" Fitz said. "Izzy and I can come and watch you, you know, lend a little moral support."

Mary beamed, and I could hardly get out of it now. Fitz smiled warmly at Billy, who sighed and resigned himself to his fate.

"Oh, very well," Billy said to me. "But you'll definitely come and watch us, won't you?"

Before I could object, Fitz led the way.

I looked back to the others, to Jane, talking to Charlie, and to Lydia and Kitty who were flirting with the band. Other than Caroline, who was shooting me daggers, they looked perfectly happy where they were. I sighed. I supposed it wouldn't hurt to delay leaving for a little while longer.

With as much grace as I could muster, I followed the others carefully down the stairs to the bar area. We could hear a pack of weres singing their rendition of "Blue Moon," and it wasn't half bad. They were still on stage when Billy and Mary put in for the next song.

"What did you pick?" I asked.

"'Relax,'" Mary said.

I died a little on the inside. "Mary, I really don't think that's a good choice."

"Oh, don't be such an old fuddy-duddy," Mary replied. "It'll be fun, you'll see! Everyone loves the old songs."

I glanced up at Fitz, who was pretty tight lipped about it. I thought it an inappropriate song for a girl her age, but if he thought so too, I couldn't tell. He looked as enigmatic as ever.

Behind me, I heard laughter. Lydia and Kitty had followed us down with the band and were already bending over the bar. Lydia's butt was exposed for the world to see, and Kitty, who was a little older, after all, and should have known better, did nothing to dissuade her.

"I wish they would raise the drinking age for witches to twenty-one, like the numpies," I observed.

Fitz nodded. He was staring at Lydia. "Yes, I imagine that you would. They're not quite mature enough at seventeen to handle it."

"No."

"But then I suppose," Fitz continued, "you all look out for each other."

"Yes, yes, we do," I said. For some reason, I was relieved he was taking a lenient view. "My younger sisters can be pretty wild, but they are good girls at heart."

At that precise moment, a wayward elbow knocked a pint of something frothy over Lydia's skimpy top, resulting in a big cheer at the bar. I covered my eyes. There was little left to the imagination after that.

"You know it's a pity your friend is so smitten with Jane," Billy shouted over the crowd.

"Oh, why is that?" Fitz looked at his watch, and I wondered exactly what was going on in that handsome head of his.

"Because I saw her first and was hoping she would come out with me."

Fitz looked confused. "I'm sorry, I thought you said earlier you were with Izzy?"

"Well, I am now."

I shook my head violently, contradicting this.

"No," Billy continued. "Jane pushed me aside, as soon as you and your friend arrived in town. Not that I mind, mark you. Jane would be mad to turn down someone as loaded as that for me. Nope, once she realized she had a chance with him, I was history. Not that it would stop me helping your dad with his money troubles," he said to me. "Rest assured, whatever happens, his problems are safe with me."

"Err, excuse me?" I said, affronted for her. "My sister never encouraged you, loaded or not. Jane isn't a gold digger. And you shouldn't be talking about Dad's private business. Not in public!"

"I'm not saying she is," Billy said, backpedaling and entirely ignoring my comments about Dad. "I'm just saying she has excellent taste. But come on, let's be honest, you're not bad yourself, and if you fancy a quick dance in a bit, I'd be more than happy to join you."

If there had been any drink left in my glass, I'd have thrown it in his face. Sadly, it was empty.

In front of us, the weres were done with their song, and the whole bar clapped.

"Come on," Mary said. "We're up next."

My sister dragged Billy off, and if I didn't know better, I'd have said he was delighted to have an excuse to get away. *Good riddance*, I thought. The man had more gall than was good for him.

The downside was now I was stuck on my own with Fitz.

"Can I get you something?" The cheery voice at my side was Charlie. He and Jane had just arrived from upstairs.

"Just a water with lemon," I said. "Where's Caroline?" I asked, looking around him.

"Oh, she's still up there with Jed talking about his catering ideas. They'll be down in a bit. Come on, Fitz, give me a hand carrying these drinks."

The two men headed over to the bar.

At that moment, Billy and Mary started to sing. Once again, I found myself cringing. If that wasn't enough, Billy began gyrating obscenely to the beat. Oh hell. I wanted the ground to open up and swallow me whole. Witches and warlocks, was it possible this night could get any worse?

"Well, you're doing all right." I said to Jane. I was glad at least one of us was having a good time.

"He's a very nice man," Jane replied. "He was telling me about his cabin in the mountains. Maybe one day I'll get to see it."

I snorted. "Oh, come off it, Jane. He'll have you down there bumping uglies if he could before the month is out."

She blushed. "Oh, stop it, Izzy." Then she smiled. "Do you really think so?"

"Really, Jane." I laughed. "That man is besotted. He couldn't be more into you if he had your name tattooed all over his backside. He hasn't left you alone for a second."

She grinned. "He's left me now."

"Don't be silly, he's on a quest to provide refreshment for his mistress. Anyway, he's a nice guy. Let him know you like him just as much, okay?"

"I do," Jane said, "I'm listening intently to everything he has to say."

"Well, do more. Touch him up a bit. Flirt harder. You know you're hard enough even for me to read, and I'm your sister. Don't leave him in any doubt whatsoever, or some hot witch will swoop in on her broomstick and will steal him out from under your very nose, I'm telling you."

"Okay, okay. Flirt more. Touch him up. I get it. Anyway, what about you?"

I frowned. "What? Billy?"

"No, not him. Fitz. He told Caroline you have pretty eyes. Sent her off in a right hump, Charlie said. Apparently, she's into him in a really big way."

"For all I care she can have him, stuck-up twerp. It makes no odds to me what they do. I couldn't care less." Funny, though I meant what I said, I felt a twang of remorse saying it. I wondered why.

Jane gave me a knowing look and smirk, but I couldn't say anything more, because the men returned, ladened with drinks. Fitz handed me my water and looked up at the stage. Charlie handed Jane hers, but I noticed he wasn't smiling anymore. If anything, he looked a bit annoyed.

"Is everything okay?" I asked.

"Fine. I, um, I think he just shortchanged me for the drinks, that's all."

Hmm. Charlie didn't seem the type to be so easily upset. "Did you say something to him?" I asked. "I'm sure it's just a mistake."

"Oh, it's sorted," Charlie said.

While he and Jane wandered off to a private corner, Fitz's attention remained glued to the stage, and I didn't know which horrified me more, Mary's banshee howling or Billy's pelvic thrusting.

"What an interesting voice your sister has."

Caroline. My circle of shit was complete.

"Perhaps when this screeching is over, we'll get a chance to dance," she said to Fitz.

Jed was apparently immune to the noise, but eager to please his guests, he nodded. "Perhaps you're right." He caught the eye of the man managing the karaoke machine and mimicked throat cutting. The man nodded, and the music faded to gray.

Mary and Billy looked pissed and stormed off the stage in bad grace, though to yowls of delight from the banshees. Caroline smirked. I'd had enough. It was time to go.

"Look, I really need to get going," I said.

"So soon?" Fitz said. "Yes, well, if that's what you want."

"It is, but I don't think my younger sisters will be thrilled to go." I looked over to where Kitty and Lydia were having a whale of a time. I thought I ought to drag them home now, before they really showed the family up.

Fitz glanced back to where I was looking. "Go if you want to. Don't worry about them. I'm sure Charlie will take them home, if I asked him. And Caroline can drive my car and take the others. You don't mind, do you, Caroline?"

"No, not at all."

Liar, liar, pants on fire.

"Let me walk you to your car."

"Wait, what?"

Before I could object further, Fitz wandered across to where Charlie and Jane were chatting quietly at a table. They talked for a bit, and then Charlie looked my way and nodded.

Oh hell, did Fitz really think I was so feeble I needed looking after? How did I go from not wanting to dance to this?

Though Caroline pointedly ignored me and stared at the band, I could feel her festering hatred through the silence. The evening couldn't have been less perfect if it tried.

Fitz was soon back at my side, and we both deposited our empty glasses on the bar.

"All set?" Fitz asked.

"Sure."

It was surreal, but a minute later I was standing on the street, the noise of the bar behind us. My ears hummed from the change.

For a little while, we walked along in silence. The night was still cold and bright, though not bad enough for me to need a coat. I wrapped my arms around myself as we walked, and I noticed he glanced at me as I did.

"Hold up," he said. He pulled out his wand and pointed it at me. Instinctively I flinched, but he shook his head, gently. "Don't worry. It's just a heat spell. Not even a Hag would notice. *Calor!*" The tip of his wand twirled, and a second later, I was so toasty I could have been lying in bed on a warm Sunday morning.

"Thanks," I said. We continued awhile in silence.

"You're an odd one to figure out," I said, stepping off the pavement and looking left and right before we crossed the road.

"How so?" Fitz asked.

"I'd never heard of you a few weeks ago. Yet everyone I know"—I thought about Billy—"well, almost everyone, is on a first name basis with you. At the coven, my friends, the Lucases, Jed, and well, everyone. Even the damned bouncer at the Flaming Cauldron knew you by sight. Have I been living in a bubble or something?"

Fitz smiled gently. "Most people don't *know* me. In fact, I'd say only a handful of people know me really well. I guess a lot of people know *of* me, but that's not the same thing at all."

Well, that was illuminating. *Not.*

"My family is a very old one," he continued, once we were walking at a normal pace again. "We contribute to a lot of charities and organizations. I suppose the donations are quite substantial, and many people benefit from them, but we like to keep everything pretty low-key. I know I do."

This made sense but was totally at odds with what George had told me Fitz had done to him. Could a man be so generous on the one hand and so callous on the other? Half of me wanted to come right out and say it, but a wise monkey on my shoulder warned me to tread carefully. It was not my fight, after all.

"You said you knew my boss?"

His stride remained unaltered, and he didn't say anything snarky, yet there was something in the way he caught his next breath that betrayed a change in his mood.

"Yes, I believe I know him quite well." His tone was clipped, and I raised my guard, cautious.

"He only joined my firm a few weeks ago. The other partners think very highly of him."

"Yes, I understand he bought his way in."

"He did?" I said, surprised. "I heard they were desperate for him. They moved heaven and earth to get him a partner's chair."

Fitz was silent for a moment. And then he turned on me. I could see his eyes were bright with hatred, even in the pale moonlight. "Have you ever stopped to think about where that information came from? That what people say and what is actually true are not always the same?"

"Of course," I said, my own bile rising against his bitterness. "I work in the legal business, for Wicca's sake. But I also trust my instincts, and I like to put a little faith in people. I'm not going to dislike people because some random stranger tells me to do so."

"I'm not telling you to dislike anyone." Fitz huffed.

"Sounds like it to me." I continued at a pace, and for a while, Fitz just stood where I left him. Fine. He could turn around now for all I cared. But then I heard the sound of running, and I glanced over my shoulder, and sure enough, he had caught up with me again.

"There's no need for you to come any farther," I said. "Feel free to go back to the others if you like. I'm perfectly capable of walking on my own."

"I said I would see you to your car, and that's what I'm going to do," he said.

"You know, I'm not some helpless young witch in need of looking after. I can look after myself perfectly well."

"I never said you were," Fitz said. "But I'm doing this anyway."

I stopped and rounded on him. "Look, I'd rather you left, actually. I'd feel a whole lot better if you did. I don't want you hanging around, okay? I don't care what everyone else says. I. Don't. Like. You."

Fitz looked as if I'd slapped him in the face. "Well, if that's what you really want." His gaze searched mine, one last time. He was clearly pissed about something, but I didn't give a fig what it was.

"Are you done?" I asked, hands on hips.

Fitz bit his lip. "I suppose I am," he said. "I guess I was wrong about you. My mistake. Good night."

I didn't respond. Instead, I just stared at him, fuming. Seeing he wasn't even going to get a civil good night, he finally took the hint and left. For a moment, I stood fixed to the spot, watching him retreat in the dark. Screw him. That fight had come out of nowhere, and I'd be damned before I let him talk to me like that again. Who the hell did he think he was, anyway?

Enough! I turned myself and, without looking back once to see where he was, continued the short journey to my car, alone at last, and hating him.

Chapter Sixteen

HOLY WATER

MARY KING WAS AN EARLY BIRD WHO WAS TYPICALLY IN THE OFFICE long before I was. Not that I followed her comings and goings that closely. Maybe she was taking a sick day or something.

George wasn't in yet either, so I opened my computer and answered a few emails. I found it hard to focus: fairy solicitation and goblin obscenity complaints just couldn't hold my attention today.

Funny. The more I thought about it, the more I realized I had no real feelings for George after all. I mean, he *was* seeing someone else, and although he was hot, my heart felt no *bada bing* when he walked in the room. That had to mean something, surely?

No. It was that damned Fitz. I'd let him get to me, and that so wasn't like me. I minimized my Outlook and wandered over to the kitchenette. It was still early, and I needed caffeine, lots of it.

The bell hanging over the office door jingled, and I stole a glance over my shoulder. It was George, and even from here he looked like shit. His five-o'clock shadow seemed twenty-four hours old, and his cheeks were oddly hollow. His clothes, however, were as impeccable as ever. He headed straight toward me.

"I'll have some of that if you're making extra," he said.

"It's a Keurig." *Get your own damned coffee* was on the tip of my tongue, but I couldn't forget that he was my boss. "European roast?"

"Sure, and black. I need it."

George waited, evidently conscious of his stubble because he kept rubbing it.

"Busy weekend? Do you need me to go out for a razor or something?"

"What? Oh, no," George replied. He rubbed his chin again. "I've got something in my office."

I removed my French Vanilla pod out of the holder and tossed it in the trash by the machine. I slipped a fresh pod in for him and slid his mug into the slot.

"So..." I pulled the tab from a half-and-half, poured it into my mug, and then did the same again. I liked my coffee creamy. "What happened to you? You're not your usual chipper self."

George shook his head. "Don't ask."

I raised my eyebrows but kept my mouth shut.

"Fae dumped me," he said.

I wasn't expecting that. "Did she say why?"

"She wasn't exactly explicit, but it boils down to *Daddy* not liking me."

"Oh. Oh, George, I'm so sorry." I handed him his coffee as a surge of pity rose within me. "That succubus sucks. Is there anything I can do?"

"No, no, it's just one of those things. I'm a big boy. I can take it."

Yet there was something about his look. I couldn't say what exactly, but I'd have bet a Leprechaun's pot of gold that there was something he wasn't telling me.

"I guess that's why you didn't show on Friday. I'm sorry."

George sipped at his mug and backed off. He didn't answer, and I wasn't going to press.

"What time do we have to be at Rosings Park tonight?" I asked.

"Well, I have a light day today, so I'll be taking off once I've checked my emails. If you want to do the same, that's fine since you'll be working later. I can pick you up at your place, if you like. Say seven?"

"Sure. Well, I'd like to take off, but we need at least one paranormal legal in the office, and Mary seems to be off today."

"Oh, she's not off. She's just running a little late."

"Oh, she telephoned in?"

George hesitated before replying. "Err, yeah. She won't be long. She's running some errands or something."

Hmm. A little bell was dinging in my head.

He headed off to his office, and I watched him go. So George was a free agent now, once the ache in his heart was mended. Still, after all my lusting, now he was free, I didn't want him. I was sure of that now. I felt sorry for him, but that was all.

The door jingled again, and this time it was Mary arriving. I sauntered back to my desk, arriving around the same time as she did, and settled down to skim through my emails.

"Good weekend?" Mary asked over the cubicle.

"Me, not bad," I replied. "The concert was good. We all had a nice time. How about you?"

It went quiet for a while, and then she echoed my response. "Not bad. I can't complain."

That little bell dinged a lot louder. *Hmm.* So Mary had a secret too. There must be something in the water in this place. I put my coffee mug down, jumping to the obvious conclusion. Whatever. I had shit to do.

There was an interview with a Golem open in front of me. I didn't like Golems—they terrified me. They were large, ferocious, and wholly without empathy. This one had been accused of the murder of his creator, and accordingly to the notes, he was pleading not guilty.

Haggerston Lowe usually gave his work to Mary, but since she hadn't been in this morning, he'd given the file to me. Despite my dislike of Golems, it looked like an interesting case, and I was grateful for the work.

The Golem, who was currently enjoying the hospitality of the Hags at their magical prison Bitterhold, claimed that his master wasn't dead at all but had simply disappeared. He knew him only as *Master*, which had made it impossible for anyone to track him down. The case against him was pretty weak, mostly circumstantial. Golems were notorious for murdering their makers. Rather like Frankenstein, they looked human but had poorly developed reason and emotional systems, childlike at best. Once they had served the purpose for which they had been created, their makers often abandoned them, resulting in rage and mishap. And sometimes murder.

This Golem, Goulding, was a sorry-looking Golem indeed. He'd had an indifferent creator; his gangly arms and fingers were too long for his body, and his legs were like matchsticks, too thin for his body. One good kick would probably snap him in two. It was hard to believe someone so frail-looking could inflict physical damage upon anyone, but these supernatural beings often possessed inhuman strength.

I worked on the file for the rest of the morning, putting everything together. By which time I knew everything there was to know about Goulding the Golem, and all of it was encased in the shiny ring binder I had compiled for Mr. Lowe.

It had been the most interesting file I'd worked on since George joined the firm, and I found myself half wishing he hadn't joined us at all. I liked the kind of files the partners had given me before, and I missed it.

"Okay," I said at last, shutting everything off and grabbing my empty coffee mug. "That's me done. I'm out with the boss tonight, meeting this vampire, so I'll be gone for the rest of the day."

"That's nice," Mary said. There was none of the usual jealousy in her voice, and my Spidey sense had a pretty good idea why.

"I guess something kept you up last night," I said, glancing over the top of the cubicle.

At that precise moment, the door to George's office opened. He had his jacket on, ready to go.

Mary smiled. "You could say that."

"Oh. I. See." Well, that had been a no-brainer.

Without asking anything more, I wandered over to the kitchenette to rinse out my coffee mug.

George was over by her cubicle now, and though his voice was lowered, his smile was intimate. So *poor George* hadn't wept for Fae that long. Pity. I suspected Fae deserved better.

I totally ignored Mary's smug look and pretended like I hadn't noticed a thing. They were a witch and wizard, both of age, and it was none of my business, after all. Good luck to them both. They were going to need it.

It was still early in the evening, and the clouds overhead were heavy and gray, fit to burst at any moment. I glanced up the moment I climbed out of the passenger seat of George's Beemer, hoping the rain would hold off long enough for us to get inside.

"If we hurry, we should make it," George said.

Taking my lead from him, I dashed over the gravel drive and made it to the door just in time. A loud thunderclap behind me preceded the downpour, and as I reached the safety of the building, there was a massive roar, and the heavens opened.

"Phew," I said.

George had just made it, also, and I saw Matthew's papers tucked safely inside the front of his jacket. A nun approached us as we entered.

"Good evening, Mr. Wickham. You're here to see Matthew?"

"Yes, we are, Sister Angelica," George replied. "Is everything okay?"

"Oh yes, sir. He asked me to inform you he is dining early this evening. He is in the restaurant, having supper."

"Thank you. I know where that is," said George.

Once again, I was struck by George's familiarity with the place. I'd lived in Misty Cedars my whole life and knew very little about Rosings Park, beyond the fact of its existence. George had been here two minutes yet seemed to know all about it.

I trailed behind him, and we walked down a corridor to the right, my sneakers squeaking on the marble flooring as we passed endless side tables filled with lavender.

"I'm glad you know where you're going," I said. "It's dark down here and kinda spooky."

"Yes, for good reason. The vamps who prefer to sleep in their coffins are down that corridor to the left. Hold up."

George paused at a font by the last vase of lavender and dipped the tips of his fingers into it, smearing the water on his neck, like aftershave. I did the same. It was holy water, and although Matthew was a "friendly," who would vouch for the others? Better safe than bitten. And we were right by their dining room. The vampires would be thinking of food.

I looked down the corridor with doors to the coffin rooms.

"Why did we see Matthew in a room upstairs, and not in his coffin?"

"All of the guests here have both. The coffin rooms are unhallowed, and the nuns refuse to attend to them there. Plus, you know, the rooms are much nicer. The rooms down that corridor are little more than crypts with no windows and nowhere to sit. They're not suitable for guests."

"The corridor of the dead. Eww."

"Just don't wander off alone down there. Let's get going. This place feels like death, and it gives me the creeps. I want this business wrapped up. If I never see this house again, or your *friend* Matthew, it'll be too soon."

There was a sneer in the way he said friend, which annoyed me. He was a client. The vampire deserved our respect.

"I'm guessing you weren't able to find what you were looking for in his will? The location of the Moonstone?" I said, putting all my cards face up on the table.

George looked down at his feet, thinking. "No. I could not. Look, I'll be honest with you. I need to find their burial place, Goody's and Matthew's. There has to be some kind of code because he wasn't explicit in the will. Well, I certainly couldn't find it."

I knew he wasn't interested in placing flowers on Goody's grave.

"Look, I'm a treasure hunter. I've never lied about that. I've examined his will from front to back, and there's nothing in it at all about the site or the stone. If you don't get something out of him, it might never be found. Is that what you want, for it to be lost forever?"

"It doesn't matter to me, one way or another. Personally I think it's a good thing if it's lost. It didn't do Goody any favors. Anyway, what makes you think he has it? I thought he just said he wanted to be buried with her. He never said he had the stone."

"No, but it's all I've got."

I shrugged. It sounded like grave robbing to me, and I wanted no part of it. Treasure hunting wasn't a sin, but I didn't like the way he went about doing it. Using Matthew. Using me. No way on earth I was going to help him.

Inside I ached to hear more of Matthew's story, but I wasn't going to help my boss try to hoodwink him, even if he was scheduled to die tomorrow. I'd rather let Matthew face the eternal nothing with his tale untold than lift one little finger to help George. He was on his own from now on. Screw him.

Matthew dabbed his lips on a napkin, leaving a smear of red on the pure white linen as it left his mouth. He merely glanced at George but smiled warmly at me as I approached.

"Ah."

He was attended to by a nun, who he waved off dismissively with a flourish of his hand. Unoffended, the good nun ventured off, carrying a tray containing nothing but a white cloth, the used napkin, and a drained bag of donor blood with a red crucifix on it, the symbol of the Vampire Sisters of Mercy.

He held out his hand to George, who gave him his executed papers. "Thank you." He put them down on the table and turned his attention back to me. "And how are you, my dear?"

"Very well, thank you," I replied. "George was telling me you entered into a period of grace. Is tomorrow...still a thing?"

Matthew rubbed his lower lip, exposing more than a hint of fang. "Tomorrow is always a *thing*, as you say. What that *thing* will be is promised to no man. Or vampire."

He looked thoughtfully at the envelope sitting unopened on the table and tapped it with his fingers. "George. I would be greatly obliged if you would take this up to my room. I would walk a little, but I don't enjoy the stairs after a heavy meal."

"But I...err."

"Thank you. If I can't trust my own lawyer on such a mission, who can I trust?"

George looked at me. "I'm not sure I..."

"I give you my word, the pretty witch will be perfectly safe with me. In any case, as you saw for yourself, I have dined already. She will have nothing to fear. Make haste, George, for the sooner you leave us, the sooner you can return. But please, don't hurry on my account."

I tried to hide my smirk as George snatched the offered envelope from Matthew's fingers and stood watching as he stormed off back along the corridor.

As soon as he was out of earshot, Matthew turned his attention to me.

"Come, my dear, I would have a little time alone with you. You are not afraid of me, are you?"

"Me? No. Not at all. Should I be?"

"No. You will be quite safe, I give you my word." He put his gnarled hand to his heart as a gesture of goodwill.

I nodded, accepting he would honor his word.

"Very good. Come, if we hurry, he won't be able to see which direction we took, and it will take him a little while longer to catch us up. Are you afraid of vampires?"

"Generally, yes," I confessed. "Why? Are we going back through the coffin rooms?"

"Yes," he said. "If you have the stomach for it? George Wickham wouldn't dare follow us that way."

I nodded again. "I trust you."

"Come then." Matthew led us out of the dining room and back to the corridor of the dead. My skin crawled as we made our way along it.

"Are you afraid of dying?" I whispered.

"Afraid? No. Curious? More than a little."

I wanted him to talk. I wanted him to distract me from the misery that slept behind these doors. The despairing undead. I could sense them, with my witch's insight. It left me cold and empty.

"What do you want to happen?" I continued. "If you um, go?"

"I'm not looking for answers, if that's what you mean. What I seek more than anything is peace."

That, at least, I could get my head around. I stared warily at the doors on either side of us. How many were occupied I couldn't say and had no wish to find out. I touched the part of my neck where I'd dabbed the holy water and wondered how much protection, if any, it would give me?

Matthew looked at me and smiled. I guessed he knew I'd done it, but if he had an opinion about it, he didn't share it.

We came to the end of the corridor, not soon enough in my opinion, and to a double set of dark, glass doors. Like a true gentleman of his age, Matthew opened the door and made way for me to pass before him. I slipped under his arm, grateful to be away from that creepy place, and was just breathing a sigh of relief when a sudden gust of wind took my breath away. I almost backed into Matthew.

"What the—!" I gasped.

A tall, wiry old woman with bloodshot eyes, dark graying hair, and sharp, pointed teeth stood right in front of me. Where she'd come from, I couldn't tell. She'd materialized in an instant. For fae's sake, I so hated vampires.

I wasn't the only one startled. The old vamp must have sensed the holy water because she jumped back at once. She looked me up and down, her eyes narrowed, and her lips curled in contempt.

"A witch," she creaked, withdrawing her skinny fingers and weathered nails that had been mere inches from my face. "I thought it was food. Why did you bring her here?"

"My business is none of yours, Octavia. Now if you'll excuse me, time is pressing."

Octavia opened her eyes to protest, but then she thought better of it. She smiled at me, not in a nice way, but like she would smile at a dog she really hated. Then without another word, she stood to one side and let us pass.

As soon as she was out of earshot, I had to ask, "Who was that?"

"Octavia Bathsheba Harrington," Matthew replied. "You would do well to keep clear of her. She had no love of your kind. She lost her first love to a witch."

"And who was that?" I asked.

"Me. Not that anything came of it. We had—what would your generation call it—a fling? That was long before I met Goody. Be warned, Octavia would bite you just to spite you."

"Good to know."

"She was beautiful in her youth, as only vampires can be, but now, like me, she has had enough. We have that in common at least."

I nodded. The old vamp had what my mother would call good bones. It wasn't too hard to picture her as a great beauty, once. She was anything but, now.

Matthew led us through another set of doors and out into the open. The rain had stopped, thank goodness, but there was hardly any light here. The windows to the lower crypt rooms had been blacked out, and there was a deliberate lack of lighting along the walk. When the door closed behind us, we were in total darkness. I pulled out my wand, ready to light the way, but Matthew held out a hand to stop me.

"Don't be afraid. The darkness protects you. The night is not evil. Only people are."

I pictured George in my mind. He would have gotten to Matthew's room by now and would be heading back down to look for us. And he'd be pissed. Playing errand boy would not be his thing.

"Do not worry about George," Matthew said. It appeared he didn't need to be inside my mind to read it. "He will not find us for a while. We are not as well-versed in the ways of magic as you, but we have a kind of our own. We can walk undisturbed for a while."

It was hard not talking, when I had so much I wanted to ask him. Not just about Goody, but about George too. Matthew obviously knew what my boss was about. The old vampire was no fool.

We began to walk along the side of the house. I could barely see him, so I focused my attention on the sound of his footsteps on the gravel path.

"What George seeks, he will never find because he has no soul. He's a cliché—a bloodsucking lawyer with no sense of honor."

"Why did you hire him?"

"Because he's also efficient and ruthless. Sometimes these qualities are invaluable too. Most especially in a lawyer."

I thought I might as well come out and say it. "Do you know where the stone is?"

His footsteps stopped before I realized he had. I stopped too, listening intently to what he intended to say. "Sometimes I think with nostalgia about the past. There are things in my life...moments...that given the chance, I would like to live again. But there are other moments, bitter ones, that are best left where they are. Safely behind me.

"I remember days where I dreamed of a wonderful future with Goody. What we would do, where we would live. The imaginary children I knew we would never have, but I dreamed of them anyway. Of course, we had no future. No amount of wishful thinking would have changed that. It occurred to me, if I had sought the stone for myself, things might have been different. But by then, Goody was already dead, and no amount of luck can change that."

"So what did you do?" I asked.

"Her sister was a good woman too. We became friends for a while and were very fond of each other. Nothing romantic you understand; lightning doesn't hit the same spot twice. I remember warm summer nights, strolling through the grounds at Dark Coven, telling her about the secret places Goody and I would meet. Perhaps I should have kept our secrets to myself, but I had to share with someone, see? Through Eleanor, I was able to keep those memories alive, at least for a while. Anyway, we would often wander around the park, and like her sister, she would indulge me in my foolish love of pixies, and we would often sit near the small pond there, remembering happier days, watching the pixies in the magical twilight hours before the moon reigned and the day slept.

"One morning, when we were ready, Eleanor and I wandered down to the subbasement. I hadn't been near it since Goody had died—I detested the place. There was a fissure in the center of the circle. Eleanor told me Thackeray Collins had driven an iron rod into it to desecrate what he'd daubed the witches' lair. It didn't work, of course. From what I was told, his very act had served only to strengthen the magic." Matthew paused, and his tone changed entirely. "Ah, George, we were wondering where you had gotten to. Did you get yourself lost?"

I turned and could just make out George's outline in the dark.

"I think I took a wrong corridor," George replied. I was right. His tone was clipped, and boy, did he sound pissed, no matter how hard he tried to hide it. "What did I miss?"

"An old vampire's tittle-tattle, that is all. You know, I'm a little tired after all. Perhaps we should head back? I have quite a day tomorrow, and I have a lot of ghosts to make peace with before a new dawn arises."

"What time...?" I couldn't bring myself to finish the sentence.

"Rosings Park prefers to let us ponder our decisions overnight. My, um, journey, if you would, is scheduled to end at four a.m., a few minutes before the sun rises."

I hated to think of him all alone at that time. "Um, would you, I mean, if you would like, I could be there for you? So you're not alone?"

We were back at the door, and Matthew opened it so that George and I could pass through.

"You are very kind, but it is not necessary. Octavia and I had a little talk, and we'll be doing this together. For moral support, if you like?"

It wasn't my place to feel about this, one way or another, but nevertheless I was still glad he wouldn't be facing the dawn all by himself.

"And George will be there, won't you, George? I do believe there will be some final affidavits to sign. It will be nice to say good-bye knowing my trusty lawyer will be standing by me to the very end."

George's "Uh-huh" was more of a grunt.

I did not relish the prospect of the grilling George would give me on the way back home, yet I was still smiling. In the end, the wily old vamp had foiled him. And I was glad about that. For now.

George didn't waste any time. We'd been in his Beemer less than a minute before he went on the attack.

"So what did he tell you?" he asked.

I gripped my knees. He was driving uncommonly fast. "Nothing. Matthew didn't tell me a thing."

"I wasn't born yesterday, Izzy. Why else would he have bothered to send me up to his room like that? He had to have told you something."

"Maybe because it's his last night on this planet and he wanted to spend it with a friend, not his lawyer," I conjectured.

"He's not your friend. He's a client."

"I don't see why he can't be both."

George turned the next corner a little too sharply, and though the Beemer hugged the road well, I didn't like his crazy driving.

"Tell me what he did say, then. Vampires are notoriously shifty. Perhaps he said something important, and you didn't realize it."

And now he was calling me stupid too. Even if Matthew had told me something, wild horses wouldn't have dragged it from me now. *Go, screw yourself, asshole*, was what I thought. Like it or not, George was still my boss, so what I actually said was, "As I said, I asked him directly about the Moonstone, and he told me nothing. Sorry, George, I can't help you. Why are *you* so desperate to find it? Do you have a demon on your back or something?"

"I told you, I'm a treasure hunter. This kind of thing is a big deal. The Moonstone is famous, and it would be the find of the century. I would go down in history as the warlock who recovered it. Can't you see how important that would be to me? To anyone?"

"I'm really sorry, George. I wish he'd told me something to help you, but he talked about love and life and, well, about tomorrow. I think he just wanted someone to say good-bye to."

He gripped the wheel a little more tightly, but at last, George took his foot off the gas and resumed driving at a normal speed. I could sense his frustration, but what an asshole. He'd been risking my life over a damned stone.

"Look," I said. "You're seeing him again in the morning. Why not come out and ask him? If he knows anything, he might tell you then, kind of like a last hoorah?"

George looked at me like I was some kind of simpleton and sneered. "Just like that? Blurt it out?"

"What have you got to lose?"

George pulled slowly onto our drive, put the Beemer into park, and turned to face me.

"Izzy," he said. "I'm under a lot of stress right now. I'm sorry about... back there." He gestured behind him, indicating the drive. "I do have...my reasons. You might not like them, but they are what they are. I'm sorry. This isn't your fault. I just got a little carried away."

I nodded and was prepared to leave it at that.

As I opened the door, he said, "Friends?"

That I wasn't so sure of, but I stayed in the car a little longer. "Hey, good luck at the...thing...tomorrow. I hope it goes as well as it can."

"Thank you," he said. "And I really am sorry."

I nodded once more, but I got out of the car this time and went inside.

Chapter Seventeen

FLAT TIRE

"For pity's sake!"

I stood by the side of the road and stared at what was left of my tire. Like an idiot, I'd left my wand at home, sitting on my dresser next to my manicure set. Great. It wasn't much use to me there. Since there was nothing else for it, I kicked the air and opened the trunk. Dang! The spare wasn't there, either.

Lydia. She's been looking for a tire for a swing, and I would bet my monthly paycheck she'd found one in the back of my car.

Sighing, I pulled her name up on my phone and hit the green call button.

"'Sup?" Lydia sounded half-asleep still. I had probably woken her up. *Good.*

"Hey, dear sister! I've been meaning to ask, did you ever make that tire swing?"

"Uh...yeah?"

"Lots of fun, was it?"

"Sure. What are you—?"

"Where'd you get the tire, Lydia?"

"Uh...why are you asking this now?"

"I'm standing by the side of the road, wondering how I'm going to get to work on time. Would you like to take a stab at why?"

"Er..."

"You stole my goddamn spare tire, Lydia, that's why. I've got a flat, and my car's going nowhere. Where's Dad?"

"Dunno."

"Great. Look, I need a ride to work. Can you come get me? I'll worry about the tire tonight."

"S'pose. Where are you?"

"By the bank."

"Can't you call an Uber?"

"Are you kidding me? This is your fault. Come fix it. You can be here quicker."

I heard her sigh down the phone. "Oh, okay, I can be there in ten minutes."

"Try to make it five. I'm already late, thank you very much."

I sighed and put away my phone. I loved Lydia, but sometimes...

I looked at my watch. Seven thirty. Earlier this morning, Matthew would have said his good-byes to the world and would now be experiencing the eternal nothing. I shuddered. In the end, I had wanted him to change his mind so badly, but ultimately, it wasn't my decision to make. That didn't stop me feeling like shit, though. I wondered how George had got on.

Fifteen minutes later, Lydia pulled up beside me on her little moped, and with a sigh, I hopped on behind her. She was late, but there was no point whining about that now.

"Let's get going, shall we?"

"Hold tight."

My little sister hit the throttle, and a moment later, we were on our way. I wished she'd worn a helmet, because her curly black mop whiplashed me as we drove along, and I found myself spitting her hair out more than once or twice.

Lydia pulled into the parking lot at the office, and to my surprise, instead of turning about and heading home, she jumped off her moped and started hopping about.

"Sorry. I need to pee."

"Why didn't you go before you came to get me?"

"I didn't think!"

I shook my head, but since I could hardly leave her to relieve herself on the asphalt, I crooked my head and beckoned her to follow me into the building.

"Oooh, I've never seen where you work," Lydia chirped.

I was wearing purple slacks and a blue shirt—clearly a witch but totally professional. In contrast, my sister was wearing cutoff jeans that showed more ass cheek than was necessary and a teeny-tiny pink tee that just covered her boobs. It had WICKED emblazoned on the twins. Needless to say, we got some strange looks as we climbed into the elevator.

I kept my mouth shut and my focus glued to the floor, but my ears were burning, and I could hardly breathe. Oh, Lydia.

The elevator doors took forever to open, but when they did, things only got worse. "Good morning, Izzy."

Mary and George were having a tête-à-tête right in front of us. *Why, oh why, do they always lock the bathroom on the main floor?* I thought.

Mary looked Lydia up and down and sneered. "Bring a friend to work day?"

George, who didn't look affected at all by the Matthew business, also checked my sister out, but in quite a different way. His gaze roamed over her Lydia without disguise, and he licked his lips, like he was contemplating dinner. I didn't know which was worse.

Lydia beamed and assumed the little minx stance. She was leaning to one side to exaggerate her ample curves, one hand splayed over her hip, the other oh-so-casually flicking her lustrous hair away from her now pouting face.

"Come on, let's get you to the bathroom so I can get on with work." I pushed Lydia out of the elevator ahead of me, conscious they were both watching us as we left and annoyed that my hormone-crazy sister kept glancing over her shoulder and grinning wickedly at George.

I just knew his gaze was glued to her ass. And probably, so did Mary. That thought, at least, made me smirk.

"Can you lay it off, just for a second?" I bit my bottom lip and gave her the big sister look. "This is where I work."

"Lay what off?" Lydia asked.

I opened the office door, which jingled, and when we reached the bathroom, I pushed Lydia inside. "Hurry up. Come and find me when you're done. My cubicle is over there, by the purple dragon."

I pointed to the fluffy toy peeking over of the top of my workspace. Lydia nodded, disappeared, and I walked over to my desk.

This was a shitty start to the week already, and I dropped my bag in a huff.

I hadn't even switched on my computer when George appeared at my side. Last night he'd been pissed as anything with me, yet today it was like none of that had happened.

"Morning, Izzy," George said. "I have some news you might be interested in."

"Oh?" That got my attention. I'd been pulling my workable files from their locked drawers but stopped in my tracks. I sat back in my chair and looked up at him. He looked positively pleased with himself. Perhaps Matthew had told him where the moonstone was, after all?

"He didn't do it." George sounded happier than I would have expected. "The old goat had a change of heart and pulled the chicken switch. Him and some other vampire, Ortense or something."

"Octavia?"

"Yes, that's it. Seems the pair of them were up all night talking, and instead of pulling the plug, they checked out of Rosings before the sun came up."

"And did he tell you about the Moonstone?" At least that would explain George's glee.

"Um, no, with all that was going down, I didn't get the chance. But I thought you'd want to know, you two being *friends* and all."

I ignored the trace of sarcasm, because I couldn't have felt more relieved. Good for Matthew! I knew George was only happy because this gave him a second shot at the pot, but I didn't care one fairy-poop about that.

"Awesome!" I said. "Will I get to see him again, then?"

"I know I will, so maybe. Oh hi."

Lydia stood by his side, pulling on her T-shirt, deliberately drawing George's attention to her feminine assets. Oh heck, sometimes my sister was such a tart. I shot her my darkest look.

"George, this is Lydia, my kid sister, who wanted to see where I worked. Lydia, this is George, my boss." *The womanizer.*

Lydia beamed at him. "Oh, I've heard a lot about *you*, George."

"Really? All wicked, I hope." He gazed with unabashed admiration at the words on her T-shirt.

At this point, I might as well have been invisible. He only had eyes for Lydia. And she was looking at him as if he was a teen rebel in leather who'd just rode into town on a Harley. Witches and werewolves, he had to be twelve years older than her. More to the point, she was twelve years younger than him.

"Yes, well, time to start work. Let me walk you back to the elevator."

I got up, and steering my kid sister away from real trouble, I marched her off double quick. I hit the down button twice, just to be sure. The moment the elevator doors opened, I pushed her inside.

"Go home. Next time, put on some clothes. You look like a streetwalker. And wear a helmet, dammit."

As always, Lydia didn't respond to my gibes. She just smiled to herself, a stupid dreamy expression glued to her face. I didn't breathe again until the doors closed quietly behind her, and she was out of sight and out of mind.

Chapter Eighteen

AT THE PLAYGROUND

My phone dinged, I thumbed the screen and saw a new text message.

Jane: Looking forward to dinner with Billy tonight?

I swiped back: I'd rather suck troll toes.

Jane: I am the bearer of good news. Billy can't make it! Warlock meeting at the Lucas place tonight, manly men only, cloaks and pointy hats, must be serious business! How sad for us!

Me: Imagine my disappointment.

Jane: *Oooh,* incoming msg from Caroline she's much more important ha-ha talk later.

Hoorah! Billy had been glued to me like a wart lately. At last I had a chance to breathe! And maybe play with a little magic, which I hadn't been able to do much of, either.

So when I got home from work, I was in a super mood, ready for a much-needed bit of me time.

"Where's Jane?" I asked, dumping my bag on the kitchen table and kicking off my shoes over by the door. She was usually in the kitchen this time of day, fixing grub.

Mom raised her gaze to the ceiling. "She's up there. She said she had a bit of a headache, so I've left her alone."

"How long has she been up there?" I asked.

"An hour. Maybe two. She came home early and more or less went straight up."

That wasn't like Jane at all. I took the stairs two at a time and knocked gently on her bedroom door.

"Come in," came the weak reply.

I found Jane facedown into a pillow, the curtains drawn and her legs dangling languidly off the end of the bed.

"What's up?" I sat on the end of it.

"I think Charlie's dumped me. He didn't even have the guts to do it himself! He got Caroline to send me a message."

"Who did? Charlie?"

"Who else?" She pulled herself up into a seated position.

"Wait a minute. What? What did he say?"

Jane's phone was on the table by her bed. She picked it up and swiped it, then handed it over to me before flopping back down on her mattress. "Here. You read it. You might as well see for yourself."

Sorry sweets, I know this is last minute, but Charlie had to scoot over to NYC to meet some girls with Fitz. No idea when they'll be back, if at all. He might text you later. Have to cancel dinner tonight - much apologies, but my life is as chaotic as ever. So much going on but will hook up soon. Love and kisses. C.

That was mean, I thought. She could shove her love and kisses up her... "That's nothing. That's just Caroline putting her nasty witch spin on it. You'll have a message from Charlie before you know it, you'll see."

I dropped the phone and flopped on the bed beside Jane.

"I don't suppose you're in the mood for a little fun spelling then?"

"Not really," Jane said. "Do you mind if I pass this time?"

"No, sure, don't worry about it." I focused on my toes as I wiggled them and imagined spelling daisies in between the digits. I slumped deep into a pillow. I'd been so excited not having Billy around, but now this. Poor Jane.

"I wonder what these girls are like?" Jane mused.

"Which girls?"

"The ones in New York."

"Pfft. If they even exist."

Jane turned on her side and stared at me. "Why wouldn't they? Caroline's never lied to me."

"Who knows? Look, you know I've never liked her. Would I put it past her to make up something like that just to spite you? Not at all. But she's not Charlie. Anyone who saw you two together could see he was crazy about you, whatever Caroline says."

"Maybe."

Jane rolled off the bed and checked her face in the mirror.

"Poop, I look like shit," she said. She picked up a hairbrush and started fixing her hair. "You're right. I'm being an idiot. Charlie will call me later, I'm sure of it."

I knew from her tone she didn't believe a word of it, and my heart was breaking for her. I wanted to punch that Caroline in the face. She could say what she liked to me, I didn't care, but not my sister. Jane was off-limits.

With a sigh, I pushed myself up off the bed. "That's it. We're going out. Go wash your face, and we'll go have a few at the Cauldron. I'm not gonna let you sit around like this and mope. Let's go out and party."

Jane shook her head. "No, you go if you like, but I'm not in the mood. I think I'll just stay in and relax for a bit. You don't mind, do you?"

I wandered over to where she sat at her dresser and kissed the top of her head. "If you say so."

Still, I didn't like it. I knew Jane well enough. If it had happened to me, I'd have laughed it off, but *she* would sit at home all night and watch the phone. That on its own made me angry, but there was nothing I could do.

"I suppose I could go out with Lydia and Kitty."

Normally this would have got a chuckle out of Jane, but not tonight. "Sure. I think they walked down to the park."

Jane stood up, picked up her phone, shook her head sadly, and fell back down on the bed. She turned over and stuck her face in the pillow, lost in her own thoughts.

I left, closing the door quietly behind me.

The company of my younger sisters was rarely my first choice. Half the time they acted like a couple of pea-brains, and the other half they weren't acting.

But Mother Gaia was calling me out tonight, so I decided to seek them out.

Dad was sitting on his rocker at the front door, people watching.

"Hey," I said. I sat down on the porch for a minute to speak to him.

"Ah, Izzy. Are you going out again?"

I felt a little twinge of guilt. Perhaps I was out rather a lot at the moment. "Yes, I was going to join Kitty and Lydia over in the park. It's a nice day. I don't suppose you fancy a walk?"

He smiled but shook his head. "Not today, love. I'm fine sitting just where I am, sipping your sister's fine lemonade and pondering the world. How is Jane by the way?"

"She'll be all right. Lover's tiff, I think."

"Ah, I figured." He stared down into his drink, pensive.

I hoped everything was all right. "How are things going with Billy? Was he able to help at all?"

"Perhaps. He's pushing for a second mortgage, and though I don't fancy that interest rate, I don't have much choice. It's that or a reverse mortgage, although he says the house isn't worth very much and he's not sure how much we would get. I've never understood this numpy finance stuff. I wish your mother's crystal ball did more than just decorate the mantel in the living room. Ah well."

"I'm sorry," I said. "Let me talk to the partners. I have an idea."

I stood up and brushed the dust off my black leather goth pants. "I won't be long. Is there anything you want me to get while I'm out?"

"No, nothing I can think of. I'm enjoying the peace and quiet while Billy's not around. He does seem to spend a lot of time buzzing around you of late." Dad's eyes were full of mischief.

"What can I say, the man really likes me. He must be in want of a wife."

"Over my dead body." Dad laughed.

"And mine. I'd tell him to get lost, but I'm worried he'd do something silly with the loan. He might change his mind or something."

Dad frowned. "Don't you worry about that. That's my problem, not yours. If he's making a nuisance of himself, you just tell him where to go."

I grinned. "Thanks, Dad. Well, I'll be back in a bit."

"Take your time. Enjoy the evening. I think I'll read for a bit and then maybe have a nap. Go keep those two out of mischief. They cause trouble wherever they go."

"Don't they just."

I strolled along our dirt drive and was soon out on the street. Haye Park was on the edge of town, less than a mile from our home. There wasn't much of a play area, just a few apologetic swings, some climbing frames, and a dead-beat paddling pond that hadn't seen any water in years. There was a fairly decent path that ran the circumference that was great for walking dogs or jogging, and it had a fair view of the mountains, currently hidden under the dense green foliage of all the maples and pines.

I spotted Kitty all on her own, sitting on a swing. Lydia was nowhere in sight. Kitty looked up as I approached and for once looked genuinely happy to see me.

"Hey, Izzy, what's up?" She had been swinging halfheartedly, and now she brought the swing to a dead stop by dropping a foot to the ground. Her seat wobbled from side to side for a bit, and she swung contrariwise for a moment to get it under control.

"Where's Lydia?"

Kitty, who was never any good at telling a lie, reddened and took a sudden interest in her shoes.

"Tell me!"

"Um, I dunno."

"You don't know where she is? Didn't you come out with her?"

"Keep your wand in your pocket, Izzy. She had a text from someone, that's all. She said she wouldn't be long."

"And how long has she been gone?"

"Not long, about an hour."

"An hour! And she didn't mention who this someone was?"

Kitty shrugged and got up from the swing and wandered over to the climbing frame. I took her place and pulled my wand from my bag.

"What are you going to do with that?" Kitty's pretty forehead crinkled.

"I'm going to poke it up your nose if you're not careful. As a matter of fact, I'm going to practice some spells. I didn't see any Hags about, did you?"

Kitty shook her head. "Not a one."

"Well then, we might as well while we wait. That is, unless you object?"

Kitty shrugged and walked over to the slide. She sat on the bottom and looked up at the sky. Lydia could be anywhere. What annoyed me more than anything was she was quite happy to leave Kitty hanging about, waiting indefinitely. My kid sister could be a real piece of work.

I passed the time using the *crear ás e voar* spell, turning plain flies into butterflies and back again. It sounded simple, but it was a complex little spell that had taken me ages to master as a kid.

Kitty just sat there, staring into space, her mind probably as empty as the cloudless sky.

We were there for about ten minutes when I heard footsteps. Sure enough, there was Lydia, looking like she hadn't a care in the world and whistling her merry way over to join us. I looked around to see if anyone was with her, but she appeared to be quite alone.

"Where in Hades have you been?" I shoved my wand in my purse and waited for Lydia's response.

"Since when were you the boss of me? I can see my friends when I want to."

"Do you have any idea how long you left poor Kitty on her own?" I shook my head in disapproval.

Lydia grinned and walked over to pull Kitty up from the slide. "Oh, Kitty doesn't mind one bit, do you, Kitty?"

Kitty opened her mouth to respond but never got the chance.

"And I *am* the boss of you," I continued. "At least when Mom and Dad aren't around. They expect *me* to watch out for you, and I expect *you* to behave!"

"Well, I didn't do anything I shouldn't, so there." She poked her tongue at me and pouted, like the spoiled little tyke she was. "Come on, Kitty. I'm hungry as heck, let's go home. Jane will have fixed something by now."

I doubted it. And the last thing Jane needed was this pair of buffoons asking her questions. Mad as I was, I decided to buy them lunch, if only to give Jane a break. "Jane isn't well. Come on, I'll buy you McDonalds."

In an instant, Lydia was all smiles. I shook my head, dumbfounded by my kid sister's shameless attitude. One of these days...

Chapter Nineteen

A BIG FAVOR

I HAD THE DAY OFF. I HADN'T TAKEN ANY VACATION DAYS IN A WHILE, so I'd booked one with no intention other than to be a lazy slug.

Jane, bless her, hadn't heard a word from Charlie, and although she looked peaky, she'd gone into work anyway. Mary, Kitty, and Lydia, in some rare show of unity, had all gotten up early and gone into town with Mom. Dad was in his hidey-hole, reading or something, so I practically had the whole place to myself. So I sat at our kitchen table, sipping good coffee and pondering the uncommon day of absolute bliss that lay before me.

And then the doorbell rang.

It was Billy.

I opened the inner door and talked to him through the screen.

"Hello, Billy," I said. "Have you come to see Dad?"

"Um, no, not exactly."

"No one home?" he asked.

"Dad's about somewhere," I said. "Everyone else went shopping."

He half pushed me aside and wandered straight in, the storm door slamming rudely behind him as he made his way over to the coffeepot. Without so much as a by-your-leave, he poured himself a mug of the strong black stuff and chugged a huge mouthful of it down.

"I needed that." Billy gasped.

"So I see."

I sat down at the end of the kitchen table and sipped quietly at my own coffee, hoping the man would take the hint and leave.

But he didn't. Instead, he was pacing about like an actor rehearsing his lines.

"You know, I've been hoping to catch you alone for some time. But you're quite the busy lady, and finding time to be intimate with you has proved something of a challenge."

As he said the word *intimate*, I moved to get up, but Billy put out his hand and urged me to sit back down in my seat. Disgruntled, my eyes narrowed, but I did as he asked. For the moment.

"No, no. Please say nothing for a minute. I need to get this out." He took a deep breath. "I think you know what I want to ask you, and it's not like we have to jump into matrimony or anything. I consider myself rather modern that way. No, on the contrary, I'm perfectly happy trying this out for a bit, and we can talk about marriage down the road."

I felt I had to say something at that point, but Billy put his finger to his lips and urged me to be quiet. Oh well. This was his funeral.

"Of course, my career is paramount, but I believe Kate De Bourgh would like you. You're spunky enough. I can't see how she could do anything but approve of my choice. And your mom certainly likes me. She was more than willing to get your sisters out of the way so you and I could have this little chat."

Hmm. I must have words with them all later.

"Of course, as I said, I'm a modern man. I would be perfectly happy for you to continue in magic after we tie the knot. Of course, you won't be required to practice anything *too* radical, after all. We have my career at the bank to consider, but I think you would do very well mixing herbal potions and charm spells with the other board wives at their little shindigs. What do you say?"

I didn't say anything. I was too shocked by everything I had just heard. Plus I wanted to punch him in the face.

He had to be joking, right? But then I remembered this was Billy Collins, and if there was one thing Billy wasn't famous for, it was a sense of humor.

I cleared my throat.

"I should probably mention that if we were to get hitched, I would make good on your father's loan. After all, it would look pretty bad if any relative of mine went under—I have my career to think of. Having an in-law default on a mortgage would look terrible. So I'll make sure your father, mother, and sisters are all taken care of, once we tie the knot."

He smiled affectionately, as if he'd just delivered the sweetest love poem in the universe. And then, to my utter horror, Billy dropped to one knee and put his hand on my leg. Shit. Was his gaze traveling up my skirt?

I swung away as fast as I could and jumped up from the table, almost knocking him to the ground as I made my bid for freedom.

"Look, you're very sweet and all that, but really, my answer has to be no. I'm not in love with you, and I don't think I ever could be." Straight and to the point, I thought, was the way to go.

Then I thought about him making good on Dad's mortgage, and for a moment, I felt sorry for my answer, so I added, "It was very kind of you to think of me like this, but no. I don't want to marry you. Or anything."

Billy's confident smile wavered a tad, but then he got up and wandered over to the sink. "I think you're teasing me," he said. "I mean, think about it. Look at your options. You're a very pretty girl, sure, but you really can't be seriously turning me down. Who else around here is likely to make you such a generous offer? You must understand I'd be doing you a huge favor. Now why don't you just say yes and let's get on with it? Where's your dad? We should probably tell him first."

I was sorry I'd left my wand upstairs because I wanted to hex him so bad.

"Are you listening to me?" I cried. "If you were the last warlock on earth, I'd demand a recount. I could never marry you. Not ever! The very thought of your hands on me gives me the willies. And your friend, *Whatsherface De Bourgh*, she can go jump for all I care. Herbal potions and charm spells, my ass. You know what you can do with them all."

I was crazy mad and running around the kitchen like a harpy. Billy was slowly backing into the wall, evidently still not taking my no for a no.

"But your mother said..."

"Forget my mother, Billy. She doesn't know diddly-squat. You two shouldn't be scheming behind my back—jeez, it's so childish. I'm not twelve! If you'd have asked me up front, I'd have told you straight off—you and I are never gonna happen. *Comprendez?* Can I say it any plainer than that?"

Billy looked ready to make another argument.

"GET OUT, damn you!" Rather than stick around, I barged out of the kitchen and ran up the stairs. My blood was boiling—what damned cheek!

I stood at my bedroom door, refusing to go back down until he left. I imagined my father, who had to have been inches away from it all, laughing his ass off on the other side of the kitchen wall. Only I wasn't laughing with him. I was fuming.

You must understand I'd be doing you a huge favor.

Did he really think that? What kind of imbecile was he? I stood, trembling with fury, listening intently for the only sound I wanted to hear, and that was the door as it hit him in the ass on his way out.

Chapter Twenty

SECRET LOVERS

It was no secret that my mom liked to shop. There wasn't a shopkeeper in Misty Cedars she wasn't on a first name basis with, and when the mood took her, she could be out from dusk 'til dawn, buying crap she didn't need, for spells she had no idea how to conjure. But it made her happy, and we left her to it. She wasn't the only one—my sisters were just as bad. If there was a new style out there, they would have to have it, whether it looked good on them or not.

So it was something of a surprise when she and my sisters burst into the kitchen without a shopping bag between them. They swarmed around me at the kitchen table, my sisters all ready to laugh at whatever I had to tell, and my Mom desperate to wish me joy.

"Well!" Mom's eyes were wide and full of hope, and although I was half annoyed at her for setting me up, I couldn't blame her for wishing for a solution to all our financial problems. "Did Billy come round? What did he say?"

"Sure, Billy came round," I said, feigning ignorance. "He finished off the coffee, and then he left."

"Yes, yes, but what did he say while he was here?" Mom sat down in the chair beside me, practically panting for news.

It sucked to have to tell her.

"He talked about how well he was doing at the bank, and how much his boss likes him, and how talented he is, and how good-looking he is, and how big his car is. Just the usual Billy, you know?"

Emotional electricity hummed in the air, and I couldn't torture them any longer. "I told him no."

"No? NO? Are you insane?" Mom almost barked the words. "That warlock is loaded. He would have magicked us out of this mess in a wand swish. Do you have any idea?"

"Yes, I understand totally, Mom, and I'm sorry for it, but if you think I could even, ugh!"

Mom kept shaking her head in disbelief, but my sisters were grinning like idiots.

"Did he go down on one knee?" Lydia mocked.

"Was he drooling?" Kitty added.

"How much money do you think he has?" Mary said.

"I bet he's a demon in bed."

"That's enough from you, Lydia," I said.

Mom was close to hyperventilating, and though she had my sympathy, I was still annoyed. "Why is everyone putting all this on me? I've never liked him, never will, and have done nothing to encourage him. I think you're all being totally unreasonable."

"But..." Mom began.

Clearly stronger words were needed. "He's a slimy, ingratiating, self-important hot-air balloon that's full of shit. He doesn't need to worry about anyone loving him—he loves himself plenty already. He pushed his way in here and said he'd be doing me a favor by marrying me. Doing *me* a favor!"

They were all staring at me as if they expected me to explode at any second. Which was a distinct possibility. I took a deep breath. Then another.

"You actually had the audacity to try to set me up with *that?* Think again, Mother dear. From now on, you will stay out of my personal business. No more matchmaking, ever. And Billy Collins will not be invited here for dinner again. Am I making myself clear?"

"MR. BENNEEEET!"

Mom's cry brought Dad out from his hiding place. He looked perfectly calm, and though I knew he'd heard every single word spoken, he still feigned surprised at seeing us all gathered in the kitchen.

"Is anything up?" His tone was innocent, his eyes wide in mock wonder.

"Billy asked Izzy to marry her." Lydia snorted.

"And she turned him down," Kitty added.

"And what of it?" Dad asked. "It sounds like a decision has been made. What do you need me for?"

"You must make her change her mind!" Mom gasped. "He was going to take care of us all. It was a wonderful and generous offer. Izzy should be thankful. For the love of weres, talk some sense into her, will you? She won't listen to me."

Dad sat at the end of the table and stretched out his arms, as if preparing for battle. "I see. Well, Izzy, is there anything I can say to change your mind? Because if there is, you're not the daughter I raised. I say well done. The man is a total bore. I know I wouldn't marry him."

"Mr. Bennet!" Mom looked ready to fall off her seat.

Even my sisters were stunned by Dad's response, and they all stared down the table at him, their mouths wide open. Only I remained calm, and thankful for his support, I rose and strolled over to where he sat and kissed him affectionately on the head.

"Thanks, Dad," I said. I gave them all my best withering look and retreated up to my room, leaving them to talk about me. I'd seen frank admiration in Kitty's eyes, the glow of understanding in Mary's, and complete incredulity in Lydia's, as if the idea of a woman refusing a man's proposal was alien to her. Well, two out of three wasn't bad. Dad was probably fanning Mom with a dish towel, again. I hoped she'd get over it soon.

"That must have been awkward," Jane said. "I mean, I feel a little sorry for him. It couldn't have been easy for him, either, but all the same, I'm glad he didn't latch on to me. "

"No kidding," I said. My crochet needles clicked frantically as they slowly circled each other in midair. I had finally mastered the casting-on spell and was imagining intricate patterns to weave for my next project.

This new fire-resistant blanket for Mary was almost finished. I'd offered to make her one out of wool, which was cheaper, but she'd asked for one made from cashmere, which was much softer, but the thread had cost me a small fortune. "Oh well, it's done now. He'll get over it."

"Maybe. I guess it depends on the depths of his feelings. Some people get over things a lot more easily than others."

I knew she wasn't thinking about me and Billy now. I shoved some loose bales of wool into my carriers and stowed it on top of my armoire. "Have you heard anything? Anything at all?"

Jane sighed. "Nothing. Caroline was right. He couldn't have cared for me after all."

"Hmmm, somehow I doubt that." It was very strange. In my mind, I had absolutely no doubt Charlie loved her; everything he did, every step he took had proved otherwise. No, there had to be something else, some other obstacle was stopping him from reaching out to her. If only I knew what it was.

The only good to come of it all was that his friend, the god-awful Fitz Darcy, was gone with him. Every cloud had its silver lining.

I said, "You know, I was thinking..."

"Yes?"

"I think Auntie Bri mentioned something about visiting New York with Uncle Ed."

Jane winced, like the very mention of New York gave her pain. She put down her book and sighed. "What of it?"

"What if you were to go with them? I mean, they always love seeing you, and who knows who you might bump into while you're all out and about?"

A little spark lit behind her eyes, and she sat up straight. "Do you really think they would let me?"

"Sure, I don't see why not. You were always their favorite niece, after all. Why don't you call her and ask?"

Some color came to her cheeks, and I knew I'd kindled some hope in my sister's heart. Hope really was the best kind of magic.

Jane put down her book and disappeared. I knew she would call them straight off, but she would prefer to be alone when she asked—she was private like that. I smiled, feeling I had done a good deed and confident that if the stars were aligned, she and Charlie would soon be back on track.

A few minutes later, she came back into my room, and the huge grin on her face told me everything I needed to know.

"Well?" I asked anyway.

She nodded. "They've rented an apartment in Brooklyn and have a spare room I can crash in. I'm sure work won't mind. I'll text Caroline in a minute and let her know I'll be there. Maybe we can get together for lunch or something?"

"Actually, if I were you, I wouldn't text anyone. Just turn up, sniff around, and see if you can orchestrate some kinda, 'OMG, fancy meeting you here,' thing. Auntie Bri has to know some people, right?"

"No, I couldn't do that. He'll think I'm some kind of crazy stalker and will run a hundred miles."

I doubted it, but it was her party.

"She also said why don't you come as well? Apparently, there's plenty of room."

"I dunno…I'm not sure I could get the time off at such short notice," I said. "But anyway, I think that calls for a celebration. Fancy a stiff one down at the Cauldron?"

"Sure, why not?"

"Awesome." I slipped on some sandals and grabbed my bag, and then Jane and I ran downstairs. We jumped into my car, which now had four good wheels, plus a spare, and was raring to go.

All the way there, Jane kept glancing at her phone.

"Expecting something?" I asked, smiling.

"Yes. I texted Caroline a few minutes ago. It says seen, but she hasn't replied yet. Maybe it's not a good time for her?"

Bad idea, Jane. "Yeah, maybe."

This time, there was a spot just in front of the Cauldron, and I steered into it with ease.

It was early still, but judging by the auras, the place was packed with a professional crowd of weres, witches, and warlocks, all in for the happy hour that went on until six.

As always, Benny was working his ass off behind the bar, but he still managed to send us a quick nod as we walked inside. Jane and I took our usual table over in the corner, and a minute or so later, Sue popped over. Somehow, she looked even more anemic than usual, and I noticed the new choker she wore around her neck.

"What can I get you two?" she asked. She picked up the empty glasses while her lemon-scented cloth worked its magic on our table, cleaning up the spills.

"How about a couple of Chardonnays?" I said. "We're celebrating."

"Something fun?" Sue asked.

"Oh, just love and the universe," I said.

"Seems there's a lot of it about." As she left, Sue nodded to the back of the bar near where we'd stood the night The Brew had played. There were a couple of cozy little tables, partially hidden from view back there. Only one was occupied now, and there was a kissing couple going hard at it, making the most of the little amount of privacy the spot afforded.

At first, the man had his back to us, completely concealing the woman, but then, even the most dedicated lovers eventually had to come up for air.

"Is that...Billy?" Jane gasped.

I looked over her shoulder. My mouth dropped open. "Holy trolls, you're right. And that's Charlotte!"

I couldn't have kept my voice down if I tried. Only a short while ago, the man had been down on bended knee, swearing his eternal love and devotion, and now, no time later, here he was, his tongue down my best friend's throat.

I didn't know whether to laugh or—seriously, the other option was still to laugh.

Realizing they'd been spotted, the two of them looked totally red-faced, and jumping up, Billy, his face covered in lipstick, bolted for the bathroom. Charlotte, abandoned by her hero, wiped her lips and came over to join us.

"Err, hello," she said, not avoiding my eyes, but not quite looking into them either. "I suppose you're both wondering what's going on?"

I didn't answer. I didn't need to—I'd pretty much figured that out all by myself.

"He came over earlier and needed a shoulder to cry on. I brought him here to maybe drown his sorrows, and well, one thing led to another..."

Jane had her head down, trying to hide her smirk, and I, well, I had no clue what to say. Billy and Charlotte. It wasn't as if they hadn't known each other forever, and for them to suddenly get it on like this seemed totally surreal. Still, they were grown-ups, and one thing was for sure—I didn't want him.

"Would you like a drink?" I said. Her lips were puffed from kissing, and I guessed she needed one more than I did right now.

"Errr, no. Billy will be back in a moment, and I suppose we'd better get going. You, um, well, you don't mind, do you?"

I shook my head and grinned. "Perfectly fine by me. Knock yourself out."

She nodded, and we all spotted Billy as he walked cautiously over from the bathroom to his own table, where he picked up his beer glass and came over to join us at ours. Dutch courage, maybe? Or a shield perhaps? Probably both.

"Hey, Billy." My smile was huge, and I fully intended to milk this for all it was worth. "Having a nice time?"

He coughed and took a gulp of beer before answering. "I am. That is to say, well, I mean, actually, well..." He downed the rest of his glass and then appealed to Charlotte for help.

Charlotte, in contrast, had recovered sufficiently to have full control of her voice. "As I said, we were about to go. We'll catch you both later, if that's okay?"

"Sure," I said. "Already looking forward to it." My lips tweaked at the corners, and it was all I could do to keep my emotions under control.

"See you around."

I waved as they retreated, Billy following Charlotte like a lost sheep. The moment they left The Cauldron, all restraint was over. Jane and I took one look at each other and burst into a fit of uncontrollable laughter.

Chapter Twenty-One

A SURPRISE AT WORK

I hadn't heard nor seen much of George for almost a week now. Not that it meant anything—it wasn't unusual for the partners to take off and do their thing. They weren't required to clock in and out like the rest of us peons, and they sure as heck didn't have to check in with me.

The funny thing was, Mary didn't seem to know much about where he was, either. Weird, since they were supposed to be a thing now, but I didn't need my superwitch senses to figure out all wasn't well with Mr. and Mrs. Newly Naughty.

Twenty-four seven phone checking and heartfelt sighs were not the signs of a contented lover—I should know, there was a lot of that about of late—but I didn't know her well enough to just come right out and ask her. She'd probably tell me it was none of my business anyway. Oh well.

The completed Golem file was set in front of me; Mr. Lowe had dropped it on my desk this morning to stash in our archives.

I opened the binder and read Mr. Lowe's latest note on the top. Oh. So the Hags had let the Golem out of Bitterhold, then. Bummer. There wasn't much they could hold him on, I supposed, not without an actual body. It sucked, but what could they do? Even paranormals had rights.

Now Goulding had been set free, and if the notes were to be believed, he was staying at digs on 100 West Main Street, with nothing but a large brown wallet containing seven dollars and a small black Nokia phone to his name, which they'd taken from him when he was arrested.

It wasn't much to show for a life, I thought, as I closed the ring binder. I picked up my wand from the tabletop. "*Cuir cartlann orm,*" I said, and watched as the file took to the air and weaved its way to the back of the office and turned the corner to the archive room, and out of sight.

100 West Main Street. Hmm, that wasn't horribly far from where we lived. I thought I'd better warn my sisters there was a monster on the prowl. Or a suspected monster, anyway. The Hags might not have found enough evidence to chuck Goulding in prison forever, but something in my gut told me he needed chucking in.

Another big sigh came from the other side of my cubicle, possibly the fourth this morning, and I wondered if Mary was being deliberately loud on purpose. Maybe she wanted to talk after all.

Needing to stretch anyway, I got up and wandered round to see what she was up to. I found her staring at her phone, and I knew the look. I'd seen my sister staring at hers in exactly the same way.

"Penny for your thoughts," I said. Boy, did I sound like my mother sometimes.

Mary dropped her phone on the table and looked up at me. She appeared well enough, her hair was tidy, and her makeup was fresh and well applied. Yet there was none of the usual snarkiness in her expression. If anything, she struck me as a bit tired. But otherwise she looked good.

"George dumped me," she said. "Well, he didn't *dump* dump me. He's just not responding to my texts."

"Well," I said reasonably. "Give him time. He might not have read them yet?"

"Yeah, right. All two hundred and seventy-three of them?"

"Wow." I glanced at her phone, half expecting it to explode in a thousand sparkles. "What an ass."

"Me or him?"

I laughed. It was the first time I'd ever heard Mary crack a joke.

"Him."

"You got that right," she said.

"Hey, cheer up, he could be in a hospital ER somewhere with tubes in his head, unable to remember his own name, never mind look at his phone."

I couldn't help feeling a little bit sorry for her. We'd never sat under the stars drinking cherryade and laughing about leprechaun farts or anything, but that didn't make her a bad person. We just weren't besties.

"When did you see him last?" I asked.

"I dunno, a while back?"

"Well, he'll have to show his face sooner or later. He's a partner. If he doesn't, questions will be asked."

"Yeah." There was something about the way she said *yeah* that caught my attention. I leaned in a little closer and lowered my voice.

"Yeah?"

There was no one else about, but Mary looked around anyway. Seeing the coast was clear, she put her face close to mine and whispered, "I heard he hexed his way in?"

"What?"

"Yeah."

I shook my head. George might be an idiot, but he was a paranormal lawyer. Something like that could get him disbarred. "I don't believe it. How?"

Mary nudged in closer still. "All right, maybe not directly, but didn't you ever ask yourself why he's so into old vamps? I mean, a good-looking stud lawyer being *that* into geriatrics. It just ain't natural."

I nodded. George's preoccupation with the elderly had always seemed kind of weird to me. It just didn't sit well with his face. "Go on. Do tell."

Mary's eyes gleamed as she warmed to her theme. "The truth is, he's very good with befuddlement charms. I saw him doing it on an old person in a retirement home. He seeks out the ones close to death and hexes them so they leave him some of their money. Not too much, mind you. If he got greedy, they would catch him quick enough, but no. Our George takes just enough to keep him above any kind of suspicion."

I shook my head again. "But he's a lawyer. Surely the partners would see the pattern. They see the accounts. Hell, I see the accounts. I've never noticed anything weird in the billing."

"Nope. He doesn't do it through the partner accounts. He's too shrewd for that. No, I think he stashes it all away some place so it can't be traced

back to him. I saw some letters on his desk in his bedroom—some fund."
She blushed, but I kept a straight face, wanting her to continue. "The truth
is George isn't a great lawyer. He's just a devious one. And he bought his
way into this partnership. With the property of the dead."

How very dramatic, I thought. "I never saw him do anything like that,"
I said. "He's a total asshole, but I never saw him try anything funny on
Matthew Devereux. Or anyone else, for that matter."

"Well, he wouldn't," Mary replied. "Not with a vampire. Befuddlement
doesn't work on a vamp. Well, not on the really old ones. Their minds are
too powerful."

"Oh, for the love of fae," I whispered. "If the partners ever found out
he was milking their clients, they'd have his crystal balls for breakfast."

Mary raised her eyebrows in understanding, giving me the impression
she'd rather hoped they would.

"Are you done with that Golem file yet?" The deep baritone voice of
the senior partner, Mr. Lowe, almost made me jump out of my skin.

"Err, yes, yes. I just sent it to archives." I stepped out of Mary's cubicle
and returned to my desk, where Mr. Lowe was waiting for me with more
files.

My cheeks were flushed, and I prayed to fairyland that he hadn't
heard us.

"Step into my office in ten minutes, will you?"

My heart skipped a beat, and though I glanced over at Mary's cubicle,
she never made a sound. I imagined her hunkered down low on the other
side of that partition, praying to Gaia he wouldn't say anything to her after
me. Even my purple dinosaur didn't seem to want to look me in the eye.
Oh, pixie poop. What have I done? I'm in for it now.

Haggerston Lowe's office was a treasure trove of magical books, demon
texts, and legalese. There wasn't much room for anything else beyond the
enormous partner's desk and a large, purple orbuculum that turned red
whenever someone was telling a lie.

Mr. Lowe did give up a little of his office space to a set of barrister's
bookcases, which lined the wall nearest the door. It contained some

numpy's legal artifacts, including a lie detector that he would sometimes pit against his orbuculum, a set of handcuffs, a judge's gavel, and a British judge's wig with a black cap, showcased on a dummy's head. When I had the time, I would check these over, but not today. I was too worried about what was coming next.

I imagined Mr. Lowe putting the black cap on his head, looking very stern before he axed me.

"Sit down, Izzy," Mr. Lowe said, as he joined me in the office and closed the door. "I'm sorry I kept you waiting, I wanted to consult with HR before I talked to you, and they only just got back to me."

Oh shit, this is it! What the hell am I gonna tell Dad now?

Tight-lipped and anxious as hell, I did as I was told and slid into the seat in front of his desk.

Mr. Lowe, who was old enough to be my grandfather, sat in the chair across from me and pulled a file toward him. He peered at it over his horn-rimmed spectacles. "Well, Izzy, I'm at a loss for words."

My stomach sank. Any sentence begun this way did not bode well for me. I bit my lip. Perhaps if I beat him to the punch and apologized for my conversation with Mary, that might save the day? Then again, maybe it was better to hear the indictment before pronouncing myself guilty.

"Sir?"

"Well, after you reached out to me, I talked to HR about the possibility of you borrowing against your IRA, but that's not possible. If we'd had a 401(k) plan, things would be different, but the IRS rules are the same for us as the nonmagical people, and our plan doesn't allow it. I'm sorry."

"Oh." *Darn. Well, it was worth a try. At least I'm not getting fired.* "Thank you for looking into it anyway." I moved to stand up to go back to work.

"Not so fast."

I sat down again.

"I've talked it over with the other partners, and we feel we would like to do something for you and your house situation. A personal loan. Would that be acceptable to you? We would make the rates favorable, so you'd be no worse off than if you borrowed against your pension, and we can sort out the repayment particulars once you agree. Would that help?"

"Why, um, yes, thank you, I'd be open to that." I hardly knew what to say.

Mr. Lowe looked at me over his spectacles, and then after a moment, he scratched something down on a piece of paper. He slid it across his desk to me. I looked down at the slip of paper and caught my breath. He'd been more than generous.

"I can loan up to such a sum. Go home, discuss it with your family, and think about it overnight. There's no rush. You can borrow all of it or just some of it. Let me know what you need and can afford, and consider it done."

I clutched the paper in my hand and beamed at him. It sucked to ask for so much, but I couldn't fault him for his kindness.

"Thank you, sir," I said. "I surely shall."

"Well, then, pop off back to work, I'm sure you've got plenty to do."

I rose from my seat and was about to leave when a thought occurred to me. "Sir?"

"Yes?" Mr. Lowe asked.

"Will George, um, I mean, will Mr. Wickham be coming back to the office any time soon? I'm running low on work."

A shadow crossed the old man's face, and he looked at me thoughtfully. "I'm afraid I can't discuss that with you, Izzy. That's all I can say on the matter."

Wow, that sounded ominous. I thought it best not to respond, but waved the piece of paper I still held in my hand at him. "Thank you for this," I said.

Mr. Lowe nodded thoughtfully, but said nothing more.

My mind was racing as I closed the door to his office behind me. Well, well. It sounded like George had been a naughty boy. Perhaps his wickedness had finally caught up to bite him in the ass after all. Though, like everyone else, I'd have to wait and see.

Screw him. There were more important things, and I couldn't wait to tell Dad what had just happened. I ran back to my cubicle, and with a heart much lighter than it had been in a while, I picked up my phone.

Chapter Twenty-Two

POTBELLIED PIGS

"It's just not fair. I'm a fan of the band too. Why didn't they invite me?" Kitty slumped on the sofa, crossed her arms, and pouted.

"I don't know. Maybe because I'm prettier?" Lydia suggested.

"Lydia!" If I had a penny for every time I had to scold that girl, I'd be a rich woman.

"Well, whatever it is, they invited me and not Kitty, and that's that."

I chomped on my piece of toast while also digesting this latest bit of news. Millicent, sister of Denny, the lead singer of The Brew, had invited Lydia to Coney Island to follow the band. Lydia was gonna be a groupie. I winced.

My internal alarm bells were ringing. Denny wanted Lydia alone with him on Coney Island? It struck me that perhaps our local boy who'd made good maybe wasn't as wholesome as he pretended to be. "I'm a one woman sort, I am. I'm waiting for that special someone..." Yeah, right. One woman at a time, and they were all special, I'd bet.

"Well," I said, "before you get all hyped up about it, you better have a word with Dad. You're not eighteen yet, which makes you legally his responsibility. You can't do jack without his permission. Chances are, he won't even let you go, not on your own, anyway."

Lydia stole my second piece of buttered toast and sauntered over to the window. "Well, as it happens, Dad's already said yes! I spoke to him a few minutes ago, and he didn't have a problem with it at all."

"Say what? I don't believe that for a second. It's going to be way too expensive. And weren't you supposed to be starting a job over at Walbrooks? What happened to that?"

Lydia shrugged and took another mouthful of toast. "Yeah, well," she said between chomps. "I don't think I'm gonna go for that. They wanted me to work on weekends, and there's no way that's gonna happen."

"Then how on earth can you afford it? Did Dad say he would pay for it?" I frowned as I thought about the money I'd just given him. He'd better not be giving Lydia any of that! And as for her turning down a paying job, that twisted my panties something terrible. Who did this little madam think she was? I'd have to talk to Mom and Dad about this and apply the thumbscrews.

"Well, Miss High-and-Mighty Snootypants, it just so happens I don't have to pay for a thing. Millicent's going to pay for everything, so there."

Lydia poked her tongue out at me and then went over to where Kitty was lying on the sofa, her arm over her face, hiding her misery. Lydia began to bounce on top of her, and as soon as the squealing started, I left them to it and rapped on the door to Dad's annex.

"Come in. Ah, Izzy." Dad looked up as I approached. "I guess you've heard the news." He nodded in the general direction of the living room.

"Do you really think that's a good idea, letting Lydia go off on her own? You know what a pea-brain she is—she's bound to get herself in trouble."

"You're overreacting, I'm sure. Millicent will keep an eye on her. She's a sensible girl. And Lydia's almost seventeen. Sooner or later, she'll be flying the nest anyway. She might as well do it now as then. At least I'll have some peace and quiet. It'll be worth it, just for that."

I perched on the windowsill and folded my arms in front of me.

"There's more to it than that though. Without us lot to keep her in check, Gaia knows what she'll get up to. You know what she's like with boys. She's a sitting duck for any warlock with a smooth tongue and an impressive wand. Really, Dad, I really think you should rethink this and tell her she can't go."

Dad waved his wand, and a book left the shelf behind him. It floated over his head and landed in his hand. I recognized Dad's personal ledger at once. He opened it and perused it for a moment before snapping it shut.

"Izzy. Look, we're not out of the water yet. I'm still going to have to borrow from the bank, and yes, your help was wonderful, but sadly, it wasn't quite enough." He reached for my hand and squeezed it gratefully. He'd been delighted when I told him about Mr. Lowe's offer, but I was stunned to learn he still needed more. The house that had once been bought for a song now cost a king's ransom. So Dad had still had to turn to Billy and his dubious investment scheme. It sucked.

"I have to say," Dad continued, "that a few weeks without Lydia can only help the situation. And this Millicent woman sounds decent enough. She called me earlier, asking for my permission, and told me about where they'd be staying and what their plans were. If I was a young warlock myself, I'd want to go too."

"Look, I want her to have fun, too, but..."

"Sweetheart, I get where you're coming from, but really, don't worry so much. Everything will work out for the best, I'm sure it will. Now just relax. Nothing bad will happen, I promise you."

I wanted to scream. I rarely disagreed with Dad, but this time, I felt he was so wrong. The ledger returned to its place on the shelf, and I knew the subject was closed. I shook my head as a final display of discontent, but there was no point arguing. Dad's mind was made up.

The door to the annex opened. Kitty stood there, red-faced, and with a sigh, Dad ushered her in. It was also my cue to leave.

I pushed my backside off the windowsill and left them to it. I needed the company of sensible people, but since Jane was still in Brooklyn, the pickings were slim.

I thought about Charlotte. I hadn't seen her since the night we'd caught her with Billy, and it was time we hooked up. I went up to my room and made the call.

Since she'd started to see Billy, Charlotte had pretty much gone underground. I didn't know if it was embarrassment or what; I certainly felt no ill-will toward her, quite the reverse, but disappear she had. I did think she was Looney Tunes, but that was a different thing altogether. Oh well, it was her choice. After all, Billy wasn't all bad. Just a bit of a twit, and he was making good money. That would always appeal to some.

Even so, it still took me by surprise when I heard the latest news.

"Guess what?" Charlotte said.

"What?"

"I moved in with Billy!"

"No blinking way." I gasped, forgetting myself. "You what?"

Charlotte remained calm and matter of fact. "Yes, that's right. He asked me, and I moved into his apartment. I think Dad was a bit relieved. I think he thought I'd never move out."

"But, Charlotte," I said, unable to get the shock out of my voice. "Are you sure that's a good idea? I mean, a quick grope and a cuddle in the back of a bar is one thing, but this is *serious*. Don't you think you should think about it first? Get to know him a bit better?"

"Oh, I know him well enough. Anyway, it's done. Look, it's no biggie. I'm twenty-one for Gaia's sake, Izzy. Isn't it about time I got out there and experienced life a little? Me and Billy get on just fine. I know that must sound weird to you, but he makes me laugh. If it all goes pear-shaped, so what? It shouldn't matter to anyone but us."

"You're right, of course. If he makes you happy, then go for it. You deserve some fun."

"Thank you."

The phone was silent for a moment. And then I remembered why I'd called her in the first place. "Um, we haven't seen each other in a bit. You fancy a drink tonight? Jane's gone to Brooklyn, and the others are driving me *insane*. What do you think about meeting up for a few at the Cauldron? My treat."

"Oh Izzy, I'd love to, but I've already got plans for tonight."

"Poop."

"Hey, why don't you come, too? The family is having dinner over at The Cedars. I'll treat you. What do you think?"

"Oh, I love The Cedars. Lucy Long still own it? Does she still do that delicious potbellied pig roast? Oh, it's fancy. I've lived here my whole live and have only been a couple times. I don't even know if I have anything to wear..."

Charlotte chuckled at my enthusiasm.

"Sure, what time?"

"I can pick you up at eight, if you like," Charlotte said. "Then you can have a drink."

"Awesome. I'll see you then."

I put down my phone and wandered over to my closet. The Cedars was posh and would require something super swanky just to fit in. The fact was, I was a little short on swanky at the moment, and my assortment of homemade sweaters weren't quite up for the job. I pulled out my wand. Some special magic was needed tonight.

When I heard the horn, I ran out of the house, only for my gut to plummet when I saw Billy at the wheel. Charlotte was in the passenger seat beside him. She rolled the windows down and grinned at me. *Dammit, Charlotte, you'd said you'd pick me up at eight, but you never mentioned Billy goddamn Collins.*

"You look fantastic. Is it one of yours?"

"Yes. Just finished it, fairy godmother–style with a wand and some silvery sparkle."

I was delighted with the little black cocktail dress. I'd conjured it out of embroidered lace, with sheer fabric adorning the bustline. There was more of the same peeping out from the sleeves. But I hadn't focused just on the dress. Sparkling pearls were woven into my braids; they faded from magical green to white, and I was very pleased with the effect.

"Yes, you look very nice," Billy agreed. "Don't worry about your clothes being homemade. Only people who know will be able to tell the difference."

Twit.

"Billy!" Charlotte said, giving his arm a playful slap, much to the insensitive twit's surprise. She grimaced in apology.

I shrugged, pretending it didn't matter, but it really did. I opened the back of Billy's Ford Taurus and climbed into the rear seat.

"All set?" Billy asked.

"As I'll ever be."

The drive was painfully slow, Billy not risking a single mile over the limit. A few times I wanted him to stop the car, so I could drive us, but I resisted the urge to volunteer and just ground my teeth until we got there.

The Cedars was a beautiful restaurant, designed in the Tudor style with beams and lead casement windows. It was surrounded by trees, set on around one hundred exquisitely manicured acres. There was a small pond, just in front of the building, and wild fairies zipped close to the surface like dragon flies, their wings glowing all the colors of the rainbow and more. Rows of cars were parked alongside the pond, and Billy took a while squeezing into a spot anyone else could easily park a bus in.

We all climbed out of the car, and instead of rushing inside, I took my time, admiring the view.

At the side of the restaurant, an old seventeenth-century waterwheel still churned, and excitable pixie children splashed in the spokes, flitting in and out in some daring game of chance.

Two puffed-up gargoyles flanked the entrance. By night, they returned to the neighboring church, but in the day, they were paid to stand sentry. It was all a little overdone, but my inner child adored it.

"Come on, let's get inside. We don't want to keep Kate De Bourgh waiting."

I stopped in my tracks. "I thought this was a family thing?"

"It is," Billy explained. "All of Charlotte's family are here. And Kate is as good as family, in my opinion. Come, come, I'm sure she'll like you. You don't have to worry."

I didn't. I shot Charlotte a knowing glance. She smiled, knowing me well enough, and then hurried her steps to follow Billy inside. I took a deep breath and followed them both.

The inside of The Cedars was as magical as I remembered it. The waiters were all elves, and they floated elegantly around the dining area floor, taking orders, talking to the guests, delivering food.

In the center of the dining area was the star attraction. Three potbellied pigs floated over an open green fire. There was no visible means of support, yet each pig turned beautifully in the air. The air was heavy with the scent of delicious roasting pork, and I licked my lips, desperate to have some.

"The Lucas party," Billy said to the ridiculously handsome maître d'. The elf had reddish auburn hair, was clean shaven, and had the most beautiful eyes I had ever seen, though they were characteristically mournful.

"Is Kate De Bourgh here? I hope we haven't kept her waiting too long."

"I believe you are the last of the party, sir. Please follow me."

I'd follow you anywhere, handsome, I thought. But I didn't utter a word. I just bustled behind the silk-toned elf, past all the round tables filled with happy customers stuffing themselves silly on pork, and onward to a slightly elevated, round booth right in the corner of the restaurant. Bingo. It was the best seat in the house, surrounded by windows with a perfect view of the pond.

I recognized pretty much everyone at the table. There was Charlotte's mom and dad, Bill and Linda Lucas, of course, and Charlotte's younger sister, Maria. The only person I didn't recognize was a very elegant woman I hadn't seen before. That had to be the famous Kate De Bourgh.

Kate oozed designer label, right from her Gucci dress down to her coordinated Louis Vuitton shoulder bag. She was very elegant, if a little older than I'd expected. Her gaze swept me up and down, and I felt myself wrapped, tagged, and bagged in under a second.

She smiled at me as we approached, and once everyone was introduced, I slid across the seat in the booth until I found myself directly opposite her.

Once we were all settled, and I'd said hi to Linda, Bill, and Marie, the gorgeous maître d' smiled and put his hands together. "Your waiter's name is Ithil. He will be with you shortly." He bowed just a fraction and then half walked, half floated away, his hips poetry in motion.

I noticed Kate was as enthralled by him as I was. In her case, her desire was a little more obvious. Maybe she didn't care who noticed.

"Well," she said, once he was gone. "I do so love coming here. Lucy simply has the finest eatery in town. Lucy, I said, last time I saw her—she and I are excellent friends, you know. Lucy, I said, you really do make *excellent* pork. *Nobody,* just nobody knows pig like you do. And you know what she said when I suggested she add a little more paprika to her secret sauce?"

Billy and Charlotte shook their heads, eager to learn. "Well, she *laughed* and she laughed. Kate, my dear—she calls me dear—Kate, she said, what a fantastic idea. I knew I should have come to you first. My business would have taken off so much sooner. Oh, what a wonderful woman she is, she truly is. She always appreciates my tips and suggestions. She's such a darling!"

"Well, if the aroma is anything to go by, she gets my vote."

Kate paused in her Bostonian eloquence to stare at me. "So you're one of the Bennet gals, from Misty Cedars?"

"I am Izzy Bennet, yes."

"Not one of the Boston Bennets, then?"

"Not that I'm aware of."

"Pity. Now that's a *very* old magical family. I believe they came over with the *Mayflower*. Wonderful, wonderful people." She narrowed her eyes as she looked me up and down. I suspected she hid a razor-sharp mind behind all that hoopla.

"I think we're pretty wonderful, too," I said, and I saw an amused twinkle in her eyes. Even better, I noticed Billy's widened eyes and his raised eyebrows, as if I'd broken some unspoken rule by talking to his boss.

The waiter, Ithil, who was as drop-dead gorgeous as the maître d', only black-haired, joined us and passed around some beautiful-looking menus made of glass.

"What's this?" I asked, as he handed me mine. "Ooooh, these are new."

"We've just got them," Ithil said. "Chef prefers them. You can order directly by touching the screens, and well, not to be indelicate, they're a lot cleaner. Chef insists on hygiene in everything."

I noticed that even though I handled the glass, I left no fingerprints or smudges. There was a hint of Tinkerbell sparkle as the menus cleaned themselves. I wondered what would happen if I dropped it on the floor.

"Good to know," I said.

While Ithil took everyone's drink order, I took a moment to peruse the menu. There weren't a lot of items. The restaurant clearly preferred quality to quantity. Still, it was a waste of time reading it. I'd made up my mind the second I'd walked in the door.

"And what can I get you to drink, madam?"

"I'll have the house wine." I handed him my menu. "You can take that away. I already know what I'm having." I nodded to the roasting pigs in the middle of the room. "The house special, please."

Ithil turned just a fraction to be sure of where I was pointing and then turned back. "Ah, an excellent choice, madam. Are you all decided? If you are, I'll take back your menus."

"I am," Kate said, handing her menu over straight after me. "I want the avocado salad with pork chops on the side."

Ithil looked expectantly at everyone else. Billy was still scanning frantically, desperate to catch up. Charlotte smiled and lowered her glass menu to the table. "I think we'd like a few minutes longer, if that's all right?"

"Very good, madam," Ithil replied. "Just tap when you're done." He turned and disappeared.

While the others perused their menus, something buzzed on the table. Kate picked up her gold-encased phone and stared down at it. Her curious look quickly broadened into an exquisite smile.

"Ah. It looks like our little party just got a little bigger."

"Oh?"

"Yes, indeed. My nephew is on his way. He said he might join us, but I never hoped...well...I should have known better. Young Darcy would move heaven and earth to be with me. I am totally his favorite aunt."

"Darcy?" I exclaimed. "As in, Fitz Darcy?"

"Oh? You know my nephew?" Kate asked. "I suppose it was unavoidable in a town of this size. But yes. He should be here any minute. Billy dear, if you could catch the eye of our waiter. We should have him chill another bottle of that excellent wine."

She had no sooner asked than Billy practically climbed over Charlotte in his quest to find Ithil.

Why was my heart racing? It was as if everyone in our booth had suddenly turned and were staring at me. I wish I still had my menu. At least then I would have something to hide behind. Not that glass was much use in the concealment department, but at least it would be something to hold on to.

No one was really looking. Except maybe Charlotte. That girl was too good at mind-reading. Really. That was a truly annoying gift she had. Maybe she was part vampire—ha-ha!

"So," I said. "Does everyone else know what they're having?"

The Lucases all nodded, and Charlotte put down her menu, indicating she was ready.

"Of course. Since he will be a while, I don't think Darcy will mind if I order for him. He and I share exactly the same taste."

No one responded. Why would they?

I thought about the last time I saw Fitz, and the words that had passed between us. Boy, was this ever going to be awkward. I wondered if he even knew I was here. If he didn't, he sure was in for a surprise.

Billy and Ithil returned, the latter carrying a freshly opened bottle of wine.

"Shall I pour, madam?" Ithil asked.

"No, just leave it there, will you? We'll see to it ourselves when my nephew arrives."

I glanced around the table at the near-empty glasses, thinking some of us could use a top up now. But I was a guest, so kept my mouth shut.

Ithil collected the remaining glass menus and took the one verbal order.

"So how is your casting-on spell coming along?" Charlotte asked. She was chomping on the end of a breadstick.

"I think I've mastered it," I replied.

"Oooh, magical design work. I'm all for that," Kate said. "All it takes is practice, practice, practice. I would make clothes myself, and if I did, my clothes would be excellent, if I ever got around to it. But alas, I never have the time. Ah, here's my nephew."

My head felt funny. Looking up should have been the most natural thing in the world to do, yet I had to tell my head to turn toward him. What was wrong with me?

"Ah, Darcy, my dear, there you are. Come on, Billy, squidge round and make room for him. Come, darling, come sit by me, and tell me all your news. I've been starved for news of late."

To my astonishment, Fitz didn't seem the least surprised to see me here. As everyone shuffled, he stared at me, and I got the impression I was supposed to read his thoughts, like we were connected somehow. Puzzled, I looked away, ignoring him. Maybe he'd forgotten our last painful discourse at The Brew concert, but I hadn't. He blushed, but remembering we were not alone, he soon recovered and smiled at his aunt, who was patting the empty spot beside her. He slid in as directed and politely kissed her on the cheek.

"Hello, everyone," he said. He smiled at everyone but me. "Excellent choice. I love the potbellied pig here."

"Oh, really? Darcy, you know you like the salads here—I ordered you the same as me."

Fitz shook his head, half smiling, but didn't contradict her. "Never change, Aunt Kate. I love you just as you are."

Satisfied, Kate preened herself while Fitz poured wine for everyone. He paused when he got to my glass.

"Designated driver tonight?" That same smoldering look.

I coughed to clear my throat. "Me? No. Not this time. Pour away." I loved the sound made by the wine as it gurgled into my glass. "Thanks."

Fitz was definitely handsome, but in the casual black sweater he was wearing right now, he was more than just good-looking. He was practically edible. It took all my self-discipline to remind myself what a total moron he was.

I tried not to look at him like a tiger in want of a meal. Where was my pork, dammit? I glanced at the display and saw one of the pigs had been removed, probably taken into the kitchen for carving.

"So, Darcy, darling. How was New York? Did you have a lot of fun in Manhattan? Tell me everything. I want to hear all the juicy news. Was Charlie there? And Caroline? Oh, how I love Caroline. You should make an honest woman of that girl someday, you really should."

My attention returned to the table and to my surprise, Fitz was gazing at me. Really gazing. My cheeks began to burn, and I instinctively turned to Charlotte, who was staring from him to me and hiding a smirk behind her hand. I wiped my lips, wondering if I had leftover dip there or something.

Fitz turned from me to answer Kate. "Caroline and I are just friends, Aunt. We don't feel that way about each other."

Kate was also gazing at me, but her shrewd eyes were cold. "Oh, come on now, sweetie. You can't fool me. I'm your auntie. Us ladies have a sixth sense about that sort of thing."

Fitz clearly thought it was useless to argue with her and could only shake his head.

"Yes," I said. "How are things in the Big Apple? Oh, did you happen to run across Jane? You probably wouldn't. She's in Brooklyn, visiting with our aunt and uncle."

Darcy picked up his glass and took a sip. This time I noticed he didn't look at me at all. His aunt, however, sat straighter in her seat, and she shot Darcy a smug side glance.

Fitz toyed with the rim of his glass. "I, um, no, I didn't know. Has she been there long?"

"Oh, funny," I said, warming to my theme. "I know she's seen Caroline. But perhaps she didn't mention it. She only saw her the once, I think. Caroline says you guys have been really busy."

"Oh, busy isn't the word," Kate intervened. "I've been getting emails from Caroline every day. The Empire State Building one day, Wall Street the next. You young people are just go, go, go, I can hardly keep up."

"Well, she'll be coming home soon, anyway," I said. "Perhaps we can all go out together when you get back to Misty Cedars. It would be great to catch up." *And get Jane and Charlie together again.*

"I'm not sure we'll be coming back," Fitz said. "Not for a while, anyway. Charlie is expanding his business in Manhattan, and I've been helping him. It might be quite some time before we can return to Pennsylvania."

"But what about Dark Coven?" I said. "He just took out a lease. Surely he's not going to give it up so soon? Everyone will be so disappointed. They all loved worshipping there, and we'd all love another chance to see the ghost. That was amazing."

The Lucases were listening intently. I knew they agreed with me. Billy didn't know what to say, and Charlotte, well, as always, my friend was wisely keeping her thoughts to herself.

"That may be, but I really can't speak for Charlie. It's his decision to make, not mine."

I shut my mouth and tried not to look as annoyed as I felt on the inside. Everyone in Misty Cedars would be so mad to hear he wasn't coming back. But then I wondered. Would they? It wasn't as if he'd been there long. He'd hardly laid down any roots. Perhaps only Jane would miss him. After all, she was the only one with an emotional tie to Charlie. So maybe it wasn't such a big deal after all. Perhaps. Even the Lucases would probably welcome everyone returning to their barn for coven meetings.

Thank Gaia they brought the food. I'd already run out of conversation. This guy really got on my nerves, and I wish I knew why.

Chapter Twenty-Three

SMALL TALK

I WASN'T IN MY BEST MOOD. SOMEHOW, FITZ'S SHOWING UP HAD completely spoiled the evening for me. Well, maybe not the potbellied pig, that had still been delicious, but the man made me feel really uncomfortable, him and his pretentious aunt. It was obvious they had both sprung from the same gene pool.

So I indulged in a sigh of relief when the check came and was presented to Bill Lucas. Charlotte had invited me, sure, but I reached for my purse, ready to pay.

"How much do I owe?" I asked. I noticed no one else was making the same gesture.

Charlotte's dad smiled jovially and brushed my offer away. "Oh, no, it's quite all right. I've got this." He beamed. He glanced across to Kate De Bourgh, who nodded her approval. *That's big of her,* I thought.

As we made ready to leave, Kate suddenly exclaimed, "Ah, look, it's Lucy herself. I just knew she wouldn't be able to resist popping over to say hello."

Lucy Long was a Chinese woman, dressed impeccably in a shimmering gown of pure white. She smiled graciously at the customers as she weaved her way over to our booth, pausing once or twice to smile and talk with anyone she recognized.

Kate spread her arms wide, ready to embrace Lucy the moment she arrived.

"Kaaate! So wonderful to see you!" Lucy squeed.

The two fell into a hug. Though somehow, they barely touched each other. The Lucases and Billy were beaming, delighted at being so highly honored by a visit from the owner.

"You look so fabulous!" Kate crooned. "That dress looks amazing on you. Have you lost a little weight?"

"No, I don't think so," Lucy replied, her smile never faltering and ignoring the bait. "You look fabulous. How was your meal? Did you enjoy it?" I liked her already.

"It was exquisite," Kate answered for everyone. "Just a little more seasoning, and it would have been perfect!"

"You don't need to wash my plate," I added. "I licked it clean."

Lucy turned to look at me curiously while the others gasped, horrified. But I was delighted with myself and glanced at Fitz, expecting a stare of disapproval, but he surprised me. Instead, he was looking away, trying to hide a smile.

"Well, I'm glad you all enjoyed yourself," Lucy said. "I hope to see you all again, soon."

"Absolutely," Kate replied. "As soon as my busy schedule allows."

"Good-bye!"

I was grateful to get back out into the fresh air. Now that the sun was down, the fairies on the pond looked even more beautiful, and the restaurant windows were adorned with candle lights. The wheel was lit up, but I knew the pixie children would have gone to bed the second the sun set in the sky. The place was enchanting.

Kate reached for her keys, but before she could open the door, her nephew intervened.

"Um, don't you think you've had a little too much to drink to be driving?" Fitz said.

"Nonsense, I only had one or two."

"Bottles," Fitz argued. "I'm sorry, Aunt, but I must insist. Let me drive you home."

"That's very kind of you, but I'm perfectly capable of driving myself. Anyway, you live all the way over on the other side of town."

"Nevertheless."

Billy piped up. "Why don't we take you? We're practically neighbors anyway. It would be no trouble at all."

Kate glared over at Billy's Ford Taurus with some trepidation. I knew how she felt. The possibility of spending another minute in close quarters with that insidious man filled me with dread.

"Is there enough room in that thing for the four of us?"

"Plenty," Billy said, failing to pick up on his boss's sarcasm. "But of course, you must sit up front. We'll just have to move a few coats and things in the back, Charlotte and Izzy will be perfectly comfortable there."

Kate turned from Billy's car to Fitz's Bugatti Chiron—I had looked it up. "Well," she said to Billy, "I suppose you *are* on my doorstep. But I am in something of a hurry. There's a call I'm expecting. Would it be too much to ask to drop me off first? You can take Izzy home after me. I'm sure you don't mind, do you?"

"Um, you know, I could take Izzy home," Fitz said. "It's not much out of my way, and you all wouldn't have to make a second journey."

Darcy's eyes were wide with hope, and I had the sneaky impression this was what he'd wanted all along. *No*, I thought. *Surely, I'm wrong.*

"Absolutely not." The vehemence of Kate's words left us all slightly horrified. I didn't like her high-handedness, and frankly, it was a bit of cheek, her expecting everyone to run around after her like that.

"I think it's a great idea," I replied. "Bye, all. Thanks for the great dinner. Great meeting you, Mrs. de Burgh. Text you later, Charlotte."

Before anyone could protest, I wandered over to Fitz's posh car and was about to reach for the handle, when the door locks popped up. Startled, I halted, giving Fitz just enough time to open the door for me.

"Well, I never," I heard as I slid inside. "Frankly, I'm surprised you haven't had enough of these Bennets. Thank Gaia my nephew had the good sense to save Charles from that gold-digging sister of hers. I just hope he has the wits to treat this other one with the same disdain."

Fitz climbed into the car beside me and turned on the engine. It had a low roar, like a wildcat, and I could only image the power under that hood.

He paused and stared at the steering wheel. A second or two passed, and I imagined he was conjuring up some excuse for himself. Or his aunt. In the end, all he said was, "You all buckled up?"

I nodded and turned away from him to look out of the window. Charlotte kissed her family good-bye, and as soon as they were gone, she shuffled awkwardly into the back seat of the Taurus. Billy stood holding open the passenger door for Kate, like the good little lapdog he was. Kate, on the other hand, remained resolutely on the asphalt, staring daggers my way. She was the only reason I didn't jump out of the car, right now.

"She means well," Fitz said. "She's just used to getting her own way."

"Over the way of others," I observed.

"Sometimes."

We drove on in silence. We might as well have been in different cars. I felt a wall between us, more powerful than magic and harder to break down. He had built it himself, brick by brick, with his haughtiness and lack of consideration.

"So how are your family?" Fitz said at last. "Is everyone well?"

I could handle small talk. It took my mind off the tempest raging inside me. "Yes, they're all good. Insane as ever."

"Good, good."

He went silent again. I wondered if he stopped the car, how long it would take to walk home. If I did, I might never get a chance to speak to him again. Not that I cared for myself, but my friends were owed answers. More small talk was needed. "What brought you back into Pennsylvania? Was it to see your aunt?"

"Partly. I don't see her as much as she would like, but when I can, I try to make the effort. It keeps her from coming up to the house in Maine."

I was pretty sure I'd heard the house mentioned before, but I guess I'd forgotten he had one. "Is it nice?"

"Sure. Beach front. Wild dragons. Very nice."

"Sounds it." I imagined something garish and tacky.

"I don't spend as much time up there as I should. My business affairs in New York take up a lot of my time. The renters see more of it than I do."

"Renters?"

"Yes. We have some cottages on the estate we let out in the summer. I have a butler, an old wizard with no family of his own. He takes care of the place and looks after the cottages, but sometimes I think the man is more at home there than I am."

"I see."

Fitz slowed as he approached a red light. As he shifted down, my focus dropped to the silver skull ring on his finger. And his hands. He had nice, manicured nails. Too bad they were attached to such a loser.

I stared at the rather intense-looking audio system and thought better about trying it. I might blow up the world.

Fitz glanced at me sideways and began again. "I, um, I'm glad I had this chance to talk to you on your own."

"You are?" *This should be good.*

"Yes. I...well...I didn't exactly come back to meet with my aunt. That was more of a bonus, really. A duty to get out of the way."

"Oh?"

"Yes. As a matter of fact, I really wanted to see you."

That was unexpected. I thought I'd stopped breathing. "Me? What for?"

"Hold on."

While Fitz pulled over onto the curb, I focused on his built-in navigator, which not only showed the roads, but also was spelled so I could see the people walking down the street in the shadows. Not that there were many at this time of night, but it was a very useful tool to help with driving in the dark. Was that...a deer? I stared at the animal. Anything rather than give my attention to the man beside me.

He put the car in park and turned to face me.

"I came back because for some stupid reason, I can't seem to get you out of my mind. It's crazy, I know. You've made it clear time and time again you don't like me, I know, and I've done my best to feel the same about you, but it's no use. When my aunt told me you might be coming tonight, I had to see you." He paused, running his fingers through his hair, his focus shifting from my face and down at that complicated audio console before he continued. "As insane as it is, I...I think I've fallen for you, Izzy. I remember the first time I laid eyes on you at the Cauldron with that ridiculous hairdo. I hoped it was nothing, but you looked so different at the coven—less garish." His focus drifted, as if he were reliving that moment. Then he blinked and ran his hand over his hair, as he prepared to finish his explanation. "I wanted to say something to you after the concert, but your family was so...I don't know. What I do know is that I can't get that image of you out of my head."

"What image?"

"You, standing in the street—your temper flaring, wild, insane, and utterly beautiful. From that day to this, you're all I've thought about. You're like a disease with no cure, and there's nothing I can do about it. I love you. I want you to go out with me. That's what I came back to ask."

Okay. So he's not the most eloquent man in the world. I would rate this proposition as marginally better than Billy's, but not by much. And he hadn't said a word about Jane, and he must have heard his aunt—surely, he knew that was all that mattered to me. Fitz had wealth and money, sure, but where was his class? Where was the compassion?

"Well, that came out of nowhere," I said.

Fitz said nothing, but just waited as lights reflected in his eyes. Eyes that would not stop looking at me.

"I'm not sure I've ever been called a disease before..."

"That's not what I meant."

I waved my hand, resisting the temptation to hex him right there on the seat—Hags be damned. "It's okay. I guess you can't help being a jerk. Gimme a minute to think." There were things I needed to know. Important things. Jane wasn't the only life he'd interfered with.

Perhaps the wine had loosened my tongue, but I found myself blurting, "So tell me about George. You two obviously had a thing between you. What was that about?"

A small twitch pulsed beneath his right eyelid at my question, but he rubbed the bridge of his nose, head shaking as he answered. "I, um, I'd rather not talk about him if that's okay. Certainly not right now. It was an ugly business, but it's behind me, and that's where it needs to remain. In the past. I want to talk about us."

"Um, last time I checked, there was no *us*. And there never will be if we can't be honest with each other. Look, I'm not going to lie to you. What he told me about you was pretty bad. I don't think I can give you any sort of answer unless you tell me what went down."

Fitz gripped the steering wheel hard, and I could almost feel the thoughts swirling in his head. "What did George say? I'd like to know what he's telling people about me."

I felt like I was back in school, telling tales in dark corners.

"Come on," he pressed. "You started this. You can't clam up now."

"Tell me about the trust fund."

"What about the trust fund? Why by Hades would George of all people tell you about that?"

"You don't deny it?"

"That depends on what the a—on what he told you."

"There's no need to shout. You know what I'm talking about. He said you blew him off because you didn't like him."

"And you believed him?" His voice was clipped now, like he was ready to explode, but at least he kept his temper. Somehow, I managed to do the same.

"Why shouldn't I? He's a lawyer and my boss. Why would he lie to me?"

"And you always trust lawyers, do you?" Fitz fell quiet for a moment, but he'd narrowed his eyes, and I could see his mind continuing to race behind them.

"I wish I'd never..." The words escaped his lips before he could stop them.

"You wish you'd never what?"

"If you must know, I wish I'd never come to Pennsylvania. It's been nothing but trouble from start to finish. All this business with George, and then your family, and this stupid infatuation with you."

"Say what?" I sat stiffly in my seat. "What about my family?"

It was Fitz's turn to look out of the window.

"Well? Spit it out. Since we're putting all the cards on the table, let's hear it all. *Well?*" My blood was boiling.

What had my freakin' family got to do with any of this? Fitz had crossed the line, again, and I doubted anything he'd have to say would calm me down now.

"Look, you have to admit, some of your family are a bit ridiculous. Charlie is on his way up. He needs a partner who can help him get there and share his goals. His face is everywhere as it is. What do you think the magical tabloids will make of your sister Lydia's antics? Believe me, I know they're not going to be kind. They will be hunting Lydia and Kitty down, photographing every second of their days, sticking cameras in windows, waiting for them to do something indecent.

"As for Mary, they'll be recording every ear-splitting banshee note she insists on singing. Mixing with your family would be the ruin of him, and I told him as much before we left for New York.

"And yes, since we're telling the *whole* truth, I knew your sister was in Brooklyn, Caroline told me, but we thought it best to keep it from Charlie. We'd both worked damned hard to persuade him she didn't like him, and I wasn't about to let your obvious scheme bring him down."

"My obvious *scheme*! Damn you, Fitz! Damn you to the Hereafter." I fumbled with the car door, struggling to open it.

"Oh, come on, Izzy. We need to talk about this."

I turned back for a moment and looked him straight in the eye. "You're right, we do. You know, from day one you've been a pumped-up, arrogant, goblin booger with your head so far up your backside, you never see what's going down.

"My sister is no gold-digger, and you know it. She's shy, and half the time even I can't tell what's she's thinking, so what makes you think you know better? The truth is, you see what you want to see, period. I don't think I've ever met anyone so ready to dislike people in general. Who the hell do you think you are, disrespecting my family this way? You're nothing, a no one, a trumped-up little rich boy who thinks he's better than everyone else because his family has cash.

"There is nothing you can say, or do, that will convince me otherwise. I hate you, Fitz. Stay away from me, and stay away from my family. I don't ever want to see you again. *Comprendez*?"

I got the door open, and I jumped out. It was still a couple of miles from home, but there was no way I was going to spend another second in the car with that idiot.

I marched down the street, with only his words for company. *Disease. Idiot. Ridiculous.* What kind of warlock was he? I didn't want to cry. I wanted to punch something. Hard. My fury gave me speed, and I bolted along, my breathing rapid, and I had no desire to calm down.

But there was another voice in my head, one I was trying desperately hard to blot out.

"*I wish I'd never...*"

"*...met you,*" I finished for him.

I listened to the purring sound of his car engine behind me. Would he dare follow me, now? After all we'd just said? I looked back over my shoulder, preparing myself for another battle of words. But then his headlights swung away, and I watched as his rear lights receded into the night. Good riddance.

Chapter Twenty-Four

THE ORBUCULUM

I SAT ON THE BENCH IN THE GARDEN, ENJOYING THE EARLY-MORNING sun, watching Jane as she moved about inside the coop, dropping feed for the chickens. She looked like she'd shed a couple of pounds—as if she hadn't been eating much lately. She was also a lot quieter than normal. I wished I'd never suggested she go to Brooklyn. If anything, it had made things much worse.

"So you didn't see Charlie at all?" I asked anyway, even though I already knew the answer.

Jane shook her head but continued to feed the chickens. "No, just Caroline. I'm sorry to say I think you might have been right about her. I mean, it took her long enough to respond to my text, and when she did, she could barely spend more than an hour with me. I don't know what I did, but she doesn't seem to like me anymore. I just don't understand it."

"You didn't *do* anything, I'm sure of it. She's just a bit of a Hag. They should hire her. She'd be good at it."

Jane stepped outside and closed the coop.

"You ever thought to feed them with a spell instead?" I asked. "I did it all the time you were gone, 'cos that chicken poop sure gets old. I had to wear sandals, for Gaia's sake."

Though not today. I looked down at my bare feet and wiggled my toes.

"I prefer doing it myself," Jane said. "I like the exercise. If we used magic for everything, we'd soon be as big as houses. Not to mention ugly. Less is more."

"Speak for yourself." I laughed. I took a quick peek at my butt anyway, just in case. "Anyway, I can think of better ways to keep in trim other than chasing after chickens."

Jane smiled faintly. "I won't ask. So did anything exciting happen while I was gone?"

There was a knock on the window behind me. Thank Gaia—excellent timing. My emotions were still raw from last night, and I wasn't quite ready to share what I felt with anyone—not even Jane.

"Oh, there you are, Izzy," Mom cried. "Come on in, hurry up. Your aunt and uncle are getting ready to leave. Auntie Bri has something she wants to ask you."

I left Jane fussing about in the yard and went straight in. I had a lot of time for Auntie Bri. She had a good head on her shoulders and had owned several successful boutiques in downtown Misty Cedars. They had long since sold them off and were living the life, now. Uncle Ed had married well.

I found Auntie Bri sitting at the table in the dining room. She was dressed in well-fitting jeans and an elegant blue cardigan I had just knitted for her. Uncle Ed was with Dad, talking over some pot plants in the kitchen window. Mom wasn't in the kitchen.

In front of Auntie Bri was a souvenir from their trip to New York. It looked like a snow globe had mated with a crystal ball.

"Oooh, that looks fun," I said. "What is it?"

"No, it's a quartz orbuculum," Bri said. "Not a real one, of course. It doesn't tell the future, only specific shadows of the past. It captured moments of our trip to Brooklyn in it. Go on, have a look. It's rather wonderful. It captures the most special moments."

"How does it do that?" I asked.

"It reads their emotions. Anyway, it saves having to cart about a clunky camera all over the place."

"And cart that about instead?"

"No," Bri laughed. "You can leave this in your room. It doesn't have to be with you all the time."

I picked it up.

"How does it work?"

"Just shake it," Auntie Bri explained.

I did as she told me and peered inside the ball. The quartz grew cloudy and then became almost crystal clear.

Images of their trip formed. I saw Uncle Ed laughing on top of a tour bus when they ventured into Manhattan. Too often, I saw Jane looking sad and wistful as she sat at a window, looking out at the world beyond their apartment. There were no prizes for guessing where her thoughts were at the time.

Still, Uncle Ed and Auntie Bri looked chirpy enough. They were super fit for their age; probably because they were both avid cyclists and had biked a fair way across America. In spite of Jane's heartache, it was clear the two of them were having a blast.

"Nice." I popped it back down on the table. "So what's up?"

"Oh, we were just wondering, since we took Jane to Brooklyn, whether you might like to come visit us up in Maine? I mean, it's not as exciting as being near Manhattan, of course, but the scenery is pretty spectacular, and there are some wonderful trails for you to walk. And of course, dragons. Your dad told me you haven't been anywhere this year. Is that right?"

Dad didn't turn around, but I knew he was listening. I guessed this was his way of thanking me for the loan.

"I'd have to get permission for some time off work, but sure. I don't think it would be much of a problem. When did you have in mind?"

"Is a week's notice too soon? You don't want to miss the best part of the season. It starts getting pretty cold after that. The fall is definitely my favorite time of the year. The trees will have turned, and the colors are spectacular. Leave it much later, and you could get caught in the snow."

"You had me at a week's notice." I laughed.

"Good. Do you mind flying?"

My stomach flipped over. I had never flown before, and well, those planes went an awful long way up.

"Could I maybe drive, Aunt? Would you mind? Only, well, you know."

Auntie Bri knew about my fear of heights, but she didn't answer at once. In fact, she looked quite serious. Her gaze fell on the wall, and I knew her well enough to know she was thinking about my car sitting right outside.

"Are you sure your little Beetle will make it? It's an awfully long way."

"Well..."

"I tell you what," Bri said. "How about you let us treat you to a nice rental? I don't mind you driving, but I'd feel better knowing you were in a reliable car."

I smiled. After everything that just happened, her timing couldn't have been more perfect. Time alone to think. It was just what the doctor ordered. "Deal. Thank you, Aunt." I kissed her on the cheek.

Bri looked delighted. Deep down, I knew I'd always been her favorite niece. I grinned, and grabbing the orbuculum in both hands, I ran off in search of Jane to share my good news.

Fitz had left me feeling like dirt, but he wasn't done yet. After my aunt and uncle left, I saw I had an email from him on my phone. I frowned. I didn't recall ever giving him my address.

Not knowing what it contained, I left Jane to it and wandered over to the back of the garden where I could be alone. There was an old maple near the back fence, and Lydia, bless her darling heart, had hooked a rope over one of the branches and made a swing of it. With my former spare tire. Classy.

I sat on it now, and with my arms wrapped around the ropes, I opened the email.

Izzy.

I've typed and typed this same message a thousand times since you left last night. But you deserve the truth. So here it is.

George Wickham and I were never truly close. We grew up together, yes, but I would never have called us buddies. A few years ago, he had a fling with my sister. Georgie wasn't underage, but she was barely legal, around Lydia's age, I think. I knew how he was with women. I'd seen him toss enough of them aside, but that wasn't my chief concern. I don't know if any of the others mentioned it, but my sister is on the autistic spectrum. She's highly functional and can play the piano beautifully, but she has some difficulty controlling her emotions. He toyed with her lack of understanding and preyed on her disability. The man has no sense of decency.

However, Georgie liked him, still does as a matter of fact, and for a while I hoped he just meant to amuse her. He'd known her for years after all. In the end, though, it was obvious to me he had his eye on her money, and when I heard her mention marriage, I almost flipped. There was enough gossip about him in Camden for me to be absolutely sure he didn't love her. His liaisons with other women were well talked of.

So before he destroyed Georgie completely, I paid him off. I gave him more than the value of the stipend, just to ensure he left both the town and my sister alone. He took it gladly, though what he did with it was his business. Georgie cried for days.

Think what you will, but my sister's happiness means everything to me. Without me, she'd fall prey to any bastard who came sniffing around. And George was the worst of them all. I did what I thought was right.

As for your sister, perhaps I was a little hasty in dragging Charlie away. I am sorry if I read the situation wrong, but really, although your sister clearly liked him, it didn't look to me like she was in love. Your other sisters, though, well, I said all I plan to say about them in our discussion last night.

The fact remains, Charlie and I had worked so hard to get his business up and running. Making a go of it meant everything to him—I couldn't risk all that being destroyed over a senseless, casual fling. Charlie has a good heart, and well, before anything else, I am his friend. I am sorry if I read the situation wrong.

Your friend,

Fitz.

My first thought was to send him a link to the word *friend* on the Urban Dictionary. Every feeling I'd felt last night, every burst of anger resurfaced, and I started to type an angry reply.

Damn him. However eloquently he'd dressed it up, however noble he'd thought himself to be, he'd still been an interfering troll turd who had destroyed all Jane's hopes for happiness. Even a stupid stink imp could see she loved Charlie. And he'd probably made all that stuff up about my boss, George. Not even he could stoop so low.

Or could he? My fingers paused over the letters, and I sat back in the swing and took a breath. I thought about everything I knew about George. What Mary King had told me, what Wickham himself had told me. I thought about his dealings with Matthew Devereux at Rosings Park, and the look on Mr. Lowe's face when I'd mentioned George at work.

Had he ever told me anything that wasn't a lie? Or taken a step to help anyone but himself?

I stopped the swing and let my phone arm flop to my lap. One of them had to be lying to me, and the more I thought about it, the more I felt it had to be George.

As for the Jane business, well, Fitz should have kept his nose out of it, but the fact was my younger sisters *were* a little wilder than they ought to be, and I could hardly condemn him for thinking the same thing I'd often thought myself.

I took a deep breath and deleted the response I'd intended to send. The warlock was an idiot. But there was no message I could send that would do anything to change that. I popped my phone in my pocket, pushed myself off the swing, and with a heavy heart, walked slowly back inside.

Chapter Twenty-Five

THE GEOMANCER

It had been a solid eight-hour drive from Misty Cedars to Camden, Maine, but I had Paranormal FM for company, and I was in a pretty good mood. As I drove into the coastal town, I zipped down the window on my shiny Audi A2, courtesy of Uncle Ed and Auntie Bri, enjoying the smell of new rental car while I listened to The Brew's brand-new release, *Banshee Screamer*. They were topping the para charts and were getting played twenty-four seven.

I turned off the radio to enjoy the more indigenous cry of the screeching gulls overhead, slowing to avoid the tourists as they left the numerous souvenir shops and crossed at pedestrian crossings. The air was crisp, and I filled my lungs with air rich with sea and lobster.

Auntie Bri must have set the watch a while back because she was there waiting for me as I pulled into the drive. There was nothing shabby at all about Bri's charming Cape Cod, right in the heart of the town of Camden. They had a lovely view of Penobscot Bay, and over the years they had expanded and renovated the property, until it was quite the prettiest little homestead in town. I loved it and wished it were mine.

"Come on in, come on in, you must be exhausted!" Auntie Bri cried. "I've just boiled a kettle and will make you some tea. Leave your things in the car. Your uncle can get them later. He went down to the lobster dock to get some fresh lobsters. He won't be long. I thought you might prefer to eat in tonight after your long drive. Is that okay?"

I hugged her hard and, after setting the alarm, followed her into her home. "Sounds perfect to me."

Auntie Bri had a small porch outback, overlooking the bay. There was no place in the world I would rather eat.

For now, I followed her into the kitchen and slumped in a chair while she fixed us both a drink. Auntie Bri's kitchen was a wonder of witch pots and pans, bundles of herbs, boxes, spell books, cookbooks, and lanterns. Her home was infused with the aroma of various oils and potions, as well as my favorite scent in the whole world: the smoke from a wood-burning fire.

For decoration, Auntie Bri had collected an assortment of brooms, which adorned the walls, and she had a thing for ceramic owls, which were shoved into every spare nook and cranny.

Her cat, Salem, was a black-and-white tuxedo who was at least twenty pounds. No matter what they fed him, the poor kitty never seemed to be able to lose any weight. He was a happy soul, and he wobbled over to me as soon as I sat down and weaved his chubby bod around my tired legs. Then he stared at my lap and, by some magic of his own, found the strength to jump into it.

I tickled the nape of his neck and watched as my aunt poured the tea through an infuser. She slid a mug over to me and settled down on the other side of the island.

"It's my official duty as your aunt to ask you if you're seeing anyone?" Bri grinned. "There. That's done. I've got it out of the way. Now I can enjoy my tea."

My smile was equally well meant. "Um, no, not at the moment." I thought about George, who was never mine, and Fitz, who never would be. "I'm just not meeting the right people, I suppose. Maybe I'm too picky."

"Nonsense," Bri said. "At your age, you should just think about having a good time. Talking of, how is poor Jane? That was a sad affair. Is there nothing to be done about it? It's such a pity. Charlie Van Buren seems decent enough. We met him, last summer, while he was up visiting the Darcy Farm."

My mug suspended midair. "You know Fitz and Charlie?"

"Sure. Well, I wouldn't exactly say I *know* the Darcys. We attend the same coven, but he's so much younger than we are, and you know, young people like to mix with people of their own age. Mind you, he outranks Ed at the Coven, and he's always polite, but that's as far as the relationship goes."

A little light illuminated my aunt's eyes, and a wry grin crossed her lips. "You know him then, I take it?"

"I...um...yes, that is to say, I've met him a few times. We're not exactly friends."

"Oh?" Her eyes still carried mischief. That witch was too shrewd by far.

I stared down at my tea, pretending to be fascinated by the loose leaves in the bottom of the mug. Salem, feeling ignored, raised his head and butted my hand, forcing me to pet him. I scratched his ears and listened to his rather loud, contented purr as he settled back down on my lap.

I tried to sound as casual as I could. "We haven't known them long. They were at our coven meeting." I felt my face redden, as it always did when I felt awkward. I decided to change the subject. "Ooh, did I mention, I saw my first ghost? That was exciting. We confirmed it was Goody Becker, a witch they burned at the stake back in the seventeenth century."

"Well, that's hardly a surprise, not if Fitz Darcy was there."

Puzzled, I asked, "Why do you say that?"

"The Darcys are part warlock, part geomancer. They have a particular affinity with the dead—well, some of them do. Was he wearing a silver ring shaped like a skull?"

"Uh-huh."

"And was your meeting held deep underground?"

"Yes. Quite deep."

"Well, then that's probably why she showed up that day. Geomancers can channel spirits through stone, sometimes even without being aware they're doing it. Funny. I knew his father had the gift, but I hadn't realized his son had it as well."

Wow. How did I miss that one? Geomancers were like the superstars of the paranormal world. Like their close cousins, necromancers, they could raise the dead, but that wasn't their main goal. They had an affinity with the earth and rocks; they understood them, could interpret them, and to some degree, were able to read into the future. They were as close to Gaia as anyone could get, without becoming gods themselves. *Hell. No wonder everyone sucked up to him the way they did.*

"Are you sure? After all, there's been talk of Goody for years. It wasn't like it was the first time we'd heard of her."

"I'm sure, but it takes a geomancer for a ghost to actually cross over. I remember my first ghost. Gosh, it was exciting. Was yours good or evil?"

"Good, I think? She seemed rather interested in me."

"Well then, did you help her out?"

"I'm sorry?"

"Ghosts don't futz around for the fun of it. If she focused on you, there must have been something she wanted you to do for her. I wonder what it was?"

I thought about Matthew. "I met her former lover. He'd checked into a suicide facility, but he changed his mind. Maybe that's what she wanted me to do, talk him out of it. Maybe that was it?"

"I don't know. There's only one way to be sure. If you see her again, maybe she'll let you know."

"I don't see how. She had no voice."

Bri smiled and took another sip of her tea. "She'll find a way, honey. Just you wait and see. Ghosts are smarter than they look."

"I wonder why he didn't tell me he was a geomancer," I mused. I'd never met one before. I'd always thought they were cool. Until now.

"Why would he?" Bri replied. "Did you ask him?"

"Umm, no. I guess not."

"Well, there you *are*, dear. Geomancers are spirit channelers, Izzy, not mind readers. I'm sure if you'd have bothered to ask him, he'd have told you all about it."

I shrugged and finished my tea. So Fitz Darcy was a geomancer. It was an uncommon gift, which shoved him right to the top of the warlock food chain. That at least would explain the elder's deference to him that day at Dark Coven.

Hmm. It would have been cool to get in contact with Goody again. But now the one man who might be able to help me was off-limits. *Great. Just my luck.*

Chapter Twenty-Six

UNCLE ED AND AUNTIE BRI

I'D SEEN MANY BEAUTIFUL PLACES IN THIS COUNTRY, BUT OF ALL OF them, Maine had my heart. I sat on the deck outside the house, chewing toast for breakfast and watching the boats as they sailed in and out of the harbor.

The skies were clear of clouds, but I kept looking up, hoping to see one of the famous Maine dragons. Yet in all the years I'd visited, I hadn't seen a single one. Half of me believed they were a myth.

Hundreds of different colored buoys dotted the surface of the bay, each one marked for its owner, and I passed the time imagining how deep the lobster pots went and how many lobsters were already trapped inside down on the seabed.

On the other side of the bay, boats of various shapes and sizes were gearing up for the day's pleasure cruises. I hoped we'd have some time to get out there. I hated heights but loved the water.

Not too far away, an old man was out walking his dog. The goldendoodle was unleashed, and he ran a little ahead of his walker. As the old man approached, he nodded, and I smiled back and said, "Hello."

He stopped. "Good morning. Don't mind old Chudley. When it's quiet like this, I sometimes let him run off his leash, but he's a good dog. He won't bite you."

The old man looked weather-beaten. His skin was a deep brown, his blue eyes lost in merry wrinkles, but there was a twinkle in them, and I knew he was one of us, not a numpy. His aura reeked of wizard, through and through.

"Ah, Reynolds. How are you this morning?"

Uncle Ed had popped out on the deck, sleepy-eyed and shirtless, showing off his tan. He had a watering can in his hand and began watering Bri's geraniums.

"Morning, Ed," said Reynolds. "When did you get back in town? I haven't seen you for a while. Are you back for the rest of the season?"

"We are, we are. We got back a little over a week ago now. We'll be staying a few more weeks to shut the place up, and then zip zip, down to Florida we go."

"You snowbirds. You're always flitting about from one place to the next, I dunno." He paused and looked at me. "And who is this lovely lady?"

"This is my niece," Uncle Ed explained. "My sister's kid, Izzy. Izzy, this is Reynolds."

"Hey," I said. "Nice to meet you. Are you local?"

My uncle grinned. "Reynolds, you were born here, weren't you?"

"And I'll die here, too, if I have anything to do with it. Come here, Chudley. There's a good boy."

I looked along the road to see Chudley had gone a little too far away and was peeing up against someone's picket fence. Not bothered by this rude interruption, the dog dropped his leg and bounced merrily back toward us. He ran a circle around Reynolds and then jumped up the fence, panting furiously and pawing at me. I reached down to pet him.

"Down boy, down!" Reynolds commanded. The dog did as he was told but still seemed happy enough. He clearly had a lot of energy and a playful disposition.

"Good boy." Reynolds looked at me thoughtfully. "How long are you in town for?" he asked.

"Oh, just a week, though I would happily stay here forever. I love this town."

"Yep, so do I." He turned to Ed, who was now on the other end of the deck, deadheading some of the flowers. "What do you say you bring this lovely lady up to the old house? I could show her around the place. Maybe flirt a bit. Don't judge a book by its cover, hon. This old dog has a few tricks in him yet." Reynolds flexed a bicep, and I laughed.

"That might be fun. I'd love to. Where is it?"

"Up at the old Darcy household. I'm the manager there."

I froze. He had to be kidding me. I'd been sucker-punched, and I hadn't seen it coming. I didn't know if he caught the look of horror on my face, but my uncle unwittingly came to my rescue.

"Yeah, sure, if you're serious. Bri and I have always fancied taking a look at the place. When were you thinking?"

"I'm free this afternoon if you are. The house is quiet now, and I don't have much to do, not now the season's nearly over. If you're lucky, I might even put out a tray of sandwiches."

"Oh, I dunno," I said, backpedaling. "We don't want to put you to any trouble or anything."

"It's no bother at all, believe me. I get lonely sometimes, up there all on my own. You'd be doing me a big favor."

"All right. We can be up there about four," Ed said. "Is that okay?"

"But what about, um, Fitz? Is he still in New York?" I asked.

"Oh, I didn't realize you knew him. It just so happens he *is* still in New York, but he's coming back tomorrow, I think. Not that there's much for him to do, the place practically runs itself."

"Perfect," Ed said, before I could say anything else. "I'll go and tell Bri. She'll be delighted."

"Good. Four o'clock, got it. So it's settled then. Chudley, come on, there's a good dog. See you all later."

Reynolds and Chudley carried on down the road, but as soon as they were out of earshot, I rounded on my uncle.

"I, um, don't you think we're being a little intrusive?" I asked. "I mean, it's Fitz's home after all. He never invited us. What if he finds out we were there? Won't he think it a bit odd that we just barged in like that? He'll think we're snooping or something."

"Nonsense," Ed said. "It'll be all right, don't you worry. Reynolds has people up there all the time. It really is a lovely house, and it has some of the best views in all of Camden. Anyway, you heard him—Fitz won't be home until tomorrow, so don't worry."

"But I..."

"Oh, hush, kiddo, you'll enjoy yourself. I wouldn't have agreed to it if I didn't think you would. To tell the truth, I'm pretty pumped about going inside the house myself. I've seen it from the outside plenty of times, and if that's anything to go by, we're in for a treat. And I've heard stories of dragons near the shoreline up there. I've never seen one, but the locals sure go on about it."

"Well, that's something. I've always wanted to see a dragon."

"Well, there you are, then. Now, let me go and grab Bri. She's going to be so excited!"

I was glad one of us was. My uncle left me to it, and I slumped down on the railing, my gaze transfixed on a buoy in the middle of the bay. Not that my brain even registered it. Instead, I was racking my mind, trying my damnedest to find a way to wriggle out of this unexpected and unwelcome invitation. A headache maybe? Or sunstroke? It sucked, but I knew if I tried something like that, Ed and Bri would both know I'd done it on purpose, and that would make me the most horrible niece in the whole wide world. Nope, after all the trouble they had gone to in bringing me up here, the least I could do was go with them to a place they'd always wanted to visit. I'd just have to suck it up and go along with it.

Oh well. At least Fitz was still in New York. That was something. If we'd met Reynolds just one day later, things could have been a hell of a lot worse. I had to pull up my big girl panties and get on with it. After all, it was just for a few hours. It would be over before I knew it.

Nothing pleased me more than getting in harmony with nature, kicking off my shoes and rolling in the dry dirt to worship Gaia and all things earthy.

Rain. Not so much. I hated getting wet, usually, but today was different. I stared out of the window and prayed. A few minutes after meeting Reynolds, the clouds had rolled in, the heavens had opened, and buckets of big, fat, heavy rain, the kind that would flash flood, came down. Maybe we wouldn't be able to see the Darcy house after all. Oh well. Bummer.

I slid off the window ledge and was about to do a victory dance when

Ed and Bri came into the front room, all dressed up and ready to go. Perhaps they hadn't noticed the downpour?

I crooked my finger and pointed over my shoulder at the scene behind me.

"Um. Have you looked outside? I think we're going to have to canc— um, postpone our plans."

"Nah, don't you worry about that." Bri's face was a picture of happiness as she looked beyond me to the fast-moving clouds. "It'll blow over in a minute. That's a storm in a teacup. They never last long. I'll make us a quick cup of tea, and then we can get going. Are you going to change, or are you going like that?"

I looked down at my ripped jeans and black tee with *The Brew* slashed across my boobs. "It'll do, won't it?" I asked. "I don't think I need to dress up to look at a house, do I?"

"No, you look just fine," Ed said. "And we'll have an early dinner over at The Bug and Black Bat when we're done, and you're fine for that too. I just booked it."

The Bug and Black Bat was an awesome para pub, nestled on a twisty, narrow street overlooking the harbor. It attracted a good blend of numpies and paras; the food was incredible and too good to pass up, so was always packed. The place was tight, with lots of nooks and crannies, and it was my favorite place to eat in Camden.

I smiled. I knew it was Ed's way of making the first trip up to the Darcy house a little more palatable in my eyes.

Bri bustled about with the teapot, and resigned to my fate, I trotted up to my room to check my appearance and to have a quick wee before we left.

I slumped on the end of my bed and stared at the mirror in front of me, but without registering my own reflection. Fitz Darcy. I couldn't stop thinking about him, and it was making me sick. He was an asshole who didn't deserve a moment of my time, yet there he was, stuck in my head, not budging an inch.

Riffraff. Ridiculous. Pig.

Stuck-up. Judgmental gnome fart.

Utterly beautiful. I love you.

I...

It was all just so impossible. I had said I never wanted to see him again, and now here I was, hardly two minutes later, ready to bang on his front door and potter about his stupid house. The muses were having fun with me, that was for sure.

"Izzy, are you ready? The rain has stopped!"

On hearing Auntie Bri, I looked out of the window, and sure enough, the clouds were parting, and the sun was breaking through. Oh well, might as well get it over with.

"I'm coming! Just a minute." *Maybe if I twisted my ankle running down the stairs? Oh, shut it, Izzy! Just be a big girl and get ready.*

I pulled my sandals on and went to join them. Auntie Bri's convertible Miata was up front and ready to go. Resigned to my fate, I slid into the tight rear seat and got comfortable.

"Is it far?" I asked.

"Not very," Bri said, climbing into the driver's seat and belting up. "Just sit back and enjoy the ride. You're going to be blown away, I promise you."

Ed got in beside her, and Bri pressed a button, and a garage door closed a few feet behind us. We were on our way.

The roads were drying as we left the heart of Camden. Bri turned to take us along a road I hadn't traveled before. We began to climb a steep road, until at last, the harbor was left behind us and there was nothing but the road and the ocean.

I gasped. The clouds had dispersed, and the sky in front was a glorious, unblemished blue. The ocean, once wild and dangerous, had calmed, and it was so quiet I could hear the rush of the waves below, even over the hum of the car engine as we cruised along the cliff top.

Out on the ocean, a few lobster men were returning from their dawn excursions, and behind them, a small cluster of islands broke the horizon.

My uncle turned in the passenger seat and smiled at me. "Not a bad view, eh?"

Speechless, I shook my head. *If this were mine, I could never leave it*, I thought.

"Wait 'til you see the house."

My imagination near imploded with possibilities. The homes along the cliff edge were few and far between, but they were glorious, expansive, and well beyond my means. I pictured myself in all of them, each one a different life, a life I was never meant to live. Yet how I wondered. Material wealth held little charm for me, not in itself, but the idea of waking up here, to these views, every single day of my life was more temptation than I could withstand. I wanted them. I wanted them all.

"I wouldn't say no if someone offered me one," I said coyly.

Ed grinned and turned back to enjoy the view.

Bri slowed the car and pulled into a gated drive. I expected to see a great house, but there was a cluster of small cottages inside the gate, looking over the water.

"Those are the vacation cottages," Ed explained over his shoulder. "I heard they're gorgeous inside, though I've never seen one. The family is well-known for looking after their guests and making sure they have a good time."

They were certainly cute, some of them nested precariously along the cliff edge, but they were well-maintained nonetheless, with well-watered flowerpots and fresh paint and shutters. I pictured myself alone, with nothing but my needles and spell books for company. Heavenly.

We drove past the six cottages all, Bri keeping her foot off the gas, giving us all a chance to enjoy the pretty view. As the last passed us by, she drove a little faster, and though I looked ahead, there was no house in sight.

I was beginning to think I'd missed it when Bri eased off the gas again.

"Take a deep breath," she said. "I think it's just around this bend."

I sat up stiffly, expecting to see yet another great house, but as Bri took the corner, my heart skipped a beat.

The Darcy home wasn't the grandest house we had seen in Camden, nor was it probably the most expensive. The two-level cedar shake home was quite expansive, boasting perhaps five to six bedrooms, and had a small courtyard-like drive at the front, with parking for numerous cars. It was relatively small, discreet, but exquisite. A few gothic touches here and there betrayed a para architect, one with an infallible sense of taste and proportion.

The house appealed to me on every level, and a small voice in my head opened her mouth for the very first time. *Idiot. This could have been yours. Eventually.*

Auntie Bri pulled up in front of the house and turned to see my reaction for herself. "Well. What do you think?"

I couldn't stop shaking my head and realized my mouth was still open.

"That's what we always thought." She laughed.

"Of course, we've only ever seen it from out there on a boat." Ed nodded toward the ocean. "But now I'm really excited to see it from the inside."

He didn't wait for me to respond, but slipped out of the passenger seat and surveyed the property. I climbed out and, standing beside him, did exactly the same. From somewhere inside, I could already hear Chudley barking.

"Not bad," Ed said. "Not bad at all."

As soon as Auntie Bri joined us, we walked to the front door, and my nerves returned as Ed leaned on the doorbell.

Chudley was scuffling on the other side, and through the frosted glass I could see Reynolds.

"Come here, boy."

Reynolds bent over to secure the dog, and then he opened the door.

"Ah ha!" he cried. "I'm so glad you could make it. I thought that rain might have put you off coming."

"It would take more than a few drops of rain to put us off." Ed laughed.

Reynolds stood to one side so we could pass. His grip was firm on Chudley's collar. "If he bothers you, I can tie him up for a bit. He's a good boy, but he's a bit excited right now. He'll calm down in a minute, once he's had a good sniff of ya."

"He doesn't bother me in the least," I said. "Let him go, if you like. We might as well let him get over it."

"My thoughts exactly," Reynolds said.

"Fine with us," Bri said.

A moment later, Chudley was jumping up and down like a lunatic, but only for a second or two. Once he'd completed his meet and greet, he scampered off to his bowl someplace, and we could all hear his slurping as he lapped something down.

The house was as tasteful on the outside as it was on the inside. It was decorated in pastel shades of blue and lemon, creams, and whites. A few occasional tables decorated the entryway, each adorned with freshly picked flowers.

Reynolds took us first into a large kitchen and breakfast room. The first thing I noticed was a huge marble island, covered with several platters of the delicious-looking sandwiches he'd prepared for us. An assortment of well-maintained copper cooking pots and pans were suspended over one side of the island, and similar pewter pots and pans—for potion brewing—were hung from the other.

Behind the island, under a window, a huge Viking stove dominated the back wall, with a great stainless-steel air vent above it. I smiled. Both looked like they had seen a fair bit of action and were not just there for show.

Something delectable was cooking on the stove, and I caught the aroma of beef and broth in my nostrils. I looked inside, mesmerized by the stew that appeared to be stirring itself.

Apart from the stewpot bubbling magically away, everything else was neat and tidy. Reynolds kept clutter to a minimum, and I had no doubt he looked after the property with as much care and attention to detail as he did this kitchen.

I had a quick look at some of the books on the spell side of the kitchen. The Darcys had a copy of *The Elements of Earth* by Meryton Stone, my favorite para author. My gaze fell on a few titles, and I smiled, spotting quite a few familiar names. Whoever purchased these had tastes very similar to my own.

"You like to read?" Reynolds asked from over by the island. I turned to see him pouring iced tea into tall glasses while a set of napkins twisted and turned in the air, forming themselves into pretty little roses and landing gently in front of my aunt and uncle.

"I do," I confessed. "Some of these spell books look incredible."

"Well, our volumes have certainly grown over the years, though young Fitz is a most avid collector. He brings home so many books, I hardly know where to put them, sometimes."

Hmm.

Drawn by the tantalizing clink of ice cubes, I picked up my glass from the island and walked over to the other side of the breakfast room.

There was a comfortable sofa, and more tables and books, but what really caught my attention was the most exquisite view of the ocean I could imagine. The large French doors opened out onto a Maine-red deck, which overhung the rocky edge of the coastline and looked directly out across the bay.

"May I?" I asked Reynolds, pointing outside.

"Be my guest," he said. Reynolds opened the large doors for me, and I stepped out into a small slice of heaven. Gaia had inspired this setting. I could feel it in my chi.

"Breathtaking," I said.

"I couldn't agree more." Reynolds joined me on the deck and took a position beside me as I admired the view.

"I've lived here my whole life, and though I know there's a whole world out there, you can keep it. I was born here, and I'll be happy dying here. I've no hankering in my bones to see any place else. My heart is in Camden, and this is where I'll stay."

"You grew up in this house?" I asked.

Reynolds chuckled. "Oh no, not me. No, I grew up down in the harbor, back in the early days when it was all para and no nonmagical folk. Camden is in my blood and always will be."

"Have you always looked after the property here?" I asked.

"No, not in the beginning. When I was a young wizard, I was a teacher. I suppose I still am in some ways, though it's been a while since I had any students. I taught the young Fitz, and his father before him. He wasn't a bad boy as they go. After all, boys will be boys, but he was a good kid."

"Oh?" I thought about the stuck-up, proud little troll-twit who had asked me out. He could hardly have been a saint, I thought.

"Fitz went to the local school? In Camden?"

"Oh no, he was homeschooled. In some ways it's a shame, because it made him somewhat people-shy and awkward. But the boy had a good heart, just like his parents. I had no trouble with him at all. Now if we were talking about his friend George, oh boy, was he ever a piece of work. I could tell you some stories about him."

"George?" I guessed he meant my boss, but I wanted to be sure.

"George Wickham, yes. He was brought in to give the other one some company, but he was a nasty little brat. We all breathed easier when that boy skipped town."

Reynold became quiet and looked thoughtfully out to sea again, but I really wanted to hear more.

"What did he do that was so terrible?"

"Ha! How long have you got? I could tell you tales to make your young toes curl. Well, for one thing, he near broke my darling Georgie's heart. Have you met Fitz's sister?"

"No. I haven't had the pleasure. Not yet, anyway."

"Ah well, she'll be here tomorrow. She's staying in town with him now, but he's bringing her home soon. I love that little girl. She's the sweetest thing that ever lived. So pretty, so kind and gentle. You would hardly know she has a disability, but those who are close to her know well enough."

"I heard she was autistic?"

"Yes. And so trusting." He looked like he was about to say something horrible but caught himself in time and stopped himself. "I tell you, if that George ever comes near her again, I swear, I'd face the Hags and swing for her. He was a horrible brat as a kid, and nothing changed when he became a man. I heard he went into the law. Now there's irony for you. I'm sorry, I'm rattling on, and you don't even know him." He shook his head, as if he was shaking George out of there. "I'll shut up now."

"Perhaps this George is not as bad as you think," I suggested. "We all have light and dark in us, don't you think?"

"Ha. Usually. But not in this case. Believe me—Izzy, is it?"

"Yes."

"Izzy, if your path ever crosses George Wickham, take a black salt bath and protect yourself. That boy is wicked. Head to toe. Don't think otherwise. No good ever came out of him, and no good ever will."

Bri and Ed had been munching on the sandwiches Reynolds had put out in the kitchen. Ed's voice was a little louder, and I knew it was his way of letting me know he was eager to move on.

Reynolds, savvy old wizard that he was, caught it too and returned with me to the kitchen.

"Right then," he said. "Let's all go take a look at the rest of the house, shall we?"

There were a series of rooms, all very tastefully furnished, and really, I would never have known this to be a paranormal house were it not for the contents of the bookshelves and the occasional pots of salt on display in every room, for emergency magic. Still, I thought, with a few gentle touches, I could make it work, ha-ha!

The bedrooms we just skimmed through, although we took a little more time in the master bedroom, as it, too, had a fabulous view of the bay.

"Master Fitz sleeps in this room," Reynolds explained. "Georgie's bedroom is across the way, but if you don't mind, I won't show you that one. She can become upset if anything changes, so I prefer to not show it, if that's okay?"

"Oh, we quite understand," Bri said. "Look at that view, Ed. Is it okay if we take a closer look? Can we go out on the deck?"

"By all means," Reynolds replied. A second later, the door was opened and out they all went. Except me. I stayed back to take a moment for myself.

Fitz's bed was painted in various mellow shades of gray and blue. It was masculine, but not harsh, and there were several books by the bed. I wandered over to see what he was currently reading.

There was a small dresser along the wall, and glancing at it, I saw one of those small orbuculums Auntie Bri had brought for us after her trip. Without thinking, I picked it up and shook it.

As the opaque gray sphere began to smoke, I watched with wonder as the images came into focus. Was that...the Flaming Cauldron? I peered closer, fascinated by the images that were oddly familiar in this strange place.

There was Charlie, of course, and then there was a memory of me, and the band, and then me, and Jed, and Denny and me. Lots and lots of me.

I saw myself through Fitz's eyes and was stunned by how he saw me. I was laughing, I was dancing, I was a total minx flirting with everyone, yet sometimes I was serious or thoughtful. His eyes had missed nothing, and I found myself wondering, hell, had I even been in the same bar?

I sat down on the end of the bed and shook it again.

"See anything you like?"

Witches and warlocks! I almost died. Fitz was smirking in the doorway to his bedroom, and I was sitting right on the edge of his bed! *Shit, shit, shit, shit, shit, shit, shit.*

I dropped the orbuculum on the mattress and jumped up, my brain a mess of random expletives. I didn't know what to do. The blood rushed to my face, and I had no words. Standing there, I felt a total idiot.

There was only one thing I could do. I bolted right past him, running like crazy, blind to everything, running in a total frenzy and not taking a breath until I was out of the house, bent double and panting by Auntie Bri's car. I looked up and saw Fitz's gleaming Bugatti was parked alongside. It was him, all right. The son of a bitch had returned home a day early.

Chapter Twenty-Seven
CALMER WATERS

I HEARD FOOTSTEPS APPROACHING BEHIND ME, AND EXPECTING IT TO BE Auntie Bri, I looked up. But it was Fitz.

Overwhelmed by my sense of shame, I just stood there, gawping at him like some immature schoolgirl with no control over her emotions. For the first time in my life, words failed to come to my rescue. I would never recover from the shame of this. Never. Ever. He'd found me sitting on his bed, for Gaia's sake! Looking at pictures of me on his orb! That was almost as bad as going into someone's browser history and checking out their porn links!

"Look, really, it's okay," Fitz said, making placating gestures with his hands. "Calm down, really."

I shook my head, less able to forgive myself than he appeared to be.

"No, really, I shouldn't be here. I'm so sorry," I panted. "Only my aunt and uncle were eager to see the place, and I, well, oh Gaia, I'm so embarrassed. Can you tell?"

Fitz smiled, and it was a warm understanding smile, nothing at all like his usual grimace.

"Hey, forget it. The summer guests ask to see the house all the time, so I'm used to it. Do you like it?"

In some regards, he reminded me of a small boy, seeking approval. My heartbeat began to slow, and I felt more like myself again.

"Yes, I like it a lot."

"Did Reynolds take you downstairs yet? It's pretty spectacular. We have an awesome coven room."

"Um, no, not yet. To be honest, we haven't been here long. We just saw the view from the kitchen and then your...um." I couldn't say bedroom. "I'm so sorry. We were told you were still in New York and wouldn't be back before tomorrow. We can leave now, sorry. We won't invade your privacy anymore."

"You're not invading my privacy at all. And yes, well, I was supposed to come home tomorrow, but I had some business in Massachusetts that over ran, and I thought, hell, at this point I might as well just go home, and the others can catch up when they can."

Typically, I'd only ever seen him in casual clothes, but Fitz was all dolled up in a pretty smart business suit. He looked hotter than ever, even if he did look a lot more formal than I was used to. His manners, however, were polar opposites. He couldn't possibly have appeared more relaxed.

"Anyway, they'll be coming to Camden tomorrow at some point. So really, don't worry about it. You couldn't have known, and well, it was a nice surprise to see you. Come on, let's go back inside. Who was that you were with? They look sort of familiar."

"Um, that's Uncle Ed and Auntie Bri. Ed is my mother's brother. Auntie Bri ran some boutiques down in Misty Cedars, but they're both pretty much retired now. Maybe you saw them down at the harbor—they have a house down there."

"Ah, maybe."

He started walking back in the house, and being totally confused and not knowing what else to do, I followed him.

Reynolds, Ed, and Bri were all in the kitchen, nibbling on sandwiches and no doubt wondering what the hell was going on.

They looked surprised to see me and Fitz standing together in the doorway.

"Err, this is Fitz Darcy. And this is Uncle Ed and Auntie Bri. I was just telling Fitz about your home in the harbor."

"Ah," Bri said. "Yes, I mean, it's nothing compared to this, of course, but we love it. It's very nice to meet you."

They all shook hands, and then without ceremony, Fitz grabbed hold of one of Reynold's sandwiches and took a big bite. "Sorry, everyone, but I'm starving. I haven't had a thing since breakfast. I hope you don't mind." He covered his mouth with his hand while he talked, which I thought was quite polite of him.

"Not at all." Ed laughed. "I mean, they're *your* sandwiches after all."

"Ha, yes, but they were made for *you*. So, Ed, do you like dragon stalking? We have some awesome underground lairs on the property. They're kind of a family secret. We keep quiet about them because we don't want the tourists messing with the nests, but there's a whole honeycomb under these cliffs, and I'd be happy to show them to you."

"I don't know about Ed, but I wouldn't mind taking a look at those myself," Bri said. "I love dragons. I haven't seen an actual nest since I was a child."

I stared at Bri in amazement. "You never mentioned you'd actually *seen* one before."

"Well, you never asked," Bri replied.

"Well then," Fitz continued. "There's a secret entrance off the family coven room downstairs. If you've time, I'd love to show them to you."

Ed and Bri were ecstatic, and to be honest, I was super psyched about it myself. I'd never seen an actual dragon, let alone a dragon's lair or nest.

"All right, let me just get changed out of this and into something more comfortable." He gestured to his suit.

"Oh, of course, take your time," Bri said. "Reynolds has been keeping us entertained, and these sandwiches are excellent."

"Yes," Ed chuckled. "If you're hungry, you'd best take a handful, or they'll all be gone by the time you get back."

Fitz grinned and grabbed another shrimp salad on rye. "So noted."

As he turned, I caught Auntie Bri looking slyly at Ed. I didn't need an orbuculum to interpret that look and shot them both a warning glare.

"Don't even go there," I mouthed.

Bri just smiled.

My gut was reminding me it was time to eat, so I grabbed a sandwich of my own. I was halfway through chewing it when I realized I'd picked the exact same sandwich as Fitz. Of course, no one else had noticed, and I was hardly going to make a point of it—they would have teased me rotten. But it made me think. So we both happened to like shrimp salad on rye, so what? It didn't mean we were fated to be lovers or anything. *Perish that stupid thought. I mean, just perish it.*

I left them all yapping, and needing a moment to myself, I stepped out onto the deck. My attention shifted to the gorgeous horizon. My earlier shame had mostly subsided, but my heart was still a torrent of emotions. I'd have to be standing in calmer waters than this, I knew, to understand what was going on inside me.

I realized I liked Fitz more than I knew. He'd been nothing but a sweetheart since arriving, and he really couldn't have been kinder to me. Yet I couldn't forget Jane and his meddling in her affair with Charlie. Nor could I forgive him for his insults to my family. I imagined taking him home with me. *Hey, everybody, here's Fitz, my new boyfriend, the one who hates you all! What's for dinner?* I couldn't ignore that just because he smiled like a boy and looked really nice in his business suit and kept dragons.

What a mess! I decided the best thing to do was just to be polite, at least for as long as Bri and Ed were around. Otherwise they would think I was plain nuts.

I thought of the coven and the peace that could only be achieved at our gatherings. I needed that calmness right now. I needed my soul to be quiet. I listened to the gentle roar of the ocean and knew Gaia was with me. And she was talking to me, waiting patiently to be heard. I just had to be still enough to hear it.

Chapter Twenty-Eight
THE DRAGON'S LAIR

FITZ HAD BEEN IN SUCH A HURRY TO RETURN, HE'D FAILED TO DRY OFF properly. His white shirt clung to him in places it was rude to look at, and I found myself smirking, in spite of myself. Auntie Bri noticed it too, and we were two girls together, grinning like idiots.

"Well now," Ed said, sparing our stupidity, "that didn't take you long at all."

"I, um, well, I didn't want to keep you waiting." There was a final sandwich on the platter. "Anyone want this?"

Ed patted his belly. "No, go right ahead. If I eat anymore, I think I'll pop, and we're supposed to be having dinner out tonight too."

"Not that a few sandwiches would stop you." Bri laughed. "My Ed eats like a horse. So go ahead, I'm full. How about you, Izzy?"

"Yeah, I could do with another." I reached for the sandwich but stopped when my fingers were an inch away. The disappointment in Fitz's expression would have made me laugh out loud, if he hadn't also made me feel terrible. It was like stealing candy from a little kid who just didn't understand why. I felt shame. I forced a smile, taking my hand away, and said, "Nah, just kidding."

"Awesome." Fitz snatched up the last sandwich and wolfed it down.

"Master Fitz," Reynolds said, "if you don't mind, I'll finish cleaning up and then will head off home. Is that okay?" Reynolds glanced at Ed and Bri, his meaning clear—did Fitz want them to stay or go?

"Absolutely," Fitz agreed. "I can take care of our guests. And thank you."

Reynolds smiled and began to load the dishwasher.

"Thank you," I said.

"It's my pleasure, Izzy."

We all followed Fitz out of the kitchen and back to the hall. Fitz opened a large door, revealing a stairway that descended into inky darkness. He paused. "I will warn you now. We're going rather a long way down. Some people find the climb back up a little too much."

"Oh, don't mind us," Ed said. "My wife and I are as fit as fiddles; we don't mind at all. As for my young niece here, well, she's like a gazelle. We'll be fine."

Even so, I was relieved and delighted to see a handrail. Fitz set off down the steps, Ed and Bri went after him, and I followed close behind, eager to see where it would lead to.

The stairs twisted and turned several times, but I was never out of my comfort zone and was only surprised at how many steps there were.

Down and down we meandered, until I was almost dizzy from all the twists. "This used to be an open spiral staircase leading down into a large cave," Fitz explained. "There were no walls, but my mother was afraid of heights, so Dad replaced them with these. Some people still find them a little daunting, but believe me, the descent is much better than it used to be."

My stomach lurched just thinking about it, and I found myself grateful for his dad's thoughtfulness. And empathic toward his mother.

"When we get to the bottom, you will notice our circle is a little unusual. You'll see some strange markings, and although they may seem random, they are not."

"Geomancer stuff?" I asked.

"Exactly." Fitz paused and looked back at me. I guessed he was surprised I'd learned of his rank, but he said nothing and carried on.

My curiosity was certainly aroused. Eventually, we made it all the way down, and I wondered what had surrounded us, on the other side of this very domestic staircase.

When we reached the bottom, Fitz said, "*Acende*," and the cavern was instantly illuminated by oddly lit shapes, dotted around the walls.

"Are those...mushrooms?" I asked.

"Yes, in a way," Fitz replied. "They are magic phosphorescent fungi. They form quite naturally from the droplets of dragon perspiration that permeate the caverns. There's not enough light for them to react naturally down here, we're too deep, but my spell enables them. The good thing is, the light I create helps strengthen the dragons, so the relationship is perfectly symbiotic."

"How many dragons are there?" I asked.

"Two, I believe. We had more in the past, but many of the entrances had to be sealed, and the dragons are very territorial. They don't like to share a space."

"Why did you seal them?" Ed asked.

"The tourist industry. My family cast enchantments along the coastline, so the lobstermen wouldn't spot them from their boats, but as the tourist industry grew, we found it harder to protect them. We sealed off the more visible entrances, forcing the dragons to find safer lairs. So now we just have two."

"And they live together okay?" I asked.

"For now. It's a mother and her baby. Dragons are fiercely protective of their young, so while she's a baby, they'll get along just fine. It'll be different when the baby grows, but that's many years off yet."

"Oh. How old is the baby?" I asked.

"Two days. Reynolds told me she hatched while I was in New York."

I paused. "Um. Are you sure this is safe? Will she be close to us?"

"As long as the mother is gone, yes. I'll check when we get closer, just to be sure."

"So what are all these markings for?" I asked.

I took a moment to stare at them. They were etched in random spots around the floor and on the walls of the cavern, though I suspected they were anything but random. I had no idea what they meant.

"My family has been blessed with the gift of geomancy for many generations. There are multiple spiritual ley lines crossing in these caves, and where they cross, our ability to read the future intensifies a thousandfold."

"You can tell the future?"

"Me, not so much. I'm more of a channeler. The dead seem to find me."

"Do you encounter many ghosts down here?" I asked. "Like you did in Dark Coven?"

"No, not a one, we're too far from a burial site I believe. Anyway, I don't seek to channel the dead, but it happens sometimes. I can't help it."

"So I saw," I said, thinking of Goody. "It can have its uses though. It is something that can be learned?"

"Channeling through the earth? No. I think you have that gift or you don't. But I do think you can learn to summon the dead. I have numerous texts on the subject upstairs if you'd like to borrow them."

"Yeah, that sounds cool. I might take you up on that, thanks."

Bri smirked at me. *What was it with aunts and matchmaking?* I walked off on my own and pretended to study the walls and the floor. In the center of the cavern was a large circle, just like many I had seen before, only Fitz's circle was marked by a series of dots. It kind of reminded me of a cribbage board, though I thought it might be impolite to say this.

Fitz was quiet for a while as we studied the markings and strangely lit mushrooms. Perhaps it was because of what I saw in the orbuculum, but I imagined his eyes on me all the time as I toured the cave. It made me a little uncomfortable, but a part of me kind of liked it.

I was staring at an unusually seated cluster of mushrooms when I heard a small puff, rather like the sound of hot air being forced through a tunnel.

"What is that?" I asked.

Fitz smiled, and I couldn't help thinking how gorgeous he looked in the magical light.

"You're near the secret entrance to the dragon's lair," he explained. "The nest is on the other side of the wall."

"Can we see it?" I asked. I prayed to Gaia he would say yes.

Fitz closed his eyes as if deep in thought. "Yes, I believe we can, but we must be quick. The mother is not far away."

"She doesn't like witches, then?"

"She doesn't like anyone who threatens the well-being of her baby."

None of us were a threat, but I supposed the mother dragon wouldn't know that.

"Cell phones off, please. We should proceed with caution."

As soon as all phones were muted, Fitz stepped between me and the cavern wall and pulled his wand out from a pocket.

"The entrance to the lair is concealed, not only to protect the dragons, but also to protect us from them. Remember, they are wild creatures, so be watchful, and have your wands at the ready in case Mom decides to make an appearance. If she does, I can protect you, but keep your eyes open just the same."

I nodded and saw Ed and Bri do the same. With some trepidation and a bucketload of excitement, I stood behind Fitz and waited as he raised his wand and pointed it at the cavern wall.

"*Aberto.*"

As he spoke the words, the wall of the cavern began to crumble, and the now tiny rocks rolled to one side, leaving an opening just large enough for a person to pass through, if they bent over.

Fitz broke a piece of fungi from the wall. "Grab a little. It gets pretty dark in the tunnels. Is anyone claustrophobic?"

We all shook our heads. I snapped a piece off, and it felt a bit like rubbery polystyrene. Not quite as bright as a firefly, but it would do.

Fitz led the way, holding his luminous mushroom ahead of him, and we all crouched and followed. I wondered how small a baby dragon would be, and what it might smell and feel like. Would I be allowed to touch it?

We kept going along a long tunnel. Bri was the shortest, but even she couldn't stand up. Luckily, I didn't mind tight spaces, or I might have freaked out.

"The baby may or may not have fire yet. That usually starts around the third or fourth day, but if it does, just use the *Cesar* spell, and that should stop it."

"So what's the right thing to do if Momma does turn up?" I asked.

"Have you used the *Aturdir* spell before?"

"The stun spell? Yeah, but not since I was a kid. And never on anything as big as a dragon." *Phasers on stun*, I thought. *Aye aye, Cap'n.*

"Her size is irrelevant if you do it right. Just say it clearly and slowly. You don't have to be loud; the cavern will take care of that."

"This is fun, isn't it?" Bri said.

"Witches," Ed sighed.

Fitz slowed, so we did the same. He now spoke in a whisper. "The last time I was here, the nest was just around the corner. A baby dragon won't have learned to fear us, but he has little control, and if he has fire, he could burn you accidentally, so take care."

We all nodded.

Fitz stood to one side, and after he signaled the coast was clear, we followed him through into the main underground chamber. It was big, though not as vast as I expected, and the cave ground and ceiling were illuminated by oddly crooked, phosphorus stalagmites and stalactites, scattered randomly around. Some were broken off, possibly knocked down by the motion of the she-dragon. There really wasn't a lot of room for her to fly around.

"How big is she?" I asked. "Mommy?"

"I would say she has a five-foot wingspan. She's not as big as some I've seen, but don't let that fool you. She is very, very strong and could carry off a horse if she had to."

I looked around for bones but could see nothing. "Oh? What does she like to eat?"

"Dead dragons."

"Nice," Ed said. "Eco friendly."

"Where's the baby?" Bri asked.

I looked around too. Nothing.

"Oh, sorry." Fitz stepped to one side, and right behind him was a small nest, rather like a bird's nest. Only rather than being made up of twigs and leaves, the nest was made up of small bones and bird feathers. And curled up in the center, with its tail wrapped all the way around its body, was a small grayish and white dragon. He was about the size of a springer spaniel, and his markings were similar.

"There's your bones," Ed said.

"Oh Gaia, how adorable," Bri gasped.

"And how tiny," I added. "I thought it would be bigger. Can we pet it?"

"Okay," Fitz replied, "but be gentle. His scales won't have hardened yet, so he's very vulnerable."

"We'll be super careful."

Bri and I dashed over, and I raised my hand, curious about how it would feel.

"Wait," Fitz cried.

His attention was alerted to something up ahead, and I froze, my hand still extended toward the baby dragon.

"Wands out," I said instinctively, and watched as everyone pulled theirs and aimed them into the darkness at the rear of the cave.

The mother flew in so fast we barely had a chance to respond. Fitz turned, forcing Bri and Ed back inside the tunnel, but I stood my ground, my wand raised, determined to give them cover.

The she-dragon landed a few feet away. She was beautiful but oh so pissed. She eyed my wand warily and began to circle the nest, so I did the same, keeping the baby between me and her.

My back was against the wall of the cave now, and I climbed onto a short ledge to get away from her. Dang. There was no way out of this but up. I was okay for the first few feet, but the higher I climbed, the more my knees trembled. "Oh no, oh no." I could go no farther. I had to get back down, but the dragon was right there, sensing her victory, waiting. I was stuck. *Oh, Gaia, no.*

Fitz came out of the tunnel.

"Turn around, look at me, turn around," he shouted. The dragon spun at the sound of his voice. I was terrified. She was too close—she only had to lash out with her powerful claws, and she could kill him.

I really didn't want to use *Aturdir.* She was a nursing mother, for Gaia's sake, and I wasn't sure what effect the spell would have on her.

Fitz's wand was out; any second now he would stun her regardless. I only had seconds to think.

All I needed was a distraction. "*Tricotar unha manta xigante!*" I cried.

In the blink of an eye, a giant, fire-resistant blanket knitted itself in front of my eyes, the needles clacking frantically, faster than I'd ever moved them before! "*Cubra-la!*" I finished. The checkered blanket flew over the she-dragon, wrapping itself around her head and momentarily blinding and confusing her.

At first the mommy twisted and turned, trying to claw the obstruction from her face. And then great bursts of fire escaped her mouth, and I knew it wouldn't be long before she was free again.

"Run," Fitz cried. "Just a few feet higher there's another tunnel. Run!"

Run I could not. With sweat pouring from my forehead and with my back flat against the wall, I inched slowly along the ledge, praying my legs wouldn't buckle underneath me. And then I froze. Turning my head, I could see the small exit, and though it was just feet away, it might as well have been miles. I was petrified.

Beneath me, the dragon was almost free. Loose strands of blanket covered her head, and her talons were shredding what was left. If I didn't shift now, I'd be toast. Literally.

"Run!" Fitz cried again. "Run!"

I suspected if I didn't bolt, Fitz would stay to protect me, and the dragon would kill us both. Slowly I began to ascend, adrenaline forcing me along the ledge. I was almost there, yet it still seemed so far away. And I was so dreadfully high.

She was free! The dragon roared with anger, and to my horror, she turned on Fitz first.

I pointed my wand at her backside. "*Píchea!*" I cried. It was only a pinching spell, but the dragon yelped and turned from Fitz to me.

There was no time. I pulled up my big girl panties and, taking a deep breath, bolted for the exit. I heard the she-dragon do the same, only her gasp was followed by a burst of flame. I dived inside the tunnel, not knowing what was waiting for me inside it. All I knew was I had to go, so I fled, the heat of the dragon's anger just inches behind. Bright-orange light illuminated my tunnel for a second, and I knew I'd only just avoided having my ass singed.

Only I ran headfirst into trouble. No sooner was I out of range of the dragon's breath than I found myself ensnared in another trap. Fitz grabbed me as I bolted down the tunnel to freedom. He must have doubled back and circled around fast to get here! He scooped me up in his arms, and I stared at him, shaking from fear and excitement. It was crazy, but for a second, I thought he was going to kiss me. Then he seemed to recollect himself, and frowning, he let me go.

"Come on," he said, "before she catches up with us. Although I think she'll go back to the nest. But let's play safe, just in case."

Chapter Twenty-Nine

THE BUG AND BLACK BAT

"ARE YOU OKAY?" FITZ ASKED.

I couldn't see too well—it was darker in the tunnel than in the cave—but I felt okay, if a little shaken.

"Unless my butt's on fire, I think I'm good."

"No, it looks pretty good to me."

"What?"

"Not on fire, I mean. Your clothing isn't scorched or anything."

"Well, good." I held my tongue, stopping my next words. I'd been about to thank him for inspecting my ass. How weird would that have sounded? Almost as weird as his choice of words, which I put down to our circumstances. It had been quite a thrilling moment, being chased by an angry dragon mom.

"How are my aunt and uncle?"

"They're fine," Fitz said. "Worried as hell about you. We'd better get back."

"Oh, of course."

"Take my hand. I know these tunnels better than anyone."

I took a deep breath, and before I could think or say anything, Fitz took my hand and began to pull me back down the tunnel. For once, I was glad of the dark. His touch had sent a thrill through me, and thank Gaia, he hadn't seen me blush. I decided not to remind him we had perfectly good wands.

"The dragon, she'll be okay, right?"

"Yeah. We just surprised her, that's all. They're never vicious. I've never met anyone who was killed by a dragon, though I know a few hunters who have gone after them...and were never seen again, needless to say. But they're protected on this estate, and most of the time they leave us alone. It was silly of me to disturb a she-dragon with a baby, but I guess I..."

"What?" I asked.

"Well...well, I guess I wanted to impress you."

"It was certainly a hot date." I laughed.

"Enough with the puns, already."

"On a scale of one to ten, I'd give it a ten."

He groaned, which I liked.

It was a short walk along the tunnel, and I could hear voices up ahead.

"Oh Gaia, Ed, what would we tell your sister if anything happens to her?" That was Bri.

"I dunno," Ed replied. "But we'd be sending her a postcard from Siberia."

"It's okay," I called. "I'm perfectly fine. We'll be there in a second."

"Izzy, is that you?" and "Oh thank Gaia, you're all right!"

There was a flicker of light up ahead from the glowing mushrooms. And then we saw them, and letting go of Fitz's hand, I ran straight to Auntie Bri, who wrapped me in a bear hug.

"I'm okay, I'm okay," I said. "No bones broken, and I'm not on fire. Are you two okay?"

"Yes, yes, we're fine. Fitz got us to safety, but we were all worried about you."

"Come on," Fitz said. "Let's get you upstairs to the light. I think we could all use a drink about now. I know I could!"

I couldn't have agreed more. Fitz ushered us all back along the tunnel and to the stairs. He led the way while my aunt and uncle chattered excitedly behind us. I was grateful for the opportunity to be silent. My emotions were still running riot. The last twenty minutes were so surreal, I didn't know what to make of them. And I was conscious of my right hand.

Somehow his hand kept connecting with mine, and I didn't know whether to brush him away or let our fingers entwine.

I said, "I don't know about you all, but all this excitement has left me famished. Will our reservations at the Bug and Black Bat still be good?"

"I don't see why not," Ed replied. "We still have plenty of time. Fitz, would you care to join us? I would like to buy you dinner. It's the least we could do for all the hospitality you've shown us."

I caught my breath, almost afraid to hear Fitz's answer. I wanted him to say yes, almost as much as I wanted him to say no.

"Are you sure I won't be imposing?"

"No, not at all," Bri said. "You'll make a four, and that would be perfect."

I caught the exchange between my aunt and uncle and sensed a little matchmaking was afoot. The funny thing was, I didn't mind one bit. I grinned and flicked Fitz's hand away one more time. I didn't need an orbuculum to see where this was going. Dinner was going to be fun.

While I found myself liking Fitz a little more—his actions and words suggested he wasn't the dark streak of misery I'd assumed him to be when we first met—I didn't forget what he'd done to Jane and how he'd insulted Lydia and Kit and Mary. Not to mention, me. But now I was willing to give him the chance to explain himself further. Perhaps dinner would offer him that opportunity.

The Bug and Black Bat was filled to capacity. From their speed, I could guess the waitstaff were mostly vamp, although the hostess was a fae who had nothing but fluttering lashes for Fitz.

Like all fae, she was tiny, about three to four feet at most. She was also exceedingly pretty, with large green eyes and wavy blond hair that floated about her face as if she were in water. Her green-tinted fluttering wings were swaying temptingly, right and left.

"If there's anything more I can get you," she tinkled to Fitz. "Just crook your finger and I'll be right here!"

"Thank you, I will." Fitz pulled out a seat for me, and I treated her to a warm smile. She bit her lip and flitted off, her wings buzzing harder than I guessed they usually did.

There was a cute lily arrangement in the center of our table, with miniature bats flying in and around the long stems. While the rest of us perused our menus, Bri pulled out her phone to take a picture of it.

"Oh! I almost forgot." I'd turned my phone off back at the cave and had forgotten to turn it back on. I pulled it out and pressed the power button. There were several quick dings in succession—and I saw two messages pop up at once. They were from Jane.

"Do you mind if I take a quick look?"

"Go right ahead," Bri said. "If the waiter comes, do you want me to order you a cider?"

"Sure, that sounds great." I was a little distracted. Jane loathed texting, especially when I was on vacation, and I knew it had to be something important for her to bother me up here. I clicked on the first. It read:

Lydia is missing. Kitty thinks she has run off with your boss, George, but no one can confirm this. Mom and Dad frantic. Any ideas?

The second message read:

Mary got hold of Kitty's phone, and we can confirm Lydia is with George and they're off to Vegas to get married. Kitty thinks Lydia used a love potion. The Hags will be after her if we don't stop her. We have to find them. Can you come home?

Using any spell for financial or emotional gain was illegal. And Bitterhold was no place for a silly young girl like Lydia to spend her days. She'd come back white-haired and shaking from her own nightmares!

"Witches and warlocks!" I nearly dropped my phone in the lily bowl.

"What is it?" Bri asked. They were all looking at me strangely.

I took a deep breath and tried to think of a better way to say it, but I really couldn't come up with anything that didn't make Lydia sound like an idiot. "Okay...it looks as if...Lydia has run off with George. For some reason, Kitty is under the impression she used a love potion on him...and... well, they're off to Vegas to get hitched."

Everyone looked shocked. We all knew the law. This was deep shit for Lydia—if it was true.

Fitz bit his lip and looked sour. I could easily imagine what he was thinking.

"Who's George?" Ed asked.

"My boss, well, my ex-boss—a miserable excuse for a man who preys upon vulnerable women."

"I couldn't agree more," Fitz said. "I know him. He lived up this way for a while, but possibly before your time, I don't know. He's a nasty piece of work."

"Oh, for Gaia's sake, why is Lydia always so stupid?" Ed asked. "Doesn't she know it's against the law to use a love potion to induce marriage? They're as bad as roofies. She'll get us all shunned. The first whiff of Hag trouble, and they'll treat the whole family like pariahs."

"Hey, she's not stupid," I said. "She's just led by her heart. Lord, I hope she's okay. Anyway, it doesn't matter if Lydia knows the law or not. George will. He's a lawyer, for fae's sake! If Kitty's right, Lydia's going to be in deep trouble. Shit, she's still underage, so our whole family could be ruined."

"Has anyone tried to stop her?" Ed asked.

"No," I said, shaking my head. "It looks like no one knows where she is. They were hoping I would know, since he's my boss, well, my former boss, but really, I don't have the faintest clue."

Bri shook her head. "Maybe George isn't so bad? Maybe we could remind him she's so very young and doesn't know any better? Perhaps he won't press charges against her."

This time Fitz shook his head. "I wouldn't put your hopes into it. I know George better than anyone; he loves money above all things, and your sister just put a slam-dunk case for damages right into his lap. He would be well within his rights to take your whole family for everything, and believe me, if he can, he will."

"This all assumes my family are right about the love potion," I reasoned. "Kitty could be wrong after all. I wouldn't put it past him to lure Lydia to Vegas with sweet talk. I mean, she's an attractive girl—with assets —and he has recently been dumped. Kitty might have got it backward. If only I was home."

Fitz pushed back his own chair, and his gaze locked on mine. I could see the concern reflected in his.

"If it'll help, I'll book a flight for you so you can shoot straight over to the airport."

Ugh, flying. Really?

Bri squeezed my hand. "I can mix a potion for you, dear. It will take the edge off your fear, and the flying won't be so bad, I promise."

Well, this was an emergency. I didn't like it, but what choice did I have?

"That's very kind," I said. My heart sank. Fitz was no longer looking me in the eye. I wished I knew what he was thinking. If Kitty was right, would he shun us too?

Out of the corner of my eye, I could see the pretty little fae, hovering a few feet away from our table. No doubt she was wondering what was going on.

"I'm terribly sorry," I said to her. "But something just came up, family emergency. No one's hurt or anything, but we have to leave now."

"Oh, that's awful. I hope everything's okay. Don't worry about your table, and I hope to see you here again soon. Please take care."

Ed waited for Bri to get up and then ushered her ahead of him over to the exit. Fitz remained at the table, frantically typing into his phone.

"There are two direct flights out tonight," he said at last. "You'd have to hurry if you were going to make the first one. The second leaves around midnight. You could make that one in good time."

I turned to Bri. "How quickly could you mix up that potion?"

"It just takes a few minutes. No time at all really."

"If you could put me on the first flight possible, I would appreciate it," I said to Fitz. "The sooner I get back home, the sooner I can try to track them down."

"It will be difficult to track them down if they don't want to be found, but I have contacts in Vegas. I'll ask them to keep their eyes, and their orbs, open." Fitz punched one last thing into his phone and looked up at me. "There. You're all set. I'll just text you the details now. Let me drive you to the airport."

"Err, no, I mean, thank you. That's very kind, but I have a rental car to return. I'd better drive myself."

"As you wish, but you've no time to waste," Fitz said. "Come on then." He waited for me to pass and followed close behind me. I was conscious his hands weren't seeking mine now. Once we joined Ed and Bri outside the restaurant, he turned and looked over to the taxi rank.

"You guys get going. I can make my own way home."

"Are you sure?" Ed asked. "I don't mind dropping you off."

Fitz smiled gently at me. "You don't have much time." And then he took my hand and squeezed it softly. "I'm sorry. I really am. If only..."

He didn't finish what he was going to say. I didn't want to know how that sentence ended. Oh boy, life could be so cruel. Just a few hours earlier, how different things had seemed. I looked sadly down at our hands. This could potentially be our last contact ever. I didn't want to think about it anymore, so I nodded, and without even thinking to thank him for the flight he'd just bought for me, I slipped into the back seat of my aunt's car.

Lydia. Stupid, stupid Lydia. What had she done? And then my uncle turned on the ignition, and we were leaving The Bug and Black Bat behind. I didn't look back over my shoulder, I knew Fitz would be standing there, watching. Right now, I didn't think I could bear to see his disappointment. *Damn you, Lydia. And George. Damn you, too!*

Chapter Thirty

NO NEWS

I'D BEEN SCRYING WITH OUR NEW ORB, THANK GAIA JANE HAD THE sense to buy one, and had been trying to track Lydia down or at least pick up her trail, but with no luck whatsoever. In the end, Jane had pulled me off, worried I'd been staring into it for too long.

She was right to. My head was spinning, and we were all out of headache potion, so I went down to the kitchen to cook up a new batch.

Mom was whining so loudly it was almost impossible to think. She kept pacing the kitchen, throwing her hands up in the air, blaming everything but Lydia for this unfortunate turn of events.

"Ugh," she cried. "I took twice as much Xanax, and it's not done me a bit of good. Oh Izzy, is that a headache potion you're making?"

I nodded.

"Good. Make some extra for me because I know I shan't sleep a wink until we hear from my baby girl! Ugh, that dreadful, dreadful man. This will be all his fault, you know. My dear, sweet little girl wouldn't have dreamed of anything like this if he hadn't encouraged her. Poor Lydia! I can hardly bear to think of all our neighbors talking about her. Oh, well, how long will you be with that potion? Oh, how my head hurts!"

Kitty, who had known something of Lydia's scheme, sat sullenly in the kitchen window, staring outside and pulling what we all called *the face*. Dad had grounded her, and she had nothing but his reprimands and our Mom's tantrums for company.

"Look, are you really sure about that potion?" I asked her.

Kitty rolled her somewhat reddened eyes. "I told you all for the one-hundredth time, *yes*. It was supposed to be a joke. Maria Lucas made a pot of the stuff, and Lydia asked for some so she could try it out on George."

"I called Maria myself," Jane said. "She did indeed give her some of it."

"But was it any good?" I said. "As I recall, Charlotte's sister couldn't make a decent pot of tea, let alone a potent love potion."

"It did nothing for Freddy Stone," Kitty said. "And he downed half a cup of it."

"Kitty! You used some, too?" I gasped.

"Oh, it's okay," Kitty reasoned. "I had no intention of marrying him. I just wanted to see how he'd react."

I rolled my eyes in despair, wondering if either of my sisters had half a brain between them.

"I don't suppose potency matters anyway. If George has a mind to say it worked on him, Lydia's screwed anyway."

Mary had put down her Kindle and was listening intently.

"Did she say anything to you?" I asked.

Mary scoffed. "Like when does she ever?"

I scowled at her.

Mary half shrugged. "No. She said nothing to me. I guess you had no luck with the orb?"

I shook my head and started on my potion, just as the phone rang. Jane, who was closest, answered it. From what I gathered, she'd already called everyone on her contacts list, but no one had seen or heard from either Lydia or George. Maybe someone had thought of something to help us, so I was all ears.

Jane lowered the phone to her lap, and gazed at me in despair.

I stopped stirring my potion and looked over.

"That was Billy," Jane said.

"Ugh." I picked up my lavender oil and poured three drops into my cauldron. "What did he want?"

"He said we were not to lose hope, but if the allegations prove true, the bank could foreclose on the mortgage. He said that might be a blessing in disguise, because he knows a property developer who would pay a good price for the lot. The numpies are short on housing, and he says they'd pay top dollar for it."

"Did he indeed?" I wanted to reach down the phone and throttle him.

"Yes." Jane pulled a funny face, and I knew there was more.

"What else did he say?"

"Um, only that after all this blows over, if Dad survives the worst of it, we might be able to find a small place to settle out in Birchwood, Ohio. He said he'd help us find somewhere, um, suitable, and since no one would know us there, we'd be able to carry on with our lives, as if nothing had happened."

If steam could come out of my ears, I'd be whistling. "Screw Billy. Trust him to use this to try to turn a deal."

"Well, Lydia may have just handed us to him on a plate."

"Look, George is a dick. Chances are he's as guilty as she is, if she's guilty at all. Let's all calm the fae down, wait until they're discovered, and then find out what really happened directly from them. It might all prove to be nothing after all. Maybe, Kitty got it all backward or something."

"Wouldn't be the first time." Jane managed a weak smile.

"Exactly. Everyone's jumping the gun, and it just isn't helping."

Jane nodded. "So what do you propose we do?"

"Well, when I go into work tomorrow morning, I can make a few discreet inquiries. I mean, George might be a partner, but he probably has to check in with someone, right? Or maybe Mary King knows something? I'll ask her."

"As long as you don't get into trouble."

"I won't. I won't do anything I shouldn't. They've been good to me at the firm, and the last thing I want is to get into trouble with the Hags myself. One sister facing Bitterhold is quite enough, don't you think?"

"Sure. In the meantime, I'm going to call everyone I know again. Sooner or later, someone will hear something, surely."

I wasn't so sure, but if making those calls made Jane feel any better, then I was hardly going to object.

I stared ahead at Dad's door. I needed to speak with him, yet right now, I dreaded facing him. I knew he'd be beating himself up for letting Lydia leave us in the first place.

I lowered my voice. "How's Dad been?"

Jane grimaced and was about to answer when the door to the annex opened and Dad came out. The last few hours had aged him considerably. He stared straight at me and turned his head, motioning for me to come over.

Jane jumped in to take over stirring the potion, and I followed him into his annex. I closed the door quietly behind me and perched my backside on the window ledge, waiting for him to talk.

Dad rubbed his chin and sat down. "Thank you for not saying I told you so."

I would have contradicted him, but Dad anticipated that and raised his hand.

"It's okay, Izzy. I'm a big boy. When I'm wrong, I'm happy to admit it. I just wish I didn't have to. Anyway, Gaia knows I can ill-afford the flight, but I've booked myself to go out to Vegas. I would take you with me, but I'd feel better knowing I was leaving at least one person with a brain behind."

"I can help with the flight if you need me too," I volunteered.

"Thank you, but no. I've accepted enough of your help as it is. It's time I did something for myself. I am supposed to be the responsible one, after all."

"But would you even know where to begin?" I argued. "I mean, they could be anywhere."

"True, but I have to do *something*. It's my fault Lydia is the way she is. I've been too free and cavalier in raising her. I should have been stricter and set a few more rules. Ah well, as they say, you reap what you sow."

"Jeez, Dad, don't be so hard on yourself," I said. "You raised us just fine. You couldn't possibly have foreseen this. And like I was telling Jane, we don't even know if what Kitty said is true. She could be wrong, and everything could still turn out just fine."

Dad picked up a piece of paper and stared at it. "Think that, if it brings you comfort, Izzy, but the harpies are already swarming."

He handed the piece of paper to me. I gasped. I knew by the orange hat on the letterhead who had sent it.

"How do the Hags know already?"

"Who knows?" Dad said. "But they want me to go in for questioning. I haven't told your mom yet. Gaia knows she's distressed enough as it is. They want to see me first thing, so once that's done, I'll be off to the airport. You can keep an eye on things here, and I'll call as soon as I find anything out."

"Okay. But call me before you board." I didn't want to say that I was afraid the Hags might detain him. Instead I said, "I'll be asking around at the office tomorrow. They might have heard from George."

Dad nodded. Dark circles had formed under his eyes—he looked so beaten and tired, and I wanted to hug him and tell him everything would be okay, but we'd both know that would be a lie.

"I'd better get back and finish my potion," I said.

"Yes, indeed," Dad replied. "I hope you made a lot of it. I have a feeling we're going to need it."

Closing the door softly behind me, I went back to stirring the spell pot. Jane gave me back the spoon. This was such a dreadful business. And as my mother wailed like a banshee, I thought of the quiet, dignified man on the other side of the wall, and something broke in me, and I wanted to cry.

I was scarcely out of the elevator when Mary came scuttling along the hall and accosted me.

"Mr. Lowe has been asking for you," she said. Her face was an odd mixture of triumph, concern, and glee. Two out of the three were genuine enough. "He said to tell you to go into his office as soon as you got in."

"Thanks," I said. I tried to sound nonchalant, though I knew it was pointless. By now everyone in Misty Cedars would have heard about Lydia and George, and the community juries would be gleefully hanging our reputations over the nearest trees.

Let them. Right about now, Dad would be with the Hags. I had more important things to worry about than the local jungle drums.

"I wonder what it's about," Mary said. She bit her lip to hide a smile.

"I can't imagine." I bit mine to stop myself from biting her. "I guess I'll know soon enough."

I dropped my things off at my desk and marched straight to his office. If the ax was going to fall, I might as well get it over with quickly.

Mr. Lowe's door was closed, so I knocked a couple of times and waited. "Come in," he said.

I took a deep breath and opened the door.

Mr. Lowe was sitting behind his desk, and the large, purple orbuculum he usually kept in his barrister's bookcase was on the desk in front of him. I stared at it ominously. Was I about to be subjected to a lie detector test? I couldn't think what that would achieve, but Mr. Lowe was a smart man, and I knew better than to go on the defensive with him.

"Close the door and have a seat," he said politely, ushering me into the chair in front of his desk.

I did as I was told. Turning, I saw Mary straining in her chair to watch us from her cubicle. I smiled at her as I closed the door and then walked over and sat down.

"I won't beat about the bush," Mr. Lowe said. "It has come to my attention that your family are experiencing some, shall we say, difficulties?"

I didn't dare ask him who had told him.

"Anyway, our mutual friend suggested I may be able to help."

Mr. Lowe pointed to the large orbuculum in front of him. "Naturally you know what this is, but I suspect you don't know everything my crystal ball can do."

I shook my head, a little wrong-footed by the direction of this conversation.

"No, sir, I'm afraid I don't."

"You are, I believe, aware that it's impossible to locate a witch or warlock concealed by an obscurity charm?"

"Yes, sir." Dammit, no wonder I'd gotten a headache trying to find them with my orb. I should have guessed that was what was blocking me.

"Of course. But what you might not know is the charm cannot project into the future."

"I'm not sure I follow," I said.

"Let's just say, should, um, subject G or subject L do something in the future, someone with the power of divination, say, might be able to detect where they *will* be, even if they can't see where they *are* in the present. Obscurity charms have no power on the future."

"I think I understand you..."

Mr. Lowe's tone remained patient. "Let me put a simple case to you.

Imagine subject G, or subject L, planned to be married in a paranormal chapel in Vegas tomorrow afternoon. Pure speculation, of course. No witch or wizard would see the wedding as it happened, unless, of course, they were actually there. But my orbuculum might see them, since the obscurity charm only has power over the moment it's protecting."

"So you're telling me it's possible to find Geor—G and L in the future, if we knew where to look?"

"Exactly so. Anyway, our, umm—shall we call him mutual friend?—made a few phone calls to Nevada chapels and narrowed the search down to three possible sites. And then he called me and asked me to help, as he's a long way from consulting his own crystal ball. So what do you say to a little wedding crashing this morning?"

I was just wondering—and half hoping—about who this mutual friend might be, when Mr. Lowe opened his hand over the sphere, and I spotted a rather expensive-looking ornamental silver skull ring on his pinky. I recognized it at once. It was the same ring Fitz wore. It had to be him. Fitz was helping us! I knew I had seen Fitz's ring some place before!

I couldn't help grinning and nodded like an idiot. Then I concentrated and stared hard inside the purple ball.

At first there was nothing but a thick, purple fog, but then the image began to clear, and some shapes began to form. After a moment, I realized I was looking inside a pure white room, with a purple carpet boasting a white pentagram in its center.

For a few seconds, nothing happened, but then a funny little man dressed like the Wizard of Oz walked into the room, and he stood at the edge of the pentagram. A series of tacky red electric candles flashed on, and an organ played the theme tune to *The Addams Family*.

"Could be worse," I suggested.

"If you say so," Mr. Lowe said, grimacing. "Though I can't imagine how."

"Could be a fake Elvis."

We shared a chuckle and then both continued to watch the ball.

A moment later, George walked into the chapel. Bingo! Mr. Lowe had lucked out on his first go, though I strongly suspected that more than luck was in play today.

"You found them!" I cried.

"Keep watching," Mr. Lowe said.

Next, I noticed that George walked in an odd, stiff way, like he was in a trance or something. However, whenever the funny Oz man had his back to him, he seemed to relax a little. And then my goofy sister walked into the room.

Lydia was wearing an off-the-rack, inexpensive white gown that she'd probably rented for an hour from some store on the strip. Her mop of hair was piled very prettily on her head, and she carried a neat little purple posy in both hands. She was grinning from ear to ear. It was clear to me that at least she was serious about this marriage, whatever people might choose to say later.

I noticed that in contrast, whenever she caught George's eye, George appeared totally normal, as if he wasn't under the influence of magic at all.

He was faking it, and I knew it. I had a strong suspicion George knew the same development company our cousin Billy did. *The bastards!*

"You said three possible sites. Which is this one?"

"I believe this is the Little Witch Chapel, although you'd better look it up to be sure. As I recall, the, um, Wizard works exclusively at that site, whereas Merlin and Sabrina are contracted to multiple chapels. You're lucky. This makes your task simpler."

I could have kissed my boss, old and wrinkly as he was. But then a thought occurred to me. George was a partner here, after all. It would have made more sense if Mr. Lowe had tried to hush this up. Yet he was helping me.

"Um, I was just wondering..."

Mr. Lowe raised a hand. "There are few things in this world I can't abide," he said. "And one of them is being hoodwinked. I wish you every success with your venture, Miss Bennet, and if I were you, I'd get a move on. I believe this event is scheduled for tomorrow morning. And as ever, that clock is still ticking. Take a day off. In fact, take two if you need it. Just get going, and good luck to you."

As I stood up to thank him, the image in the orbuculum began to fade, obscured by the purple fog that soon engulfed it.

Mr. Lowe smiled a rare smile and waved me off.

"Thanks, Mr. Lowe. You're a sweetie."

My heart racing, I snatched up my purse and ran to the elevator, ignoring Mary's astonished look. On the way down, I called Dad on my cell phone. He'd probably left the Hags by now, but if I hurried, I might be able to catch him before he boarded. If I did, then perhaps I could go with him. Screw my fear of flying. There was still a drop of Bri's potion I could chug, and it would be totally worth it.

All I knew was if we stopped the wedding, there was a chance Lydia and Dad would be out of trouble. But first we had to find them.

Chapter Thirty-One

THE LITTLE WITCH CHAPEL

I HAD NEVER FLOWN TO THE OTHER SIDE OF THE COUNTRY. MY GENERAL dislike of heights kept my feet firmly rooted to the ground, but this was an emergency, and I still had a fair amount of Auntie Bri's chill potion in my purse. The caramel-flavored liquid had taken the edge off my fear and made the whole thing bearable.

Jane had wanted to come with us, but we just couldn't afford the extra ticket. I left with a thousand assurances that I would let her know as soon as we found Lydia and George.

Once the seat belt signs were off, we were free to retrieve our luggage from the overhead bins. I was still a little dopey from the potion, so Dad reached up and collected my carry-on for me.

I watched as each passenger stepped off the plane. A tall, dark-haired airport official flourished a copper wand before each of us.

"What is she doing?" I asked.

There was a short werewolf in front of us. He was exceptionally hairy, probably because last night was a full moon. I looked down at his fingernails, which were pretty dark, confirming my suspicions.

He turned around. He carried a well-worn leather carry-on bag over his shoulder, and I suspected he visited Vegas a lot. "She's checking for gambling charms and cheats. They're funny about magic here—

understandably." He kept looking at his watch. "By Gaia, I hate lines, don't you?"

"What happens if you're caught cheating?" Dad asked. "Do you get thrown into Bitterhold?"

The were's frown broadened. "Oh, they have much, much worse things than the Hags out here. Trust me, you don't want to find out what I'm talking about. Play nicely and they leave you alone. Step over the line..." He drew a finger line across his own throat.

I got the message.

The next passenger off the plane wore a long, black shroud and put me in mind of the grim reaper. He had passed my seat just the once during the flight, but even then, his austere presence had given me the willies. I couldn't see his face as he kept the hood closed, and his aura was a strange murky gray. I wondered what that meant.

The tall man didn't object to the copper wand as it approached his face. In fact, he barely reacted at all.

"Raise your arms," the official said.

The tall man did as he was asked, and his sleeve slid down, just a fraction. His hand and wrist were misshapen and unusually thin for a person of his stature. The official waved him on, and the strange man left the plane.

"You see all sorts in Vegas," the were said. "Um, are you here for business or pleasure?"

"Neither. I'm here to stop a wedding. My sister's."

"Ha, that's one I haven't heard before. Oh, look, do me a favor, will you? Would you mind holding onto my bag while I go back and use the bathroom? I should have gone earlier. I'll meet you out there in the terminal. Don't worry, I'll find you."

He held his bag out to me as if it were the most natural request in the world. Did he think I'd been born yesterday?

"Sorry, I'm allergic to leather. Guess you'll have to take it with you."

The were scowled but was pushed forward by the other passengers, all eager to get off the plane.

"Hey now, just wait a—"

He almost fell in front of the official, who immediately waved her wand over him. The tip suddenly glowed red, and two Hags came out of nowhere and grabbed him by the arms.

"Wait a minute, that's probably just my lucky dice," the were cried. "Have a look in my bag, you'll see what I'm talking about."

One of the Hags mumbled something, and I heard an exasperated, "No, of course I didn't plan to use them. They're a present—from a friend—"

I didn't hear the rest of it. I glanced at Dad, who exchanged a frightened glance. Sometime soon that might be Lydia. Or us.

The airport was buzzing with tourists and slot machines. Another time I might have slowed down to explore, but not today. Lydia might be married at any moment, and if we missed her by just a few seconds, I would never forgive myself. And neither would Dad.

We headed straight for the taxi rank, and I thanked Gaia there wasn't much of a line.

The taxi driver was a rather rough-looking elf, which was still pretty good-looking as elves went. His dark eyes suggested a lot of late nights behind the wheel, but elf drivers were famous for their quick reflexes and light foot—which made them excellent drivers in an emergency situation. Most of the ambulance drivers in Misty Cedars were elves. The license in his cab read Aloysius Riverdale.

"Where to?" Aloysius hit the meter, which started spinning at once.

"The Little Witch Chapel. Do you know it, Alo, All...?"

Before he answered, Aloysius spun the taxi out of the rank and went zipping along the road, weaving in and out of the heavy tourist traffic like a pro. "Sure, I know it. And just call me Al. Everyone else does."

Thank Gaia for that, I thought.

"So," Al said, as he swerved to avoid a mile-long limousine. "You two getting hitched then?"

Dad chuckled. "I should be so lucky. Izzy is my daughter."

"Oh!" Al said, sitting up more pertly in the driver's seat. "Well, if you need someone to show you the city, hell, baby, I'm your elf!"

"Um, perhaps another time." I had no idea where The Little Witch Chapel was, but I kept looking out of the window, expecting it to pop up any moment.

Al pulled off the main strip and drove us up some long back road. Just as I was beginning to think he was taking us the scenic route, he pulled onto a ramp and started zipping past some of the older casinos. The place certainly had atmosphere. All that was missing was Frank Sinatra and Dean Martin and the Rat Pack.

"Is it far?" I asked. "We're in a bit of a hurry."

"Don't you worry," Al said. "I'll get you to the church on time." He cackled at his own joke.

He pulled down a side street, and a second later, he had us in front of a rather boring looking building that could have been anything, a pet store, a gun shop, or maybe just a plain old-fashioned warehouse. It was nothing like I imagined a wedding chapel would look. There were a few other cars in the parking lot, but nothing else.

"Is this it?" I asked.

"If you're looking for The Little Witch Chapel, it is. And it looks like someone's about to get spliced."

"How can you tell?"

Al pointed to a red light over the door that had begun to flash. "Show time." He pointed to his meter. "I can keep your tab running if you like?"

"Oh Gaia, Dad, you get it. Let me get inside."

While Dad fumbled for his credit card, I scrambled for the passenger door and made a beeline for the entrance.

I opened the door, and there were several paras sitting or standing in the lobby, waiting for their turn. There was a long glass counter, full of last minute gifts, such as wedding albums, cheap rings, and bubble-blowers. The whole place was decorated in tacky shades of pink, from the painted walls to the shag pile carpet. I saw all this in an instant, but what I didn't see was either Lydia or George.

"Where are the weddings?" I cried.

Everyone turned to look at me, and a small fae carrying a purple posy just like Lydia's pointed to a door near the back of the lobby. I ran straight to it.

"Wait, you can't go back there! There's a wedding in progress!"

I ignored the somewhat portly fairy with a half-broken wing behind the counter and ran over to the door. I prayed it was my sister on the other side, fearful I might already be too late, and just as worried it wouldn't be them and I was about to barge into some poor stranger's wedding.

There was nothing I could do about that now. I burst open the door and was taken aback by the surprisingly beautiful chamber in front of me. Pretty little purple butterflies and fireflies danced over an ornate silver arch, and a tall wizard, dressed like the Wizard of Oz, presided over the wedding. And there, standing on either side of the pentagon, dressed just as I'd seen them in Mr. Lowe's orbuculum, were Lydia and George.

"Holy Gaia, what are you doing here?" Lydia gasped. "I told Kitty not to tell anyone. This was supposed to be a surprise."

George looked an odd mixture of surprise, anger, and frustration. He did not, however, look like he was under the influence of any potion.

"Am I too late?" I gasped.

"No, I suppose not." Lydia pouted. "You can be my bridesmaid if you like. We're about to get started, but really, I wish you'd picked something more suitable to wear."

"Shall we continue?" the wizard asked.

"This wedding cannot go on," I said. "My sister administered a love potion—the groom has not given his legal consent."

"Oh, we don't care about that sort of thing here in Vegas," said the wizard, reopening his service book. "What happens in Vegas, stays in Vegas."

"Maybe not here, but it matters in the rest of the country. How could you be so naïve?"

"Oh that? Really, Izzy, it was a bit of fun. That stuff just gives you a warm tinkle. It's not a real love potion, even George knows that. He drank it quite willingly, you know."

"You silly, silly girl! You have no idea what you've done!"

At that moment, Dad caught up with us. When Lydia saw how angry Dad looked, some of the bravado left her face, and she became rather coy. George attempted to blend back into the shadows. He glared at me, unable to hide his anger.

"Are we too late?" He gasped. "Did they do it?"

"No," I replied. "But we were just in time though."

The chubby fairy from the lobby now joined us. "What the heck is going on?" she asked. "You people have no right to be here. This is a private wedding."

"We're relatives of the...bride," I said, nodding to Lydia. "But the wedding can't go on. The groom has been given a love potion."

"Well, give him an antidote and see if he still wants to continue. We sell them behind the counter, you know, at a very reasonable rate." With one sweep of her arm, she conjured a dozen vials filled with colored liquids that floated in the air, inviting us to select one.

Lydia looked hopefully across to George, but if anything, George backed farther into the shadows.

"George?" Lydia said.

But George walked around the edge of the room, and as he reached us, he shot me another ugly glare.

"Why is everything always about you?" And without so much as a glance back at my sister, he stormed from the chapel, leaving us all to sort out his mess by ourselves.

Lydia stamped her foot and cried, "NOW look what you've done! You are the worst sister ever!" And then she ran after George, crying his name. I caught her just as she reached me, and she slumped and burst into a fit of tears.

Chapter Thirty-Two

RSVP

I TOOK ADVANTAGE OF MR. LOWE'S OFFER AND CHOSE NOT TO GO INTO work in the morning. I rolled over in bed and stared blankly up at the ceiling. The second dose of potion had left me drowsy, but better that than deal with my anxiety on the plane.

On the upside, it had helped drown out Lydia's endless whining, who even now still failed to see how anything she had done had been wrong.

I suspected that Dad would be devoting the rest of his life to teaching her the errors of her ways. Good. It was about time someone reined in my wayward sister. I don't think she realized how close she'd come to a spell in Bitterhold. Not even now, when both Dad and I had been going on at her for almost a day, and after he'd banned all concerts, parties, and most things nonfamily related for the foreseeable future. She'd squirmed, squealed, and objected, but most of all, I got the feeling we were boring her.

I closed my eyes but found it hard to find peace. Perhaps we had saved Lydia, but at what cost? Oh Gaia, I was so conflicted. Fitz had probably saved us from total ruin, but he was still the asshole who'd destroyed Jane's hopes of happiness, and how could I forgive him for that? Ever? And even if I could, would he even look at me now? He had no love for my family, that was obvious, and this latest escapade would hardly endear him to us now, even if we had dodged a shunning.

Oh, for the love of pixies, why did I even care? I had spurned him once, and thought it all over, yet every time I'd convinced myself I had no feelings for him, his face popped back into my head. Now which sister was being foolish? I felt like I didn't know myself at all.

I pulled a pillow over my face and growled into it.

"Is this a bad time?"

I pulled off the pillow to see Jane standing in my bedroom door.

"You not going into work either today?" I asked.

"No. I had a day off. You taking a sickie?"

"Something like that. The flight potion knocked me out. I'll be all right in a bit."

Jane perched on the end of my bed and handed me a small white envelope.

"That just came for you," she said.

I sat up and turned the envelope over in my hand. It felt silky, very expensive, and the handwriting was unfamiliar to me. The style was very old-fashioned and very beautiful. I had no idea who had sent it.

I sniffed it, and it had an earthy smell to it. Curious, I ran my finger along the top and opened it. Inside was a single card, with a silver rim and very similar, elegant writing.

"Oh. It's a wedding invitation," I said.

"Who's it from?" Jane asked.

"Matthew and Octavia. From Rosings Park."

"Oh?" It took a moment for Jane to realize who they were, but then she smiled.

"Well, that must be a relief," she said.

"It's certainly better than the alternative," I agreed. I stared at the date. "They're getting hitched next week. They're not wasting any time, that's for sure."

"Why would they?" Jane mused. "From what you told me, she's been waiting long enough."

I nodded. Matthew and Octavia, eh? Well, that was a surprise for sure. I thought about Goody. Their love had been such a long time ago. Perhaps this was what she had wanted all along. I found myself itching to commune with her, to see if she was at peace, or if this new development would only bring her further torment. If that were true, perhaps it would be best to let sleeping ghosts lie?

Once again, my thoughts returned to Fitz and his gift for channeling the dead.

"Are you going to go?" Jane asked.

"Sure. I mean, I've never been to a vampire wedding before. It might be fun. I wonder what they'll be serving for supper?"

"Just make sure you stay off the menu."

I laughed. "I don't think they would eat their own wedding guests. Matthew at least would consider that most impolite."

I noted the ceremony was scheduled for midnight and was to be held at St. Judes, an unconsecrated church on the outskirts of Misty Cedars.

"Grab me a pen," I said. "Might as well respond now."

Jane picked one up off my dresser and handed it to me.

"It says *and guest*. Do you want to come with me?"

"Sure, if you want me to. I'm not that keen on being up so late, but if you want someone to go with, that's fine."

I marked guest plus one on the RSVP, then kicked myself off the bed, and pulled on a sweater and some jeans.

"You going out?" Jane asked.

"Just for a walk. I need to stretch my legs."

"Okay. Well, I'm off to feed the chickens. I'll see you when I get back."

I could just as easily have popped the card in the mailbox, but I needed to clear my head. The post office was a short walk from home, and it looked nice outside, so I thought why not? I brushed my teeth and fixed my hair before going down.

Downstairs, Lydia was with Mom in the kitchen. Mom was simpering and cooing over her darling girl, but Lydia was peevish and only scowled in return. Kitty and Mary were probably out somewhere.

Lydia shot me a nasty glare as I passed by, but I didn't rise to the challenge. She could sulk all she wanted to. Though she'd protested her love for George all the way on the flight home, I knew he hadn't written to her, or texted her, or made one overture of love since he'd abandoned her at the altar. Maybe in time she would come to forgive me, maybe not, but it didn't matter one iota. I had done the right thing. For everyone. Including her, whether she saw it or not.

I grabbed one of Jane's cookies off the counter and held my head high as I left her to Mom's fussing. Neither of them said a word to me directly. I didn't care.

"Isn't is great to live here in this nice house, with a roof over our heads? Yeah, it really is. Don't you agree, Lydia?"

I closed the door behind me, setting out on foot, basking in the glorious sunshine and trying desperately hard not to think of Fitz as I walked off our drive and into the street. I wasn't thinking of him at all as I waved to some of the neighbors, or as I passed people walking their dogs.

Strewth, this was annoying. I couldn't function with him always in my head. There had to be a way to rout Fitz out of there, before he drove me insane. What I needed was a distraction. Not that I hadn't had plenty of late, but I desperately needed a new one.

Surely, he had to be responsible for Lydia's timely rescue. I couldn't think of anyone else who would even bother. I mean, the band liked her, but what would an eloping groupie be to them? They would probably say she'd been far out for attempting it. It had to be a coven thing. That ring was too much of a coincidence. Maybe this was Fitz's way of saying he was sorry. Or maybe it meant something else? Maybe I should call him and ask? But what if I was wrong? Gaia, my head was spinning just thinking about it all.

There was a line at the post office, but since I didn't have to wait to post a single letter, I walked around them all and dropped my reply into the mail slot. When I turned, I was surprised to see Charlotte had walked into the post office, a worried look on her face.

"Hey, Charlotte, what's up?" I asked.

She bit her lip and looked down at her feet. Shit. This must be serious. She was carrying a copy of the *Misty Cedar's Times* in her hand and, frowning, handed the newspaper over to me.

"You might as well hear about it now, since you'll hear it sooner or later, I'm sure."

"I don't understand," I said.

"Second page. Just look."

Confused, I opened the newspaper but didn't have to scour the headlines. There was a picture of George in the center of the page and another, smaller picture of Billy at the bottom of the article. The photographer had chosen the most unflattering shots imaginable. The two men looked anything like their usual professional selves. Instead, they looked suspicious and shifty, and I looked up at Charlotte, perplexed.

"Read it," she said.

I scanned the article.

Following an anonymous tip-off, George Wickham, recently dismissed partner from the reputable law firm, Lowe and Wyatt, is wanted for questioning by the Witchfinder Financial Regulator on several counts of investment fraud. Our source, a former client and upstanding member of the paranormal community, has provided irrefutable evidence, citing a number of counts of embezzlement and misrepresentation.

His accomplice, Mr. William Collins, once esteemed Bank Manager of Misty Cedars Banking and Loan, has been reprimanded and is currently being questioned by The Hags in connection with this matter. Our source says there are potential misdealings from that establishment, dating back as far as the seventeenth century.

If the allegations are proved correct, a spokesperson for the bank has indicated they will make good on any investors who were innocently bamboozled by these schemes. There is no word on the current whereabouts of George Wickham, although a former girlfriend has indicated he is also being tracked down by his abandoned Golem, who may have a different kind of justice in mind. The seven-foot giant was last seen in a gray coat with a hood, outside The Little Witch Chapel in Vegas. This newspaper is offering a reward to anyone with fresh information on this matter.

As ever, we will endeavor to bring you the latest as it happens...

I hadn't realized my mouth was wide open. "Are you kidding me?" I said. "Is this for real?"

"I don't think they would print it if it wasn't." Charlotte couldn't have looked glummer. "The Hags came for Billy late last night." She lowered her eyes. "The saddest thing is he didn't even try to deny it. He just looked at me, and I knew. Anyway, I saw you come in here, and I thought well, you might as well hear it from me as anyone."

I gave her arm a gentle squeeze. "None of this is your fault," I said. "You couldn't possibly have known—how could you?"

"No, I know, but people will think I did. I'm gonna have to leave town, I'm sure."

"Oh, come on, you only just met him. No one's going to think you knew what he was up to. This has been going on for years. Shake those thoughts away, sweetie."

Charlotte was famous for her level-headedness, so seeing her so close to tears like this was heartbreaking.

"Everybody knows you. They'll know you had nothing to do with it. People will be kind, you'll see."

"Will they?" Charlotte didn't look so sure.

I handed her back her paper, noticing for the first time that everyone in the post office was dead silent and were listening in. "Well, it's not like you married him. You could always move back home."

Charlotte didn't look too thrilled at the suggestion.

"Come on, let's get you out of here."

Everyone was staring at us, and my back bristled. My blood was up, and I turned on them all.

"Oh hey, Mr. Mendelson, does your neighbor know you encourage your dog to poop on his lawn? How are you, Mrs. Harrison? Is the secret ingredient you put in your cakes still prune juice? Good to see you, Mr. Richards. Usually I only see your eyes through the gap in the blinds when you watch me walking by your house."

Suddenly everyone's attention was on the counter, as they waited their turn to be served.

Charlotte giggled a little, and I was thankful.

We stepped outside, and I walked along with her for a little while. We were both lost in our separate thoughts. I could guess what she was thinking, though my own musings were on the anonymous informers. For some reason, Matthew's name kept popping into my head. Although the partners had many clients, any of whom could have talked to the press, it was the reference to the seventeenth century that aroused my suspicions. Billy's ancestor, Thackeray Collins, had persecuted Goody Becker, and I couldn't help but make the connection between him and the old vampire. I suspected Matthew was settling old scores and revenging the murder of his beloved Goody at last. Wow, these vampires really knew how to hold a grudge.

As for the second informant, it had to be Mary King. I couldn't prove it, of course, but Mary and George had been intimate, and she might have learned of the Golem through him. All my instincts told me it was Goulding, the same Golem I had read about at work and suspected was on our plane to Vegas. Regardless, nothing would change the fact that George was in deep, deep doo-doo.

Poor George. Golems were single-minded creatures. Once they were set on a task, nothing could stop them from carrying it out. Goulding would follow George relentlessly. One way or another, he'd be looking over his shoulder for the rest of his life.

"I'm sorry if your family were hurt by any of this," Charlotte said. "I've no idea how he embezzled from them, but at least the bank has promised to make good on any losses."

"Yes," I said. "And I know Dad will be thankful for that. Anything they can do will be a big help. It would be nice if my dad didn't have to worry anymore."

We came to a crossroads. Charlotte's home was one way, mine another.

"It's going to be rough, Charlotte, I know," I said. "But you're my friend, and I love you. Nothing Billy or George did is going to change that. Call me or text me, any time you need to talk. Don't be a stranger, okay? And let me know if you need any help moving out."

Charlotte squeezed my hand and smiled. "Thank you. All I can do is take it a day at a time. So mote it be."

She turned, and I watched as she continued along the road. I thought about Billy, and how, in some bizarro parallel universe, I might have been making that same walk to a lonely place. And then I remembered how much he annoyed me, and after shaking my head at such a stupid thought, I turned and headed home.

Chapter Thirty-Three

TEA LEAVES

THINGS WERE LOOKING MUCH SUNNIER NOW. THE BANK HAD WRITTEN to Dad regarding Billy's unprofessional shenanigans and had offered a generous settlement by way of an apology, but there was still one dark cloud of gloom hovering over us, and that was my dear sister's broken heart.

For some time now, Jane had been putting on a brave face. Of course, no one beyond the family would know this—she generally hid her emotions quite well—but we knew the truth. Though weeks had passed since she'd seen Charlie, her spirits remained pretty low. Aside from getting up and going to her daycare job, and coming home every day, she wasn't doing much of anything.

She'd just come out of the shower and was brushing her long, wet hair in her bedroom. I was passing her open room door, when Mom came bounding up the stairs, still in her dressing gown, faster than I'd seen her move in years.

"Oh my word!" she cried. "You'll never guess what I just read on Wartbook."

She bustled me into Jane's bedroom and practically forced me down on the bed, she was flailing so much. Jane put her brush on the dresser and waiting patiently for Mom to speak.

"What is it?" I asked. It had to be something important for her to be lathering herself into such a state. "Somebody die?"

"No, no, no, don't be so morbid, Izzy. No, it's great news, well, good news. My, my, I'm not sure why I'm so flustered since it's nothing to us at all, but oh well, something may come of it. Who knows? It's just a bit of gossip, really."

"What?" Jane and I cried in unison. "What is it?"

"Charlie Van Buren is coming back to Misty Cedars! Tonight! Apparently, he put in a whopper of an order of groceries from Fae Gourmet and renewed his cleaning contracting with Harpy Helpers. Dang, Linda Lucas got the news first and already has more than a hundred likes on her post. Blast. If only I'd heard about it before she did."

I was gobsmacked. Jane, on the other hand, turned in her seat and continued to brush out her hair. Seeing neither of us were as excited as she was, Mom huffed. "Well, I'd better finish getting dressed and get myself into town. I, um, have a bit of shopping to do myself. You sure you don't want to come with?"

I shook my head, and Jane did the same. As soon as Mom left, I shuffled over to the other side of the bed and stared at Jane's reflection. I'm not sure what I expected—a spark of hope, maybe, or a flush of color. If anything, I would have said Jane looked sadder than ever.

"Aren't you a teensy bit excited?" I asked, clasping my forefinger and thumb to make a point.

Jane shook her head. "Why should I be? If he was coming for me, I would have heard first, wouldn't I? But he hasn't called or emailed me or nothing. If anything, this proves that he's not interested at all. At least, that's how I'm reading it. Even Harpy Helpers knew he was coming before I did."

"Oh, I don't know," I reasoned. "Maybe he plans to surprise you. There could be a million and one reasons why he hasn't contacted you yet. And maybe he has. Have you checked your mail this morning?"

"No." Jane picked up her phone and swiped. Then she put it down again and resumed brushing out her hair.

"Well?"

"Nothing. Just as I thought."

"Then screw that guy. He doesn't deserve you." I kissed her on the cheek and left her to mope, since there wasn't much I could do to help.

Perhaps I should go into town with Mom after all. I liked to get my information firsthand, and maybe I could learn something that would cheer Jane up.

"Hold up, Mom," I shouted as I traipsed down the stairs. I'd been right to hurry. Mom had thrown on a multicolored frock and pulled her mop up into an updo. Usually the last to be ready, she wasn't taking any prisoners today.

"Jane not coming?" she asked, looking behind me hopefully.

"Not right now," I said. "Shall we go in my car?"

"If you like, as long as you cleared out the trunk?"

"Yeah, we're good. Come on."

A few minutes later, we were both safely buckled in my old Beetle and were whizzing down the street somewhat over the speed limit. Normally Mom would have chewed me out, but not today. I guess she was as eager for gossip as I was.

"Of course, we have to find a way to get Jane and Charlie together," Mom said. "We'll have to be more forceful this time. They're both a couple of shy bears, and I'm afraid unless my daughter accidentally falls on top of him, I don't think they'll ever move further along."

"Mom!"

"Oh, don't pretend to be all coy, missy. You know as well as I do how all that business works. You guys have the Internet these days. I suspect you know more about it all than I do."

I couldn't help my grin and turned to look out of the window.

I had to admit I felt a little weird. Change was hovering in the air, and I could almost touch it. What it meant, I wasn't sure. I had no gift for divination, but my skin tingled with it. Even the air seemed different.

There was a free parking space right in front of Walbrooks, and Mom jumped out of the car even before I'd put it in park and turned off the engine.

I knew what she was about. She was buddies with Hill, the witch who ran the coffee counter here in the store. They were both members of the local coupon club, and if anything was happening in town, Hill was always the first to hear about it.

Hill was working behind the counter, steaming up a pumpkin latte for a tall wizard with a cart full of goodies. Pumpkin was always in season in Walbrooks, and the air was thick with it.

She grinned at us but carried on serving the man, and I groaned as Mom began foot tapping beside me, afraid the man might take it the wrong way and take offense. I needn't have worried. He paid for his drink and, without a backward glance at us, continued on his way.

"I know why you're here," Hill said, leaning conspiratorially over the counter. "I saw it on Mrs. Lucas's Wartbook post."

"Yes, yes, never mind that," Mom said, irritated. "Just do your thing?"

Hill wasn't bothered at all by Mom's abrasiveness. She grinned and nodded, and reached for a medium-sized mug. I wondered what she planned to do with it, but then she ripped open a tea bag, and then it dawned on me what this was all about. "These aren't the best, but we don't sell loose-leaf here anymore. But this can be just as good. I'll pop an ice cube in it so you can drink it fast."

When the tea was ready, Hill came from around the counter and half sat, half leaned over our table. Her gaze was on the coffee station, in case any new customers arrived. Mom took the cup and took a gentle sip to test the temperature, and reassured it was cool enough, she drained most of the mug in a single chug. When she was done, she slid the mug back toward Hill.

"Well," Mom asked, her knee bouncing wildly under the table like she needed to pee. "What do you see?"

Hill closed her eyes and spun the mug in a single circle, and then she put it down on the table so the leaves could settle. We all huddled in closer, anxious to learn what the leaves would tell.

"Ooh! I see a wedding. And not too far off!"

Mom sat back and clasped her hands together with glee. "I knew it! Gaia be praised, my beautiful Jane will be jumping the broomstick. Ooh, I can't wait to order her a bright-red gown for her coven meetings! Oh, wait until I can tell Linda Lucas. My girl married before her Charlotte! She'll have a fit!"

"Um, you might want to hold up on that order," Hill said. "It's not Jane I'm looking at. It looks like a...vampire union?"

"Wait? What? What are vampires doing in my tea leaves? Shake it up, you're looking into the wrong future."

"Um, no. I mean I don't see you here, but I see one of your daughters." Hill looked directly at me.

"Actually, Mom, I have been invited to a vamp do. But why are the leaves showing that to us? Mom isn't going."

"Doesn't matter," Hill explained. "The leaves show what they want to show. I can't ask for anything specific. It doesn't work that way."

"But what does it mean? How can a vampire wedding affect us, or Jane, even if one of my daughters is on the guest list? Why would it show us that?"

Hill shrugged. "It must have some meaning. I just can't tell you what it is. I can only read what it shows me."

Mom slumped in her seat and picked up the mug. She looked disgusted, and since she didn't have the gift herself, she put it back down and folded her arms. I glanced in the mug also, just in case, but all I could see was Bugs Bunny's head and ears. Freud would have been fascinated.

"Oh well, I suppose I'll have to wait and see what they do next. But someone needs to give those two a little shove, really they do."

Mom reached for her purse, but Hill shook her head. "That one's on the house."

Mom's smile returned. "Thank you. You won't get in trouble, will you?"

"Nah. It's just a tea bag. Those things rip all the time."

We all got up at the same time. "Sorry if it's not what you wanted. We could always do another reading tomorrow? Maybe the leaves will show us something else."

Mom's smile became more natural. "Yes, that's true. Well then, I guess I'll be seeing you tomorrow. All right, Hill. Thanks for taking a look."

"No problem, anytime."

Hill went back to her post behind the counter, and I went off in search of a cart. I was less disappointed in the reading than Mom had been. I had no idea what the tea leaves were saying, but the fact was, I was going to a vampire wedding, and clearly something important was going to happen there. I just had to put my trust in Gaia and let events unfold as they should. Naturally. And then, well, who knew?

Jane was stowing the last items in the refrigerator when we heard a car pull up on the drive outside.

"Are we expecting someone?" I asked no one in particular.

Jane shrugged, Mom shook her head, and Mary didn't look up from her Kindle. "Maybe it's for Lydia or Kitty?" She swiped her page and continued reading.

"Can't be for Lydia, she's grounded until the year 3000," I said.

Jane popped the milk on the bottom level and reached for something else, and I went over to the window. I could not believe my eyes. "Oh, blessed be! I don't believe it!"

"What?" asked Jane.

"It's Charlie. And Fitz!"

The two men were climbing out of Fitz's Bugatti Chiron, looking around and then looking at the house. Charlie said something to Fitz, who nodded. I would have sold my knitting needles to know what they were talking about. I hoped it was Jane. It better be. They both walked to the front door, looking very serious.

Jane froze mid pork chop, but it was Mom who jumped into action when the doorbell rang.

"Oh, leaping leprechauns! Come on, girls, quick. Let's put this stuff away before they see it. They'll think we're a bunch of slobs."

"Don't be silly, Mom," I said. "Everyone has to put groceries away. They know that. Even rich people."

"Maybe, maybe not. You said that Fitz guy is with him?" Mom snorted. "Gaia alone knows what he wants, but whatever. As long as Charlie is here, I'll keep my mouth shut, but I must say, that man pushes all my buttons every time I see him."

"Err, maybe someone could get the door?" Mary said dryly.

"Why don't you?" Mom snapped, as she squeezed a bag of frozen peas into an already overstuffed freezer. "Or is manual labor beneath you?"

Mary slid out of her window seat, and after wriggling her nose at Mom, she sauntered out into the hall. The next few seconds were manic. I had never seen Mom or Jane move so fast, but by the time Charlie and Fitz made it to the kitchen, the place had never looked more organized.

"Well, hello." Mom beamed, pulling out two seats at the kitchen table and ushering the two men into them. "Can I get you something? A cup of tea? Or coffee? If you're hungry, we have plenty in. I could fix you both a sandwich. Anything? Or maybe you'd like something stronger? Oh dear, we don't keep a lot of alcohol in the house, but I'm sure my husband has some sherry or something. He's not at home right now, so I can't ask him, but I'm sure he wouldn't mind."

If there had been a spell to shut Mom up, I'd have used it. When she did finally take a breath, I grabbed the opportunity to step in. "So the magical lure of Misty Cedars just wouldn't leave you alone. Staying long?"

"For a while, I hope," Charlie said.

His attention kept flitting to Jane, but though I could detect she was a little flushed, she kept her eyes downcast. I could only imagine how hard this must be for her.

"Our plans aren't quite settled as yet," Fitz continued. "It's going to depend on the outcome of...some business."

"How are the girls doing?" I asked. "Still partying hard?"

"Caro and Lou chose to stay in New York," Charlie offered. "She said she has, um, allergies."

I bet she does. "Well, it's lovely to see you both," I said, since everyone else apparently had nothing to say. "Perhaps we could all meet up at the Cauldron for some drinks or something?"

Charlie nodded rapidly.

Fitz looked directly toward me. "Yes, we'd like that very much."

For a few seconds, nobody spoke. Desperate to fill the void, Mom stepped forward and violently shook Charlie's hand for no reason at all. "It really is so lovely to see you again. And...err...your friend." She looked Fitz up and down like he was a hissing reptile.

She turned to Jane. "My daughter, Jane, is lovely as ever, don't you think?"

As luck would have it, Jane's natural embarrassment brought a bloom to her cheeks I hadn't seen in weeks. Jane stared at the floor, unable to lift her gaze.

"Um, yes. She looks...err...very beautiful."

Charlie's own blush matched Jane's, and I think if he could, he'd have conjured a hole in the ground to swallow him up.

Another silence.

Fitz leered at Charlie, silently urging him to carry on, but it appeared

Charlie was fresh out of words.

"Well, it was lovely seeing you all," Charlie said at last.

I thought it was a strange thing to say, seeing as they'd both just got here. Even Fitz, normally so on top of things, turned to stare at his friend. Charlie fidgeted with his cuff like a naughty schoolboy caught in the act, and I wondered what the hell was going on.

"Anyway, hopefully, we'll see you all again soon. Bye."

To our astonishment, Charlie marched from the room, and we soon heard his footsteps on the gravel outside.

"Um, excuse me," Fitz said and went after his friend.

"Well, what on earth was that about?" Mom asked as soon as the front door closed.

I raised my eyebrows. "Damned if I know."

We heard a car engine ignite, and I watched from the window as the two men pulled out of our drive.

Jane remained exactly where she was, and turning around, I saw her face had turned so pale now, it was as if she'd been completely drained of blood.

"Are you okay?"

She nodded faintly and then sat down at the table. "I suppose that could have been worse."

"I don't see how," I said, mad as hell at both men for messing her about. Again.

I was about to join her when we heard another car pull back into the drive. I turned to look out of the window again, thinking it might be Dad, but no. It was Charlie and Fitz again.

Charlie still looked nervous, but Fitz towered over him, waving his arms about like a deranged monkey. Something had bothered him. I'd have given anything to hear what was being said, but whatever it was, Charlie didn't appear to like what he was hearing. He kept shaking his head and wandering back and forth. He would take one step to the house and then another back to the car. I watched, incredulous as he did this over and over, clearly unable to make his mind up about what he wanted to do. I hunkered down at the window, desperate to stay out of sight so as not to scare him off.

At last, Charlie nodded and, squaring his shoulders, marched alone to our front door. Fitz returned to his car.

"What the—" I said.

"What?" Jane asked.

Before I could answer, there was a very determined knock at the door. Mary went to open it, and a second later, Charlie was once again in our kitchen, this time looking a hell of a lot more confident than he did before.

"Please, don't say anything, but there is something very important I need to ask. I need to speak to Jane. Alone."

We all stood dumbfounded, but Mom regained her senses first and ushered us all from the kitchen. "Come on, girls. Let's do as he says. Charlie and Jane have some very important things to discuss."

We left them to it, but no sooner did the door close than we all huddled up to the keyhole and listened for all we were worth. I wished I had my wand on me to amplify the sound, but they would have been able to hear it too.

"This is *so* awkward," Charlie said. "You must think I'm a complete idiot for staying away for so long."

To her credit, Jane said nothing, though I wanted to shout "yes, you utter moron" through the kitchen door. But Mom kicked me gently, and I grinned instead.

"My reasons for staying away, well, I won't bore you with the details because they were utterly stupid. But I'm back now, and oh Gaia, I'm making a real hash of this, aren't I?"

Again, Jane did not reply. *Yes, you are,* I mouthed, half laughing. Even Mary managed a snicker.

"The thing is, Jane, darling, well, the truth is, I'm in love with you. Have been since the moment I first saw you. I thought maybe you didn't love me..."

I heard a silly giggle. "Oh, you silly love, I can barely speak I love you so much. Just the same as you, from day one."

I imagined tears in my sister's eyes, and for a moment, there was nothing but silence on the other side of the door. Then Charlie spoke again. "Then you'll marry me?"

I wanted Jane to shout, "Not before you give me a bit more explanation, you asshole!" *You're really letting him get away with that?*

We couldn't hear or see Jane's answer, but things had become awfully quiet on the other side of that door. Then Mary accidentally leaned on the door handle, and we all went tumbling inside the kitchen, almost falling on the floor. Somehow, we all caught ourselves in time.

Jane and Charlie were locked in a tight embrace, and from the tears of joy in her eyes, we didn't need to ask how she'd responded. That, and the flashy diamond on her finger that was large enough to pay for this house.

"Thank Gaia for that!" Mom gasped, holding onto her chest as she tried to breathe. "Any longer, and I'd have had to ask him for you."

Hugs were had all around. My heart danced to see my sister so happy. Her cheeks were flushed again, but this time with joy, and Charlie looked like he'd won the lottery. He was going to marry my sister, so in my book, he just had.

I'd just pulled out of a bear hug with Charlie, when another car pulled into the drive, and I could see this time it was Dad. He stared curiously at the other car in the driveway, but soon came inside to join us. His attention went straight to Jane and Charlie, who were holding hands as if their life depended on it.

"What's all this?" he said. "I'm out of the house for five minutes and come home to madness and mayhem?"

"Don't be silly," Mom said. "Charlie has just proposed to our Jane—isn't it marvelous?"

It was Dad's turn to square his shoulders. "Oh, he has, has he? Well, Charlie, do you think you can just swan in here and whisk my eldest daughter away because you want to? Have you any idea how miserable you've made her these last weeks? I think you've got a damned nerve!"

"But DAAAAAD!"

"Be quiet, Jane. I think this young man has something to say to me, do you not?"

Charlie coughed and, stepping forward, tidied his shirt collar. "I, um, I would like your permission to marry your daughter?"

"Yes? Which one?"

"DAAAAAD!" Jane cried.

"Jane. I would like to marry your daughter—Jane."

"And you think you'd be able to support her in the manner she deserves?"

"I, um, err, that is to say, well, I'd like to think so."

I wanted to laugh but held my tongue. I knew Dad was messing with him, but Charlie didn't. This was too much fun.

"Well then," Dad said. His serious gaze flitted between Charlie and Jane. "It seems my daughter can't be happy without you, so..."

Dad's grin couldn't have been broader. He held out his hand to shake Charlie's. "So welcome to the madness!"

The room burst into excited chattering, and for a moment, everyone was hugging and kissing each other.

"About time," I said to Charlie.

He grinned.

"Well, good news all round then, I suppose," Dad said.

"What's that?" I asked.

"I've just got back from a meeting at the university. They've asked if I could do some freelance work for them. It's all work from home, of course, but they have plenty for me to do."

Dad was beaming as he said this, and I couldn't have been happier for him. This latest news was just pure icing.

"Congratulations," I said. I kissed him on the cheek and gave him a big fat squeeze. My gaze fell on the window. I knew Fitz was sitting in his car outside, and I was just wondering if he was coming in to join our celebrations, when the Bugatti went into reverse and backed out of our drive.

My heart sank. Why was he leaving? I wanted him to come inside, to thank him. I wasn't an idiot. All this good luck wasn't ... falling from the sky into our laps. And no one else had the power to wield it so freely as he did.

Thankfully, everyone was so wrapped up in our good fortune that no one noticed as I slipped off to be alone. Why had Fitz left us, ... as everything was looking so perfect?

He'd said he'd loved me once. Yes, all right, I'd scorned him, twice, but things were different now. I'd changed. But had Fitz changed, too? I crawled up to my room, happy for my sister and Dad, but I felt so lonely on the inside. Had I left everything too late? If I had, I was the biggest fool in Misty Cedars. I stared out of my bedroom window and tried not to think about Fitz, and what might have been, if I hadn't gone and screwed it all up.

Chapter Thirty-Four

NICE DAY FOR A BLACK WEDDING

"WHAT THE HECK SHOULD I WEAR?"

Jane already looked fabulous in her cornflower-blue dress and braided updo.

"Personally, I think the beige dress is really pretty," Jane said. "The pink is nice, but it's a bit hot for that tonight."

I held the pink dress up against me. It was my favorite, but Jane was right. It was nearly eleven o'clock, but outside it was still over ninety degrees. The dress was one of the few I had purchased, but the pretty material was super heavy, and I would die in it in this heat. I tossed the pink on the end of the bed and slid into the lighter, beige dress. It was one I had made myself, so at least I could be sure no one else would be wearing it at the wedding.

"Your car is here!" Mom shouted up the stairs.

We had ordered an Uber so we could both drink.

"Be there in a minute, Mom. Tell him to wait." I took one last glance in the mirror. Hair loose, makeup perfect, dress on, all good. I'd toned down my goth girl look for the night. There would be a lot of vamps at this gig, and I wanted to stand out.

I slipped into my sandals and picked up my shoulder bag and grabbed the large, gift-wrapped box off the end of the bed.

"How do I look?"

"Fantastic. That dress really suits you."

I took a deep breath. "Awesome. Let's get going then."

We walked down the stairs and both kissed Mom good-bye. Kitty and Mary were out, but Lydia was sitting in Mary's usual window seat and scowling. She'd not said a word to me since Vegas, but oh well. I'd saved her from a miserable future, and maybe she couldn't see that now, but she would, in time. Mom had told her about George, the financial scam, and the Golem, and even my immature sister would soon see the sense in what we had done. She looked me up and down as we made ready to leave.

"You look nice," she said.

"Thank you."

It was a beginning.

The Uber driver was a numpy. He looked nervous at having a pickup at a para address, but as of now, there were no para alternatives. Driver choice was the luck of the draw. He barely looked at us when we got into the back seat, but no matter. I was in a good mood, and not even a grouchy numpy was going to change that.

As the car pulled off the drive, I stared out of the window. I'd been on tenterhooks since Hill's reading. The tea leaves showed the wedding, which meant something of import was going to happen. Plus, I was delighted that Matthew had chosen to live and was about to begin that new life.

"What is he like?" Jane asked. "The vampire. You said he was very old. I've never seen a really, really old one before."

I could believe that. Most of the super-old ones became recluses once their looks began to wither. Most of them left society completely, emerging only to feed. And then they were only seen by their victims.

"I definitely wouldn't call him pretty. But I think he was handsome once. I'd say the same for the bride, Octavia. They're both very haughty."

"Aren't all vamps? Oh well, so long as we stay off the menu. I know vamps don't like to eat witch, but there's always an exception to the rule."

"Don't worry, I can speak for the bride and groom—you'll be perfectly safe."

"It's not the bride and groom I'm thinking of. It's all the other guests."

The driver was listening intently though he remained tight-lipped. I nudged Jane. We might be safe from the bites of the undead, but the driver was a numpy, and I could see he was worried. The sun had been down for a while, and now was the usual feeding time for Nosferatu.

"If you like, you can drop us off down the road from St. Judes?" I offered. "At the crossroads?"

The man nodded frantically and began to relax, though his foot remained heavy on the gas pedal. I could tell he wanted a quick in and out on this fare. After all, it was still pretty close to a host of hungry vampires, in the middle of nowhere, where no one would come if he screamed. Still, at least he didn't kick us out of the car, and I was thankful for that.

We soon arrived at the crossroads. The fare had been paid in advance, so the second we closed the door behind us, the driver was gone. I can't say I blamed him. Poor guy, he looked positively terrified. I wondered just how many vamps were attending and prayed that either Matthew or Octavia had the sense to include a shitload of lavender in the wedding flowers. Which reminded me.

"Oh poop, I forgot. Are you wearing your crucifix?"

Jane wore a long chain around her neck and pulled out the crucifix neatly hidden under her dress. "Oh boy, am I."

Phew. "Good, good."

Picking out a present for a four- to five-hundred-year-old vampire hadn't been easy. Jane and I had spent some time deliberating on the most perfect thing, and then it had come to me. Goody had once made Matthew a cloak so they could enjoy the twilights and sunsets together. We would do the same for Octavia.

"You want help with that?" Jane asked, as I shuffled the gift box to balance the load.

"Nah, it doesn't weigh much. It's just bulky," I said.

"Even so. Why carry it when you don't have to?" Jane whipped out her wand and pointed it at the box. I held it out as far from my body as I could. "*Levitar.*"

A moment later, the box hovered in the air, and all I had to do now was push it along with my finger until we reached the church.

"Thanks," I said.

Boy, what a difference a few days had made with my sister. It was like a heavy weight had been lifted from her heart, and I almost imagined she was even happier than she'd been before. The rock on her finger was a keeper, and even now I saw her stealing glances at it and grinning when she thought no one was looking.

St. Judes was an old, abandoned church, normally covered in graffiti and half the windows had been smashed out. The graveyard was unattended, and half the headstones had been damaged and desecrated. At least, that's how I had always seen it.

Today, there were no signs of any of such vandalism. The church had been miraculously altered by charms and enchantments, the great Gothic entrance had been restored to its glorious heyday, and great candles burned in the restored glass windows. I suspected the glass art wasn't original. There were no haloed angels or images from the Bible. Instead, there were some pretty raunchy images of dancing satyrs and steamy succubi, and these were not static depictions but were animated and fascinating to watch. Since the church had been unconsecrated, I guessed it was okay.

Across the street was a large black marquee that I'd missed on the approach, but someone was lighting the candles inside, causing the canvas to glow. I smiled when I saw the catering truck with FCC, Inc. emblazoned on the side. I immediately looked around for Jed Colonel, though if he was here, I couldn't see him.

The parking lot was full to the brim. From the make and model of the cars, we could tell this was an elite gathering; over the years, Matthew and Octavia would have brushed shoulders with some wealthy and powerful paras and numpies, and it certainly showed today. The guests were still hanging out in the parking area. I could tell most were vamps, but there were all sorts here tonight, dressed in their finest and seeming awfully classy.

I looked down at my dress and felt a bit country bumpkinish as we walked up to the Gothic doors.

"Do you want to stay outside and mingle, or shall we go in?" Jane asked.

"Let's go in. I don't know any of these people. I'd feel a little odd just standing about." My gaze fell on a rather fashionable yet emaciated vamp who was looking me up and down. I couldn't tell if she was checking out my dress or deciding whether or not to eat me. "Plus some of them look a little hungry."

Jane laughed with me.

From somewhere nearby, I could hear the howl of wolves. I wondered if they were calling naturally, or whether they'd been hired by the wedding party for ambience.

I was about to remark on this to Jane when my heart almost stopped. Because there, right in front of me with a huge grin on his face and a bunch of wedding programs in his hand, was Fitz Darcy.

"Fitz! Oh, by Gaia, what are you doing here?"

"Hello to you, too," Fitz said. "I'm here as an usher. I saw you were on the guest list and wondered when I'd see you."

My mouth was still open as he handed me and Jane a copy of the program.

"I didn't know you were friends with Matthew Devereux," I said.

"I'm not," he replied. "Well, I know him, of course, but not well. Octavia is my godmother. I'm here for the bride."

"It's lovely to see you again," Jane said. I was glad one of us had kept our manners.

"And congratulations to you," Fitz said. "May I see the ring?"

Jane didn't need to be asked again, and Fitz took her hand and admired the rock Charlie had planted there. "Very nice," he said. "I couldn't be happier for you both. I think you'll make each other very happy." His grin was sincere, and his eyes were twinkling. I wondered what exactly he'd said to Charlie to turn things around. "Come on, let me take you to your seats. You're both on the groom's side. You can leave your gift on a table at the back of the church. In fact, allow me."

He pushed the large box through the doors leading into the church and over to a table decked with more presents than I had seen in my life. "*Pinga*," he said.

The box dropped gently and landed perfectly balanced on top of some others. He turned and walked us both down the aisle toward the altar. The traditional cross had been replaced by a floating crescent moon, its pale light reflecting off the white irises that swamped the rest of the altar.

As we walked down, it dawned on me I had nothing left to reproach Fitz for. It sucked to think I had blown it, romantically, but that had been my fault entirely. Now, as I walked behind him, all I could think was how handsome he was, and how good he looked all dressed up for this wedding. And his ass. That was a topic all by itself.

"I'll catch you both later," Fitz said, flicking through the wedding programs with his thumbs. "Duty calls."

I didn't want him to leave us, but like he said, he had shit to do. While Jane read the program, I cast my gaze around the church. We were surrounded by all sorts of para, mostly vampires, and I was surprised to see my boss, Mr. Lowe, sitting in one of the pews along with his family. Perhaps I shouldn't have been so surprised. In fact, I now saw that a few people in the congregation were wearing that same ornate silver ring. I suspected there were more geomancers assembled in this church than had ever been gathered together in history. I wondered if we'd see many ghosts.

Now that we were closer to the altar, I could see two coffins propped against each wall. Matthew and Octavia would be inside them, as was the tradition, and they would rise on the first stroke of midnight, when the ceremony was scheduled to begin.

"I wonder if they're both texting each other in there," I whispered to Jane. We both chuckled.

I glanced at the program. It was very brief. There was a welcome, a hymn, and the exchange of vows. Very nice. The service was going to be performed by the Reverend Josh Pratt, Necromancer.

When I looked up, there he was. Reverend Josh wore a black suit with a red shirt, the classic formal garb of necromancer officials. He was a lot younger than I expected—I figured he could be no more than twenty-five, tops, but he looked as sincere as any minister of sixty years or more. Except a lot hotter.

There was a single unlit candle by his side, larger than any of the others lighting the church. He ran his hand over the top of it, and the wick ignited.

"Welcome, friends, as we come together tonight to witness this honorable union of the undead. Please stand as we celebrate the dedications of Matthew Cornelius Xavier Devereux to Octavia Bathsheba Darcy Harrington as they promise to walk the night together."

His voice was very velvety and soothing, and I could imagine him calling on the dead and them responding. We all rose in unison.

As soon as we all stood, we heard the creak of the coffin hinges as the lids opened, and the two ancient vampires rose from their home earth beds, arms folded across their chests, as was the tradition.

Very solemnly, to match the occasion, the two vampires climbed from their coffins and walked gracefully into the center of the church, taking their places facing each other in front of Reverend Josh.

Josh took a step back into the shadows, so the candle shone only on Matthew and Octavia. At that moment, all other candles in the church flickered and then blew out. There was a great hush, and we all listened as the couple prepared to make their vows. In the distance, a lone wolf cried out to the moon. Bang on cue. These wedding planners were awesome.

Matthew and Octavia clasped their hands and stared directly at each other. This they recited in unison:

> *We will cherish our love, which is stronger than blood,*
> *We will share our home earth, which will bind us.*
> *This undead vow we make in honor and trust,*
> *Devoting our time to the night, which conceals us.*
>
> *We pledge all that we have, and all that we own,*
> *Promising no harm will befall one another.*
> *Our undead oath we swear to this crowd,*
> *Two lost souls finding peace in each other.*

Once their vows were spoken, Josh stepped out of the shadows, and the candles in the church rekindled. This time he held open a book. I wondered what kind of book they would have at a vampire wedding, never having seen one before, and made a mental note to myself to ask about it later.

On the open page of the book were two amethyst rings. They were so beautiful; the purple stones were so clear the candlelight reflected directly through them.

"I am charged to ask you all, at mortal peril of your souls, those of you who have one, if you know of any reason why these two vampires cannot be joined together in eternal matrimony?"

The hush was replaced with an air of expectation as Josh waited the required time before continuing with the ceremony. The moment was over, and Matthew and Octavia were reaching for their rings when a rush of extreme cold air flooded the center of the church. I looked over to the aisle, and there, floating toward the bride and groom, was Goody Becker, just as I had seen her before.

"Witches and warlocks!" I whispered to Jane. "Oh shit, this is gonna be awkward."

Matthew, however, didn't look too surprised at seeing her there. Perhaps Octavia looked a little ruffled—this was her wedding day after all —but Matthew's eyes were full of tears as his old love approached the couple. We all felt the ache inside him, and my own heart was torn in two seeing her there at the altar with him. He had loved Goody once, still did most likely, even though he probably loved Octavia too.

We all sat in silence, wondering, dreading how all this was going to play out.

"It is good to see you, Goody," Matthew said simply.

"And I you, Matthew."

I was stunned. Her voice was high and sweet, like a child's, and I was surprised she could speak at all. There was no malice in her tone, only a deep yearning, and my eyes misted over and filled with tears.

"I have come to give my blessing to your marriage." Goody reached out to Matthew and, taking his hand in her own, put something in his palm. None of us could see what it was, though I had my suspicions. Then Goody turned to Octavia, and reaching out, she touched the old vampiress gently on her arm.

"The love I have for Matthew is my gift to you, which I offer with this kiss."

To the congregation's astonishment, Goody rose up in the air and kissed Octavia on the forehead. As she pulled away, the old vampiress began to transform. Her crepey skin tightened, her eyes became larger, and her flesh filled out with the tone of youth. The wrinkly and gnarled fingers that had just reached for her wedding band were now fully rejuvenated. They were long and slender, pale and beautiful. Octavia had become young once more.

In the same breath, Goody kissed Matthew, though this time her kiss was on his lips. Perhaps I imagined this, but I thought she lingered a little longer this time. When she pulled away, the years melted away, but it wasn't only Matthew who changed. I could see her clearly now and watched openmouthed as the ravages of the flames left her face and her scars faded to nothing. She was herself once more, both enchanting and lovely.

Screw me sideways, I thought. I looked at Jane, and she was as wide-eyed as I was.

Goody held Matthew's hand one last time, and I imagined them just as they had been, a long time ago, when they had first met each other in Matthew's garden, in 1652. It was almost like I was there, when they were young and in love, long before the world stepped in and tore them both apart.

Goody's image began to fade. She smiled one last time, letting go of his hand, closed her eyes, and was gone.

After the shock of the ceremony, we headed outside the church and walked over to the black marquee set up for the wedding supper. There was now another van parked next to the FCC truck, and Jane pulled my arm with glee.

"Look," I cried. "They've hired The Brew. This is gonna be awesome."

Better and better, there was someone else outside the marquee to gladden her eyes.

"Charlie!" Jane ran across the street and flung herself into his arms, and he twirled her around. When she was back on terra firma, she looked up at him and smiled. "What are you doing here? I didn't know you were invited."

"I wasn't, but Fitz called me and told me to get my butt over for the wedding supper, so how could I refuse?"

"That's awesome," she said. "Where have they put you? Are you sitting with us?"

"I think so." Charlie pointed to the tent. "I didn't see a seating plan, so I think it's a free-for-all. We can sit wherever we want." He planted a big soppy kiss on her lips, and though I was happy for my sister, I started to feel like a bit of a gooseberry. I lowered my gaze, not wanting either of them to catch what I was thinking.

My sister was a lot sharper than I thought. "You don't mind, do you, Izzy? We promise to behave."

"No, not at all." I didn't mind. Not really. I wished for a little of the same for myself.

We all strolled into the marquee, and I could see Jed casting spells, getting everything ready. There were large tubs filled with a dark liquid, and I shuddered to think what might be inside those. At least the food provided for the nonvamps smelled good. I caught the distinct aroma of roasting beef and gravy and realized how hungry I was.

Denny Finn and the band were busy setting up their equipment, and seeing us come in he waved but carried on with what he was doing.

More and more guests were filing in, so we laid claim to a table close to the food and the band. I watched as Jane and Charlie laughed and talked. They didn't mean to be exclusive but couldn't help it, I supposed. Couples were notoriously oblivious to everyone else when in love.

I found myself looking for Fitz, my gaze glued to the entrance of the marquee, waiting for him to come in. At first, I thought he might be busy with the photographer, but then I remembered reading someplace there were no photographers at vampire weddings, since their image couldn't be captured.

Matthew and Octavia came in and took their seats at the newlywed's table. I still couldn't get used to them looking so young. Matthew was impossibly handsome; he had towered over Goody's ghost, whereas Octavia was a few inches shorter than he was. I had to admit they looked fantastic together. Since her transformation, there was something different about Octavia, and it wasn't just her sudden youthful appearance. But what was it?

I watched as the new wife took Matthew's hand in her own and kissed it.

That was it. She looked softer, gentler, possibly less bitter than she had as an old woman. Goody had gifted her with her love, which had changed more than just her looks. Matthew's happiness was assured, and my one reservation for their future was put to rest.

More announcements were made, food was eaten, and then the band began to play. The first song was a tribute to the married couple. It was Elvis's "Can't Help Falling in Love." As soon as I heard the opening line, my heart melted.

I watched mesmerized as the invigorated couple took the dance floor for the first dance. They looked so happy together, like young people in the first blush of youth more than centuries-old vampires.

When the dance was over, The Brew started performing some of their own songs, and Jane and Charlie were up in a flash, shaking their butts to "Toil and Trouble." I wondered if anyone else saw the humor in their choice.

Not in the mood to dance alone, I felt the sudden urge to get some fresh air. I pushed my half-eaten plate away from me, grabbed my purse from the back of my chair, and strolled out of the marquee.

There was so much good luck all around me, and I knew I should be thankful, and I was, really, but none of it compensated for the feelings that I'd been nurturing of late for Fitz. He had loved me, and I had blown it. That was the truth of it, and no magic in the world could put that right. Not unless I wanted a visit from the Hags.

Some rogue clouds drifted over the full moon, dimming most of the natural light around me. The trucks were between me and the marquee, and I found myself in almost total darkness. I remembered Dad once told me—the dead of night, not midnight, was the time for wishes.

I closed my eyes and wished for...well, I didn't know what I wished for. A little of what Jane had found? That wasn't too selfish of me, was it?

There was a fluttering sound behind me, like the fizzing sound a match made when it was struck. I turned, not realizing anyone else was with me.

"Who's there?" I asked, squinting into the darkness. I could see no one and immediately pulled out my wand, just in case. Any asshole who lunged at me out of the dark was going to get a fireball in the mouth.

One by one, tiny amber lights began to glow, and I realized what I was seeing were small fireflies, glowing in the darkness. It was unusual for them to be out so late, so intrigued, I watched them.

Any fireflies I had seen before had floated at random spots, but these seemed to be forming an arrow, one that led away from the marquee and over to the cemetery by the church.

Okay. My curiosity got the better of me, and I followed them, holding my wand ready, ready for anything.

Behind me, the beat of the band grew a little fainter, and I was thinking of casting a light spell when the clouds slipped past the face of the moon and the light shone fully on the church. And there was Fitz, standing in the cemetery, waving as one by one, the pretty fireflies escaped the tip of his wand.

My heart danced to see him, but still unsure of myself, I held myself back, walking steadily but surely, waiting to see what he would do next.

As I came right to him, Fitz lowered his wand, and the fireflies flew off into the night.

"I was wondering if you would come for me," he said.

Fitz was so close now. I could smell the sea air on him, and I thought about Maine and his life up there. His aroma made me giddy with desire.

"I—I wanted to thank you. For all that you've done. I know it was you who helped us. It wasn't exactly hard for me to figure it out."

Fitz's gaze was gentle as his eyes probed mine. "Then I think you're smart enough to know that everything I did was for you."

I nodded. Maybe I hadn't let myself believe it, but deep down, in those places that couldn't be reached by magic, I think I'd known all along.

"You said you hated me once," he said. "If that's still true, tell me quickly, and I swear before Gaia I will never bother you again. You have my word. As a Darcy."

I stepped as close to Fitz as I could get and raised my hands to his shoulders. In the paleness of the moonlight, I could see his eyes dancing with hope, and his lips were only inches away from me now. All I had to do was tilt my head and I could kiss him.

"I never really hated you," I said, as my lips ached to kiss him. "I thought you were a bit of a bastard, I suppose, but then, aren't all heroes bastards, in the beginning?"

"And now?" he said. Fitz leaned in a little closer, and the heat of his breath tickled my lips.

"Now? Well, let's see, shall we? One step at a time. I like to take things nice and slow."

I closed my eyes and, bringing my lips to his, waited for the true magic to begin.

EPILOGUE

"Okay, if you must know," I said, "I'll tell you one thing about me and Fitz, and one thing only."

Charlotte's lips curled into a mischievous grin. "Go on, then, before he comes back."

I leaned in close and pretended to whisper, but made sure all the other guests could hear. "He's a really good kisser."

Charlotte laughed. Thankfully, she was already over Billy. We'd opened an account for her in Magical Moments, and she'd already seen a couple of hot prospects off the site. Billy had moved back in with his mom and was keeping a very low profile, working part time in the family's general store. I really didn't expect him to ever show his face in Misty Cedars again, which suited me just fine.

"I still don't get how she was able to speak to Matthew and Octavia," Charlotte said. "You said she couldn't speak last time, but this time she could?"

I shrugged. "Fitz said it was probably because there were so many geomancers in the room. That was a helluva lot of energy for her to channel, so she was able to have a voice. I wish you'd seen it, Charlotte. It was such a beautiful moment. Hold up a minute."

I left her for a minute to look out of the window.

Charlie and Jane were having a low-key engagement party at Dark Coven. Fitz was out back in the kitchen, getting some catering tips off Jed Colonel. He'd thought this was a good idea, since I'd told him I was a terrible cook, and we both agreed at least one of us should know what to do in the kitchen. Practical romance at its best.

"Are they here yet?" Jane asked.

We were all on the lookout for Matthew and Octavia. I'd introduced them to Jane and Charlie later during their wedding, and we were all becoming firm friends. Matthew and Octavia were back from their honeymoon in Paraland, a theme park down in Florida, and they had promised to join us all just before sundown, so we were holding off eats until they arrived.

A darkened SUV pulled into the drive and advanced slowly up toward the house. "Oh, look, I think that's them now."

Charlie was right behind me, a bottle of champagne in his hand, and he filled my glass for the umpteenth time. To be honest, I was a little tipsy, but in a good way, my witch blood dancing with the fizzy bubbles.

If Mary was affected by the booze, she didn't show it. On arrival, she'd made a beeline for Charlie's bookcase and, having selected something she liked, settled down for the duration.

Lydia, reprieved for the night, was out in the kitchen with the guys, flirting like crazy with all The Brew members—Denny Finn noticed me looking and winked to let me know he'd make sure she didn't get up to too much mischief—and Kitty remained in the room with us, quietly people watching. If one good thing had come out of the whole George Wickham affair, it was the impact on Kitty. She no longer worshipped Lydia as she had once done, and with Jane's help, she'd put in a number of applications to various colleges around the state. I had high hopes for her and, along with the rest of the family, had vowed to do whatever I could to support her. Which, since hooking up with Fitz Darcy, turned out to be rather a lot.

I watched as Matthew and Octavia got out of the SUV and was delighted to see them both wearing their cloaks. After saying hello to a few people at the front door, they soon joined the party.

Charlie put a glass of something red into Octavia's hands, but Matthew waved the offer off and came over to me, still in his cloak.

"Forgive my directness, but there is something I would like to discuss with you before sunset. Would you do me the honor of taking a stroll around the estate?"

It wasn't the first time Matthew had spoken to me since his transformation, but like before, I was taken aback by the formality of his speech. It had seemed right and fitting on the old Matthew but didn't quite work with the new one. He sure looked hot though.

"Sure," I said, downing the remains of my champagne and setting my glass on a nearby mantel. "I would love to."

I followed Matthew out of the room and passed the kitchen. Fitz looked up and, seeing Matthew, waved at us both, but then his attention returned to some cutting skill Jed was demonstrating with his knife. The blade blurred, and suddenly a cucumber became one hundred perfect slices, forming a perfect circle around the outside of a salad bowl. I guessed we were going to be eating a lot of salads.

Outside, the frogs and crickets were doing their thing, but other than that, the grounds were silent. We were well away from the noise of the roads, and since The Brew were attending as guests, not musicians, all was quiet.

"If I remember, there is a pretty little wilderness around the back of this house," Matthew said. "There used to be a small pond and a walled shrubbery with an arched gate. I would like to see if it's still there."

I followed Matthew around the side of the house. Sure enough, there was an arched gate built into an old stone wall, and together we passed through it.

In the center of the enclosure was a fountain, with a large fish pumping water through its mouth. Matthew smiled. "In my day, that was an Eros. Otherwise, the pond looks exactly the same."

I stared down at a well-fed white koi that popped its head out of the water through the lily pads.

"Goody and I used to come here all the time," he said. "And here"—he pointed to an old stone bench—"here we sat the day she left me." He stared at it for a moment and then decided to sit on it. "Hmm. The last time I sat here, she broke my heart. But I return to it with a heart that is whole again. Perhaps that's the true nature of luck. Seeing the good, where once you only saw bad."

I smiled faintly at him, and at first, I thought he was staring into nothing, but he turned his head, and I realized he was focused on something in particular.

"That is a particularly beautiful Elder tree, don't you think?"

I followed his gaze and nodded. "Yes, very pretty," I said.

"It was her favorite tree. I liked kissing her under it. Would you mind if we went there for a moment?"

As long as you don't try to kiss me, sunshine. Heck, what would I do if he did? "No, not at all."

We both left our stone bench, and Matthew led me around the square pond and over to the tree. He rubbed his hand against the bark, and I smiled at the initials M & G, etched forever into the trunk. It was a miracle they had lasted so long.

"Young people do such foolish things, do they not?"

I laughed a little, thinking of me and Fitz. "Yes, yes, I suppose so."

At the base of the trunk was a large stone. Matthew knelt down, and he grinned. I had seen that grin once before.

"Is that a pixie rock?" I asked.

"Yes. A very old one. I put this one here, many, many years ago." He patted the grass at his feet.

He smiled. "She is here. I wanted you to know that."

I didn't say a word but just nodded.

Matthew put his hand inside his cloak and pulled something out from the pocket. He didn't have to tell me what it was. I knew it was the Moonstone. It was a glistening pale-blue stone, the size of a pebble. I leaned over to get a better look at it, and to my surprise, the center seemed to shift a little, like it was made of molten rock. Mesmerized, I could see why Goody had asked to keep it. I wouldn't have been averse to keeping it myself.

"My friends have guarded my love all this time. I think it only fair to return this gem to them."

I nodded again.

Very carefully, Matthew lifted the rock, and a group of very curious pixies stood beneath it, hands on their hips, wondering what he wanted. Matthew found an empty spot near them and then pressed the stone into the ground.

The pixies ran to it at once, and though they were too tiny for me to hear their cries, I could see they were really excited. Ever so gently, Matthew lowered the stone, and together we stood up again.

When I looked up at him, Matthew was smiling, and in that moment, I knew both he and Goody had made their peace, and all the hurt was over.

I stepped up to the handsome vampire and felt no fear as I kissed him on the cheek. Only gladness, for having met him. He had said good-bye to his past, and now it was time to move on.

Matthew smiled at me and fondly brushed my cheek.

"Ahem! I hope I'm not interrupting something?"

I turned to see Fitz Darcy, smiling at us.

"I fear I must return to the house," Matthew said. "My bride awaits. If I may, I will leave this wonderful young witch in your charge."

I backed into Fitz, who wrapped his arms about me. I loved feeling protected by him. Or at least his impulse to protect me. "I'll look after her, have no fear."

Matthew nodded, and we watched as he returned to the house.

As soon as he was gone, I turned around in Fitz's arms. "Jealous, were you?"

Fitz's mouth twitched playfully. He crooked a finger under my chin and tilted my head upward. I loved it when he did that. His soft, sweet lips parted, ready to kiss me. "The only thrall I want you under is mine."

A grin pulsed at the corner of my mouth as I lifted my fingers and ran them through his beautiful hair, pulling him into a kiss that left us both a little breathless. When at last I came up for air, I brushed his cheek, loving all the things he told me with one silent look. "Too late, I'm afraid. I enthralled you first."

Fitz's gaze danced with amusement before he moved in for another soft kiss. "So mote it be."

***

Thank you for reading! Did you enjoy? Please add your review because nothing helps an author more and encourages readers to take a chance on a book than a review.

And don't miss more in the Soul and Shadows series with book 2, SENSE AND SUCCUBUS, coming soon!

Until then read more paranormal romance like EDGE OF THE WOODS by City Owl Author, Jules Kelley. Turn the page for a sneak peek!

You can also sign up for the City Owl Press newsletter to receive notice of all book releases!

SNEAK PEEK OF EDGE OF THE WOODS

By Jules Kelley

The sun crested the horizon, lighting the inside of the truck with an orange glow, and Leland stretched, trying to work eighteen hours of road stiffness out of his shoulders. In the distance, mountains rose above the scraggly pines like towering angels against the brightening sky, welcoming him to paradise instead of throwing him out. He spared one hand off the steering wheel to knuckle the dust and sleepless itch out of his eyes and wished for another cup of coffee.

Taking the job in Pine Grove had been a risk, but as far as he was concerned, it was already paying off. He'd washed off the last of the dust from the Arizona desert at a gas station somewhere north of Salt Lake City, and now, watching the foothills of western Montana fill his view, he barely remembered what Tucson looked like.

When he'd interviewed with the Upham County Sheriff's Department, Sheriff Rylan had told him that Pine Grove was the basement office of deputy assignments.

"'Bout once a month, you'll have to go out on the nature preserve to find some birdbrain out-of-towner who got lost on the full moon. The town trades on old folktales 'bout werewolves in the woods, and some people are dumb enough to go lookin'. Other than that, hope you like sittin' around with your thumb up your ass waitin' for somebody to lock themselves out of their house."

That sounded just fine to Leland. Hell, he might even have time to go fishing every now and then. The fancy fly rod he'd bought himself a couple of years ago hadn't been doing anything except collecting dust in his closet, and the Tucson PD staff therapist had brought it up in his final session.

"When's the last time you took some time off to just enjoy a hobby?"

Well, no time like the present.

A flash of movement on the side of the road caught his attention—an animal stumbling up out of the ditch right in front of him—and he swore as he stomped on the brakes, pulling hard on the steering wheel. His heartbeat thudded in his ears as the vehicle skidded sideways, tires squawking as they jumped and bounced over the asphalt. The SUV finally came to a stop with one tire in the ditch, and he pried his shaking hands off the steering wheel to scrape them over his face.

He turned to look at the animal he'd almost hit and sucked in a sharp breath when he realized it wasn't a bear or a deer, but a human, naked and filthy, hunched over as he lurched unsteadily across the pavement.

Leland was out of the driver's seat in an instant, automatically reaching for his handset to radio Guerrera, and then swore when he remembered. He wasn't in uniform. He wasn't in Arizona. Guerrera was twelve hundred miles away. He wasn't even a police officer anymore. He patted his pockets instead, looking for his phone and digging it out as he cautiously approached the man.

Boy, he corrected himself as he got closer. It was hard to tell what his face looked like under streaks of dirt—*And is that dried blood?*—but he was small, slender, his dark eyes large in his ashy brown face. Late teens, Leland guessed, forcing down the itch of memory at the back of his mind: another young face, another pair of haunted eyes. He didn't have time for that right now.

"Hey," Leland called, one hand out to him, moving slowly. "Are you all right, kid?"

The boy didn't answer him, but he watched Leland warily. He drew in several quick breaths through his nose, and after a moment, Leland realized he was sniffing the air. His mannerisms were more animal than human, but his hair was shaved close on the sides, a stylish—and recent—

haircut, and a diamond earring glinted from the dirt caking his right ear, so he hadn't been out of civilization that long.

"It's all right. I'm here to help you," Leland tried again, keeping his voice calm and quiet. He thought of the legends of werewolves in Pine Grove that Rylan had told him about and just as quickly shook off the idea. The boy, naked and bloody, had clearly been through *something*, but Leland knew intimately that run-of-the-mill humans were more than capable of incredible cruelty without any supernatural assistance.

"Can you tell me your name?" Leland said, trying to keep the boy's attention as he inched back toward his SUV. Somewhere in the meager life's belongings in the back seat of the vehicle were clothes that might fit the kid, at least enough to cover him up and keep him from freezing. The day was rapidly warming as the sun rose, but spring nights in Montana were still chilly, and he'd obviously been out for at least a few hours.

Leland checked his phone as he sifted through one of his duffel bags. One bar of signal. Maybe it would be enough to call somebody, see if he could get an ambulance on the way. He only had two local numbers—the Upham County sheriff's office and the Pine Grove Wildlife Preserve. The sheriff's office was in Red Horse River, another hour and a half up the road, and Rylan *had* said that the preserve director would be his point of contact for problems with wayward tourists, lost hikers, and animal attacks.

Well, here goes nothin'.

He tucked the phone between his ear and shoulder, listening to it ring as he finally found a pair of sweat pants that looked like they might fit the kid if he pulled the drawstring tight.

There was a click, then silence, and Leland waited to hear someone on the other end. "Hello?" Nothing. "Hello, can you hear me?"

The beep of a dropped call mocked him, and he huffed out a frustrated breath. "Dammit."

The young man twitched, seeming to focus on him for the first time, his gaze confused and curious—but finally human, not glassy and alien.

"Who're you?"

"Hey, kid," Leland said, immediately pocketing his phone again. "My name's Leland Sommers. I found you out here on the road. You remember how you got here?"

The kid looked around, frowning, and Leland guessed the answer before he shook his head. "Where the fuck is *here*?"

He shivered, and Leland held out the sweat pants in offering. The kid's nose wrinkled, but he took them.

"You're on Route 23, right outside Pine Grove, Montana." He cleared his throat. "What's your name?" He focused on keeping his voice steady and warm. The boy didn't seem especially volatile, but neither had that one girl he'd found stoned out of her mind on the floor of her boyfriend's meth lab—until she'd damn near taken a chunk out of his arm.

This guy looked more like something had already taken a bite out of *him*, Leland thought, eyeing a fresh-looking wound on the kid's left shoulder.

"My name's Diego." Diego wet his lips, pulling the drawstring on the pants as tight as they would go. They still sagged on his narrow hips, the *Arizona Coyotes* logo down the leg looking bigger than his entire body.

Leland's phone rang in his pocket, and Diego flinched and immediately looked around as if he'd lost something, swearing under his breath. Leland guessed he'd had a phone with him before whatever had happened. But he'd have to ask questions later; the call was coming from a local number.

"This is Leland Sommers."

"You call this number a minute ago?" The woman's voice on the other end of the line was brusque, no-nonsense. "This is the Pine Grove Nature Preserve's ranger station."

"I did." Well, at least something was going right. "I'm the new sheriff's deputy, coming to fill the position in town. I'm stopped on Route 23 out here east of town with a young man who was in the road with no clothes on. Is there an emergency response service that I should call?"

The woman on the other end made a noise that might have been a snort. "Closest hospital's at least an hour away. Can you get him into your car and drive him in, or do you need a backboard and a neck brace?"

Leland darted a glance over at Diego, evaluating him. He was trying to pick the leaves and twigs out of his hair now; it didn't seem at all like he was nursing a spinal injury.

"No, he's ambulatory." Diego gave him an odd look, frowning, and Leland had a sudden flash of another kid—younger, smaller, but with the same mix of wariness and cautious hope on his face. He looked away. "Where should I take him?"

"There's a clinic. When you're coming in to town, turn left at the stoplight, and you'll see it in about half a mile. I'll call Haley and Doc Fenton, let 'em know you're comin' in."

"Which stoplight?" Leland asked, and the woman laughed.

"The only one in the whole town. Anything you want me to tell the doc when I call her? Injuries, things like that?"

"Just some contusions, abrasions. It does look like he got attacked by an animal, maybe. Large wound on his shoulder might be a bite mark."

The woman went so quiet that Leland pulled the phone away from his ear to see if the call had dropped.

"Hello?"

"I'll let them know," she said and hung up without a good-bye.

The clinic had a single lightbulb above the door, glowing brightly in the misty morning, and one lonely car parked in the parking lot.

Diego was shivering by the time Leland helped him down from the passenger's seat, teeth chattering, little muscle spasms shooting through him.

"You're gonna be all right," Leland murmured, supporting him carefully, noting the feverish heat in his skin. A peek at Diego's face confirmed that his eyes had gone glassy again, little beads of sweat at his hairline. "We're here at the clinic. We're gonna get you taken care of."

The door was locked, and Leland pressed the button labeled FOR SERVICE AFTER HOURS. Within seconds, a woman in jeans and flannel with short-cropped gray hair unlocked the door and pushed it open with an urgency that Leland appreciated.

"You're the one that called in to the preserve?" the woman said, already reaching for Diego, gloved hand brushing his hair out of his face to look at his eyes.

"Yeah." Leland lifted Diego over the threshold when the kid couldn't seem to pick his feet up enough to get past the doorstep. "You the doctor?"

"I'm Dr. Fenton." She locked the door behind them and led them through the empty lobby, the fluorescent lights flickering and buzzing to life when she flicked the switch. "Can you help me get him to the exam room?"

"Nice to meet you, Doc." Leland grunted at the unexpected weight as Diego went almost limp against him, and he hitched his arm more securely around Diego's middle. "I'm Leland." As an afterthought, he added, "His name's Diego."

She swept ahead of them into an exam room and helped Leland get Diego up onto the patient table, the white paper crinkling loudly.

A buzzer sounded, and Diego groaned, covering his ears.

"That'll be Haley," Dr. Fenton said, changing out her gloves for fresh ones. "The preserve director. Do you mind letting her in for me?"

"Yeah, I got it." Leland steadied Diego before finding his way back through the clinic toward the front door. When he first saw the girl standing on the other side of the glass, he wondered if maybe it was someone's daughter instead of Haley Fern, Director of the Pine Grove Nature Preserve. Nothing about her, from her blond ponytail to the soft roundness of her face and generous curves of her figure, matched the gruff, no-nonsense voice he'd heard on the phone that morning. Then again, she was clutching a travel mug with LUANN'S DINER emblazoned on the side like it was the only thing keeping her standing, so maybe that was just how she sounded when she got dragged out of bed at the crack of dawn on a Saturday morning.

When he approached the door, she lifted the huge sunglasses that had been covering half her face, and wow, those big, brown eyes could stop a full-grown man in his tracks. They almost did.

He fumbled the door open a crack and leaned out a bit, staying cautious in case he was wrong. He'd been wrong before. "Can I help you?"

She squinted up at him, her nose wrinkling under a dusting of dark freckles. Christ, she was so cute it was almost illegal.

"I'm Haley Fern, the preserve director," she said, and he knew immediately it wasn't the same person he'd talked to that morning. Her voice was too sweet for that. "And you are?"

He had the oddest impulse to take his cap off, but he just held the door open wider for her instead. "Leland Sommers, the new dedicated deputy. I called the preserve this morning about a kid I found on the way in. That wasn't you I talked to, was it?"

"Oh, no, that was my ranger, Michele." She ducked in under his arm as he held open the door, still eyeing him like she was sizing him up. "You're the one they hired to take George's place? We weren't expecting you until tomorrow night."

She was half his height, but he felt almost scolded. It was all he could do not to feel like he was telling his teacher why he didn't have his homework. "My lease was already up at my old place, so I figured I'd come up a couple days early, start getting settled in."

He locked the door behind her, and when he turned around, she was rubbing one eye and biting back a yawn. No one had a right to be that cute and that intimidating at the same time.

She caught him watching her and waved one hand apologetically. "Sorry. Not a morning person. Michele said the boy you found was injured?"

He nodded, shortening his stride so he could walk beside her down the hall. "Bite marks. Looked like maybe a dog or coyote from glancing at it. 'Bout the right size and depth, compared to other likely things." At her sideways glance, he shrugged, guessing at her unasked question. "Saw a few animal attacks on the force in Arizona."

He shut his mouth, clenching his jaw against the echo of snarls and growls that were even louder than the screams...

Haley pushed the door to the exam room open, and Leland was grateful for the opportunity to focus on something else. Diego sat on the bench, his knuckles almost white where his fingers were curled around the edge, his jaw clenched so hard the tendons were standing out in his neck.

"Diego, this is my friend Haley," Dr. Fenton said. "She'd like to talk to you about what happened last night, if that's okay."

Leland was several feet away, but he could still hear Diego's breathing go ragged, the whites of his eyes visible as he started shivering.

"You don't have to," Haley said quickly as Diego swayed, and Leland stepped forward, bracing Diego gingerly by his upper arms. The boy twitched at his touch, but his skin was clammy and cold underneath a thin layer of sweat. "Karen, I think he's..."

Dr. Fenton nodded, opening a drawer and pulling out a plastic-wrapped syringe.

"Can you breathe for me, Diego?" she said calmly as she pulled the wrapper apart. "Your heart is beating very quickly, so I'm going to give you something to relax you, but can you help me by focusing on your breathing? Breathe in...and out. In...and out." She kept up the soothing breath count while she plunged the needle into a bottle, pulling the clear liquid up into the syringe. "That's it. You're doing great."

Diego flinched when he saw the needle, but when he pressed backward, Leland was there, blocking his route. Dr. Fenton kept talking to him in a calm, soothing voice as she slid the needle into his arm, and within seconds, Leland felt Diego relaxing, starting to slump over.

He lowered the boy to the padded bench, moving out of the way when Haley appeared with a soft blanket that she wrapped around Diego's torso, tucking it under him gently. She didn't seem to notice Leland watching her as she leaned forward to look at the bite mark on Diego's shoulder, and... was she...sniffing him? Maybe to see if he smelled like alcohol, but Leland hadn't noticed any indication that the kid might have been drinking.

"I appreciate your help, Deputy Sommers," Dr. Fenton said, drawing his attention. "He's lucky you found him when you did."

Seems like it would've been luckier if someone had found him earlier, Leland thought, but he just nodded. "Glad to help," he said instead. "Sorry to ask, but do you have a restroom I could use?"

"Of course. Down the hall on the right."

He thanked her and headed toward the door she'd indicated, trying not to hurry too obviously. Now that the immediate crisis was over, his body was reminding him that he was only human, and he'd had approximately a gallon of coffee since he'd left Arizona.

As he washed his hands afterward, he caught sight of his reflection in the mirror and grimaced. It was a damn wonder not one of the three people he'd seen that morning had run screaming, what with the bloodshot eyes, two days' worth of stubble, and messy hair curling up from under his baseball cap. Then again, all three of them had bigger things to worry about. But so much for first impressions as the new deputy, he thought, scrubbing a hand over his whiskery jaw. Maybe Haley and the doc wouldn't hold it against him.

And maybe one of them could point him toward the best place to get another round of coffee to keep him on his feet until he could at least get his meager belongings out of the truck and into the new place. Maybe some breakfast too. He thought of the sticker on Haley's thermos and headed back down the hallway, intent on asking her for directions.

The door to the exam room was cracked open, and he could see the two women talking with their heads bent close together, though they stopped and looked up as soon as they heard his footsteps. It made him feel a little put on the spot, especially the way Dr. Fenton pressed her fingertips to her mouth like she was hoping he hadn't heard what she'd been saying.

"Sorry to interrupt," he said, trying for his best friendly smile now that he knew what a mess they were looking at. He wouldn't blame them if they'd been discussing him; he'd think twice about trusting the man he'd seen in the mirror too. "I was wonderin' if you could point me toward someplace to get some coffee and a bite to eat."

Haley's expression shifted from cautious to cheerful in the space it took her to blink. "I'll do you one better," she said. "I can't ask Diego any questions until he wakes up, and Karen says he needs to rest for a while, so why don't I just take you?"

The parking lot at Luann's was about half full, probably peak breakfast crowd, and Haley wrinkled her nose. A good half her pack was here, and if there was one thing she knew about small-town werewolves, it was that they stuck their noses into everyone else's business, especially hers. All part of being the alpha, her mother used to say.

But Haley couldn't imagine anyone sticking their nose in her mother's business and living to tell about it, so maybe it was just all part of her whole pack having known her since she was knee-high. Either way, they were all going to be extremely interested in the new deputy and in why Haley was out and about before ten a.m. on a Saturday, and she'd rather keep both things to herself for now.

Especially the new deputy, she thought as she watched him ease his Chevy Blazer into the gravel spot next to hers, his dusty Arizona plates catching the sunlight. Maybe it was because she'd broken up with her boyfriend before she left Seattle and hadn't been seeing anyone else in the nine months she'd been back in town, or maybe it was because the full moon was only three days away and making her antsy, but she was a little ticked off about how good-looking he was, especially when she knew she couldn't do anything about it.

"Welcome to Pine Grove, Deputy," she called as he opened his door and stepped out, moving stiffly. She guessed the long drive was starting to catch up with him. God knew that after the last time she'd driven back from Seattle, she'd shifted into a wolf and gone for a run just to stretch her legs as soon as she'd gotten home.

"Just Leland is fine," he said, removing his cap long enough to rake his hair away from his face before he settled it back on his head. "Hell of a welcome wagon you rolled out there." His smile was the barest quirk of his lips, and it did awful, terrible things to her pulse. *Dang.*

"Oh, we throw wounded kids at every new deputy that comes to town," she joked with a grimace. "He didn't tell you where he was from or anything like that, did he?"

He shook his head, and she wondered if it was bad to feel such a wash of relief. Notifying family members would have to wait until they could confirm whether that bite on Diego's shoulder had done what she thought it had, so she was glad she didn't have to make excuses for why she was putting it off.

"Nah, he didn't talk much. Barely got his name out of him. Figure it was the shock."

The bell over the door jangled as she pulled it open, and the smell of sizzling bacon hit her straight in the nose, drawing an audible growl from her stomach. She sensed the ripple of movement through the dining room as they came in, the curiosity of twenty werewolves and their family members at the sight of a new person in town.

"Haley Fern, what are you doin' out so early on your day off?" Sally called from where she was pulling down orders from the kitchen window. "And—oh, who's your friend?"

Well, whoever hadn't noticed them before sure as heck had now.

"Sally, this is Leland Sommers. He's the new deputy, just got in this morning. Leland, this is Sally Newcrow. She and her sister, Luann, own the diner."

"Nice to meet you." Leland nodded politely. "Sure does smell good in here."

"Tastes good too." Sally grinned at him as she loaded her arms up with plates of food to take out to the tables. "Well, sit your butts down, and I'll get to you in a second."

Haley led him over to the last empty booth, hoping the high benches would give them some semblance of privacy, and pulled the laminated, handwritten menus out of the holder, handing one to him as he got settled.

"You can't go wrong with anything here," she promised, looking at the menu to keep from staring at him, even though the offerings hadn't changed in twenty years and Haley always got the exact same thing.

Behind Leland, Sally caught her eye and mouthed, *He is so hot!* It took all Haley's self-control not to roll her eyes. Sally pulled her pencil out of her ponytail and flipped to a new page on her notepad as she sidled up to their table.

"It sure is exciting to get to meet the new deputy," she said brightly. "We ain't had anyone new in town since Jo Pham managed to convince Brooks Carmody to move in with her back when Haley's momma was still—"

"Sally," Haley interrupted before Sally could get off track and blurt out incriminating details. "I'm sure he'd rather order his food."

Sally giggled, waving her hand. "Oh, don't mind me, Deputy. What're you havin' to eat?"

He flipped the menu over, still scanning the list of items. "Uh, Miss Fern says I can't go wrong with anything here..."

Sally mouthed *Miss Fern!* at her over his head, and this time Haley did roll her eyes.

"So how about the pancakes and bacon?"

"You got it, sugar. And Haley's right—everything here's the best you ever had, includin' your momma's cookin'."

Leland snorted, tucking his menu back into the holder. "Well, that wouldn't be a hard standard to beat." There was a faint tension at the corners of his mouth when he said it that made Haley think there might be a story there, and she didn't realize where Sally was headed with her train of thought until it was too late.

"Well, at least that means your future wife won't be intimidated in the kitchen," Sally said cheerfully, and Haley gave her a horrified look that she didn't bother hiding from Leland. "Or are you already married, Deputy?"

"Give me the steak and eggs, Sally," Haley blurted, talking over her, desperate to stop the impending disaster of a conversation. "And coffee."

"Uh, no, I'm not married." Amusement sparkled in his eyes as he folded his hands on the table, glancing at Haley, and she wanted to slide right off the bench. "And I'll have a coffee too, please. Black."

"Comin' right up, sugar. Y'all just hang tight."

Haley shook her head as Sally walked off to put their orders in, embarrassed laughter bubbling up in her throat. "Sorry about that. It's a small town, and like she said, we don't get new residents often. People get nosy. You can tell 'em to buzz off, I promise."

Leland chuckled, leaning back in the booth. "It's all right. Small towns are like that. At least so far everybody's been friendly, not like where I grew up."

"Arizona?" Haley guessed, but he shook his head.

"Nah, Idaho."

She waited, but he didn't expand on that. "That's not too far away from here."

Sally dropped off their cups of coffee, black for Leland and with a pitcher of cream for Haley, and he hummed, noncommittal, as he picked his up and took a sip. Haley poured the whole little pitcher into hers until it turned light tan and added two packs of sugar. He didn't seem interested in talking about Idaho, and despite her rampant curiosity, she decided it would be rude to pry.

"Are you staying here in town?" she asked instead. There wasn't much in the way of lodging for visitors, just the twenty-two rooms at the Sundown Motel, the seven empty RV spots at the Timber Trails Trailer Park, and the three suites at the Carmody Bed & Breakfast. "Or did you get a place in Red Horse River?"

The county seat was where most of the rest of the sheriff department employees lived, although it wasn't a metropolis itself, by any means.

"I'm renting an apartment here, but I don't know if it's ready yet." He smiled, rolling his coffee cup between his palms. It was already half empty, Haley noticed. "I wasn't supposed to be here until tomorrow night, so I might have to get a room somewhere."

Haley blinked. "An apartment?" In Pine Grove? She couldn't think of a single place. Maybe someone was renting him a room in their house, in which case she was a little peeved that no one had told her that option was on the table. She had an empty room at her place—not that having him underfoot all the time would be a great idea. She kept catching a whiff of him on her inhales, underneath the coffee and breakfast scents of the diner. The full moon being so close meant that the wolf was right at the surface of her consciousness, harder to ignore than usual, and the wolf thought Leland smelled *delicious*.

Down, girl.

"Yeah, it's a room over the newspaper office, I think she said? The woman I talked to said it hadn't been lived in for a while." He took a sip of his coffee, watching her over the edge of the cup like he was hoping she'd have a clue what he was talking about.

"Oh!" She'd forgotten Jo used to put out a community newsletter before she'd gotten too busy with the bed-and-breakfast and then having a baby. There was a one-bedroom apartment above the old printing office that they used for storage now, and Jo must have decided to clean it up and rent it out. "Yeah, Jo used to live there when she put out the *Howler*. I forgot about that."

"The *Howler*." Leland smirked. "Sheriff Rylan said you guys have some kind of werewolf thing going on for tourists. What's that about?"

Haley laughed nervously, clutching her coffee cup. Her mother had always said she was a *terrible* liar, but when your regional alpha said that the new deputy couldn't know anything about the pack of werewolves that made up most of the town's population...well, she'd give it her best shot.

"Yeah, the original town charter has all these provisions for werewolves and werewolf-human cooperation. Nobody's sure what the founders were thinking, but it gives us a nice little draw for tourist traffic. Gotta pay for the nature preserve somehow."

"It's not a federal or state preserve, then?" Leland looked mildly interested at that, fiddling with his coffee cup—empty already, Haley noticed.

"No, it's private land. One of the town founders owned it and designated it as a preserve about the same time they drew up the charter. It's officially owned by the town these days. There's a small American gray wolf family that lives there, so at least there actually *is* something for the tourists to look at, if they're lucky enough to get a glimpse."

Sally's sudden appearance with the coffeepot as soon as Leland drained his cup meant she was hovering close enough to eavesdrop, but Haley couldn't really fault her for that. The whole diner was probably listening, putting that wolf hearing to good use. The pack already knew that the new deputy wasn't being let in on the secret, but it didn't hurt for them to know what he'd been told. The last time an outsider had accidentally found out about the town's unusual demographics was still a cautionary tale passed down through generations, and nobody wanted a repeat of that mess.

"Do you think that might have been what attacked Diego?" Leland asked, and Sally almost dropped the coffeepot. So that news hadn't spread yet, then.

"I hope not," Haley said, ignoring Sally for the moment. "They've never shown aggression toward humans before. We get campers and hikers who try to break the rules and stay overnight in the preserve, but we don't see many animal attacks. A couple of boys got scared up a tree by a bear last year, but she just ate their food and trashed their campsite before she moved on."

Leland snorted. "Guess people are the same everywhere. Can't tell you how many of my calls in Tucson were to rescue people from something that never would have happened if they'd just paid attention to the safety regulations."

Haley relaxed a little, grateful that he hadn't pushed her on it. "Yeah, some people are convinced the rules are only there to spoil their fun. In our case, a lot of people think they're also there to keep the werewolves a secret." Which was true, but that didn't mean it wasn't also for safety purposes.

"So how long have you been the preserve director?" He held eye contact with her as he took a sip of his fresh coffee, and she was struck by how *blue* his eyes were, even bloodshot and tired.

"Almost a year." Her smile felt tight and tense even to her, and she tried to relax. "My mom was the preserve director before me. I always expected to take over from her—went to college in Seattle to get a master's in wildlife conservation, even—but I just didn't expect it to be *yet*." She laughed ruefully, rubbing at her forehead. "It's been...a lot."

"What happened?" There was a gentleness to his voice that caught her attention, made her notice the way he leaned in, his face open. "Is she...did she...?"

"Got married," Haley said flatly, amused by the flash of surprise in his expression. "She met a guy while I was in college, brought him to my graduation with her, and that's when she told me she was moving to Columbus, Ohio, with him."

"Damn. That must have been a surprise."

"You're tellin' me." She shrugged. "Nobody else in town wanted to take over, and everybody figured I was going to do it anyway, so here I am."

"Funny." Leland chuckled, but Sally appeared at the table with plates of food, cutting off whatever he'd been about to say.

They got the plates arranged, silverware rolled out, and after Leland had spread butter on his pancakes and started cutting them into pieces, she prompted him.

"Funny?"

"Oh, just..." He popped a giant pancake triangle into his mouth, no syrup, and chewed it thoughtfully. "Sheriff told me nobody wanted the deputy job. You got yours because nobody else wanted it." He shrugged. "Funny coincidence is all."

Haley laughed, cutting into her steak, her mouth watering at the deep-red color inside. *Perfect.* "Well, when you go into town to do your paper work and orientation, you'll find out why nobody wanted the deputy position. This place has a *reputation*."

"Oh yeah?" Leland grinned at her, seeming more relaxed by the moment, and she felt some of the stark loneliness of the past nine months ease away, like a weight lifting. "What, because of the werewolf thing?"

Haley nodded. "That, and by extension, the tourists. You really will have more work to do around the full moon."

"That's all right. Just promise me there's no Bigfoot to contend with, and I'll cope with the werewolves." The glint of mischief in his eyes belied his dry tone, and Haley's heart skipped a beat. *Dang it, he's cute.*

"No Bigfoot that *I* know of," she promised, holding up three fingers like a Girl Scout.

He laughed, breaking off a piece of bacon and stuffing it into his mouth. "Well, you're the first person I'm calling if I find him."

Was he flirting? *Don't I wish.*

"That's fair." She shoved a bite of steak into her mouth and immediately lost her train of thought, salt and blood flooding across her tongue and soothing the constant itch of hunger at the back of her mind. She groaned, her eyes slipping closed, and let herself get lost in the taste for a moment. When she opened her eyes again, it was to see Leland watching her, one corner of his mouth pulled up in a crooked smile, and she blushed.

"Sorry," she muttered, laughing, and covered her mouth as she swallowed. "I'm really hungry."

"No apology necessary," Leland assured her, and she wondered if she was imagining the extra rasp to his voice. She didn't have much time to think about it, though, as her phone vibrated in her back pocket, buzzing loudly against the booth seat, the sound nearly making her jump out of her skin.

A glance at the screen showed that the call was coming from the clinic, and she put her fork down and sat back from the table a bit.

"Sorry," she told Leland. "I need to take this." She didn't wait for his nod to accept the call. "Hey, what's up?"

There was a clatter in the background, and then Karen said, "Haley, I'm so sorry. I know you just left, but I need you to stop back by. The sooner the better."

Haley's heart dropped into her stomach. "Of course. I'll be there in just a minute." She hung up and gave Leland an apologetic smile. "Sorry to run out on you. Do you need directions to your apartment, or do you know where you're going?"

"I can figure it out," he said, polite, giving her an easy smile. "Thanks, though."

Sally appeared with a to-go box, confirming Haley's suspicion that she was still eavesdropping, but Haley couldn't bring herself to care. She packed up the steak and bacon, pushing the plate with the eggs on it over toward Leland.

"Here, as my apology for ditching you. Plus, they won't reheat very well."

"I won't let 'em go to waste," he promised, and she grabbed her box, headed to the register to pay.

"Put his bill with mine," she told Sally quietly. "Welcome-to-town breakfast and all."

"Uh-huh." Sally grinned at her as she rang up both meals and waited for Haley to count out the cash for the total. "I'd like to eat *him* for breakfast."

"*Shh!*" Haley hissed, glancing toward the booth. She could barely see the back of Leland's head over the high back of the bench, his blue baseball cap. There was no way to tell if he'd heard, but maybe she'd gotten lucky and he hadn't. "Just let me pay and leave in peace, for heaven's sake."

"If that's what you want." Sally took the cash, counted it, and glanced up at Haley. "You need your change?"

"No, of course not." She tucked her wallet back in her jeans pocket and picked up her box. "Although I should keep the tip as compensation for all the trouble you're causing, flirting with the deputy."

Sally snorted. "Please. He's too young for me."

"Plus, you're married," Haley noted wryly.

Sally waved her off. "Emmett wouldn't care. He knows I know what side my bread's buttered on. But, girl, your toast is dry as a bone." At Haley's sharp look, Sally held up her hands, the ancient register dinging as she pushed the drawer shut with her hip. "I'm just sayin', is all."

"Have a nice day, Sally," Haley said pointedly, loudly, and then turned toward Leland. "Have a good one, Deputy."

Leland lifted his hand in a wave, throwing her a nod over his shoulder, and she felt twenty pairs of eyes on her as she waved back and headed for the doors, her cheeks warm and a tingle in her stomach that she couldn't entirely blame on her breakfast being interrupted.

The Styrofoam box squeaked loudly as she set it on the passenger's seat of her Range Rover, and her thoughts shifted to the boy at the clinic and the bite on his shoulder, the clatter she'd heard on the phone, and the restrained urgency in Karen's voice.

The chance that someone *hadn't* illegally turned a human into a werewolf on her preserve was shrinking so rapidly it wasn't even much of a question anymore. But who the heck would have done such a thing?

She thought—hoped—that none of her pack would, but if it wasn't one of hers, that meant that there were trespassers in her territory, and that came with its own set of questions. But making sure Diego was all right was her first priority, and the Range Rover kicked up gravel as she gunned it out of the parking lot.

Don't stop now. Keep reading with your copy of EDGE OF THE WOODS by City Owl Author, Jules Kelley.

And find more from Adrienne Blake at authoradrienneblake.com

Don't miss book two of the *Soul and Shadows* series with SENSE AND SUCCUBUS coming soon, and find more from Adrienne Blake at authoradrienneblake.com

Until then, discover more paranormal romance with EDGE OF THE WOODS by Jules Kelley!

There's something lurking in Pine Grove, Montana, and its bite is vicious.

Haley Fern has been the alpha of her local werewolf pack for less than a year, when their law enforcement liaison retires, and Leland Sommers, a man who knows nothing about werewolves or their world, is hired in his place.

What could be an awkward situation turns complicated when the man shows up his first day on the job with an injured teenage boy he found on the road–a boy Haley knows has just been bitten.

But discovering who bit the kid isn't as easy as it seems, especially with Leland asking questions and looking at Haley the way he does.

Can the alpha figure out who is attacking innocent people on her wildlife preserve and protect her pack? Or will the new sheriff and her growing attraction to him put her entire world in danger?

Escape Your World. Get Lost in Ours! City Owl Press at www.cityowlpress.com.

ACKNOWLEDGMENTS

I'd love to give thanks to my secret squirrel mentor. He's been there with me from the start, nudging me along and whispering encouragement in my ear. Even when I thought he was nuts. I'd also like to acknowledge City Owl Press for taking a chance on my work. Thank you.

ABOUT THE AUTHOR

ADRIENNE BLAKE is a *USA Today* bestselling author of paranormal mystery and urban fantasy. She is also an Amazon Top 100 bestselling author. Her stories blend plot, humor, and darkness, all in one sizzling cauldron. Born in the UK and writing in the US, she and her partner are managed by three ruthless cats.

authoradrienneblake.com